114

四技二專 統測

詳解本

歷屆英文試題**完全解析**

目錄 CONTENTS

全部音檔

Test 1

Test 2

Test 3

Test 4

Test 5

Test 6

114

四技二專統一入學測驗－詳解

114 年統測
試題講解

第一部分：選擇題

I. 字彙題 (114 年-2～9)

II. 對話題 (114 年-9～17)

III. 綜合測驗 (114 年-17～23)

IV. 閱讀測驗 (114 年-23～39)

第二部分：非選擇題

I. 填充 (114 年-40)

II. 句子重組 (114 年-40～41)

III. 中譯英 (114 年-41)

選擇題解答

1	2	3	4	5	6	7	8	9	10
A	B	B	C	C	A	A	D	D	C
11	12	13	14	15	16	17	18	19	20
A	C	A	D	A	D	B	C	D	B
21	22	23	24	25	26	27	28	29	30
C	B	B	A	A	C	B	A	A	D
31	32	33	34	35	36	37	38	39	40
D	C	B	D	D	C	C	B	A	D
41	42								
B	B								

114 年四技二專統一入學測驗詳解

第一部分：選擇題（84 分）

I. 字彙題

A **1.**

This child is using colored chalks to ______ pictures on a blank piece of paper.

(A) draw (B) heat (C) mail (D) type

這個小孩正用彩色粉筆在白紙上畫畫。

解析

1. (A) **draw** [drɔ] *vt.* & *vi.* 畫 & *vt.* 拉；吸引（三態為：draw, drew [dru], drawn [drɔn]）& *n.* 有吸引力的人 / 事 / 物；平局

   例: I couldn't draw a dog, so I drew a cloud.
   （我不會畫狗，所以就畫了一片雲。）
   Paul drew a stool over to the fireplace.
   （保羅拉了一張凳子到壁爐邊。）

   (B) **heat** [hit] *vt.* 使變熱 & *n.* 熱（不可數）；溫度

   例: Wax turns into liquid when heated.
   （把蠟加熱就會變成液態。）

   (C) **mail** [mel] *vt.* 郵寄（信）& *n.* 郵件（集合名詞，不可數）

   例: Some people collect stamps, while most simply use them for mailing letters.
   （有些人會收集郵票，而大多數人只會在寄信時用上它們。）

   (D) **type** [taɪp] *vt.* 打字 & *n.* 類型

   例: You should type more carefully to avoid mistakes.
   （你打字應該更細心一點，以避免發生錯誤。）

2. 根據語意，(A) 項應為正選。

其他重點

1. **a colored chalk** 彩色粉筆
2. **blank** [blæŋk] *a.* 空白的 & *n.* 空白處，空格；（頭腦）一片空白

B **2.**

The room was so ______ that I couldn't even find space for these new chairs.

(A) available (B) crowded (C) empty (D) positive

這間房間太擠以致於我甚至找不到地方放這些新椅子。

解析

1. (A) **available** [ə`veləbl̩] *a.* 可得到的；可用的；（人）有空的

   例: This new product is now available in stores.
   （這個新產品已經可以在商店裡買到了。）

   (B) **crowded** [`kraʊdɪd] *a.* 擁擠的
   be crowded with...　擠滿了……
   = be full of...

   例: Night markets are always crowded with people on weekends.
   （夜市在週末時總是擠滿了人。）

   (C) **empty** [`ɛmptɪ ] *a.* 空的 & *vt.* 使變空 & *vi.* 注入（海 / 湖 / 河等）（三態為：empty, emptied [ `ɛmptɪd], emptied）

   例: There weren't any empty seats on the bus.
   （公車上沒有任何空位。）

   (D) **positive** [`pɑzətɪv] *a.* 確信的，有把握的；積極正面的；（化驗 / 檢驗等結果）陽性的 & *n.* 優點，好處

   例: Lisa has a positive attitude towards her future with this company.
   （麗莎對自己在這家公司的前途抱持樂觀的態度。）

2. 根據語意，(B) 項應為正選。

其他重點

so... that...　如此……以致於……

例: Tom worked so hard that he eventually became a successful businessman.
（湯姆非常努力，終成巨賈。）

B **3.**

Many people have climbed the main ______ of Mount Jade in Taiwan, which is the highest point on the island.

(A) base　(B) peak　(C) shore　(D) valley

很多人攀登過臺灣全島最高點的玉山主峰。

解析

1. (A) **base** [bes] *n.* 底部，基部（= bottom [`bɑtəm]）；（軍事）基地；（棒球）壘 & *vt.* 以……為基礎

   例: The dessert has a delicious, crunchy base.
   （這道甜點的底層酥脆可口。）

   (B) **peak** [pik] *n.* 最高點；山頂 & *vi.* 達到頂峰，達到最大值

   例: Sally was at the peak of her fitness when she competed in the marathon.
   （莎莉在參加馬拉松賽跑時身體處於最佳狀態。）

(C) **shore** [ʃɔr] *n.* 岸（邊），濱，畔

例: Jason must be crazy to go fishing by the shore during a typhoon.
（傑森一定是瘋了才會在颱颱風時到岸邊釣魚。）

(D) **valley** [ˋvælɪ] *n.* 山谷

例: The spectacular view of the valley really took my breath away.
（這山谷的壯麗景色令我屏息。）

2. 根據語意，(B) 項應為正選。

其他重點

Mount Jade　　玉山

C **4.**

After looking at his grandfather's ______ on the wall, John was happy to discover that his grandfather and he really looked alike.

(A) cattle　(B) jewelry　(C) portrait　(D) whistle

約翰看到牆上的祖父肖像後，很高興地發現祖父跟他真的很像。

解析

1. (A) **cattle** [ˋkætḷ] *n.* 牛群（複數名詞，可被數量為「二」以上的數詞（如 two、three、four、many 等）修飾。）

例: The farmer wants to buy some dairy cattle.
（這農夫想買幾頭乳牛。）

(B) **jewelry** [ˋdʒuəlrɪ] *n.* 珠寶，首飾（集合名詞，不可數）

例: Nancy unlocked the jewelry box with a key.
（南西用鑰匙打開珠寶箱。）

(C) **portrait** [ˋpɔrtret] *n.* 肖像，畫像

例: Lily's great-grandmother's portrait still hangs in her father's house.
（莉莉曾祖母的畫像還掛在她爸爸家裡。）

(D) **whistle** [ˋ(h)wɪsḷ] *n.* 哨子；口哨 & *vi.* 吹哨子；吹口哨

例: The police officer blew his whistle and asked the crowd to leave immediately.
（警員吹哨要求群眾立刻離開。）

2. 根據語意，(C) 項應為正選。

其他重點

alike [əˋlaɪk] *a.* 相似的 & *adv.* 相似地；同樣地

look alike　　長得相像

例: The twins look so much alike that only their mother can tell them apart.
（這對雙胞胎長得太像了，只有他們的母親分辨得出來。）

C **5.**
It is risky for people to touch plants in rainforests because some plants can be ______ to humans.
(A) fashionable (B) jealous (C) poisonous (D) reasonable
摸雨林中的植物是有風險的，因為有些植物對人類來說是有毒的。

解析

1. (A) **fashionable** [ˋfæʃənəbl̩] *a.* 流行的；時髦的
   例: This store sells many fashionable skirts.
   （這間店販售很多時髦的裙子。）

   (B) **jealous** [ˋdʒɛləs] *a.* 嫉妒的
   be jealous of... 嫉妒……
   例: We are all jealous of Kevin's new mansion.
   （我們都很嫉妒凱文的新豪宅。）

   (C) **poisonous** [ˋpɔɪzənəs] *a.* 有毒的
   例: The factory was shut down because it was releasing poisonous gases into the air.
   （這間工廠因排放有毒氣體至空中而遭停業。）

   (D) **reasonable** [ˋriznəbl̩] *a.* 合理的
   例: The boss asked Nick to give her a reasonable explanation for his lateness.
   （老闆要求尼克為遲到給她一個合理的解釋。）

2. 根據語意，(C) 項應為正選。

其他重點

risky [ˋrɪskɪ] *a.* 危險的，有風險的
例: The patient had to go through a risky operation in order to live.
（這個病人必須動一個高風險的手術才能活下去。）

A **6.**
Governments have the ______ to punish people who drink and drive.
(A) authority (B) bargain (C) courtesy (D) infection
政府有權處罰酒駕者。

解析

1. (A) **authority** [əˋθɔrətɪ] *n.* 權力；權威（不可數）；權威人士（可數）；有關當局（恆用複數）
   例: Several countries claim authority over these waters.
   （好幾個國家聲稱對這些水域擁有主權。）

(B) **bargain** [ˋbɑrgən] *n.* 很划算的東西（可數）& *vi.* 講價，討價還價

例: The department store's 100th anniversary sale attracted many people who were looking for bargains.
（那間百貨公司的一百週年慶特價活動吸引眾多想搶便宜的人。）

(C) **courtesy** [ˋkɝtəsɪ] *n.* 禮貌

例: Even though you may not like Laura, you should still treat her with courtesy.
（就算你可能不喜歡蘿拉，你還是應該以禮相待。）

(D) **infection** [ɪnˋfɛkʃən] *n.* 感染

例: Hank hasn't recovered from his eye infection.
（漢克的眼睛感染還沒復原。）

2. 根據語意，(A) 項應為正選。

A **7.**

During the night, the sensor lights in the park will ______ turn on by themselves when someone is passing by.

(A) automatically (B) organically (C) productively (D) selfishly

晚上時，公園內的感應燈會在有人經過時自動開啟。

解析

1. (A) **automatically** [ˏɔtəˋmætɪklɪ] *adv.* 自動地

例: The lid of this trash can opens automatically.
（這個垃圾桶的蓋子會自動打開。）

(B) **organically** [ɔrˋgænɪklɪ] *adv.* 有機耕作地

例: Organically grown crops may contain more vitamins than non-organic crops.
（有機作物可能比非有機作物含有更多維生素。）

(C) **productively** [prəˋdʌktɪvlɪ] *adv.* 高效地

例: You should spend your time productively instead of playing video games all day.
（你該有效運用你的時間而不是整天打電動。）

(D) **selfishly** [ˋsɛlfɪʃlɪ] *adv.* 自私地

例: Even though there was only enough cake for one slice per person, Mona selfishly took two.
（儘管蛋糕只夠每人吃一片，夢娜卻自私地拿了兩片。）

2. 根據語意，(A) 項應為正選。

其他重點

1. **turn on... / turn... on** 打開（電器）

 例: Would you mind if I turned on the radio?
 （你會介意我打開收音機嗎？）

2. **pass by** 經過

 例: A bus passed by without stopping at the stop.
 （公車過站不停。）

3. **sensor** [ˋsɛnsɚ] *n.* 感應器

 例: The sensor will detect the slightest motion and turn on the lights.
 （感應器會偵測到最輕微的移動然後開燈。）

D **8.**

Chen Chieh-hsien (陳傑憲) ______ the WBSC Premier12 2024 MVP (Most Valuable Player) due to his magnificent performance.

(A) was named after (B) made fun of (C) was in charge of (D) stood out as

陳傑憲在 2024 年世界棒球十二強賽事中表現傑出，因而脫穎而出成為當屆比賽的最有價值球員。

解析

1. (A) **be named after...** 以……的名字命名

 例: The newborn was named after his grandfather.
 （這個新生兒取了跟爺爺一樣的名字。）

 (B) **make fun of...** 嘲笑……

 例: Tina was upset because her classmates made fun of her new hairstyle.
 （蒂娜因同學嘲笑她的新髮型而心情欠佳。）

 (C) **be in charge of...** 負責 / 掌管……

 例: Karen is in charge of her boss's schedule.
 （凱倫負責安排她老闆的行程。）

 (D) **stand out as...** 脫穎而出成為……

 例: Jay scored several slam dunks, easily standing out as the star of the playoff game.
 （傑伊多次灌籃得分，理所當然脫穎而出成為該場季後賽的焦點明星。）

2. 根據語意，(D) 項應為正選。

其他重點

1. **WBSC Premier12** 世界棒球十二強賽

 WBSC 世界棒壘球總會（World Baseball Softball Confederation 的縮寫）

premier [prɪˋmɪr] *a.* 首要的 & *n.* 總理，首相
*confederation [kən͵fɛdəˋreʃən] *n.* 同盟，結盟
2. **magnificent** [mægˋnɪfəsənt] *a.* 非凡的，華麗的

D **9.**

Mary came to me and introduced herself again. Apparently, she thought that I had forgotten her name.

(A) actively (B) entirely (C) internally (D) obviously

瑪莉走過來我這裡，又自我介紹了一次。她顯然以為我忘記她的名字了。

解析

1. 原句劃線的字有下列意思及用法：
apparently [əˋpærəntlɪ] *adv.* 顯然；據說
例: Apparently, Fred was quite upset that his friends went camping without him.
（弗雷德顯然很不高興朋友們去露營沒揪他。）
2. (A) **actively** [ˋæktɪvlɪ] *adv.* 積極地
例: A job won't fall into your lap; you need to start actively looking for work.
（工作不會從天上掉下來，你應該開始積極找工作。）
(B) **entirely** [ɪnˋtaɪrlɪ] *adv.* 完全地
例: The house was made entirely of brick.
（那棟房子是完全磚造的。）
(C) **internally** [ɪnˋtɝnlɪ] *adv.* 內心地
例: Sophia looked confident on the outside, but internally, she felt nervous and stressed.
（蘇菲亞外表看起來有自信，但內心卻感到緊張與有壓力。）
(D) **obviously** [ˋɑbvɪəslɪ] *adv.* 明顯地，顯而易見地
例: Obviously, you didn't tell me the truth.
（顯然你沒有跟我說實話。）
3. 根據上述，apparently 與 obviously 同義，故 (D) 項應為正選。

C **10.**

My sister decided to abandon her old habits and start a fresh chapter in her life.

(A) bring about (B) carry on (C) give up (D) run into

我妹妹決定拋棄她的舊有習慣，開始人生的新篇章。

解析

1. 原句劃線的字有下列意思及用法：
abandon [əˋbændən] *vt.* 放棄；遺棄

例: Vivian abandoned her opportunity to study abroad in order to take care of her parents.
（薇薇安為了照顧她的雙親而放棄出國留學的機會。）

2. (A) **bring about...** 引起 / 導致……

例: The internet has brought about a lot of changes in our daily lives.
（網際網路為我們的日常生活帶來諸多改變。）

(B) **carry on...** 繼續……

例: Let's carry on this discussion some other time.
（咱們另找時間繼續這次的討論。）

(C) **give up...** 放棄……

例: You should never give up your dreams.
（你絕不可以放棄夢想。）

(D) **run into...** 遇到……（問題、困難等）

例: Daniel's company ran into financial problems.
（丹尼爾的公司出現財務問題。）

3. 根據上述，abandon 與 give up 同義，故 (C) 項應為正選。

其他重點

chapter [ˋtʃæptɚ] *n.* 章，回，篇；一段時期；分會

II. 對話題

A **11.**

Dad: Hey, you're always on your phone!
Son: I know. I just like playing games and watching videos.
Dad: But if you use the phone too much, you might hurt your eyes.
Son: ________________
Dad: Yeah, let's go jogging. It's more fun.

(A) Then I should use it less. (B) Should I use a new phone?
(C) Do you like to watch videos, too? (D) So you should play online games.

爸爸：喂，你老是在滑手機！
兒子：我知道。我就是喜歡玩遊戲和看影片。
爸爸：但如果你用手機太久，可能會傷眼睛。
兒子：________________
爸爸：對啊，我們去慢跑吧。那比較有趣。

(A) 那我該少用一點。 (B) 我該換新手機嗎？
(C) 你也喜歡看影片嗎？ (D) 所以你應該玩線上遊戲。

解析

空格後，爸爸回答 "Yeah, let's go jogging."（對啊，我們去慢跑吧。）得知，兒子同意爸爸的話，用手機太久會傷眼，該少用一點，因此 (A) 項應為正選。

其他重點

1. **hurt** [hɝt] *vt.* 傷害 & *vi.* 疼痛（三態同形）& *n.* 傷，痛

   例: My back starts to hurt if I sit at the computer for too long.
   （如果我在電腦前坐太久，背就會開始痛。）

2. **go jogging** 慢跑

   例: Amy likes to go jogging along the beach at sunset.
   （艾咪喜歡在日落時沿著沙灘慢跑。）

C **12.**

Lucy: Do you know that plastics can take 20 years to break down?

John: That's awful! We really need to use less plastic.

Lucy: I agree. ________________

John: Great idea! I'll try that, too.

(A) No wonder I prefer buying plastic containers.

(B) So I keep using plastic straws for all my drinks.

(C) That's why I always carry my own water bottle.

(D) And I make sure to throw away everything I buy.

露西：你知道塑膠要花二十年才能分解嗎？

約翰：好可怕！我們真該少用塑膠。

露西：我也是這麼覺得。________________

約翰：好主意！我也來試試。

(A) 難怪我比較喜歡買塑膠容器。 (B) 所以我的飲料都一直用塑膠吸管。

(C) 所以我總是自備水壺。 (D) 而且我一定會把所有我買的東西都丟掉。

解析

空格後，約翰說 "Great idea! I'll try that, too."（好主意！我也來試試。）得知，露西提出了一個好方法讓約翰也想要跟著做，因此 (C) 項應為正選。

其他重點

1. **plastic** [ˋplæstɪk] *n.* 塑膠 & *a.* 塑膠的
2. **awful** [ˋɔfʊl] *a.* 可怕的；很差的
3. **container** [kənˋtenɚ] *n.* 容器
4. **straw** [strɔ] *n.* 吸管（可數）；稻草（不可數）

A **13.**

Vendor: These vegetables are chemical free.

Customer: They look great. But what about the eggs? ________________

Vendor: Of course! We get them straight from the farm every morning. They are the best.

(A) Are they fresh? (B) How much are they?

(C) Do you plant them? (D) How do you cook them?

攤販：這些蔬菜都沒有化學農藥喔。

顧客：看起來很不錯。那雞蛋呢？________________

攤販：當然！每天早上從農場直送。品質最優。

(A) 新鮮嗎？ (B) 多少錢？

(C) 你們自己種的嗎？ (D) 要怎麼煮啊？

解析

空格後，攤販說 "Of course! We get them straight from the farm every morning."（當然！每天早上從農場直送。）得知，顧客在問雞蛋的品質新鮮度，因此 (A) 項應為正選。

其他重點

1. **vendor** [ˋvɛndɚ] *n.* 小販
2. **chemical** [ˋkɛmɪkḷ] *n.* 化學（製）品（可數）& *a.* 化學的
3. **straight** [stret] *adv.* 立刻；直直地 & *a.* 直的；坦誠的；連續的

D **14.**

Ken: The line is too long! Let's cut in line, so we can get into the theater in time.

July: No way. ________________

Ken: OK. Let's go to the back of the line.

(A) Which theater do you prefer? (B) Which movie are we going to see?

(C) How much do you pay for two adults? (D) How can you even think of doing that?

肯：隊排好長喔！我們去插隊，這樣才來得及進電影院。

茱莉：不可以。________________

肯：好啦。那我們去後面排隊。

(A) 你比較喜歡哪間電影院？ (B) 我們要看哪部電影？

(C) 兩個大人要多少錢？ (D) 你怎麼會想到要幹這種事？

解析

空格前，茱莉說 "No way."（不可以。）得知，茱莉不同意肯這樣的想法，因此 (D) 項應為正選。

其他重點

1. **cut in line** 插隊

例: Even though Matt was late, he didn't cut in line.
（即使麥特很晚到，他也沒有插隊。）

2. **in time** 及時

例: If you hurry, you might get to the meeting in time.
（如果你快一點，或許可以及時趕上會議。）

3. **prefer** [prɪˋfɝ] *vt.* 比較喜歡（三態為：prefer, preferred [prɪˋfɝd], preferred）

例: Jane prefers studying in a quiet environment.
（珍比較喜歡在安靜的環境中讀書。）

4. **adult** [əˋdʌlt / ˋædʌlt] *n.* 成年人 & *a.* 成年的；成熟的

A **15.**

Dave: I'm going to a job interview this Thursday. What should I prepare?
Nancy: A good first impression is important. ______________
Dave: For example?
Nancy: A suit or something formal that looks professional.

(A) You have to dress properly. (B) You need to speak carefully.
(C) You ought to show interest in the pay. (D) You should ask questions about the job.

戴夫：我這禮拜四要去面試。該準備什麼嗎？
南希：好的第一印象很重要喔。______________
戴夫：像是什麼？
南希：西裝或看起來專業的正式服裝。
(A) 你需要穿著得體。 (B) 你該小心說話。
(C) 你應該表現對薪水的興趣。 (D) 你應該問一些關於工作的事。

解析

空格後，戴夫問南希 "For example?"（像是什麼？），南希回答 "A suit or something formal that looks professional."（西裝或看起來專業的正式服裝。）得知，南希是建議服裝方面的事情，因此 (A) 項應為正選。

其他重點

1. **impression** [ɪmˋprɛʃən] *n.* 印象；想法，感覺；痕跡
   a first impression　第一印象
2. **suit** [sut] *n.* 西裝，套裝
3. **formal** [ˋfɔrml̩] *a.* 正式的
4. **professional** [prəˋfɛʃənl̩] *a.* 專業的 & *n.* 專業人士

D **16.**

Anna: Hey Terry, do you know that Lee Yang (李洋) and Wang Chi-lin (王齊麟) won a gold medal at the Paris Olympics?

Terry: Yeah! That makes two gold medals, including the one from the Tokyo Olympics.

Anna: Their skills are incredible. And their teamwork is super impressive, too!

Terry: ________________

Anna: Exactly! That's why badminton is getting more popular in Taiwan these days.

(A) They have decided not to work together.
(B) Some people say their success was just luck.
(C) I believe they don't need to practice anymore.
(D) I think their success has motivated many people.

安娜：嘿，泰瑞，你知道李洋和王齊麟在巴黎奧運得到金牌嗎？
泰瑞：知道啊！把東京奧運那面也算進去，他們就有兩面金牌了。
安娜：他們技術超強，而且彼此合作無間！
泰瑞：________________
安娜：對啊！所以最近羽球在臺灣越來越風行了。
(A) 他們已經決定不再搭檔了。　(B) 有些人說他們的成功只是運氣好。
(C) 我覺得他們不需要再練習了。　(D) 我覺得他們的成功激勵了很多人。

解析

空格後，安娜說 "Exactly! That's why badminton is getting more popular in Taiwan these days."（對啊！所以最近羽球在臺灣越來越風行了。）得知，因為他們激勵了許多人，所以越來越多人喜歡羽球，因此 (D) 項應為正選。

其他重點

1. **medal** [ˋmɛdl̩] *n.* 獎牌；獎章
   a gold / silver / bronze medal　金 / 銀 / 銅牌
2. **incredible** [ɪnˋkrɛdəbl̩] *a.* 難以置信的
3. **badminton** [ˋbædmɪntən] *n.* 羽毛球

4. **motivate** [ˋmotə͵vet] *vt.* 促使，激發

例: The coach's speech helped to motivate the team before the big game.
（在關鍵比賽前的教練講話幫助激勵了球隊。）

B **17.**

Mom: Guess what? A high school student offered his seat to me on the bus today. He's so sweet!

Son: ________________

Mom: That's true, because I'd been working all day and I could hardly keep my eyes open.

(A) Did you say anything?
(B) Maybe you looked tired.
(C) Surely he liked standing.
(D) Was he getting off the bus?

媽媽：我跟你說喔，今天在公車上有高中生讓座給我耶！真貼心！
兒子：________________
媽媽：是沒錯，因為我工作了一整天，眼睛都快睜不開了。
(A) 你有跟他說什麼嗎？
(B) 可能是你看起來太累了。
(C) 他當然是喜歡站著。
(D) 他是要下車了嗎？

解析

空格後，媽媽說 "That's true, because I'd been working all day and I could hardly keep my eyes open."（是沒錯，因為我工作了一整天，眼睛都快睜不開了。）得知，兒子應是說媽媽是不是看起來很累，因此 (B) 項應為正選。

其他重點

1. **offer** [ˋɔfɚ] *vt.* 提供

例: Tony was kind enough to offer me a ride home.
（湯尼真好，說要載我回家。）

2. **hardly** [ˋhɑrdlɪ] *adv.* 幾乎不

3. **get off** 下（車、飛機等）

例: You need to get off at the next stop.
（你得在下一站下車。）

C **18.**

Housekeeping: May I help you?

Mrs. Liu: Yes. I'm Mrs. Liu. We've just changed rooms, from 706 to 1012. I think I lost my scarf during the move.

Housekeeping: I'm sorry. ________________

Mrs. Liu: It's blue and green, made of silk. Very expensive!

(A) Where did you lose the scarf? (B) Which room do you like better?
(C) What does your scarf look like? (D) Why did you move to another room?

客房清潔：需要幫忙嗎？
劉太太：我是劉太太。我們剛從 706 號房換到 1012 號房。我的圍巾好像在換房間的時候不見了。
客房清潔：對不起。________
劉太太：是藍色和綠色的，絲質的。很貴！
(A) 您在哪裡弄丟圍巾的？ (B) 您比較喜歡哪個房間？
(C) 您的圍巾是什麼樣子？ (D) 您為什麼要換到別的房間？

解析

空格後，劉太太說 "It's blue and green, made of silk."（是藍色和綠色的，絲質的。）得知，客房清潔應在詢問圍巾的外觀，因此 (C) 項應為正選。

其他重點

1. **scarf** [skɑrf] *n.* 圍巾（複數為 scarfs / scarves [skɑrvz]）
2. **silk** [sɪlk] *n.* 絲

D **19.**

Ms. Lee: Are you an art lover, Johnson?
Johnson: I'm passionate about art. I majored in art history and modern sculpture.
Ms. Lee: Impressive! ________
Johnson: Your focus on modern art matches my background and interests. I'm excited to use what I've learned at this job.
Ms. Lee: That's great to hear. We'll let you know the outcome as soon as possible.
(A) Have you heard the outcome yet? (B) Are you majoring in modern history?
(C) What's your educational background? (D) Why do you want to work at my gallery?

李小姐：強森，你喜歡藝術嗎？
強　森：我可喜歡藝術了。我曾經主修藝術史和現代雕塑。
李小姐：相當優秀！________
強　森：貴公司著重在現代藝術，跟我的背景興趣相當吻合。我很期待能把所學運用在這份工作中。
李小姐：很好。我們會盡快通知你結果。
(A) 你已經知道結果了嗎？ (B) 你現在主修現代史嗎？
(C) 你的學歷背景是什麼？ (D) 你為什麼想在我的畫廊工作？

解析

空格後，強森說 "Your focus on modern art matches my background and interests. I'm excited to use what I've learned at this job."（貴公司著重在現代藝術，跟我的背景興趣相當吻合。我很期待能把所學運用在這份工作中。）得知，李小姐應在詢問強森為什麼想要應徵此份工作，因此 (D) 項應為正選。

其他重點

1. **passionate** [ˋpæʃənət] *a.* 熱情的，激昂的
   be passionate about...　　熱愛……
   例: Robert is passionate about playing the guitar and writing songs.
   （羅伯特熱愛彈吉他和寫歌。）
2. **sculpture** [ˋskʌlptʃɚ] *n.* 雕刻（不可數）；雕刻作品（可數）
3. **background** [ˋbækˌgraʊnd] *n.* 背景
4. **outcome** [ˋaʊtˌkʌm] *n.* 結果
5. **gallery** [ˋgælərɪ] *n.* 畫廊

B **20.**

Paul: I read an article online. It said Thomas Edison (湯瑪斯・愛迪生) didn't actually invent the light bulb. What he did was make it work for homes.

Jack: Really? ________________

Paul: The article said it's Humphry Davy, a scientist. He created the first electric light.

(A) But who finally switched it off?

(B) Then who came up with it first?

(C) Who bought the first light bulb anyway?

(D) So who did he really invite to his home?

保羅：我看到一篇網路文章，說湯瑪斯・愛迪生其實沒有真的發明電燈泡。他所做的是讓電燈泡可以在家裡使用。

傑克：真的假的？________________

保羅：文章說是一個叫漢弗里・戴維的科學家。他發明了第一個電燈。

(A) 但最後是誰把它關掉了？　　(B) 那最早是誰弄出來的？

(C) 到底是誰買了第一顆電燈泡？　　(D) 所以他到底邀請了誰去他家？

解析

空格後，保羅說 "The article said it's Humphry Davy, a scientist. He created the first electric light."（文章說是一名科學家，漢弗里・戴維。他發明了第一個電燈。）得知，傑克在問是誰先發明電燈的，因此 (B) 項應為正選。

其他重點

1. **invent** [ɪnˋvɛnt] *vt.* 發明

例: The company invented a more efficient way to recycle plastic.
（這間公司發明了一種更有效率的回收塑膠的方法。）

2. **bulb** [bʌlb] *n.* 電燈泡（= light bulb）
3. **scientist** [ˋsaɪəntɪst] *n.* 科學家
4. **electric** [ɪˋlɛktrɪk] *a.* 電的
5. **switch off...** 關掉……

例: Please switch off the lights when you leave the room.
（離開房間時請關燈。）

III. 綜合測驗

◎ 21 - 24

Taiwan won 43 awards, including two golds, at the 47th WorldSkills Competition hosted by France in September 2024. About 1,400 students competed in over 60 skill categories __21__ robotics, carpentry, and refrigeration and air conditioning. Taiwan's competitors Tsai Yun-rong (蔡昀融) and Chen Sz-yuan (陳思源) won the top awards in cabinetmaking, and refrigeration and air conditioning, respectively. Tsai said he dedicated many hours of study and practice to his skills. Encouraged __22__ his father, Tsai tried woodworking in kindergarten. Since junior high school, he has spent 12 hours every day in the carpentry workshop to improve his skills. As for Chen, he emphasized the importance of hands-on training. Chen joined a training program in refrigeration and air conditioning at the age of 15, and __23__ the six-month course when most people dropped out. The two winners are clear examples of learning by doing. They develop their skills through direct experience and __24__ over a long period of time. The competition, also known as "Skills Olympics," provides a global stage for young people to demonstrate their talents.

21. (A) compared with (B) except for (C) such as (D) rather than
22. (A) at (B) by (C) from (D) with
23. (A) complete (B) completed (C) completing (D) will complete
24. (A) constant practice (B) giving awards (C) robotics talents (D) speech training

臺灣在 2024 年九月於法國舉辦的第四十七屆國際技能競賽中，榮獲包括兩面金牌在內的四十三個獎項。此次競賽約有一千四百名學生參賽，涵蓋超過六十個技能項目，像是機器人技能、木工以及冷凍空調等。臺灣選手蔡昀融和陳思源分別在傢俱木工與冷凍空調項目奪得金牌。蔡昀融說他投入了大量時間研習苦練以精進自己的技能。由於父親的鼓勵，他在幼兒園時便開始接觸木工。從國中開始他就每天花十二小時泡在木工場裡加強磨練。至於陳思源，他強調實作訓練的重要性。陳思源在十五歲時就參加一個冷凍空調的訓練課程，並在大多數人中途退出的情況下完成為期六個月的課程。這兩位金牌得主是「從實踐中學習」的範例。他們透過長時間的實際操作與不斷練習來培養技能。這項被譽為「技藝奧林匹克」[註]的競賽為年輕人提供了一個展現才華的國際舞臺。

註：本句中的 "Skills Olympics," 前建議加上 the。

C **21.**

解析

1. (A) **(be) compared with...** 與……相比

 例: Compared with city life, living in the countryside feels much more peaceful.
 （和城市生活相比，鄉村生活感覺寧靜多了。）

 (B) **except for...** 除了……（本身不包含在內）

 例: Except for weekends, the library opens at nine every morning.
 （除了週末外，圖書館每天早上九點開門。）

 (C) **such as...** 像是……

 例: Many fruits, such as bananas and oranges, are rich in vitamins.
 （許多水果如香蕉和柳丁等都富含維他命。）

 (D) **rather than + N/V/V-ing** 而不是……
 = instead of + N/V-ing

 例: Rather than complaining, you should find a solution to the problem.
 （與其抱怨，你應該尋找問題的解決方法。）

2. 根據語意，可知 (C) 項應為正選。

B **22.**

解析

1. 本題測試以下固定用法：

 be encouraged by... 受……鼓勵

 例: The young athlete was encouraged by his family to keep chasing his dreams.
 （這位年輕運動員受到家人的鼓勵，持續追夢。）

2. 原句實為：
Tsai was encouraged by his father, and Tsai tried woodworking in kindergarten.
上句包含兩個句構完整的子句，因兩子句有相同的主詞 Tsai，可將第一句的主詞省略，再將過去式 be 動詞 was 改為現在分詞 being 後予以省略，形成表被動語態的分詞構句。
3. 根據上述用法，可知 (B) 項應為正選。

B **23.**

解析

1. 空格前有一完整句子 Chen joined... of 15 及對等連接詞 and，依句意可推知 and 連接兩個子句，空格應置與前半句中的簡單過去式動詞 joined 對等的另一動詞，此動詞亦應使用簡單過去式，兩個子句皆是敘述過去的事實。
2. 根據上述，可知 (B) 項應為正選。

A **24.**

解析

1. 空格前有介詞 through、名詞詞組 direct experience（實際操作）及對等連接詞 and，得知空格應置 and 連接的另一個名詞（詞組），兩個名詞（詞組）皆作 through 的受詞。
2. (B) giving awards（頒發獎項）、(C) robotics talents（機器人技術方面的天分）、(D) speech training（演說訓練）置入後皆不符語意，僅 (A) constant practice（不斷練習）置入後符合語意，可知 (A) 項應為正選。

重要單字片語

1. **competition** [ˌkɑmpəˋtɪʃən] *n.* 比賽（可數）；競爭（不可數）
   compete [kəmˋpit] *vi.* 競爭
   competitor [kəmˋpɛtətɚ] *n.* 競爭者，參賽者
   例: Athletes from different countries compete for gold medals at the Olympics.
   （來自各國的選手在奧運中爭取金牌。）
2. **category** [ˋkætəˌgorɪ] *n.* 種類；範疇
3. **carpentry** [ˋkɑrpəntrɪ] *n.* 木工手藝（不可數）
4. **refrigeration** [rɪˌfrɪdʒəˋreʃən] *n.* 冷藏，冷凍（不可數）
5. **respectively** [rɪˋspɛktɪvlɪ] *adv.* 分別，各自
6. **dedicate** [ˋdɛdəˌket] *vt.* 奉獻；獻出（音樂作品、書等）
   dedicate A to B　將 A 奉獻給 B
   例: The artist dedicated her latest painting to her late grandmother.
   （這位藝術家將最新畫作獻給已故的祖母。）
7. **workshop** [ˋwɝkˌʃɑp] *n.* 實習工場；作坊；研討會；工作室

8. **hands-on** [ˋhændz,ɑn] *a.* 實際動手做的

9. **drop out** 中途退出；輟學
(drop 的三態為：drop, dropped [drɑpt], dropped)
例: Some participants dropped out halfway through the marathon because of injury.
（有些參賽者因受傷在馬拉松中途退賽。）

10. **constant** [ˋkɑnstənt] *a.* 持續的；穩定的

11. **be known / famous / renowned as...** 以……的身分而聞名
例: Taipei is known as a vibrant city full of culture and delicious food.
（臺北是知名的文化與美食滿點的蓬勃城市。）

12. **demonstrate** [ˋdɛmən,stret] *vt.* 展示，示範 & *vi.* 示威
例: Lydia demonstrated her cooking skills at the annual food festival yesterday.
（莉迪亞昨天在年度美食節上展現了她的烹飪技巧。）

◎ **25 - 28**

E-cigarettes were once advertised as a healthier choice than regular cigarettes. Their sweet flavors and cool designs have made the public believe they are harmless. __25__, the truth is e-cigarettes contain nicotine (尼古丁), which can lead to addiction and lung damage. According to an expert at the Einstein Medical Center in Philadelphia, __26__ a teaspoonful of liquid nicotine could kill a person weighing 91 kilograms. Despite the risks, the number of high school students who smoke e-cigarettes __27__ worldwide in the past five years. In Taiwan, more and more teenagers are smoking e-cigarettes. A 2021 survey found that 3.9% of junior high and 8.8% of high school students used e-cigarettes. One possible reason for this trend is the ease of buying e-cigarettes online. Sellers even deliver them to convenience stores. __28__, Taiwan's government banned e-cigarettes starting in 2023. They also reminded teenagers to follow the "Three No's Policy": no trying, no buying, and no recommending e-cigarettes. Otherwise, there would be a fine of up to NT$10,000.

25. (A) However (B) Therefore (C) At last (D) By chance

26. (A) as far as (B) as tall as (C) as little as (D) as many as

27. (A) double (B) has doubled (C) will double (D) have doubled

28. (A) To stop this rise (B) Due to the price
(C) With regard to fashion (D) Instead of taking action

電子菸曾經被宣傳為比傳統香菸更健康的選擇。它們香甜的風味和酷炫的設計讓大眾相信它們是無害的。然而真相是：電子菸含有致癮和損害肺部的尼古丁。費城愛因斯坦醫療中心的一位專家表示，僅僅一茶匙的液態尼古丁就足以殺死一個體重 91 公斤的人。儘管有這些風險，過去五年來全球吸電子菸的高中生人數仍然翻了一倍。在臺灣，越來越多青少年開始吸電子菸。2021 年的一項調查顯示，3.9% 的國中生和 8.8% 的高中生吸過電子菸。造成這趨勢的原因之一可能是上網買電子菸很容易。賣家甚至能把電子菸送到超商供人取貨。為了遏止這種上升趨勢，臺灣政府自 2023 年起全面禁止電子菸。同時政府也提醒青少年遵守「三不政策」：不嘗試、不購買、不推薦電子菸。違者將面臨最高新臺幣一萬元的罰鍰。

A **25.**

解析

1. (A) **however** [haʊˋɛvɚ] *adv.* 然而；無論如何

   例: Hank had never acted before; however, his performance tonight was outstanding.
   （漢克以前從未演過戲；然而他今晚的表演非常出色。）

   (B) **therefore** [ˋðɛr͵fɔr] *adv.* 因此

   例: The road was blocked; therefore, we had to find another route.
   （道路被封了，因此我們只好另找路線。）

   (C) **at last** 最終；終於

   例: After what seemed like hours of searching, we found a parking spot at last.
   （我們找車位時感覺花了好幾個小時，最後終於找到車位。）

   (D) **by chance** 偶然間

   例: I found out about the meeting by chance because no one informed me officially.
   （我是在偶然之中才得知這場會議，因為沒有人正式通知我。）

2. 根據語意，可知 (A) 項應為正選。

C **26.**

解析

1. (A) **as far as...** 與……一樣遠（表距離）；就……而言

   例: John can run as far as Linda.
   （約翰跑步可以跑得跟琳達一樣遠。）

   (B) **as tall as...** 與……一樣高（表高度）

   例: No one in my class is as tall as Ian.
   （我班上沒人跟伊恩一樣高。）

(C) **as little as...** 與……一樣少，僅有……（表數量極少）

例: As little as ten minutes of exercise a day can improve your health.
（每天只要運動十分鐘就能改善健康。）

(D) **as many as...** 與……一樣多，多達……（表數量多）

例: As many as 50 employees attended the meeting this morning.
（今天早上多達 50 位員工參與了該會議。）

2. 空格後為 a teaspoonful of liquid nicotine（一茶匙的液態尼古丁），並且強調 could kill a person weighing 91 kilograms（足以殺死一個體重 91 公斤的人），可知空格應與後文為對比關係。由此可知 (C) 項應為正選。

B **27.**

解析

1. 由空格後 ... in the past five years（過去五年來）可判斷時態應為現在完成式。而本句主詞為 the number of high school students who smoke e-cigarettes（吸電子菸的高中生人數）應視為單數。
2. 根據上述，可知 (B) 項應為正選。

A **28.**

解析

1. 空格前說明根據 2021 年的一項調查，臺灣的國、高中生皆有一定比例吸過電子菸，一個可能原因是網購電子菸很容易，空格後說明臺灣政府自 2023 年起全面禁止電子菸。
2. 四個選項之中：(A) to stop this rise（為了遏止這種上升趨勢）、(B) due to the price（因為這個價格）、(C) with regard to fashion（以流行為考量）、(D) instead of taking action（未能採取行動），僅 (A) 置入後符合語意，可知 (A) 項應為正選。

重要單字片語

1. **cigarette** [ˌsɪgəˋrɛt / ˋsɪgəˌrɛt] *n.* 香菸
   e-cigarette 電子菸
2. **advertise** [ˋædvɚˌtaɪz] *vt.* 將……登廣告；宣傳……
   be advertised as... 被宣傳為……
   例: This new smartphone is advertised as having the best camera on the market.
   （這款新的智慧手機被宣傳是擁有市面上最佳的攝影鏡頭。）
3. **flavor** [ˋflevɚ] *n.* 口味 & *vt.* 給……調味
4. **addiction** [əˋdɪkʃən] *n.* 上癮
5. **despite** [dɪˋspaɪt] *prep.* 儘管
   despite + N/V-ing 儘管……
   = in spite of + N/V-ing
   例: Despite / In spite of the rain, they went ahead with the outdoor wedding.
   （儘管下雨，他們仍照常舉行那場戶外婚禮。）

6. **risk** [rɪsk] *n.* 風險 & *vt.* 冒……的風險
take the risk of + V-ing　冒險從事……
例: Dan took the risk of investing all his savings in a new restaurant.
（丹冒著風險把所有積蓄投入一家新餐廳。）

7. **survey** [ˋsɝve] *n.* 調查

8. **trend** [trɛnd] *n.* 趨勢；潮流

9. **ban** [bæn] *vt.* 下令禁止（三態為：ban, banned [bænd], banned）& *n.* 禁令
例: The school banned smartphones during class hours.
（學校禁止上課期間使用智慧手機。）

10. **remind** [rɪˋmaɪnd] *vt.* 提醒；使想起
remind sb of sth/sb　使某人想起某事物 / 某人
例: Your smile reminds me of a very good friend of mine.
（你的微笑讓我想起一位很好的朋友。）

11. **recommend** [ˌrɛkəˋmɛnd] *vt.* 推薦；建議
recommend that + S + (should) + V　建議……
例: The doctor recommended that my mom get more exercise.
（醫生建議我媽媽要多運動。）

IV. 閱讀測驗

◎ 29 - 30

Answer the questions based on the poster below.

Dorothy Hodgkin: an outstanding chemist who won a Nobel Prize in 1964 for her studies in vitamins.

Grace Hopper: a mathematician who was a pioneer in developing computer technology. She served in the U.S. Navy during World War II.

Maria Mayer: a scientist who won a Nobel Prize in 1963 for her work in atomic science.

Maria Mitchell: a famous astronomer who discovered a new comet in 1847. She was the first woman ever to be voted into the American Academy of Arts and Sciences.

Nancy Roman: an astronomer who worked with rockets and space exploration. She was called a "wizard in math" while in college.

Chien-Shiung Wu: a nuclear physicist who was regarded as the "top woman experimental physicist in the world" by Princeton University in 1958. She came to the United States from China.

請根據以下海報回答問題。

桃樂絲・霍奇金：傑出化學家，以其對維生素的研究獲得 1964 年諾貝爾獎。
葛麗絲・霍普：數學家，電腦科技發展的先驅。在第二次世界大戰期間服役於美國海軍。
瑪麗亞・梅耶：科學家，以其在原子科學方面的研究獲得 1963 年諾貝爾獎。
瑪麗亞・米切爾：著名天文學家，於 1847 年發現一顆新彗星。她是第一位被選入美國藝術與科學學院的女性。
南希・羅曼：天文學家，專攻火箭和太空探險。她在大學期間被稱為「數學奇才」。
吳健雄：核物理學家，1958 年被普林斯頓大學譽為「世界頂尖的女性實驗物理學家」。從中國到美國來發展。

A **29.**

What is the best title for the poster?
(A) The power of women
(B) Wizards in World War II
(C) The Nobel Prize winners
(D) Women chemists in the world

這張海報的最佳標題為何？
(A) 女性的力量
(B) 二次世界大戰中的奇才
(C) 諾貝爾獎得主
(D) 世界上的女性化學家

理由:
根據此張海報中六名人物的共通點為她們都是傑出的女性，故 (A) 項應為正選。

D **30.**

According to the poster, which of the following statements is **NOT** true?
(A) Maria Mitchell was an astronomer who found a new comet.
(B) Dorothy Hodgkin and Maria Mayer were Nobel Prize winners.
(C) Grace Hopper and Nancy Roman were good at mathematics.
(D) Chien-Shiung Wu was a scientist born in the United States.

根據海報，下列哪一項敘述不正確？
(A) 瑪麗亞・米切爾是發現新彗星的天文學家。
(B) 桃樂絲・霍奇金和瑪麗亞・梅耶是諾貝爾獎得主。
(C) 葛麗絲・霍普和南希・羅曼擅長數學。
(D) 吳健雄是出生在美國的科學家。

理由:
根據海報的最後一句 "She came to the United States from China."（從中國到美國來發展。）得知吳健雄是從中國來的，並非在美國出生，故 (D) 項應為正選。

重要單字片語

1. **poster** [ˋpostɚ] *n.* 海報
2. **outstanding** [aʊtˋstændɪŋ] *a.* 傑出的
3. **chemist** [ˋkɛmɪst] *n.* 化學家
4. **vitamin** [ˋvaɪtəmɪn] *n.* 維他命；維生素
5. **pioneer** [ˏpaɪəˋnɪr] *n.* 先驅，開拓者
6. **navy** [ˋnevɪ] *n.* 海軍
7. **atomic** [əˋtɑmɪk] *a.* 原子的
8. **astronomer** [əˋstrɑnəmɚ] *n.* 天文學家
9. **discover** [dɪsˋkʌvɚ] *vt.* 發現
   例: We were excited to discover a beautiful waterfall during our hike.
   （我們在健行時很興奮地發現了一個美麗的瀑布。）
10. **comet** [ˋkɑmɪt] *n.* 彗星
11. **academy** [əˋkædəmɪ] *n.*（專門培養專才的）學院
12. **rocket** [ˋrɑkɪt] *n.* 火箭
13. **exploration** [ˏɛkspləˋreʃən] *n.* 研究，調查；探險，探測
14. **wizard** [ˋwɪzɚd] *n.*（某方面的）行家，奇才；男巫
15. **nuclear** [ˋn(j)uklɪɚ] *a.* 核子的
16. **physicist** [ˋfɪzɪsɪst] *n.* 物理學家
17. **regard** [rɪˋgɑrd] *vt.* 把……視為
    regard A as B　將 A 視為 B
    例: People regard Tom as a talented musician.
    （人們視湯姆為才華洋溢的音樂家。）
18. **experimental** [ɪkˏspɛrəˋmɛntḷ] *a.* 實驗性的

◎ 31 - 32

Dave is seeking Betty's advice on choosing a mobile data plan. Answer the questions based on the conversation and the table below.

Dave: Hey Betty, I need your advice on choosing a cell phone plan.
Betty: Of course. What's the most important to you in a data plan?
Dave: I need a lot of data since I play online games and watch tons of videos online.
Betty: Me too. How much data are you thinking of?
Dave: My plan with Horizon offers 10 GB at NT$ 399[註]. I'm considering upgrading to 20 GB.
Betty: If you watch videos very often, you might need unlimited data.
Dave: Unlimited? Isn't that super expensive?
Betty: Not necessarily. My plan is NT$ 699 per month with unlimited data, calls and texts.
Dave: Really? I'll switch to the same plan then. Thanks a lot!
Betty: You're welcome!

Horizon Mobile Data Plans		
Plan	***Fee / Month***	***Data / Month***
A*	NT$ 399	10 GB
B	NT$ 599	20 GB
C*	NT$ 699	unlimited
D	NT$ 999	unlimited

＊ Special discounts for students only

戴夫正在請貝蒂提供選擇行動數據方案的建議。請根據對話和下方表格回答問題。

戴夫：嘿，貝蒂，我要向妳請教怎麼選手機資費方案。

貝蒂：好啊。你在選數據方案時最看重哪一點？

戴夫：我要大流量的，因為我有玩線上遊戲，也看非常多影片。

貝蒂：我也是。那你打算選多大流量？

戴夫：我現在用的地平線方案，月租費新臺幣 399 元，流量 10 GB。我在考慮升級到 20 GB。

貝蒂：如果你常看影片，可能會需要流量吃到飽哦。

戴夫：吃到飽？那不是很貴？

貝蒂：也不見得。我現在的方案月租費新臺幣 699 元，可以無限上網、通話和傳簡訊。

戴夫：真的嗎？那我要換成跟妳一樣的方案。太謝謝妳了！

貝蒂：不客氣！

地平線行動數據方案		
方案	*月租費*	*每月可用流量*
A*	NT$ 399	10 GB
B	NT$ 599	20 GB
C*	NT$ 699	吃到飽
D	NT$ 999	吃到飽

＊ 僅限學生的特別折扣

註：金錢符號 $ 與後面的數字間不需空格。

D **31.**

According to the conversation and the table, which of the following statements is **NOT** true?

(A) Both Dave and Betty play games and watch videos online.

(B) Horizon offers two different types of discounts to students.

(C) Dave's current data plan includes 10 GB of data per month.

(D) Betty wants to upgrade her data plan to include 20 GB of data.

根據對話和表格，下列哪一項敘述不正確？

(A) 戴夫和貝蒂都會上網玩遊戲和看影片。

(B) 地平線方案提供兩種不同類型的學生折扣。

(C) 戴夫目前的數據方案包含每月 10 GB 流量。

(D) 貝蒂想把她的數據方案升級到 20 GB 流量。

理由:

根據對話倒數第六段，戴夫考慮把他的數據方案升級到 20 GB，而倒數第三段貝蒂說她目前的數據方案是 "unlimited data"（無限上網），得知是戴夫而非貝蒂想升級數據方案，故 (D) 項敘述不正確，應為正選。

C **32.**

According to the conversation, which data plan will Dave choose in the end?

(A) Plan A

(B) Plan B

(C) Plan C

(D) Plan D

根據對話，戴夫最後會選擇哪一個數據方案？

(A) A 方案

(B) B 方案

(C) C 方案

(D) D 方案

理由:

根據對話倒數第三段，貝蒂說她目前的數據方案是月租費新臺幣 699 元，可以無限上網、通話和傳簡訊，而戴夫接著說 "I'll switch to the same plan then."（那我要換成跟妳一樣的方案。）得知他選擇 C 方案，故 (C) 項應為正選。

重要單字片語

1. **tons of...** 許多的……

   例: Tons of tourists visit this beautiful island every summer for vacation.
   （每年夏天有許多遊客來到這座美麗的島嶼度假。）

2. **horizon** [həˋraɪzn̩] *n.* 地平線（單數）；範圍，範疇（常用複數）

   broaden one's horizons 開闊某人的眼界（本片語中 horizons 恆為複數）

3. **upgrade** [ˌʌpˋgred] *vt.* & [ˋʌpgred] *n.* 升級

例: I plan to upgrade my old laptop before the new semester starts.
（我打算在開學前升級我的舊筆電。）

4. **switch** [swɪtʃ] *vi.* 轉換 & *vt.* 打開／關閉（開關）& *n.* 開關

switch to sth　轉換成某物

例: I switched to a healthier diet after visiting the nutritionist last month.
（我上個月去見了營養師後，就轉換到更健康的飲食。）

◎ 33 - 35

The table below contains data on typhoons that hit Taiwan in 2021, 2022, and 2023. Answer the questions based on the table below.

Year	Typhoon Name	Warning Period (Dates)	Intensity near Taiwan
2023	KOINU	2023-10-02 ~ 2023-10-06	Moderate Intensity
2023	HAIKUI	2023-09-01 ~ 2023-09-05	Moderate Intensity
2023	SAOLA	2023-08-28 ~ 2023-08-31	Intense Intensity
2023	KHANUN	2023-08-01 ~ 2023-08-04	Moderate Intensity
2023	DOKSURI	2023-07-24 ~ 2023-07-28	Moderate Intensity
2023	MAWAR	2023-05-29 ~ 2023-05-31	Moderate Intensity
2022	NESAT	2022-10-15 ~ 2022-10-16	Moderate Intensity
2022	MUIFA	2022-09-11 ~ 2022-09-13	Moderate Intensity
2022	HINNAMNOR	2022-09-02 ~ 2022-09-04	Intense Intensity
2021	KOMPASU	2021-10-10 ~ 2021-10-12	Severe tropical storm
2021	CHANTHU	2021-09-10 ~ 2021-09-13	Intense Intensity
2021	LUPIT	2021-08-04 ~ 2021-08-05	Severe tropical storm
2021	IN-FA	2021-07-21 ~ 2021-07-24	Moderate Intensity
2021	CHOI-WAN	2021-06-03 ~ 2021-06-04	Severe tropical storm

以下表格包含在 2021、2022 及 2023 年間侵襲臺灣的颱風資料。請依照表格內容回答問題。

年份	颱風名	警報期間（日期）	接近臺灣時的強度
2023	小犬	2023-10-02 ~ 2023-10-06	中度
2023	海葵	2023-09-01 ~ 2023-09-05	中度
2023	蘇拉	2023-08-28 ~ 2023-08-31	強烈
2023	卡努	2023-08-01 ~ 2023-08-04	中度
2023	杜蘇芮	2023-07-24 ~ 2023-07-28	中度
2023	瑪娃	2023-05-29 ~ 2023-05-31	中度
2022	尼莎	2022-10-15 ~ 2022-10-16	中度
2022	梅花	2022-09-11 ~ 2022-09-13	中度
2022	軒嵐諾	2022-09-02 ~ 2022-09-04	強烈
2021	圓規	2021-10-10 ~ 2021-10-12	強烈熱帶風暴
2021	燦樹	2021-09-10 ~ 2021-09-13	強烈
2021	盧碧	2021-08-04 ~ 2021-08-05	強烈熱帶風暴
2021	煙花	2021-07-21 ~ 2021-07-24	中度
2021	彩雲	2021-06-03 ~ 2021-06-04	強烈熱帶風暴

B **33.**

Which month has[註1] the most typhoons in 2023?

(A) July

(B) August

(C) September

(D) October

2023 年哪個月份有最多颱風侵襲？

(A) 七月

(B) 八月

(C) 九月

(D) 十月

理由:

由表格可知 2023 年七月、九月、十月各有一個颱風侵襲，八月有兩個颱風侵襲，故 (B) 項應為正選。

註1：因為本句說明是 2023 年發生的事情，故動詞 has 宜改為過去式 had。

D **34.**

Which of the following statements is true?

(A) There were a total of six typhoons in 2021.

(B) There were more typhoons in 2022 than in 2021.

(C) Both typhoons MUIFA and LUPIT hit Taiwan in 2022.

(D) Most typhoons were of Moderate Intensity during the three years.

以下敘述何者正確？

(A) 2021 年總共有 6 個颱風。

(B) 2022 年的颱風比 2021 年多。

(C) 梅花颱風跟盧碧颱風都是在 2022 年時侵襲臺灣。

(D) 這三年間大多數的颱風都是中度颱風。

理由:

由表格可知 (A) 2021 年共有 5 個颱風侵襲，並非 6 個；(B) 2022 年共有 3 個颱風侵襲，所以比 2021 年少；(C) 盧碧颱風於 2021 年侵襲臺灣，並非 2022 年。故 (D) 項應為正選。

D **35.**

Which of the following charts shows the data on the table correctly?

(A)

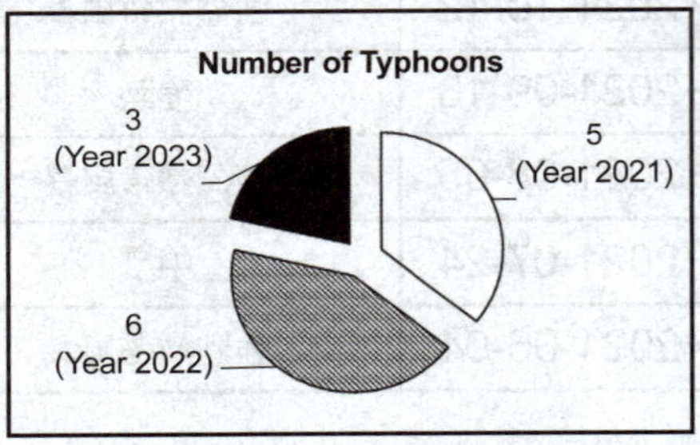

(B)

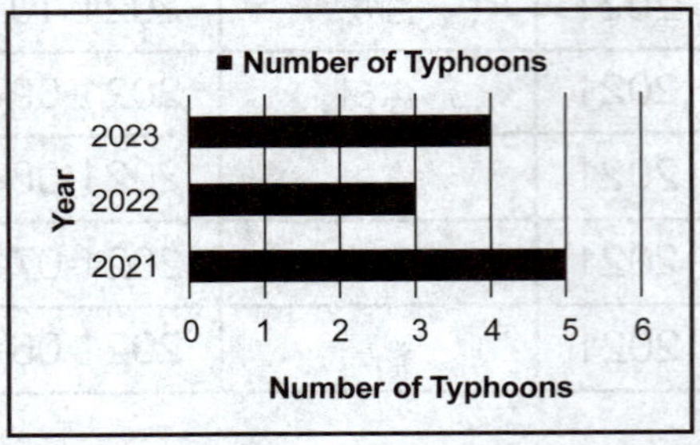

(C)

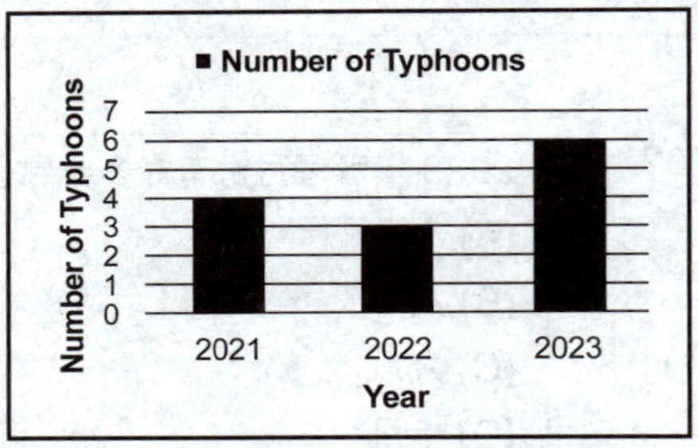

(D)

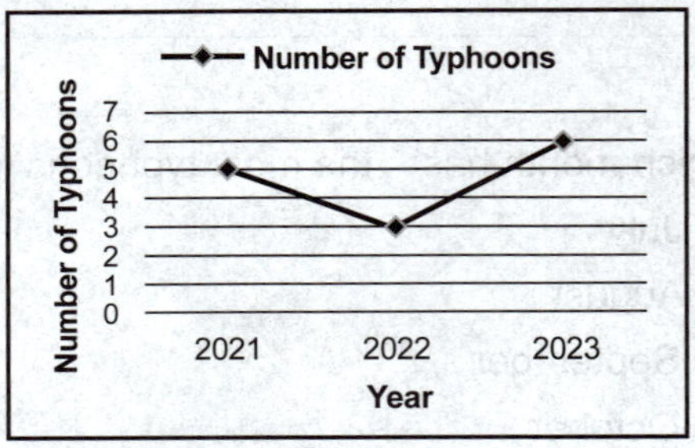

下列哪張圖表正確呈現了表格中的資料？

(A)

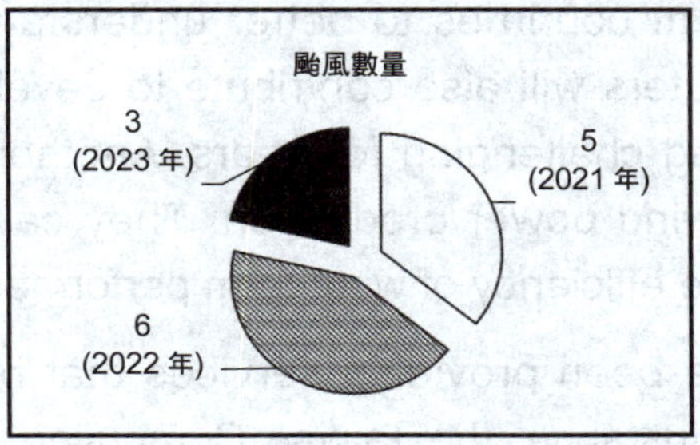

(B)

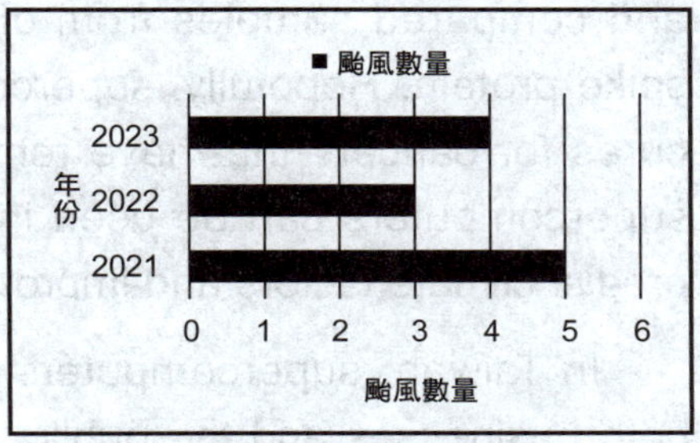

(C)

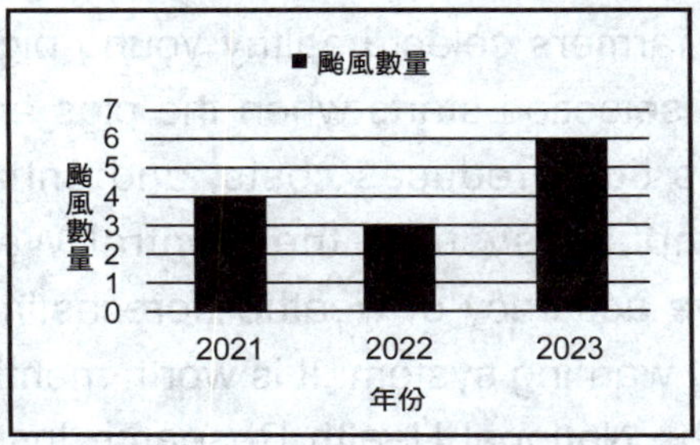

(D)

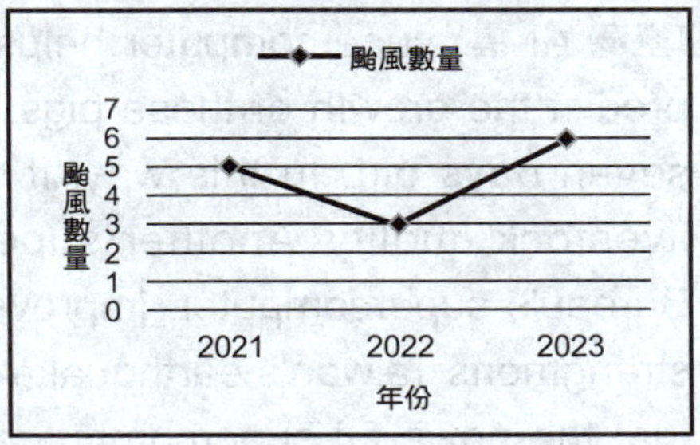

理由:

本題測驗學生理解內文表格的程度：2021 年共有 5 個颱風侵襲臺灣；2022 年共有 3 個颱風侵襲臺灣；2023 年共有 6 個颱風侵襲臺灣。故 (D) 項應為正選。

重要單字片語

1. **table** [ˋtebḷ] *n.*（用列與欄呈現數據的）表格；桌子
   chart [tʃɑrt] *n.*（用圖呈現數據的）圖表

2. **contain** [kənˋten] *vt.* 包含，裝有
   例: This box contains all the tools you need for gardening.
   （這個箱子裡面有做園藝時需要的所有工具。）

◎ 36 - 38

With the rise of AI, supercomputers have become more important than ever. These powerful machines can process large amounts of data quickly. They help drive innovation and improve efficiency in the modern economy. Increasingly, governments and companies are building advanced supercomputing systems.

Around the world, supercomputers have already made an impact in various fields. During the pandemic, a supercomputer helped scientists isolate and identify the spike protein (棘蛋白) in COVID-19 virus. **It** analyzed and compared samples from different countries to better understand the spike protein. Hopefully, supercomputers will also contribute to developing cures for cancers that have remained challenging for years. Another area supercomputers can be used in is wind power production. They can help predict climate factors and improve the efficiency of wind farm performance.

In Taiwan, supercomputers have been providing services that benefit both businesses and the public. For instance, the Taiwan Computing Cloud (臺灣 AI 雲) supercomputer helps pig farmers select healthy young pigs and predict the growth of these pigs. The selection starts when the pigs are just seven days old. In this way, it saves time, reduces costs, and enhances livestock quality. Another supercomputer system, the Central Weather Bureau's supercomputer, improves the accuracy of weather forecasting and strengthens Taiwan's earthquake early warning system. It is worth mentioning that the powerful supercomputer at the National Health Research Institutes supports advanced biotechnology and pharmaceutical projects. This contributes to better health of the population.

In conclusion, supercomputing is not just about technology; it is also about shaping the future. As computing power increases, it will enable more innovation and new creation.

隨著人工智慧興起，超級電腦變得空前重要。這種強大的設備能快速處理大量資料，推動創新並提升現代經濟的效率。各國政府與企業也正逐步建立先進的超級電腦運算系統。

在全球範圍內，超級電腦已在各領域展現其影響力。疫情期間，超級電腦協助科學家分離並辨識新冠病毒[註1]中的棘蛋白。它分析並比對來自不同國家的樣本，以深入了解棘蛋白。多年來癌症一直令醫界頭痛不已，而在未來，超級電腦有望在開發癌症療法上有所貢獻。另一個應用領域是風力發電，超級電腦可以協助預測氣候因素，提升風力發電廠的運作效率。

在臺灣，超級電腦一直都在提供裨益企業和民眾的服務。例如「臺灣 AI 雲」的超級電腦協助豬農挑選健康的豬仔並預測這些豬仔的生長情況。篩選程序從豬仔出生七天起就開始了，如此一來，既可節省時間、降低成本又可提升家畜的品質。另一個例子是中央氣象署的超級電腦，它改善了氣象預報的準確度，也強化了臺灣的地震預警系統。值得一提的是，國家衛生研究院的強大超級電腦支援先進的生技製藥計畫，有助於提升全民健康[註2]。

總結來說，超級電腦運算不僅是科技的進步，更形塑了未來。隨著電腦運算能力的提升，將會促成更多創新與新發明[註3]。

註1：本句中的 COVID-19 virus 前應加上 the。

註2：本句中的 health of the population 建議改為 public health 較為自然。

註3：本句中的 new creation 建議改為 creativity 較為自然。

C **36.**

What is the main idea of this passage?

(A) The theories of supercomputing

(B) The pros and cons of supercomputers

(C) The use and impact of supercomputers

(D) The medical practice of supercomputing

本文的主旨是什麼？

(A) 超級電腦運算的理論

(B) 超級電腦的優缺點

(C) 超級電腦的用途與影響

(D) 超級電腦運算在醫療上的應用[註4]

理由:

本文旨在介紹超級電腦在各領域的應用，包括疫情研究、風力發電、畜牧業、氣象預報與生技研發，主要強調超級電腦的用途與帶來的影響，故 (C) 項應為正選。

註4：此處語意不清，應改為 The use of supercomputing in medical practice 方指「超級電腦在醫療上的用途」。

C **37.**

What does "**It**" in the second paragraph refer to?

(A) an impact

(B) the pandemic

(C) a supercomputer

(D) the spike protein

第二段中的 **It** 指的是什麼？

(A) 影響

(B) 疫情

(C) 超級電腦

(D) 棘蛋白

理由:

前句敘述 "During the pandemic, a supercomputer helped scientists isolate and identify the spike protein in COVID-19 virus."（疫情期間，超級電腦協助科學家分離並辨識新冠病毒中的棘蛋白。），依前後句意可推知代名詞 It 指的是前句中的 a supercomputer（超級電腦），故 (C) 項應為正選。

B **38.**

According to the passage, which function is **NOT** mentioned in the third paragraph?
(A) Helping people become healthier
(B) Enhancing wind power performance
(C) Improving Taiwan's livestock quality
(D) Providing more accurate weather forecasts

根據本文，第三段未提及哪一項功能？
(A) 幫助人們變得更健康
(B) 提升風力發電表現
(C) 改善臺灣的家畜品質
(D) 提供更準確的天氣預報

理由:
第三段提及多項臺灣超級電腦的應用，包括幫助豬農挑選健康豬仔與預測成長，進而節省時間、降低成本並提升家畜的品質，以及改善氣象預報的精準度和強化地震預警系統，並能支援生技製藥計畫，促進全民健康，而提升風力發電效率是在第二段中提到，故 (B) 項應為正選。

重要單字片語

1. **innovation** [ˌɪnəˋveʃən] *n.* 創新（不可數）
2. **efficiency** [ɪˋfɪʃənsɪ] *n.* 效率（不可數）
3. **economy** [ɪˋkɑnəmɪ] *n.* 經濟；節儉
4. **impact** [ˋɪmpækt] *n.* 影響，衝擊（常與介詞 on 並用）& [ɪmˋpækt] *vt.* 對……產生影響
   make / have an impact on... 對……有影響 / 衝擊
   例: Social media makes an impact on how young people form their opinions today.
   （社群媒體對當代年輕人意見形成的過程具有極大的影響力。）
5. **isolate** [ˋaɪslˌet] *vt.* 分離，隔離，孤立
   isolate A from B　將 A 與 B 隔離
   例: The patient was isolated from others to prevent the virus from spreading.
   （那位病患被隔離以防病毒傳播。）
6. **identify** [aɪˋdɛntəˌfaɪ] *vt.* 識別，指認，認定（三態為：identify, identified [aɪˋdɛntəˌfaɪd], identified）
   identify A as B　將 A 認定為 B
   例: The museum identified the painting as an original work of the artist.
   （博物館將這幅畫認定為那位藝術家的原作。）
7. **virus** [ˋvaɪrəs] *n.*（濾過性）病毒
8. **analyze** [ˋænəˌlaɪz] *vt.* 分析，解析
   例: Scientists analyze weather patterns to prepare for extreme climate changes.
   （科學家分析天氣模式，以應對極端氣候變化。）
9. **contribute** [kənˋtrɪbjut] *vi.* 促成，導致（與介詞 to 並用）& *vt.* 捐助，貢獻
   contribute to + N/V-ing　促成 / 導致……
   = lead to + N/V-ing
   = result in...
   = give rise to + N/V-ing
   = bring about...
   例: The new technology will contribute to lower levels of pollution in urban and rural areas.
   （這項新技術將促使城市與鄉村地區的汙染程度降低。）

10. **predict** [prɪˋdɪkt] *vt.* 預測
例: Experts predict a strong economic recovery in the second half of this year.
（專家預測今年下半年將有強勁的經濟復甦。）

11. **enhance** [ɪnˋhæns] *vt.* 增強，提高
例: Regular practice can greatly enhance your performance in musical competitions.
（規律的練習能大大提升你在音樂比賽中的表現。）

12. **accuracy** [ˋækjərəsɪ] *n.* 準確性（不可數）

13. **strengthen** [ˋstrɛŋθən] *vt.* 加強，鞏固
例: Exercise and a balanced diet strengthen your immune system against diseases.
（運動與均衡飲食能加強免疫系統對抗疾病的能力。）

14. **in conclusion** 總之
= to sum up
例: In conclusion, daily reading significantly improves vocabulary and language skills.
（總之，每天閱讀能大幅增進詞彙量和語言能力。）

15. **creation** [krɪˋeʃən] *n.* 創造（不可數）；創造物，創作品（可數）

16. **the pros and cons** 優缺點，利弊

17. **a weather forecast** 天氣預報

◎ 39 - 42

Taiwan supplies a third of the world's orchids. As Taiwan's top flower exports, orchids brought in export earnings of NT$ 7 billion in 2023. The most popular export variety is Taiwan's unique moth orchids (蝴蝶蘭). Often used as gifts or for displays, moth orchids come in different shapes and colors.

Taiwan's orchid industry emerged in the 1980s. It has flourished with the use of greenhouse farming. In fact, flower exports increased tenfold between 1995 and 2008. In 2007, Taiwan lost its top position in the global flower market to the Netherlands. To cope with this challenge, Taiwan growers worked hard to make themselves different from their competitors. They began focusing on the export of orchid seedlings, young orchid plants that have just grown from seeds. In 2018, Taiwan exported about NT$ 4.5 billion worth of moth orchid seedlings to over 80 countries. The large diversity of native orchids on the island enables the creation of many commercial varieties. Growers mix different native species to develop a new variety. Taiwan has the largest concentration of orchid greenhouse growing and related services in the world.

Taiwan growers' achievements have gained worldwide recognition. In 2024, Taiwan hosted the World Orchid Conference for the first time. The main topics centered on Orchid Technology and Conservation & Preservation. The orchid industry in Taiwan uses high-tech farming and advanced technology. On the other hand, more needs to be done in conservation and preservation. The source of moth orchids for creating new varieties is decreasing. Native species have gradually disappeared from the wild. The orchid industry realized that ecological protection goes hand in hand with economic growth. This was the aim of a volunteer program that began in 2018 to replant native species in nature. Given time, orchids may not only decorate homes but also enrich Taiwan's forest ecosystem.

全球三分之一的蘭花產量都是由臺灣供應的。蘭花是臺灣最大宗的花卉出口項目，在 2023 年為臺灣創造新臺幣 70 億元的出口金額，其中最受歡迎的品種是臺灣特有的蝴蝶蘭，它常被用來送禮或展示，有多種不同形狀和色彩。

臺灣的蘭花產業啟始於 1980 年代，隨著溫室農業技術的應用而蓬勃發展。事實上，從 1995 年到 2008 年間，臺灣的花卉出口成長了十倍。在 2007 年，臺灣在全球花卉市場的領先地位被荷蘭取代。為了面對這項挑戰，臺灣花農努力讓自己與競爭對手做出區隔。他們開始專注於出口蘭花幼苗 —— 也就是剛從種子萌芽的蘭花幼株。到了 2018 年，臺灣向超過 80 個國家出口了價值約新臺幣 45 億元的蝴蝶蘭幼苗。臺灣本土蘭花的高度多樣性，讓花農得以開發多種商業用途的品種。花農將不同的本地蘭花混種，培育出新的變種。臺灣擁有全球密度最高的溫室種植蘭花及相關服務產業。

臺灣花農的成就已獲得國際認可。2024 年時，臺灣首次主辦世界蘭花會議。會中的主要討論議題集中在「蘭花科技」與「保育與保存」。臺灣蘭花產業運用了高科技農業技術，不過在保育與保存方面仍有進步空間。用來培育新變種的蝴蝶蘭來源逐漸減少，野生的本地品種也逐漸消失。蘭花產業意識到生態保護與經濟成長必須齊頭並進。為了這個目的，臺灣在 2018 年啟動野生蘭花復育志工計畫。假以時日，蘭花不僅能美化居家環境，也可以豐富臺灣的森林生態系。

A **39.**

What is the topic of the passage?

(A) An introduction to Taiwan's orchid industry
(B) The development of the global orchid market
(C) Varieties created by Taiwan's orchid industry
(D) Activities of the 2024 World Orchid Conference

本文主題是什麼？
(A) 臺灣蘭花產業簡介
(B) 全球蘭花市場的發展
(C) 臺灣蘭花產業創造的新品種
(D) 2024 年世界蘭花會議的活動內容

理由:
本文介紹臺灣蘭花產業的發展歷程、全球地位及面臨的生態保育挑戰，強調產業成長與自然保護需並行的重要性。得知 (A) 項應為正選。

D **40.**

What is the main idea of the third paragraph?
(A) The differences between native plant species and new varieties
(B) The report of the World Orchid Conference on orchid exports
(C) The operations of high-tech farming in Taiwan's orchid industry
(D) The balance between industry growth and orchid species protection

本文第三段的主旨是什麼？
(A) 原生植物品種與新品種的差異
(B) 世界蘭花會議就蘭花出口所做的報告
(C) 臺灣蘭花產業的高科技栽培運作
(D) 產業成長與蘭花物種保護間的平衡

理由:
本段說明臺灣蘭花產業雖以高科技技術著稱，卻也面臨原生蘭花資源逐漸消失的問題，因此開始推動生態保育行動，以求產業與自然環境共存共榮。得知 (D) 項應為正選。

B **41.**

According to the passage, which of the following statements is true?
(A) Moth orchids are the largest item of Taiwan's flower imports.
(B) Taiwan growers mix native species to produce new orchid varieties.
(C) The Netherlands has the world's largest greenhouse orchid industry.
(D) Volunteers removed native orchid plants from the wild in 2018.

根據本文，下列哪一項敘述正確？
(A) 蝴蝶蘭是臺灣最大宗的花卉進口品項。
(B) 臺灣花農透過雜交原生品種來培育新的蘭花品種。
(C) 荷蘭擁有全球最大的溫室蘭花產業。
(D) 志工於 2018 年移除野生的原生蘭花。

理由:
由第二段倒數第二句 Growers mix different native species to develop a new variety.（花農將不同的本地蘭花混種，培育出新的變種。）得知 (B) 項應為正選。

B **42.**

Arrange the following events according to the historical timeline of Taiwan's orchid industry.

a. Taiwan's orchid export earnings were NT$ 7 billion.
b. Taiwan lost its top position in the global orchid market.
c. Taiwan exported moth orchid seedlings to over 80 countries.
d. Taiwan hosted the World Orchid Conference.

(A) b → d → c → a (B) b → c → a → d
(C) c → a → b → d (D) c → d → b → a

請依臺灣蘭花產業的歷史時間軸排列下列事件。
a. 臺灣蘭花出口收入達新臺幣 70 億元。
b. 臺灣失去全球蘭花市場的領先地位。
c. 臺灣將蝴蝶蘭幼苗出口到超過 80 個國家。
d. 臺灣主辦世界蘭花會議。

理由:
根據本文可知 a. 項發生於 2023 年、b. 項發生於 2007 年、c. 項發生於 2018 年、d. 項發生於 2024 年。因此時間順序為 b → c → a → d，故 (B) 項應為正選。

重要單字片語

1. **third** [θɝd] *n.* 三分之一 & *a.* 第三的
a third of... 三分之一個……（當主詞時，動詞要依後面接的名詞判斷用單數或複數）
例: A third of the water in the bottle was gone.
（瓶子裡三分之一的水不見了。）
A third of the elephants in the herd were young.
（這群大象中有三分之一是年輕的。）
2. **orchid** [ˋɔrkɪd] *n.* 蘭花
a moth orchid 蝴蝶蘭
3. **export** [ˋɛksport] *n.* 輸出品 & [ɪksˋport] *vt.* 出口
例: This company exports its products mainly to the USA.
（這家公司主要將產品出口到美國。）
4. **earnings** [ˋɝnɪŋz] *n.* 盈餘（恆用複數）
5. **billion** [ˋbɪljən] *n.* 10 億
6. **variety** [vəˋraɪətɪ] *n.* 變化；種類
a variety of... 各式各樣的……
例: Debra enjoys a variety of outdoor activities, such as jogging and cycling.
（黛博拉喜歡多種戶外活動，如慢跑和騎單車等等。）
7. **come in...(sizes/shapes/colors...)**
有……（尺寸 / 形狀 / 顏色……）
例: Our screens come in five different sizes.
（我們的螢幕有五種不同的尺寸。）
8. **emerge** [ɪˋmɝdʒ] *vi.* 出現，冒出
emerge from... 從……冒出來
例: Steam emerged from the hot spring, creating a mysterious atmosphere.
（蒸氣從溫泉中升起，營造出神祕的氛圍。）
9. **flourish** [ˋflɝɪʃ] *vi.* 蓬勃發展
例: Tammy's creativity really flourished when she was exposed to new cultures.
（譚美接觸到新文化時創造力大爆發。）

10. **greenhouse** [ˋgrin͵haʊs] *n.* 溫室
11. **tenfold** [ˋtɛn͵fold] *adv.* 十倍地 & *a.* 十倍的

例: The sales of my umbrella stand increased tenfold during rainy days.
（我的雨傘攤在下雨天時銷售量暴漲十倍。）

12. **global** [ˋglobḷ] *a.* 全球的
13. **cope with** 處理

例: How do you cope with difficult customers?
（你是怎麼應付奧客的？）

14. **competitor** [kəmˋpɛtətɚ] *n.* 競爭者，參賽者
15. **seedling** [ˋsidlɪŋ] *n.* 幼苗，幼株
16. **diversity** [daɪˋvɝsətɪ] *n.* 多樣性；差異
17. **native** [ˋnetɪv] *a.* 本地的，土生的
be native to... 為⋯⋯（地方）所獨有

例: Polar bears are native to the Arctic.
（北極熊原生於北極地區。）

18. **commercial** [kəˋmɝʃəl] *a.* 商業的 & *n.*（廣播 / 電視的）廣告
19. **species** [ˋspiʃɪz] *n.* 物種（單複數同形）
20. **concentration** [͵kɑnsənˋtreʃən] *n.* 大量聚集的區域；注意力
21. **achievement** [əˋtʃivmənt] *n.* 成就
22. **recognition** [͵rɛkəgˋnɪʃən] *n.* 承認，認可；認出
23. **conference** [ˋkɑnfərəns] *n.* 會議
24. **center** [ˋsɛntɚ] *vt.* 集中於；使置中 & *n.* 中心點，中央

例: Please center the title at the top of the page.
（請把標題置中放在頁面頂端。）

25. **conservation** [͵kɑnsɚˋveʃən] *n.*（動植物）保護；（自然資源）保存（皆不可數）
26. **preservation** [͵prɛzɚˋveʃən] *n.* 保存，保護
27. **decrease** [dɪˋkris] *vi.* & *vt.* 下降 & [ˋdikris] *n.* 下降

例: The sales of electric cars decreased sharply in the second quarter.
（第二季電動車的銷售大幅下降。）

28. **ecological** [͵ɛkəˋlɑdʒɪkḷ / ͵ikəˋlɑdʒɪkḷ] *a.* 生態（學）的
ecosystem [ˋɛko͵sɪstəm / ˋiko͵sɪstəm] *n.* 生態系統
29. **hand in hand** （事物）緊密連結；（人）牽手

例: Innovation and risk often go hand in hand.
（創新和風險通常是分不開的。）

30. **economic** [͵ɛkəˋnɑmɪk] *a.* 與經濟有關的
31. **given time** 只要給予時間；如果有時間
此為分詞構句的結構，通常置於句首，原句為 If + 主詞 + is given time, 主詞 + 動詞⋯⋯，if 子句改寫為分詞構句，省略連接詞 if、主詞及 be 動詞。

例: Given time, Ted will learn to speak Korean fluently.
（只要給泰德時間，他就能學會說流利的韓語。）

32. **enrich** [ɪnˋrɪtʃ] *vt.* 使富庶，使豐富

例: The course is designed to enrich students' vocabulary.
（設計這門課的目的是為了增加學生的字彙量。）

第二部分：非選擇題（第 I 題，每格 2 分，共 4 分；第 II 題 6 分；第 III 題 6 分；共 16 分）

I. 填充

1. 這位巨星在台北三場演唱會的所有門票在五分鐘內全部售完。

All tickets for the superstar's three c___①___ in Taipei were s___②___ out in just five minutes.

① concerts　　② sold

解析

1. 本題空格 ① 的對照譯詞為『演唱會』，且空格為 c 開頭，故空格應置名詞 concert，且因前有『三場』這個量詞，所以名詞需為複數形 concerts。

concert [ˋkɑnsɚt] *n.* 演唱會，音樂會；一致，協調（不可數）

put on a concert　舉辦演唱會

= hold a concert

例: The singer is going to put on a concert this weekend.
（該歌手這個週末將舉辦一場演唱會。）

2. 本題空格 ② 的對照譯詞為『售完』，且空格為 s 開頭，前面有 be 動詞，後有介詞 out，故該句測試動詞片語 be sold out，所以空格應置 sold。

be sold out　售完，賣光

例: The cupcakes at that bakery are so popular that they are usually sold out before noon.
（這間麵包店的杯子蛋糕太受歡迎了，以致於通常在中午前就銷售一空。）

其他重點

superstar [ˋsupɚˏstɑr] *n.* 超級巨星

II. 句子重組

2. are a bad gift choice / the cutting of / Knives or scissors / as they symbolize / a solid friendship

Knives or scissors are a bad gift choice as they symbolize the cutting of a solid friendship.

（選擇刀子或剪刀當禮物是不太好的，因為它們象徵堅貞友誼的破裂。）

解析

1. 先找出開頭為大寫的詞組 Knives or scissors（刀子或剪刀）作為句首。

2. 主詞詞組 Knives or scissors 後面應接動詞（詞組）。重組部分中，are a bad gift choice（當禮物是不太好的）含動詞 are，應置於主詞詞組後形成 "Knives or scissors are a bad gift choice..."，如此形成一個完整的句子結構：主詞 + 動詞 + 主詞補語。
3. "Knives or scissors are a bad gift choice..." 為完整的句子，其後應接解釋刀子或剪刀當禮物不太好的原因，as 可為連接詞表『因為』，後面應接一副詞子句，由主詞 they 開頭代表前面所提的 Knives or scissors 及動詞 symbolize（象徵）。
4. 剩下的詞組部分，the cutting of（……的破裂）應接於 they symbolize 後面，形成 "they symbolize the cutting of..."（它們代表……的破裂），of 為介詞，其後應接名詞詞組 a solid friendship（堅貞友誼）形成一個完整的副詞子句來解釋主要子句 Knives... choice 的原因。
5. 由上可得答案：
Knives or scissors are a bad gift choice as they symbolize the cutting of a solid friendship.

其他重點

1. **symbolize** [ˋsɪmbəlˏaɪz] *vt.* 象徵
例: In many cultures, crows symbolize bad luck.
（烏鴉在許多文化中都是厄運的象徵。）
2. **solid** [ˋsɑlɪd] *a.* 穩固的；固體的
例: Open and honest communication is needed to build a solid relationship.
（要建立穩固的關係就必須要有開誠布公的溝通方式。）

III. 中譯英

3. 如果你接獲不明來電，未經確認前不要接聽。
If you receive a call from an unknown number, don't / do not answer it before checking / you check who it is.

解析

1. 『如果你』可譯成 If you。
2. 『接獲』可譯成 receive。
3. 『不明來電』表示是未知號碼的電話，可譯成 a call from an unknown number。
4. 『未經確認前』表示未經確認是誰打來的，可譯成 before you check who it is；因該副詞子句主詞與第 5 點的祈使句『不要接聽』相同，也可將此主詞 you 省略，check 改為動名詞 checking，此時 before 作介詞，譯成 before checking who it is。
5. 『不要接聽』為祈使句，省略主詞 you，此中文暗指不要接聽前面所指的不明來電 "a call from an unknown number"，此名詞詞組可用代名詞 it 代替，因此可譯為 don't answer it 或 do not answer it。
6. 由上得知，本句可譯為：
If you receive a call from an unknown number, don't / do not answer it before checking / you check who it is.

113

四技二專統一入學測驗－詳解

113 年統測
試題講解

第一部分：選擇題

第二部分：非選擇題

選擇題解答

1	2	3	4	5	6	7	8	9	10
D	B	C	D	B	D	A	C	A	A
11	12	13	14	15	16	17	18	19	20
B	B	D	A	D	D	C	C	D	A
21	22	23	24	25	26	27	28	29	30
C	C	B	A	C	B	A	D	C	A
31	32	33	34	35	36	37	38	39	40
D	A	C	B	B	D	B	B	D	C
41	42								
C	A								

113 年四技二專統一入學測驗詳解

第一部分：選擇題（84 分）

I. 字彙題

D **1.**
Johnny is wearing a very ______ hat that looks different from those of other people.
(A) common (B) general (C) regular (D) special
強尼戴著一頂很特別的帽子，看起來和其他人的不同。

解析

1. (A) **common** [ˋkɑmən] *a.* 普通的；共同的 & *n.* 公用地
例: Earthquakes are common in this part of the country.
（地震在此國家的這個地區相當常見。）
(B) **general** [ˋdʒɛnərəl] *a.* 大致的；一般的，普遍的 & *n.* 將軍
例: After reading the report, you will have a general idea of the project.
（讀完這份報告後，你會對這計畫有個大略的概念。）
(C) **regular** [ˋrɛgjələ] *a.* 經常發生的；規律的，固定的；普通的，一般的 & *n.* 老顧客，常客
例: Joyce is one of our store's regular customers.
（喬伊絲是我們店裡的常客之一。）
(D) **special** [ˋspɛʃəl] *a.* 特別的
例: What's so special about this car?
（這輛車有什麼特別之處？）
2. 根據語意，(D) 項應為正選。

其他重點

A look / be different from B A 與 B 看起來 / 是不同的
例: Gina is very different from her sister in terms of personality.
（吉娜與她妹妹在個性方面很不同。）

B **2.**
Loud noises can make it hard for me to ______, so I always find a quiet place to study with full attention.
(A) bend (B) focus (C) panic (D) wander
太吵的聲音會讓我很難專注，所以我總會找個安靜的地方專心念書。

解析

1. (A) **bend** [bɛnd] *vi.* & *vt.*（使）彎曲；扭曲（事實）& *vi.* 俯身 & *n.*（道路等的）轉彎處
（三態為：bend, bent [bɛnt], bent）

例: The strong man can bend a steel rod with his hands.
（那個大力士可以用手折彎鋼條。）

(B) **focus** [ˋfokəs] *vi.* & *vt.*（使）集中（注意力）& *n.* 焦點

例: I am so tired that I cannot focus on anything today.
（我今天太累了，做什麼事都沒辦法專注。）

(C) **panic** [ˋpænɪk] *vi.* & *vt.*（使）恐慌 & *n.* 驚恐（三態為：panic, panicked [ˋpænɪkt], panicked）

例: I panicked at the sight of the poisonous snake.
（我看到那條毒蛇時嚇得驚慌失措。）

(D) **wander** [ˋwɑndɚ] *vi.* & *vt.* 漫遊；閒逛 & *n.* 閒逛

例: An old man wandered through the streets, looking lost.
（有個老先生在街頭遊蕩，看來是迷路了。）

2. 根據語意，(B) 項應為正選。

C **3.**

Here is a helpful ______ for cooking chicken soup: add a little salt. It will make the soup tasty.

(A) lip (B) gap (C) tip (D) nap

說一個煮雞湯的實用祕訣：加些許鹽。如此會讓湯更美味。

解析

1. (A) **lip** [lɪp] *n.* 嘴唇

例: Tommy accidentally bit his lip, and it hurt a lot.
（湯米不小心咬到嘴唇，非常痛。）

(B) **gap** [gæp] *n.* 歧異；裂縫

例: Because of the generation gap, my mom doesn't share my interest in this type of music.
（由於代溝的緣故，我對這種音樂有興趣，我媽卻沒有。）

(C) **tip** [tɪp] *n.* 祕訣；小費；尖端 & *vt.* & *vi.*（給）小費（三態為：tip, tipped [tɪpt], tipped）

例: Thank you for giving me some tips on how to ski.
（謝謝你告訴我幾個滑雪的訣竅。）

(D) **nap** [næp] *n.* 打盹，小睡 & *vi.* 打瞌睡（三態為：nap, napped [næpt], napped）

例: You look exhausted. Why don't you take a nap?
（你看來累極了。何不小睡一下？）

2. 根據語意，(C) 項應為正選。

D **4.**

My grandpa sleeps at ______ the same time every day. He goes to bed at about 9 pm.

(A) briefly (B) fluently (C) gently (D) roughly

我爺爺每天都在差不多的時間去睡覺，大概晚上九點左右。

解析

1. (A) **briefly** [ˋbriflɪ] *adv.* 簡短地；短暫地

例: Please tell me what happened briefly. I don't have much time.
（請簡短說一下發生了什麼事。我趕時間。）

(B) **fluently** [ˋfluəntlɪ] *adv.* 流利地

例: Anthony speaks English so fluently that he sounds as if he were a native speaker.
（安東尼講英語十分流利，聽起來好像英文是他的母語一樣。）

(C) **gently** [ˋdʒɛntlɪ] *adv.* 輕柔地；溫柔地

例: Mary dipped her handkerchief in soapy water and washed it gently.
（瑪麗把手帕浸在肥皂水裡，輕柔地洗滌。）

(D) **roughly** [ˋrʌflɪ] *adv.* 約略地，大致上

例: Nicole roughly described the planned course of action.
（妮可大致描述了一下預定的行動過程。）

2. 根據語意，(D) 項應為正選。

B **5.**

Being friendly with your roommates can help you stay away from ______ with them.

(A) dialogues (B) conflicts (C) personality (D) relationship

跟室友保持友好可以幫助你避免衝突。

解析

1. (A) **dialogue** [ˋdaɪəˌlɔg] *n.* 對話

例: Simply reading the dialogue is not enough. You should act it out.
（光唸對話還不夠。你要把它演出來。）

(B) **conflict** [ˋkɑnflɪkt] *n.* 衝突 & [kənˋflɪkt] *vi.* 衝突，相抵觸

例: The conflict between the two countries lasted nearly twenty years.
（這兩國之間的衝突延續了將近二十年。）

(C) **personality** [ˌpɝsn̩ˋælətɪ] *n.* 個性

例: Lisa has a pleasant personality.
（麗莎的個性很好。）

(D) **relationship** [rɪˋleʃən,ʃɪp] *n.*（人、團體之間的）關係 / 往來；（兩物之間的）關係；戀愛關係

例: The relationship deepened between this powerful country and those Arab countries.
（該強國深化了與那些阿拉伯國家間的關係。）

2. 根據語意，(B) 項應為正選。

其他重點

stay away (from sb/sth) 遠離（某人 / 某事物）

例: Stay away from Owen. He's a bad guy.
（離歐文遠一點，他不是善類。）

D **6.**

Jack is a very ______ person. He will never change his decisions no matter how hard you try to persuade him.

(A) easy-going (B) democratic (C) obedient (D) stubborn

傑克是一個很固執的人。無論你多努力說服他，他都不會改變他的決定。

解析

1. (A) **easy-going** [ˌizɪˋgoɪŋ] *a.* 隨和的；悠閒的

例: Matt is a chill guy. He is easy-going and always relaxed.
（麥特這個人很酷。他隨和而且總是很悠閒的樣子。）

(B) **democratic** [ˌdɛməˋkrætɪk] *a.* 民主的

例: The president was elected through a democratic process.
（該總統是經由民主程序選出來的。）

(C) **obedient** [oˋbidɪənt] *a.* 遵守的，服從的

例: Your dog needs to learn to be obedient in a special school.
（你的狗該去專門的學校學習服從。）

(D) **stubborn** [ˋstʌbɚn] *a.* 固執的，頑固的

例: Jane would like to go to the school dance, but her stubborn parents wouldn't let her.
（珍想參加學校舞會，但她固執的爸媽不讓她去。）

2. 根據語意，(D) 項應為正選。

其他重點

persuade [pɚˋswed] *vt.* 說服

例: Try to persuade Jerry to apologize to the teacher.
（試著說服傑瑞去向老師道歉。）

A **7.**

Kuo, Hsing-chun (郭婞淳) won a gold medal in the 2020 Tokyo Olympics. I ______ her a lot and want to be like her one day.

(A) admire (B) frighten (C) impress (D) suspect

郭婞淳在 2020 年東京奧運奪金。我非常崇拜她，希望有一天也能像她一樣。

解析

1. (A) **admire** [ədˋmaɪr] *vt.* 欽佩，欣賞

   例: I admire Justin for his proficiency in English.
   （我很欽佩賈斯汀的英文造詣。）

   (B) **frighten** [ˋfraɪtn̩] *vt.* 使驚嚇

   例: You should not let your son watch that movie because it might frighten him.
   （不要給你的兒子看那部電影，他可能會嚇壞。）

   (C) **impress** [ɪmˋprɛs] *vt.* 使印象深刻；使銘記

   例: I was deeply impressed with the city's tidiness.
   （我對該市的整潔印象極為深刻。）

   (D) **suspect** [səˋspɛkt] *vt.* 懷疑；猜想 & [ˋsʌspɛkt] *n.* 嫌疑犯

   例: The police suspected Bob of committing the crime.
   （警方懷疑鮑伯犯了這個罪行。）

2. 根據語意，(A) 項應為正選。

C **8.**

Though she hurt her arm last week, Amy could still play the violin as skillfully as before.

(A) casually (B) cruelly (C) smoothly (D) strictly

雖然艾咪上禮拜弄傷了手臂，但她還像以前一樣熟練地拉小提琴。

解析

1. 原句劃線的字有下列意思及用法：

   skillfully [ˋskɪlfəlɪ] *adv.* 熟練地

   例: The magician performed his tricks skillfully.
   （魔術師熟練地表演戲法。）

2. (A) **casually** [ˋkæʒuəlɪ] *adv.* 悠閒地；隨便地

   例: On weekends, I enjoy strolling casually in the park near my place.
   （週末時我喜歡在住處附近的公園悠閒地散步。）

   (B) **cruelly** [ˋkruəlɪ] *adv.* 殘忍地

   例: The evil stepmother treated the little boy cruelly.
   （惡毒的繼母殘酷地對待這小男孩。）

(C) **smoothly** [ˋsmuðlɪ] *adv.* 順暢地，順利地

例: The graduation ceremony ran smoothly.
（畢業典禮進行得很順利。）

(D) **strictly** [ˋstrɪktlɪ] *adv.* 嚴格地，嚴厲地

例: The club strictly screens its candidates.
（那家俱樂部嚴格篩選申請入會者。）

3. 根據上述，skillfully 與 smoothly 同義，故 (C) 項應為正選。

A **9.**

May has to conquer her fear of flying if she wants to travel by airplane.

(A) beat (B) hunt (C) recover (D) select

梅如果想搭機旅行的話，她必須克服對飛行的恐懼。

解析

1. 原句劃線的字有下列意思及用法：

conquer [ˋkaŋkɚ] *vt.* 克服；征服，擊敗

例: Frank finally conquered his fear of snakes.
（法蘭克終於克服了他對蛇的恐懼。）

2. (A) **beat** [bit] *vt.* 戰勝（某問題等）；擊敗；毆打 & *vi.* 跳動 & *n.*（心臟）跳動聲；敲打聲；節拍（三態為：beat, beat, beaten [ˋbitn̩]）

例: My grandfather's ability to beat anyone at chess has weakened over the last few years.
（過去幾年來，爺爺打遍天下無敵手的棋藝漸趨退化。）

(B) **hunt** [hʌnt] *vt.* & *vi.* 獵取 & *n.* 打獵；尋找

例: Mike hunted a deer yesterday.
（麥克昨天獵到一頭鹿。）

(C) **recover** [rɪˋkʌvɚ] *vt.* 恢復；重新找到 / 拿回 & *vi.* 康復

例: Tony recovered his health.
（湯尼恢復了他的健康。）

(D) **select** [səˋlɛkt] *vt.* 選拔，挑選 & *a.* 精選的，優等的

例: Who has been selected as the class leader?
（誰選上班長？）

3. 根據上述，conquer 與 beat 同義，故 (A) 項應為正選。

A **10.**

It is against the law for drivers not to stop at the crosswalk and allow walkers to cross first.[註1] If drivers do so, they will be fined.

(A) illegal (B) national (C) political (D) unusual

駕駛人不禮讓斑馬線上的行人是違法的。這樣的駕駛人將被處以罰鍰。

註1：此句宜改為 It is against the law for drivers to fail to stop at a crosswalk...

解析

1. 原句劃線的字有下列意思及用法：

   against the law 違法的

   例: Never do anything against the law.
   （千萬別做違法的事。）

2. (A) **illegal** [ɪˋligḷ] *a.* 違法的，非法的

   例: It is illegal to park here.
   （在這停車是違法的。）

   (B) **national** [ˋnæʃənḷ] *a.* 國家的；國立的；全國的

   例: How many national parks are there in your country?
   （貴國有幾座國家公園？）

   (C) **political** [pəˋlɪtɪkḷ] *a.* 政治的

   例: Never talk about religious or political issues at social gatherings.
   （社交聚會千萬別談論宗教或政治議題。）

   (D) **unusual** [ʌnˋjuʒuəl] *a.* 不尋常的；非凡的

   例: Martin decided to give his baby an unusual name.
   （馬汀決定給他的小寶寶取一個特殊的名字。）

3. 根據上述，against the law 與 illegal 同義，故 (A) 項應為正選。

其他重點

1. **crosswalk** [ˋkrɔsˏwɔk] *n.* 斑馬線，行人穿越道
2. **allow** [əˋlaʊ] *vt.* 允許，讓

   allow sb/sth to V 允許某人 / 某事物……

   例: My parents wouldn't allow me to go out alone at night.
   （我爸媽不允許我晚上一個人出門。）
3. **fine** [faɪn] *vt.* & *n.* 罰款 & *a.* 優良的，漂亮的；晴朗的；細微的 & *adv.* 令人滿意地

   例: Bill was fined NT$6,000 for speeding.
   （比爾因超速被罰款新臺幣六千元。）

II. 對話題

B **11.**

Customer: I'd like to have one oyster omelette and fried noodles, please.
Stall owner: Ok. Your order will be ready in five minutes.
Customer: I can't use chopsticks. Can I have a fork, please?
Stall owner: ________________
Customer: Thank you.

(A) You're very welcome. (B) Of course, here you go.
(C) Oyster is also delicious.[註1] (D) Sure, we have instant noodles.

顧客：我想要一份蚵仔煎跟炒麵，謝謝。
攤商：好。您點的餐五分鐘後會好。
顧客：我不會用筷子。給我叉子好嗎？
攤商：________________
顧客：謝謝。
(A) 不客氣。 (B) 沒問題，這是您的叉子。
(C) 蚵仔也很美味。 (D) 當然，我們有泡麵。

解析

空格前，顧客問攤商 "Can I have a fork, please?"（給我叉子好嗎？），空格後，顧客回答 "Thank you."（謝謝。），得知顧客拿到了叉子，因此 (B) 項應為正選。

註1：此句宜改成 Oysters are also delicious.

其他重點

1. **oyster** [ˋɔɪstɚ] *n.* 牡蠣，蠔
2. **omelette** [ˋamələt] *n.* 蛋包；煎蛋捲（= omelet〔美〕）
3. **order** [ˋɔrdɚ] *n.* 點菜；訂購 & *vt.* 點（菜）；訂購
   take sb's order　　接受某人的點餐
   例: The waiter came to take my order.
   （服務生過來幫我點餐。）
4. **chopstick** [ˋtʃɑpˏstɪk] *n.* 筷子（常用複數）
   a pair of chopsticks　　一雙筷子
5. **delicious** [dɪˋlɪʃəs] *a.* 美味的

B **12.**

Tina: An old friend is coming to visit me tomorrow. I haven't seen him for ten years.
Mike: An old friend? ________________
Tina: He wants to tell me something about his girlfriend. They broke up!
Mike: Sorry for him.

(A) How old is he?
(B) Why is he coming?
(C) When will you see him?
(D) Who was he looking for?

蒂娜：有個老朋友明天會來找我。我已經有十年沒見過他了。
麥克：老朋友？________
蒂娜：他想跟我說他女朋友的事。他們分手了！
麥克：他真可憐。
(A) 他多大年紀？
(B) 他來幹嘛？
(C) 妳什麼時候要見他？
(D) 他在找誰？

解析

空格後，蒂娜回答 "He wants to tell me something about his girlfriend."（他想跟我說他女朋友的事。），得知麥克應該在問原因，因此 (B) 項應為正選。

其他重點

1. **visit** [ˋvɪzɪt] *vt.* & *vi.* & *n.* 拜訪
   例: Last fall, I went to visit my aunt in Spain.
   （去年秋天，我到西班牙看我阿姨。）
2. **break up (with sb)** （與某人）分手
   例: I think Susan has made a wise decision to break up with John.
   （我認為蘇珊和約翰分手是個明智的決定。）
3. **look for...** 尋找……
   例: I'm looking for a babysitter to care for my son.
   （我正在找一位保姆來照顧我兒子。）

D **13.**

Mrs. Chen: I heard that the new neighbors moved in yesterday.
Mr. Chen: ________
Mrs. Chen: No, not yet. What do they look like?
Mr. Chen: The lady is tall and thin and the man is kind of chubby.

(A) I'm glad I just met them.
(B) The neighbors have two cats.
(C) They ran a small business here.
(D) I thought you've met them already.

陳太太：我聽說新鄰居昨天搬進來了。
陳先生：________
陳太太：還沒。他們長什麼樣子？
陳先生：女的又高又瘦，男的蠻胖的。
(A) 我很開心我剛見過他們。
(B) 鄰居有兩隻貓。
(C) 他們在這裡經營一家小公司。
(D) 我以為妳已經見過他們了。

解析

空格後，陳太太回答 "No, not yet. What do they look like?"（還沒。他們長什麼樣子？），得知陳先生以為陳太太已經見過新鄰居，因此 (D) 項應為正選。

其他重點

1. **hear** [hɪr] *vt.* & *vi.* 聽聞；聽到（皆不用於進行式）（三態為：hear, heard [hɝd], heard）

   例: We were all upset when we heard the news.
   （我們得知這個消息時都很難過。）

2. **chubby** [ˋtʃʌbɪ] *a.* 圓胖的
3. **business** [ˋbɪznəs] *n.* 公司（可數）；生意（不可數）

A **14.**

Adam: We all know that the Wright brothers (萊特兄弟) flew the first airplane in 1903. But do you know which one of them flew the airplane?

Jacky: The older brother did.

Adam: I'm surprised you know that. OK. ________________

Jacky: Only about 12 seconds.

Adam: Wow, you really know a lot!

(A) How long was the flight?
(B) How old was his brother?
(C) How many times had he tried before?
(D) How far did the airplane actually fly?

亞當：我們都知道萊特兄弟在 1903 年駕駛了第一架飛機。但你知道他們兩個中是誰開的飛機嗎？

傑奇：哥哥。

亞當：你居然知道。好。________________

傑奇：只有大約十二秒。

亞當：哇，你真的懂很多耶！

(A) 他們飛了多久？
(B) 他的哥哥幾歲？
(C) 他之前嘗試過了幾次？
(D) 飛機實際飛了多遠？

解析

空格後，傑奇回答 "Only about 12 seconds."（只有大約十二秒。），得知亞當應該在問有關時間的問題，因此 (A) 項應為正選。

其他重點

1. **fly** [flaɪ] *vt.* & *vi.* 駕駛（飛機）（三態為：fly, flew [flu], flown [flon]）

   例: Can you fly the plane?
   （你會開飛機嗎？）

2. **flight** [flaɪt] *n.* 飛行；班機

D **15.**

Amy: Did you finish your report for the Performing Arts class?
Janet: Yes. ________________
Amy: Like what?
Janet: For example, women were not allowed to act on stage in the past.
Amy: That was really unfair, wasn't it?

(A) But I haven't given it to Professor Johnson.
(B) And I've read many books about famous artists.
(C) But I'm not sure if my mom allows me to act on stage.[註1]
(D) And I've gathered a lot of information about the theater.

艾　咪：妳表演藝術課的報告寫完了嗎？
珍妮特：寫完了。________________
艾　咪：像是什麼？
珍妮特：舉例來説，以前女性是不准上舞臺表演的。
艾　咪：那真是不公平，對不對？
(A) 但是我還沒有交給強森教授。
(B) 而且我讀了許多關於知名藝術家的書。
(C) 但是我不確定我媽是否會讓我登臺表演。
(D) 而且我蒐集了許多關於劇場的資訊。

解析

空格後，艾咪詢問 "Like what?"（像是什麼？），珍妮特則回答 "For example, women were not allowed to act on stage in the past."（舉例來說，以前女性是不准上舞臺表演的。），得知艾咪先前應該有表示她學到許多劇場相關的資訊，因此 (D) 項應為正選。

註1：此句宜改成 But I'm not sure if my mom will allow me to act on stage.

其他重點

1. **allow** [əˋlaʊ] *vt.* 允許，讓
   allow sb/sth to V　允許某人 / 某事物……
   例: My parents wouldn't allow me to go out alone at night.
   （我爸媽不讓我晚上一個人出門。）
2. **stage** [stedʒ] *n.* 舞臺
3. **unfair** [ʌnˋfɛr] *a.* 不公平的
4. **famous** [ˋfeməs] *a.* 出名的
5. **gather** [ˋgæðɚ] *vt.* 蒐集
   例: We need to gather information about the situation before taking action.
   （我們採取行動之前，得先蒐集相關情況的資訊。）

D **16.**

Rita: Why did you apply for this position?

Ben: I'd like to work for a large company. Your company is the perfect fit for me.

Rita: In this position, you'll have to lead a small team. How have you shown leadership at your other jobs?

Ben: ________________

Rita: That's good.

(A) I worked for my team leader in the past ten years.[註1]

(B) I'd like to apply for a perfect job in a smaller team.[註2]

(C) From now on, I'll lead a team in this large company.

(D) At my current position, I manage a team of ten workers.[註3]

麗塔：你為什麼要應徵這個職位？

班：我想要在大公司裡工作。貴公司對我來說非常適合。

麗塔：在這個職位上，你需要領導一個小型團隊。你在之前的工作裡是如何展現領導能力的？

班：________________

麗塔：不錯。

(A) 我過去十年為我的組長工作。

(B) 我想在小一點的團隊裡應徵理想的工作。

(C) 從現在起，我會在這大公司裡領導一個團隊。

(D) 我目前的職位是在管理一個有十個人的團隊。

解析

空格前，麗塔詢問 "How have you shown leadership at your other jobs?"（你在之前的工作裡是如何展現領導能力的？），空格後則表示 "That's good."（不錯。），得知班應該是說明了他領導才能相關的事情，因此 (D) 項應為正選。

註1：此句宜改成 I've worked for my team leader for the past ten years.

註2：此句宜改成 I'd like to apply for a perfect job on a smaller team.

註3：此句宜改成 In my current position, I manage a team of ten workers.

其他重點

1. **apply** [ə`plaɪ ] *vi.* 申請（三態為：apply, applied [ ə`plaɪd], applied）
   apply for...　　申請 / 應徵……
   例: Elmer is applying for admission to that university.
   （艾爾馬正在申請那間大學的入學許可。）
2. **position** [pə`zɪʃən] *n.* 職務；位置
3. **fit** [fɪt] *n.* 適合
4. **lead** [lid] *vt.* & *vi.* 帶領；領先（三態為：lead, led [lɛd], led）
   例: Gareth led his team to success in the competition.
   （加瑞斯帶領他的隊伍贏得比賽。）

5. **leadership** [ˋlidɚʃɪp] *n.* 領導能力（不可數）
6. **from now on** 從現在開始

例: From now on, you'll have to be on your own.
（從今以後，你一切得靠自己了。）

7. **current** [ˋkɝənt] *a.* 當前的
8. **manage** [ˋmænɪdʒ] *vt.* 管理

例: It takes a lot of experience to manage a big company.
（管理一間大公司需要豐富的經驗。）

C **17.**

Sue: How's the project going?

Eric: It's going well.

Sue: Oh, good. ________________

Eric: They are great, and they have a lot of creative ideas.

Sue: I'm happy to hear that.

(A) But who is not feeling well? (B) But how did they come to the office?
(C) And what are the new colleagues like? (D) And when will the project be created?

蘇：專案的進展如何？

艾瑞克：很順。

蘇：嗯，很好。________________

艾瑞克：不錯，他們有很多頗富創意的點子。

蘇：這樣很好。

(A) 不過是誰身體不舒服？ (B) 不過他們是怎麼過來公司的？
(C) 新同事們如何？ (D) 專案什麼時候會生出來？

解析

空格後，艾瑞克回答 "They are great, and they have a lot of creative ideas."（不錯，他們有很多頗富創意的點子。），得知蘇應該是在詢問某些人的狀況，因此 (C) 項應為正選。

其他重點

1. **project** [ˋprɑdʒɛkt] *n.* 專案，計畫
2. **creative** [krɪˋetɪv] *a.* 有創意的
   create [krɪˋet] *vt.* 創造
3. **colleague** [ˋkɑlig] *n.* 同事

C **18.**

Jason: Where are you? The presentation is about to begin.

Susan: I'm almost there. The traffic is terrible this morning.

Jason: ________________

Susan: Yes, please. You can make a start, and I can handle the rest of the slides myself.

(A) Do you want me to cancel the presentation?

(B) Would you like me to order snacks and drinks?

(C) Do you want me to introduce the first few pages?

(D) Would you like me to turn off the audio equipment?

傑森：妳在哪裡？簡報就要開始了。

蘇珊：我就快到了。今早的交通真是糟透了。

傑森：________________

蘇珊：好，拜託你了。你先開個頭，我可以自己簡報剩下的投影片。

(A) 妳要我取消簡報會嗎？　(B) 妳要我訂購點心飲料嗎？

(C) 妳要我介紹前幾頁嗎？　(D) 妳要我關掉音響設備嗎？

解析

空格後，蘇珊回答 "Yes, please. You can make a start, and I can handle the rest of the slides myself."（好，拜託你了。你先開個頭，我可以自己簡報剩下的投影片。），得知傑森應該是在詢問有關簡報開頭的事，因此 (C) 項應為正選。

其他重點

1. **presentation** [ˌprɛzənˋteʃən] *n.* 簡報；口頭報告
   give / make a presentation　做簡報 / 口頭報告
2. **handle** [ˋhændḷ] *vt.* 處理
   handle a problem　處理問題
   例: Kelly handled the emergency calmly and quickly.
   （凱莉冷靜快速地處理這起緊急事件。）
3. **introduce** [ˌɪntrəˋd(j)us] *vt.* 介紹
   例: The chairman introduced the speaker to the audience.
   （主席向聽眾介紹這位演講者。）
4. **audio** [ˋɔdɪˌo] *a.* 聲音的

D **19.**

Student: Sir, we are raising money to help save the rainforest. Would you like to donate some money?

Man: Are you kidding? ________________ It doesn't affect me!

Student: Well, sir, rainforests are very important to us. Many things we use are made from rainforest plants, such as the clothes we wear.

Man: Oh, I see. Young man, I'll donate NT$ 500.[註1]

(A) I'll never save the rain![註2]　(B) I won't take your money.

(C) What is your favorite clothing style?　(D) Why do I have to save the rainforest?

學生：先生，我們正在募款幫助拯救雨林。您願意捐點錢嗎？

男子：開什麼玩笑？________________ 對我又沒有影響！

學生：先生，雨林對我們來說很重要。我們使用的東西很多都是雨林的植物做的，像是我們穿的衣服等等。

男子：喔，原來如此。年輕人，我捐新臺幣五百塊。

(A) 我絕不會去儲存雨水！　(B) 我不會拿你的錢。

(C) 你最喜歡的衣服風格是什麼？　(D) 我為什麼要拯救雨林？

解析

空格後，男子回答 "It doesn't affect me!"（對我又沒有影響！），學生則接著解釋拯救雨林的原因，得知男子先前應該是在表達否定拯救雨林的事，因此 (D) 項應為正選。

註1：NT$ 500 宜改成 NT$500（即金錢符號 $ 與數字間並無空格）。

註2：此句宜改成 I would never save rainwater.

其他重點

1. **raise** [rez] *vt.* 募（款）

   raise money　募款

2. **save** [sev] *vt.* 拯救 & *vt.* & *vi.* 儲存；存錢；節省

   例: The soldier risked his life trying to save his friend.
   （那位士兵冒著生命危險，企圖拯救他的朋友。）
   You should save money for a rainy day.
   （你應存錢以備不時之需。）

3. **donate** [ˋdonet / doˋnet] *vt.* & *vi.* 捐獻（金錢、物資等）

   例: Mr. and Mrs. Smith donated one million dollars to a local charity.
   （史密斯夫婦捐了一百萬美元給當地的慈善機構。）

4. **affect** [əˋfɛkt] *vt.* 影響

   例: Over 10,000 commuters were affected by the strike.
   （超過一萬名通勤者受到該起罷工事件的影響。）

A **20.**

Jack: I got a text message from the hotel. They ask us to click on a link to confirm our reservation.[註1]

Lucy: ________ This message seems strange.

Jack: But could it be a new policy? I'm afraid our reservation would be cancelled.[註2]

Lucy: Let me call the hotel. It's better to be safe than sorry.

(A) Hey, don't do that. (B) Just click on it now.

(C) Absolutely, go ahead. (D) It's a standard procedure.

傑克：我收到飯店的簡訊。他們叫我們點擊一個連結來確認我們的訂房。

露西：________這簡訊似乎很奇怪。

傑克：但會不會是新的規定？我怕我們的訂房會被取消。

露西：讓我打個電話給飯店。安全第一。

(A) 嘿，不要這麼做。 (B) 現在就點看看。

(C) 當然好，儘管去做。 (D) 是標準程序。

解析

空格後，露西表示 "This message seems strange."（這簡訊似乎很奇怪。），露西接著表示 "Let me call the hotel. It's better to be safe than sorry."（讓我打個電話給飯店。安全第一。），得知露西先前應該會阻止傑克點擊連結，因此 (A) 項應為正選。

註1：此句宜改成 They asked us to click on a link to confirm our reservation.

註2：此句宜改成 I'm afraid our reservation will be canceled.

其他重點

1. **confirm** [kənˋfɝm] *vt.* 確認；證實

   例: I would like to confirm my dinner reservation.
   （我想確認晚餐的訂位。）

2. **reservation** [ˏrɛzɚˋveʃən] *n.* 預訂

   make a reservation for... 預訂……

   例: I'd like to make a reservation for a table of five people tonight.
   （我想訂今天晚上的位子，一共五位。）

3. **strange** [strendʒ] *a.* 奇怪的

4. **policy** [ˋpɑləsɪ] *n.* 規定；政策

5. **It's better to be safe than sorry.** 安全第一。/ 防患於未然。

6. **standard** [ˋstændɚd] *a.* 標準的

7. **procedure** [prəˋsidʒɚ] *n.* 程序

III. 綜合測驗

◎ 21 - 24

Living on Orchid Island, the Yami (Tao) people are able to keep their traditions going. The best-known tradition is the "flying fish season" of spring and summer. Flying fish ___21___ as a gift from heaven. During the festival period, the local people have to be very careful of their actions and words in order not to break with traditions. ___22___ the years, hundreds and thousands of tourists have visited Orchid Island every flying fish season. Many tourists have shown a lack of respect for local customs. Therefore, residents keep reminding tourists to avoid ___23___. One thing tourists should not do is touching the fishing boats when taking pictures. Traditionally, Yami (Tao) women and outsiders are not allowed to touch the fishing boats. ___24___ thing tourists should not do is entering the backyard of houses where local residents dry their flying fish. Acts of disrespect, according to local fishermen, would bring bad luck. Tourists should remember not to disturb normal life on the island.

21. (A) regard (B) regarded (C) are regarded (D) are regarding

22. (A) About (B) Below (C) Over (D) Without

23. (A) good manners (B) rude behaviors (C) spending money (D) showing consideration

24. (A) Another (B) Other (C) Any other (D) No other

生活在蘭嶼的雅美族（達悟族）能夠維繫他們的傳統。最著名的傳統是春夏季節的「飛魚季」。飛魚被視為上天的恩賜。在此節慶期間，當地人必須非常小心自己的言行，以免違反傳統。多年來，每到飛魚季節就有數十萬名遊客造訪蘭嶼。許多遊客並未尊重當地習俗。因此居民不斷提醒遊客要避免無禮的舉止。遊客不該做的事情之一是拍照時觸碰漁船。傳統上，雅美族（達悟族）的女人和外人是不准觸碰漁船的。遊客不該做的另一件事是進去當地居民晒飛魚的屋子後院。根據當地漁民的說法，不尊重的行為會帶來厄運。遊客要記得不要打擾島上的正常生活。

C **21.**

解析

1. 空格前 Flying fish（飛魚）為名詞，空格後接介詞 as 及介詞的受詞 a gift from heaven（上天的恩賜）。
2. 可推知空格應使用動詞，四個選項皆可作動詞，僅 (C) are regarded（被視為）置入後符合語意，可知 (C) 項應為正選。

C **22.**

解析

1. 空格所在句子之時態 have visited 為現在完成式（have / has + p.p.），因此空格應使用常與此時態並用的介詞，如 for（計，達）、since（自從）、over（在……期間）等。
2. 四個選項皆為介詞。(A) About 表「關於」；(B) Below 表「在……下面」；(C) Over 表「在……期間」；(D) Without 表「沒有」，根據空格所在句子之時態及語意，得知 (C) 項應為正選。

B **23.**

解析

1. 空格前的句子提到許多遊客並未尊重當地習俗。
2. (A) good manners（有禮貌）、(C) spending money（花錢）、(D) showing consideration（體貼）置入後不符語意，僅 (B) rude behaviors（無禮的舉止）置入後符合語意，可知 (B) 項應為正選。

A **24.**

解析

1. 倒數第六句至第四句提到居民不斷提醒遊客要避免無禮的舉止，遊客不該做的事情之一是拍照時觸碰漁船，傳統上，雅美族（達悟族）的女人和外人是不准觸碰漁船的，而空格所在的句子提到遊客不應做的事是去當地居民曬飛魚的屋子後院。
2. 由語意可知文中暗指遊客不該做的事有很多，而僅舉例兩種，因此為「非限定的兩者」，應使用 one... another...（一個……另一個……）。
3. 倒數第五句使用 One thing（一件事），則空格應使用 Another thing（另一件事），可知 (A) 項應為正選。

重要單字片語

1. **orchid** [ˋɔrkɪd] *n.* 蘭花
2. **resident** [ˋrɛzədənt] *n.* 居民
3. **outsider** [autˋsaɪdɚ] *n.* 外人
4. **backyard** [ˋbækˏjɑrd] *n.* 後院
5. **disrespect** [ˏdɪsrɪˋspɛkt] *n.* 無禮，不尊敬（不可數）
6. **according to + N** 根據……
   例: According to the weather forecast, a typhoon is coming this weekend.
   （根據氣象預測，這週末會有颱風。）
7. **disturb** [dɪsˋtɝb] *vt.* & *vi.* 打擾，使煩惱
   例: Don't disturb Mom while she is at work.
   （老媽工作時不要打擾她。）
8. **behavior** [bɪˋhevjɚ] *n.* 行為，舉止

◎ 25 - 28

The 3D printer is a machine that can create three-dimensional solid objects. In the printing process, the printer adds layers upon layers of materials until a solid object is completed. __25__, 3D printers only made small, simple plastic objects. But now, 3D printer technology can help house builders know the exact amount of materials they need even before they start construction. Therefore, building 3D printed homes requires fewer resources and produces __26__ waste than the traditional way.

The 3D printer[註1] can improve the quality of the objects they create by using artificial intelligence (AI). One of the most exciting applications of AI in 3D printing __27__ generative design. Generative design is a computer-aided design technique that uses AI to improve the design process. It helps create lighter and stronger structures. This is because AI can find the best way to reduce the weight of a structure __28__ increasing its strength. In this way, better buildings can be created.

25. (A) Finally (B) Soon (C) At first (D) In summary

26. (A) last (B) less (C) least (D) little

27. (A) is (B) are (C) has (D) have

28. (A) nor (B) since (C) unless (D) while

3D 列印機是可以製造立體的固體物品的機器。在列印過程中，印表機將材料一層一層堆疊成形，直到固體物件完成。起初 3D 列印只能製造簡單的小型塑膠物品。但現在 3D 列印技術可以讓房屋的營造商甚至在還沒開始施工前就預知所需材料的確切數量。因此建造 3D 列印房屋，比起傳統方式所需的資源較少，產生的廢棄物也更少。

3D 列印機可透過人工智慧來改進其創造物件的品質。人工智慧在 3D 列印中最令人興奮的應用之一便是生成式設計。生成式設計是一種電腦輔助設計的技術，利用人工智慧來改進設計流程。它有助於創造更輕且更堅固的結構。這是因為人工智慧在增加建築物強度的同時，還可以找到減輕重量的最佳方法。如此就可以創造更優良的建物。

註1：因本句後半部使用代名詞 they，故 The 3D printer 宜改為 3D printers。

C **25.**

解析

1. (A) **finally** [ˋfaɪnl̩ɪ] *adv.* 最後，終於

例: Finally, I'd like to thank you all for coming to my birthday party.
（最後，我要感謝大家來參加我的生日派對。）

(B) **soon** [sun] *adv.* 不久，很快

例: We'll be leaving for the trip soon, so you'd better pack your bag now.
（我們馬上就要出發去旅行了，所以你最好現在就去收拾行李。）

(C) **at first** 起先

例: At first, Kevin didn't believe what we said, but he accepted that it was the truth in the end.
（起先凱文不相信我們說的話，但最後他相信我們說的都是實話。）

(D) **in summary, ...** 概括來說 / 總而言之，……
summary [ˋsʌmərɪ] *n.* 概述，概要

例: In summary, the sales manager is not satisfied with your performance this year.
（總的來說，業務經理不滿意你今年的表現。）

2. 根據語意，可知 (C) 項應為正選。

B **26.**

解析

1. 本題測試一般比較句構用法：
less... than... 比……還少……（less 後加不可數名詞）

例: The new model of the car causes less pollution than the old one.
（新款車製造的汙染少於舊款。）

2. 根據上述用法，可知 (B) 項應為正選。

A **27.**

解析

1. 空格前有 One of the most exciting applications of AI in 3D printing（人工智慧在 3D 列印中最令人興奮的應用之一）作主詞，空格後有單數名詞 generative design（生成式設計）作受詞，得知空格應置 be 動詞 is 或第三人稱動詞。
2. 四個選項皆為動詞，惟 (B) 項 are（是）、(D) 項 have（有）分別為複數名詞用的 be 動詞及第一、二人稱動詞，(C) 項 has（有）為第三人稱動詞，但置入後不符語意，僅 (A) 項 be 動詞 is（是）置入後符合語意，可知 (A) 項應為正選。

D **28.**

解析

1. (A) **nor** [nɔr] *conj.* 也不（常與 neither 並用）
   neither... nor...　　既不……也不……
   例: Neither Jeff nor Monica can handle this difficult customer.
   （傑夫和莫妮卡都無法應付這個難搞的顧客。）

   (B) **since** [sɪns] *conj.* & *prep.* 自從 & *conj.* 由於（since 作連接詞或介詞，表「自從」時，所引導的子句或片語，一定與完成式或完成進行式並用。）
   例: Michelle has been practicing the piano for four hours a day since she started taking lessons.
   （從蜜雪兒開始上鋼琴課以來，每天都要練上四個小時。）

   (C) **unless** [ʌnˋlɛs] *conj.* 除非（之後須接主詞及動詞）
   例: Chris won't go to the party unless Jill decides to go with him.
   （除非吉兒決定和克里斯一起去參加派對，否則他不會去。）

   (D) **while** [(h)waɪl] *conj.* 當；而；雖然
   例: Tom finished reading a book while he was waiting for the bus.
   （湯姆在等公車時看完了一本書。）

2. 四個選項皆可當連接詞，根據上述用法，僅 (D) 項置入後符合語意。(D) 項 while 在原句空格內表「當」引導副詞子句時，此副詞子句中之主詞與主要子句中之主詞相同，皆為 AI，則此副詞子句可化簡為副詞片語，原句原為：This is because AI can find the best way to reduce the weight of a structure while <u>AI is increasing its strength</u>. 化簡方法為去掉副詞子句之主詞，之後的 be 動詞 is 予以省略。故原句可改寫為：This is because AI can find the best way to reduce the weight of a structure while <u>increasing its strength</u>. 由此可知 (D) 項應為正選。

重要單字片語

1. **dimensional** [dəˋmɛnʃənl̩] *a.* 尺寸的；空間的
   three-dimensional [ˏθridəˋmɛnʃənl̩] *a.* 立體的，三度空間的（= 3D）
2. **solid** [ˋsɑlɪd] *a.* 固體的；堅固的；實心的 & *n.* 固體
   例: The solid oak table in the dining room is great for parties and dinners.
   （飯廳的實心橡木桌非常適合聚會和晚餐。）
3. **process** [ˋprɑsɛs] *n.* 過程 & *vt.* 處理
   in the process of...　　在……的過程中
   例: The company is in the process of moving to a bigger office.
   （公司正在搬往較大的辦公室。）
4. **layer** [ˋleɚ] *n.* 層次
   例: There was a thin layer of dust on the old machine.
   （那臺舊機器上積了一層薄薄的灰塵。）
5. **builder** [ˋbɪldɚ] *n.* 營造商
   build [bɪld] *vt.* 建造；建立
   （三態為：build, built, [bɪlt], built）

6. **construction** [ˌkənˋstrʌkʃən] *n.* 施工，建造
be under construction　施工中
construct [kənˋstrʌkt] *vt.* 建造
例: A new shopping mall is under construction in our neighborhood.
= A new shopping mall is being constructed in our neighborhood.
（我們家附近正在興建一座新的購物中心。）

7. **resource** [rɪˋsɔrs / ˋrisɔrs] *n.* 資源（常用複數）
例: If we don't limit the use of natural resources, they will be used up one day.
（我們若不限制使用天然資源，總有一天會把它們用光。）

8. **artificial** [ˌɑrtəˋfɪʃəl] *a.* 人造的
artificial intelligence　人工智慧（常縮寫為 AI）

9. **application** [ˌæpləˋkeʃən] *n.* 應用；申請（書）

10. **generative** [ˋdʒɛnəˌretɪv] *a.* 有生產能力的

11. **structure** [ˋstrʌktʃɚ] *n.* 結構；建築物

12. **reduce** [rɪˋdjus] *vt.* 使減少；使淪為
例: The landlord is planning to reduce the rent of the apartment next year.
（房東打算明年降房租。）

IV. 閱讀測驗

◎ 29 - 30

Answer the questions based on the following timetable.

Timetable

Train No.	Operation Day	Taichung	Miaoli	Hsinchu	Taoyuan	Banqiao	Taipei	Nangang
1510	Mon ~ Fri	07:12	07:31	07:45	07:58	08:10	08:21	08:30
802	Daily	07:25	07:45	07:58	08:10	08:22	08:32	08:40
1202	Mon ~ Fri	07:21	—	—	—	—	08:07	08:15
1602	Mon ~ Fri	07:40	—	08:05	08:18	08:31	08:42	08:50
1302	Mon ~ Fri	07:53	—	—	08:27	—	08:47	08:55
204	Daily	07:48	—	—	—	08:27	08:37	08:45
606	Sat	08:00	—	08:25	08:38	08:51	09:02	09:10

根據以下時刻表回答問題。

時刻表

列車班次	行駛日	臺中	苗栗	新竹	桃園	板橋	臺北	南港
1510	週一至週五	07:12	07:31	07:45	07:58	08:10	08:21	08:30
802	每天	07:25	07:45	07:58	08:10	08:22	08:32	08:40
1202	週一至週五	07:21	—	—	—	—	08:07	08:15
1602	週一至週五	07:40	—	08:05	08:18	08:31	08:42	08:50
1302	週一至週五	07:53	—	—	08:27	—	08:47	08:55
204	每天	07:48	—	—	—	08:27	08:37	08:45
606	週六	08:00	—	08:25	08:38	08:51	09:02	09:10

C **29.**

Which of the following is **NOT** true about the timetable?

(A) Train No. 802 operates every day of the week from Monday to Sunday.

(B) Train No. 1510 takes longer to get from Taichung to Taipei than Train No. 1202.

(C) If Mr. Sakula takes Train No. 606 on Saturday, he will arrive at Taoyuan at 08:30.

(D) From Taichung to Nangang, Train No. 204 will make a stop at Banqiao and Taipei.

關於本時刻表的資訊，下列哪一項不正確？

(A) 802 車次從週一到週日每天行駛。

(B) 1510 車次從臺中到臺北的乘車時間比 1202 車次久。

(C) 如果宮脇先生於週六搭乘 606 車次，他會在八點三十分抵達桃園。

(D) 由臺中開往南港的 204 車次，會停靠板橋及臺北。

理由:

根據時刻表最後一列資訊得知，606 車次抵達桃園的時間為八點三十八分，而非八點三十分，故 (C) 項應為正選。

A **30.**

Maria is planning to take a train from Taichung to Taipei this Saturday morning. On the way, Denny will join her on the train at Hsinchu. They will be meeting Mr. Lee at Taipei station at 08:50. Which train is her best choice?

(A) No. 802 (B) No. 1202
(C) No. 1602 (D) No. 606

瑪麗亞打算這週六早上從臺中搭火車到臺北。途中，丹尼會在新竹上車與她會合。他們將於八點五十分在臺北車站與李先生會面。下列哪一班車是她的最佳選擇？

(A) 802 車次 (B) 1202 車次
(C) 1602 車次 (D) 606 車次

理由:

根據時刻表得知，週六有行駛的為 802、204 及 606 車次。由於丹尼會在新竹上車，上述三個車次中只有 802 及 606 車次停靠新竹。又瑪麗亞與丹尼必須於八點五十分前抵達臺北車站，606 車次抵達臺北時已超過九點，802 車次於八點三十二分即抵達臺北，故 (A) 項應為正選。

重要單字片語

1. **timetable** [ˋtaɪm͵tebl̩] *n.*
(公車、火車、飛機等的）時刻表
(= schedule [ˋskɛdʒʊl]）；時間表
例: Make sure to check the timetable before the trip so that we won't miss the bus.
（出發前一定要查好時刻表，這樣我們才不會錯過公車。）

2. **operate** [ˋɑpə͵ret] *vi.* 營運；運作 & *vt.* 經營
例: The machine has some problems, but it has been operating well recently.
（這臺機器有點問題，但最近的運轉是 OK 的。）

◎ 31 - 32

After the 2022 Asian Games, Minhua, Yating, and Fuhao are motivated to join the University Student Sports Clubs. Answer the questions based on the poster below.

CLUB	HOW TO PLAY	PRACTICE TIME
Badminton	Two or four people hit a shuttlecock over a high net.	Evening on Fridays
Basketball	Two teams score points by throwing a large ball through an open net.	Evening on Tuesdays and Saturdays
Cycling	An individual rides a bicycle.	Morning on Thursdays
Rugby	Two teams score points by carrying an oval ball across a particular line.	Evening on Saturdays
Swimming	An individual moves through water by moving the body.	Evening on Mondays
Weightlifting	An individual lifts heavy objects as a sport.	Evening on Tuesdays and Fridays

2022 年亞運會結束後，敏華、雅婷和富浩躍躍欲試地想參加大學運動社團。根據以下的海報回答問題。

社團	玩法	練習時間
羽毛球	兩人或四人隔著一面高的網子拍擊羽毛球。	每週五晚
籃球	兩隊投擲一顆大球穿越空心的網子以得到分數。	每週二、六晚
腳踏車	一個人騎腳踏車。	每週四早
橄欖球	兩隊帶著一顆橢圓形的球穿過一特定的線來得分。	每週六晚
游泳	一個人透過移動身體在水中移動。	每週一晚
舉重	一個人舉起重物的運動。	每週二、五晚

D **31.**

Minhua and Yating are interested in playing a team sport, which[註1] clubs are they likely to join?

(A) Basketball and weightlifting
(B) Badminton and cycling
(C) Swimming and badminton
(D) Rugby and basketball

註1：... sport, which... 應改為 ... sport. Which...。

敏華和雅婷對團隊運動感興趣，她們可能加入哪些社團？

(A) 籃球和舉重
(B) 羽毛球和腳踏車
(C) 游泳和羽毛球
(D) 橄欖球和籃球

理由:
根據本海報的第一項 "Badminton"（羽毛球）提到其玩法為 "Two or four people hit a shuttlecock over a high net."（兩人或四人隔著一面高的網子拍擊羽毛球。），第二項 "Basketball"（籃球）提到其玩法為 "Two teams score points by throwing a large ball through an open net."（兩隊投擲一顆大球穿越空心的網子以得到分數。），及第四項 "Rugby"（橄欖球）提到其玩法為 "Two teams score points by carrying an oval ball across a particular line."（兩隊帶著一顆橢圓形的球穿過一特定的線來得分。），得知 (D) 項應為正選。

A **32.**

Fuhao works in the evening on Mondays and Tuesdays. Which clubs is he likely to join?
(A) Badminton, Cycling, Rugby
(B) Basketball, Swimming, Weightlifting
(C) Rugby, Weightlifting, Swimming
(D) Cycling, Basketball, Badminton

富浩每週一及週二晚上工作。他可能加入哪些社團？
(A) 羽毛球、腳踏車、橄欖球
(B) 籃球、游泳、舉重
(C) 橄欖球、舉重、游泳
(D) 腳踏車、籃球、羽毛球

理由:
根據本海報的第一項 "Badminton"（羽毛球）提到其練習時間為 "Evening on Fridays"（每週五晚），第三項 "Cycling"（腳踏車）提到其練習時間為 "Morning on Thursdays"（每週四早），第四項 "Rugby"（橄欖球）提到其練習時間為 "Evening on Saturdays"（每週六晚），得知 (A) 項應為正選。

重要單字片語

1. **Asian** [ˋeʃən] *a.* 亞洲（人）的
   Asia [ˋeʃə] *n.* 亞洲
2. **motivate** [ˋmotəˏvet] *vt.* 激勵，激發
   sb be motivated to V　某人被激勵去做……
   = motivate sb to V
   例: According to the research, encouragement can often motivate children to study harder.
   （根據研究，鼓勵往往能激發小孩讀書更用功。）
3. **be based on...**　以……為依據
   例: The novel was based on a true story.
   （這部小說是根據一個真實故事所寫的。）
4. **poster** [ˋpostɚ] *n.* 海報
5. **shuttlecock** [ˋʃʌtḷˏkɑk] *n.* 羽毛球
6. **rugby** [ˋrʌgbɪ] *n.* 橄欖球
7. **oval** [ˋovḷ] *a.* 橢圓形的，卵形的 & *n.* 橢圓
8. **weightlifting** [ˋwetlɪftɪŋ] *n.* 舉重

◎ 33 - 35

Lina is planning a trip and comparing two hotels in a tourist spot. Answer the questions based on the information below.

Hotelcomparison ×

http://www.hotelcomparison.com

	Cruise Hotel	Universe Hotel
Facilities	Fitness center Indoor car parking Restaurants	Business center Outdoor pool Gift shop
Services	Free airport shuttle Laundry service Free Wi-Fi	24-hour room service Free Wi-Fi Car rental service
Distance from tourist attractions	Sunset Beach (1 km) Theme Park (6 km) Art Museum (8 km)	Art Museum (2 km) Theme Park (16 km) Sunset Beach (20 km)
Room rates	Single: NT$ 2,700 Double: NT$ 3,600 Triple: NT$ 5,200	Single: NT$ 1,800 Double: NT$ 2,400 Triple: NT$ 3,500

莉娜正在做旅遊規畫並比較同個觀光景點的兩間旅館。請根據以下訊息回答問題。

旅館比較

http://www.hotelcomparison.com

	航遊旅館	宇宙旅館
設施	健身中心 室內停車場 餐廳	商務中心 戶外泳池 禮品店
服務	免費機場接駁 洗衣服務 免費無線上網	24 小時客房服務 免費無線上網 租車服務
與景點的距離	日落海灘（1 公里） 主題公園（6 公里） 美術館（8 公里）	美術館（2 公里） 主題公園（16 公里） 日落海灘（20 公里）
房價	單人房：新臺幣 2,700 元 雙人房：新臺幣 3,600 元 三人房：新臺幣 5,200 元	單人房：新臺幣 1,800 元 雙人房：新臺幣 2,400 元 三人房：新臺幣 3,500 元

C **33.**

Which facility or service is provided by both hotels?

(A) Outdoor pool
(B) Business center
(C) Free Wi-Fi
(D) Laundry service

哪種設施或服務是兩間旅館都有提供的？

(A) 戶外泳池
(B) 商務中心
(C) 免費無線上網
(D) 洗衣服務

理由:

根據表格的第三列 "Services"（服務）可判斷兩間旅館都有提供的是 "Free Wi-Fi"（免費無線上網），得知 (C) 項應為正選。

B **34.**

How far does Lina have to drive to the Theme Park if she stays in the hotel closer to it?
(A) 2 km
(B) 6 km
(C) 8 km
(D) 16 km

如果莉娜住在離主題公園比較近的旅館，她開車到那裡要開多遠？
(A) 2 公里
(B) 6 公里
(C) 8 公里
(D) 16 公里

理由:
根據表格第四列 "Distance from tourist attractions"（與景點的距離）可判斷離主題公園比較近的旅館是 "Cruise Hotel"（航遊旅館），且其距離為 6 公里，得知 (B) 項應為正選。

B **35.**

Which of the following is true?
(A) If Lina likes to use the fitness center, she should choose Universe Hotel.
(B) If Lina likes to swim in the pool, she should choose Universe Hotel.
(C) Lina will have to pay NT$ 1,800 for a single room in Cruise Hotel.
(D) Lina is able to use room service anytime in Cruise Hotel.

下列敘述何者為真？
(A) 如果莉娜喜歡上健身房，她就應該選擇宇宙旅館。
(B) 如果莉娜喜歡在游泳池游泳，她就應該選擇宇宙旅館。
(C) 若要住在航遊旅館的單人房，莉娜需支付新臺幣 1,800 元。
(D) 莉娜若住航遊旅館，便可隨時使用其客房服務。

理由:
根據表格第三欄可知 "Universe Hotel "（宇宙旅館）有 "Outdoor pool"（戶外泳池），得知 (B) 項應為正選。

重要單字片語

1. **compare** [kəmˋpɛr] *vt.* & *vi.* 比較 & *vt.* 把……比作 & *vi.*（可與……）匹敵
comparison [kəmˋpærəsn̩] *n.* 比較
例: It's interesting to compare a British English accent with an American one.
（比較英式英語與美式英語的腔調很有意思。）

2. **a tourist spot** 觀光景點
spot [spɑt] *n.* 地點；斑點；汙漬

3. **shuttle** [ˋʃʌtl̩] *n.* 往返通勤列車，區間車；梭子 & *vt.* 短程運送
a shuttle service 接駁車的服務

4. **laundry** [ˋlɔndrɪ] *n.* 待洗衣物

5. **room service** 客房服務

6. **rental** [ˋrɛntl̩] *n.* 出租
a rental car 租來的車（= a rental）

7. **theme** [θim] *n.* 主題
a theme park　　主題公園
8. **single** [ˋsɪŋgl̩] *a.* 單一的；單身的
a single room　　單人房
9. **double** [ˋdʌbl̩] *a.* 雙倍的 & *vt.* 使加倍
a double room　　雙人房
10. **triple** [ˋtrɪpl̩] *a.* 三倍的 & *vt.* & *vi.*（使）成為三倍
a triple room　　三人房

◎ **36 - 38**

Jensen Huang (黃仁勳) is the chief executive of NVIDIA, a leading company that makes chips used in artificial intelligence (AI). In 2023, Huang was listed among the 100 most influential people in AI. An inspiration to many, Huang encourages young people to seize the opportunities that AI will present. Meanwhile, he reminds them to take a positive attitude towards challenges.

In a speech to university graduates in Taiwan last year, Huang shared two important lessons he has learned in the past three decades. The first lesson is not to be discouraged by failure. In 1996, his company nearly closed down due to rapid changes in the industry. They soon realized that they had made a mistake, and Huang humbly asked a major customer for help. With the customer's support, the company moved on to invent the chip that led to their future success. Huang's advice is to always honestly face your mistakes and seek help.

The second lesson is to keep going despite difficulties. In 2007, the company made an expensive investment on[註1] product improvements. The new products were not selling well for many years until they started being used for machine learning. The experience taught Huang and his colleagues to handle the pain and suffering needed to achieve their vision. Their continued efforts help[註2] build NVIDIA into a global leader in AI technologies.

Huang's life story is also about **pushing oneself to do better**. Born in Taiwan, Huang moved to the United States at the age of nine. He later earned two engineering degrees before working for two chip companies. In 1993, on his 30th birthday, he and two friends founded NVIDIA. Today, Huang often advises students to live a life of purpose, and to run, not walk, towards their goals.

黃仁勳是製造人工智慧所使用晶片的主力公司輝達的執行長。在 2023 年，黃仁勳名列 AI 產業最具影響力的百大人物榜單。啟發了很多人的黃仁勳鼓勵年輕人抓住 AI 將要提供的機運。同時他提醒他們在面對挑戰時採取積極的態度。

去年他在臺灣一場對大學畢業生的演說中，黃仁勳分享了過去三十年間學到的兩個重要教訓。第一個教訓是不要因失敗而氣餒。1996 年，他的公司因產業急速變化而瀕臨倒閉。他們很快意識到犯了錯，黃仁勳低聲下氣地向某大客戶求助。有了這位客戶的支持，公司奮勇前進，發明了後來大獲全勝的晶片。黃仁勳的建議是要永遠誠實面對錯誤並尋求幫助。

第二個教訓是不怕艱困，勇往直前。2007 年，公司動用大筆資金投入產品改良。這些新產品的銷售低迷了許多年，直到它們開始被用於機器學習為止。這個經驗讓黃仁勳和他的同事學會如何咬緊牙關，承受達成願景必須經歷的痛苦和磨難。他們不懈的努力讓輝達成為 AI 科技的全球領導者。

黃仁勳的人生故事也是**自我鞭策更進一步**的故事。他出生於臺灣，九歲時移民至美國。後來他拿到兩個工程學位，之後在兩家晶片公司工作過。1993 年，在他 30 歲生日那天，他和兩位朋友創立了輝達。現在黃仁勳常建議學生生活要有目標，要向目標衝衝衝而不要慢吞吞地走過去。

註1：make an investment 後面接的介詞為 in。

註2：本句延續前一句黃仁勳與他同事們過去的經歷幫助了輝達成為 AI 科技的全球領導者，所以動詞仍使用過去式，help 須改為 helped。

D **36.**

What is the main idea of this passage?

(A) How to come up with a speech

(B) How to succeed in chip making

(C) How to seize opportunities in AI

(D) How to deal with difficult situations

本文的主旨是什麼？

(A) 如何想出一篇演講

(B) 如何在晶片製造領域成功

(C) 如何抓住 AI 的機會

(D) 如何克服困難

理由:

本文主要談論黃仁勳的演講內容，其中提及他創業的過程和如何應對過程中所遭遇的困難。故 (D) 項應為正選。

B **37.**

According to the passage, which is **NOT** an example of "**pushing oneself to do better**"?

(A) Working for chip companies
(B) Reaching the age of 30 in 1993
(C) Earning two engineering degrees
(D) Founding NVIDIA with two friends

根據本文，下列哪一項不是 "**pushing oneself to do better**" 的例證？

(A) 在晶片公司工作
(B) 1993 年滿 30 歲
(C) 獲得兩個工程學位
(D) 和兩個朋友創立輝達

理由:

根據本文最後一段的第三句與第四句 "He later earned two engineering degrees before working for two chip companies. In 1993, on his 30th birthday, he and two friends founded NVIDIA."（後來他拿到兩個工程學位，之後在兩家晶片公司工作過。1993 年，在他 30 歲生日那天，他和兩位朋友創立了輝達。）得知，(A) 項、(C) 項和 (D) 項為正確的三個例證，(B) 項應為事實描述而非例證。故 (B) 項應為正選。

B **38.**

Based on the passage, arrange the following events in the order in which they happened.

a. New products made profits when they were used for machine learning.
b. Huang's company almost shut down because of challenges in the industry.
c. Huang became one of the most 100[註3] influential people in artificial intelligence.
d. The company admitted their mistake and obtained help to develop a product.

(A) b → a → c → d　　(B) b → d → a → c
(C) c → d → b → a　　(D) c → a → d → b

根據本文，將以下事件排出發生的先後順序。

a. 新產品用在機器學習時有了利潤。
b. 黃仁勳的公司因為產業挑戰而幾乎倒閉。
c. 黃仁勳成為 AI 領域百大影響力人物之一。
d. 這家公司承認錯誤並在開發某產品上取得協助。

理由:

根據本文第三段第二至三句得知 a. 項發生於 2007 年；第二段第三句得知 b. 項發生於 1996 年；第一段第二句得知 c. 項發生於 2023 年；第二段第四句得知 d. 項發生於 b. 項後。故 (B) 項應為正選。

註3：100 應該置於 most 之前，百大最具影響力的人物說法應為 the 100 most influential people。

重要單字片語

1. **chief executive** [ˋtʃif ɪgˋzɛkjʊtɪv] *n.*（公司或機構的）執行長，總裁
2. **chip** [tʃɪp] *n.* 電腦晶片；碎片，屑片
3. **artificial intelligence** [ˏɑrtəˋfɪʃəl ɪnˋtɛlədʒəns] *n.* 人工智慧（縮寫為 AI）
4. **influential** [ˏɪnflʊˋɛnʃəl] *a.* 有影響力的
5. **inspiration** [ˏɪnspəˋreʃən] *n.* 鼓舞人心的人；靈感，啟示
6. **seize** [siz] *vt.* 抓住

   例: Our team will seize every opportunity to win.
   （我們的隊伍會抓住每個可獲勝的機會。）
7. **meanwhile** [ˋminˏ(h)waɪl] *adv.* & *n.* 同時
8. **attitude** [ˋætətjud] *n.* 態度（常與介詞 to 或 toward(s) 搭配）

   例: Brian has a very bad attitude towards work.
   （布萊恩的工作態度不佳。）
9. **decade** [ˋdɛked] *n.* 十年
10. **discourage** [dɪsˋkɝɪdʒ] *vt.* 阻止；打消……的念頭

    例: Patty's father tried to discourage her from buying a scooter.
    （派蒂的父親試圖打消她買機車的念頭。）
11. **close down** 關閉，停業
    = shut down（shut 三態同形）

    例: Owing to poor management, the factory closed down two years after it was established.
    （由於管理不善，工廠建立兩年後就關門大吉了。）
12. **humbly** [ˋhʌmblɪ] *adv.* 謙卑地；卑微地
13. **move on to...** （往下）進行……

    例: We should start out testing on a small scale before we move on to a larger group.
    （在我們對更大的群組進行實驗前，應該要先做小規模的測試。）
14. **lead to...** 導致 / 造成……
    （lead 三態為：lead, led [lɛd], led）

    例: Rebecca's positive attitude led to a happier life.
    （蕾貝卡積極正向的態度讓她的人生過得比較快樂。）
15. **investment** [ɪnˋvɛstmənt] *n.* 投資
16. **continued** [kənˋtɪnjud] *a.* 持續的
17. **engineering** [ˏɛndʒəˋnɪrɪŋ] *n.* 工程（學）（不可數）
18. **found** [faʊnd] *vt.* 創立，開設

    例: Alex founded a hospital in his hometown.
    （艾力克斯在他家鄉創辦了一家醫院。）
19. **come up with...** 想出 / 提出……
    （come 三態為：come, came, come）

    例: Bob came up with an excuse for being late.
    （鮑伯為遲到想了一個藉口。）
20. **deal with...** 解決 / 處理……
    （deal 三態為：deal [dil], dealt [dɛlt], dealt）

    例: Kyle had to deal with the problem by himself.
    （凱爾必須自行解決這個問題。）
21. **make profits** 獲利，賺錢
    （make 三態為：make, made, made）

    例: Henry made big profits from selling stocks.
    （亨利賣股票賺了一大筆錢。）
22. **obtain** [əbˋten] *vt.* 獲得，得到

    例: You can obtain the information you need at the visitor's center.
    （你可以在遊客中心獲得需要的資訊。）

◎ 39 - 42

On October 9, 2023, Triton, the first weather satellite made in Taiwan successfully entered space. It is also the fourth satellite in the world to use GNSS-R instrument to collect weather data. Its purpose is to help us predict the weather more accurately.

This satellite is named after Triton, an ancient Greek god of the sea. The sea god commands the wind and waves. The satellite Triton is able to gather such data as wave heights and sea wind speeds. Triton uses a technique that collects signals **reflected** from the Earth's surface. It carries GNSS-R instrument to receive signals which are sent back from sea surfaces. The calmer the sea, the stronger the signal, indicating weaker winds. This information is valuable as wind speed data is not easy to collect. Such information improves the prediction of typhoon strengths and movements. Triton observes weather changes mainly in the Atlantic Ocean, Indian Ocean, and central Pacific Ocean.

Triton, started in 2014, is the fruitful cooperation between Taiwan Space Agency (TASA) and local companies. TASA developed GNSS-R instrument and key components such as the Onboard Computer and GPS Receiver. More than 20 local research groups and manufacturers participated in developing the ground station equipment. The satellite is 82% developed and produced in Taiwan.

Now that Triton is in space, we can expect it to provide more accurate information and support disaster prevention. The success of Triton contributes to global weather forecasting. It is also an important step forward for Taiwan's space engineering.

臺灣製造的第一顆氣象衛星「獵風者」於 2023 年 10 月 9 日成功發射進入太空。這也是世界上第四顆使用 GNSS-R 設備收集氣象資料的衛星，其功能是協助我們更準確地預測天氣。

此衛星的英文名「特里頓」是古希臘某位海神的名字。祂掌管風與海浪。獵風者衛星能收集如浪高及海上風速等相關數據。它運用收集從地表反射的訊號的一種技術，藉由所配置的 GNSS-R 設備接收由海平面發送回來的訊號。海面越平靜，訊號越強烈，代表風越小。這樣的資訊很珍貴，因為風速數據很難收集。這種資訊能提升颱風強度及動向的預測精準度。獵風者氣象衛星主要觀測大西洋、印度洋及太平洋中部的氣象變化。

獵風者計畫於 2014 年啟動，是臺灣國家太空中心（TASA）及民間公司合作的豐碩成果。國家太空中心研發出 GNSS-R 設備及關鍵零組件如內嵌式電腦及衛星定位系統接收器。超過二十個國內研究團體及製造商參與研發地面站的設備。該衛星 82% 的零件都是由臺灣研發及製造。

既然獵風者氣象衛星已經進入太空，我們期待它能提供更準確的資訊來協助預防災害。獵風者的成功對於全球氣象預報也將貢獻良多。它也是臺灣航太工程往前邁進的一大步。

Triton: 獵風者氣象衛星
TASA: Taiwan Space Agency 國家太空中心
GNSS-R: Global Navigation Satellite System-Reflectometry 全球導航衛星系統反射訊號接收儀

D **39.**

What is the passage mainly about?

(A) Challenges of space engineering in Taiwan
(B) The description of the Greek sea god Triton
(C) Differences in weather forecasting techniques
(D) The introduction of a weather satellite in Taiwan

本文的主旨為何？
(A) 臺灣航太工程的挑戰
(B) 描述希臘海神特里頓
(C) 氣象預測技術的差異
(D) 臺灣氣象衛星的介紹

理由:
本文旨在介紹臺灣本土製造的第一顆氣象衛星 —— 獵風者氣象衛星的名稱由來、運作原理及對氣象預測的貢獻等等，故 (D) 項應為正選。

C **40.**

Which is closest in meaning to "**reflected**" in the second paragraph?

(A) looked into
(B) made of
(C) sent back
(D) named after

哪一個字詞的文意最貼近第二段中的「被反射」？
(A) 被調查
(B) 由……製造
(C) 被送回
(D) 以……命名

理由:
根據第二段的後一句："It carries GNSS-R instrument to receive signals which are sent back from sea surfaces."（藉由所配置的 GNSS-R 設備接收由海平面發送回來的訊號。）得知，(C) 項應為正選。

C **41.**

According to the passage, which of the following is true?

(A) Triton started to collect wind speed data before 2014.
(B) All of Triton was developed and produced in Taiwan.
(C) Triton shows the improvement in Taiwan's space skills.
(D) Fewer than 20 local companies worked on the Triton project.

根據本文所述，下列何者正確？
(A) 獵風者氣象衛星在 2014 年之前即開始收集風速相關資料。
(B) 獵風者氣象衛星全部由臺灣研發及製造。
(C) 獵風者氣象衛星顯示臺灣航太科技有所進步。
(D) 不到二十間民間公司參與獵風者氣象衛星計畫。

理由:
根據本文最後一段最後兩句："The success of Triton contributes to global weather forecasting. It is also an important step forward for Taiwan's space engineering."（獵風者的成功對於全球氣象預報也將貢獻良多。它也是臺灣航太工程往前邁進的一大步。）得知，(C) 項應為正選。

A **42.**

Which of the following can be inferred from the passage about the contribution of Triton?

(A) It helps reduce damage caused by bad weather.
(B) It improves the speed and strength of typhoons.
(C) It connects the Atlantic Ocean and Indian Ocean.
(D) It measures the heights of satellites from sea surfaces.

可以從本文推論出下列哪一項獵風者衛星的貢獻？
(A) 它能協助降低惡劣天氣造成的災損。
(B) 它能改善颱風的速度與強度。
(C) 它連接大西洋與印度洋。
(D) 它能測量從海平面算起的衛星高度。

理由:
根據本文最後一段第一句："Now that Triton is in space, we can expect it to provide more accurate information and support disaster prevention."（現在獵風者氣象衛星已經進入太空，我們期待它能提供更準確的資訊來協助預防災害。）得知，(A) 項應為正選。

重要單字片語

1. **satellite** [ˋsætḷˌaɪt] *n.* 衛星
2. **predict** [prɪˋdɪkt] *vt.* 預測
   prediction [prɪˋdɪkʃən] *n.* 預測

例: It's too early to predict which team will win the game.
（現在要預測哪支隊伍會獲勝還言之過早。）

3. **accurately** [ˋækjərətlɪ] *adv.* 準確地
accurate [ˋækjərət] *a.* 準確的
4. **be named after...** 以……命名
例: The math formula was named after the great mathematician.
（這道數學公式是以這位偉大數學家的名字命名的。）
5. **command** [kəˋmænd] *vt.* & *n.* 掌控，命令
例: The general commanded the troops to fire on the enemy.
（將軍下令部隊向敵軍開火。）
6. **reflect** [rɪˋflɛkt] *vt.* 反射；反應 & *vi.* 思考（與介詞 on 並用）
例: The mirror reflects sunlight.
（鏡子會反射陽光。）
7. **observe** [əbˋzɝv] *vt.* 觀察；注意到
例: Have you observed any changes in the neighborhood?
（你觀察到這裡附近有什麼改變嗎？）
8. **fruitful** [ˋfrutfḷ] *a.* 成果豐碩的
9. **cooperation** [koˌɑpəˋreʃən] *n.* 合作
10. **agency** [ˋedʒənsɪ] *n.* 機關，代辦處
11. **component** [kəmˋponənt] *n.* 零件；構成要素
12. **onboard** [ˋɑnbord] *a.* 內建的；嵌入式的
13. **research** [ˋrisɝtʃ / rɪˋsɝtʃ] *n.* 研究 & [rɪˋsɝtʃ] *vt.* 研究
14. **manufacturer** [ˌmænjəˋfæktʃərɚ] *n.* 製造商；廠商
15. **ground** [graʊnd] *n.* 地面 & *vt.* 使擱淺；使停飛；禁足
16. **equipment** [ɪˋkwɪpmənt] *n.* 裝備
17. **Now that + S + V, S + V**
既然……
例: Now that we have a dryer, we don't have to worry about rainy days anymore.
（我們既然有了烘乾機，就不用再擔心下雨天了。）
18. **contribute** [kənˋtrɪbjut] *vi.* 促成，導致（與介詞 to 並用）
contribute to... 導致……
例: Hard work alone does not necessarily contribute to success.
（光靠努力不一定就會成功。）
19. **forecast** [ˋfɔrˌkæst] *vt.* & *n.* 預測，預報

第二部分：非選擇題（第 I 題，每格 2 分，共 4 分；第 II 題 6 分；第 III 題 6 分；共 16 分）

I. 填充

1. 你比較喜歡用現金付款或是電子錢包？

Would you p ___①___ to pay by cash or with an electronic w ___②___?

① prefer ② wallet

解析

1. 本題空格 ① 的對照譯詞為『比較喜歡』，且空格為 p 開頭，故空格應置動詞 prefer。
prefer [prɪˋfɝ] *vt.* 較喜歡；寧願（三態為：prefer, preferred [prɪˋfɝd], preferred）
prefer to V rather than V 喜歡做……甚於做……
例: Jonathan prefers to exercise outdoors rather than watch TV at home.
（強納森喜歡在戶外運動甚於在家看電視。）

2. 本題空格 ② 的對照譯詞為『錢包』，且空格為 w 開頭，故空格應置名詞 wallet。
wallet [ˋwalɪt] *n.* 皮夾，錢包
例: Max folded the receipt and put it in his wallet.
（麥克斯把發票摺起來放進皮夾裡。）

其他重點

1. **pay by cash** 用現金付款
= pay in cash
= pay with cash
= pay cash

2. **electronic** [ɪˌlɛkˋtranɪk] *a.* 電子的；用電子操作的
例: Using cellphones or any other electronic devices is forbidden during the exam.
（考試中禁止使用手機或任何其他電子產品。）

II. 句子重組

2. work on / to see that / It is good / solving pollution problems / more people

It is good to see that more people work on solving pollution problems.
（看到更多人致力於解決汙染問題是件好事。）

解析

1. 先找出開頭為大寫的詞組 It is good（某事是好的）作為句首。

2. 主詞詞組 It is good 中的 It 為虛主詞，此詞組之後應接不定詞，此不定詞為真正的主詞。重組部分中，to see that（看到⋯⋯）為不定詞詞組，形成 "It is good to see that..."。
3. that 後應接表「看到之事」的名詞子句，子句結構為：主詞 + 動詞 + 受詞。
4. 剩下的詞組部分，more people（更多人）可為主詞，work on（致力於⋯⋯）為動詞片語，形成 "more people work on..."，on 為介詞，其後接動名詞片語 solving pollution problems（解決汙染問題）當作受詞使句子完整。
5. 由上可得答案：
   It is good to see that more people work on solving pollution problems.

其他重點

1. **work on...**　做⋯⋯

   例: I've been working on this project for some time.
   （我做這個專案已經有一段時間了。）
2. **solve** [sɑlv] *vt.* 解決；解（題）
   solve a problem　解決問題

   例: Thanks to Rick's help, Laura solved the problem.
   （多虧瑞克幫忙，蘿拉把問題解決了。）
3. **pollution** [pəˋluʃən] *n.* 汙染

Ⅲ. 中譯英

3. 一些專家說今年將比去年更熱更潮濕。
   Some experts say (that) this year will be hotter and more humid than last year.

解析

1. 『一些專家』可譯成 Some experts。
2. 『說』可譯成 say，後面通常會加 that + 名詞子句，that 也可以省略。
3. 『今年』可譯成 this year。
4. 『將』表未來，翻譯時使用未來的助動詞 will。
5. 『比去年』可譯成 than last year，但須要放在比較級形容詞的後面。
6. 『更熱』可譯為 hotter。
7. 『更潮濕』可譯為 more humid。
8. 『更熱』及『更潮濕』中間需有連接詞 and 作連接。
9. 由上得知，本句可譯為：
   Some experts say (that) this year will be hotter and more humid than last year.

112

四技二專統一入學測驗－詳解

112 年統測
試題講解

第一部分：選擇題

第二部分：非選擇題

選擇題解答

1	2	3	4	5	6	7	8	9	10
B	C	A	D	B	D	D	C	A	A
11	12	13	14	15	16	17	18	19	20
D	A	C	B	C	B	D	B	A	B
21	22	23	24	25	26	27	28	29	30
A	C	B	A	D	A	C	D	D	C
31	32	33	34	35	36	37	38	39	40
D	B	C	B	A	A	C	B	D	D
41	42								
A	D								

112 年四技二專統一入學測驗詳解

第一部分：選擇題（84 分）

I. 字彙題

B **1.**

It is a big ______ for people in this small town to learn that the only movie theater is going to shut down next month.

(A) cable (B) shock (C) tube (D) zone

得知唯一的電影院下個月就要停業，這個小鎮的人感到非常震驚。

解析

1. (A) **cable** [ˋkebḷ] *n.* 電纜；（電視節目等）有線系統

   例: We have to pay to watch cable TV.
   （我們得付費才能收看有線電視。）

   (B) **shock** [ʃɑk] *n.* & *vt.* 震驚

   come as a shock 令人震驚

   例: The news that Thomas would resign came as a shock.
   （湯瑪斯要辭職的消息令人震驚。）

   (C) **tube** [t(j)ub] *n.* 管子

   例：Water will come out of this tube and flow into the pond.
   （水會從這條管子流出，再流進小池裡。）

   (D) **zone** [zon] *n.* 地區

   例: Louise volunteered to go to the war zone to report on the war.
   （路易斯自願前往戰區報導戰事。）

2. 根據語意，(B) 項應為正選。

其他重點

shut down （永久或暫時）停業

例: It's a pity that this grocery store is going to shut down.
（很可惜這家超市要關門大吉了。）

C **2.**

The animal rights group is going to ______ a party to raise money for street cats.

(A) break (B) fight (C) hold (D) spell

動物權保護團體將舉辦一個為流浪貓募款的派對。

解析

1. (A) **break** [brek] *vt.* & *vi.*（使）破碎；弄壞，損壞（三態為：break, broke [brok], broken [ˋbrokən]）

例: Chad broke his mother's vase by accident.
（查德不小心打破他媽媽的花瓶。）

(B) **fight** [faɪt] *vt.* & *vi.* & *n.* 打架；爭吵；奮戰（三態為：fight, fought [fɔt], fought）

例: My parents fought over money last night.
（昨晚我爸媽為錢吵架。）

(C) **hold** [hold] *vt.* 舉行；握／抓住（三態為：hold, held [hɛld], held）

例: We'll be holding a meeting at noon today.
（今天中午我們要舉行會議。）

(D) **spell** [spɛl] *vt.* & *vi.* 拼字 & *n.* 咒語

例: How do you spell that word?
（那個字要怎麼拼？）

2. 根據語意，(C) 項應為正選。

其他重點

raise money 募款

例: Jimmy has been active in helping to raise money for charity.
（吉米一直都很積極主動幫忙慈善機構募款。）

A **3.**

I have ______ finished writing the novel, and I'm going to complete the last chapter tonight.

(A) almost (B) already (C) always (D) altogether

我快要寫完這本小說了，今晚會寫完最後一章。

解析

1. (A) **almost** [ˋɔlmost] *adv.* 差不多，幾乎

例: Liam can play almost any sport.
（連恩幾乎什麼運動都會。）

(B) **already** [ɔlˋrɛdɪ] *adv.* 已經

例: Molly has already eaten dinner.
（茉莉已經吃過晚餐了。）

(C) **always** [ˋɔlwez] *adv.* 總是

例: Katie always takes the MRT home.
（凱蒂總是搭捷運回家。）

(D) **altogether** [ˏɔltəˋgɛðɚ] *adv.* 總共；完全地

例: There are 18 people in the meeting altogether.
（這次會議共有十八人參加。）

2. 根據語意，(A) 項應為正選。

D **4.**

In some countries, looking at someone in the eye for too long is considered ______, so you should avoid doing it.

(A) basic　(B) classical　(C) legal　(D) rude

在某些國家，盯著別人的眼睛一直看會被認為是沒有禮貌，所以你該避免這麼做。

解析

1. (A) **basic** [ˋbesɪk] *a.* 基本的

   例: Basic computer skills are required for this job.
   （這份工作要求具備基本電腦技能。）

   (B) **classical** [ˋklæsɪkḷ] *a.*（音樂）古典的；傳統的

   例: Do you like to listen to classical music?
   （你喜歡聽古典樂嗎？）

   (C) **legal** [ˋligḷ] *a.* 與法律相關的；合法的

   例: Henry went to a lawyer for legal help.
   （亨利去找律師尋求法律上的協助。）

   (D) **rude** [rud] *a.* 無禮的，粗魯的

   例: I don't like Jim because of his rude manners.
   （我不喜歡吉姆，因為他很無禮。）

2. 根據語意，(D) 項應為正選。

其他重點

1. **consider** [kənˋsɪdɚ] *vt.* 把……視為……；考慮
   consider A (to be) + N / 形容詞　將……視為……

   例: In fact, many workers considered the plan (to be) impractical.
   （實際上，很多員工認為那個計畫很不切實際。）

2. **avoid** [əˋvɔɪd] *vt.* 避免；避開
   avoid + N/V-ing　避免……

   例: Avoid cutting in while people are talking.
   （人家在講話時，要避免插嘴。）

B **5.**

If you keep blowing air into the balloon, it will ______ with a loud bang.

(A) aim　(B) burst　(C) explore　(D) shine

如果你一直吹氣球，它就會爆炸並發出巨響。

解析

1. (A) **aim** [em] *vi.* & *vt.*（使）瞄準；打算 & *n.* 瞄準；目標

aim at...　　瞄準……

例: Although Ivan was aiming at the bird, he hit the tree.
（艾凡雖然瞄準的是那隻鳥，卻打到了樹。）

(B) **burst** [bɝst] *vi.* & *vt.*（使）爆破／炸（三態同形）& *n.* 爆破／炸

例: The little boy used a needle to burst the balloon.
（小男孩用一根針刺破氣球。）

(C) **explore** [ɪkˋsplɔr] *vi.* 勘探（石油等）& *vt.* 探索；尋找

例: It is said that Columbus arrived here but did not explore the area.
（據說哥倫布到過這裡，但沒有探索這個地區。）

(D) **shine** [ʃaɪn] *vi.* 發亮，照耀（三態為：shine, shone [ʃon], shone）& *vt.* 擦亮（三態為：shine, shined, shined）& *n.* 光亮

例: Carl just had his shoes shined.
（卡爾才找人擦過他的鞋。）

2. 根據語意，(B) 項應為正選。

其他重點

bang [bæŋ] *n.* 砰的一聲 & *vt.* 猛然撞擊
with a bang　　砰然一聲

例: The angry man shut the door with a bang.
（這名生氣的男子砰地一聲把門關上。）

D **6.**

The boss agreed to increase workers' _______, so they can make more money to improve their life.

(A) permits　　(B) risks　　(C) scales　　(D) wages

老闆同意增加員工的薪水，這樣他們就可以賺更多錢來改善生活。

解析

1. (A) **permit** [ˋpɝmɪt] *n.* 許可證 & [pɚˋmɪt] *vt.* & *vi.* 准許，允許（三態為：permit, permitted [pɚˋmɪtɪd], permitted）

例: You need a permit to fish here.
（你要有許可證才可以在這裡釣魚。）

(B) **risk** [rɪsk] *n.* 風險 & *vt.* 冒……的風險
run the risk of + V-ing　　冒著……的風險

例:Parents shouldn't run the risk of leaving their children alone at home.
（父母不應冒讓小孩獨自在家的風險。）

(C) **scale** [skel] *n.* 等級（可數）；規模（常用單數）

例: Pollution has caused changes to weather patterns on a large scale.
（汙染已經大幅造成天氣型態的改變。）

(D) **wage** [wedʒ] *n.* 工資 & *vt.* 發動（活動、戰爭等）

例: The workers went on strike in protest against low wages.
（工人發動罷工抗議低工資。）

2. 根據語意，(D) 項應為正選。

其他重點

1. **agree** [əˋgri] *vt.* & *vi.* 同意；贊成
agree to + V　同意做……
例: Tom finally agreed to go to the movies with us.
（湯姆最後總算同意和我們一起去看電影。）

2. **improve** [ɪmˋpruv] *vt.* & *vi.* 改善
例: Ken would like to improve his English speaking ability.
（肯想要增進自己的英語口說能力。）

D **7.**

Since my teeth are very ______ to sweets, I don't eat candies and cookies.

(A) attractive　(B) effective　(C) positive　(D) sensitive

因為我的牙齒對甜食非常敏感，所以我不吃糖果和餅乾。

解析

1. (A) **attractive** [əˋtræktɪv] *a.* 誘人的，有吸引力的
例: Unlike her sister, Liz was extremely attractive.
（和她姊姊不同的是，莉絲十分嫵媚動人。）

(B) **effective** [ɪˋfɛktɪv] *a.* 有效的
例: Do you think this medicine is effective?
（你認為這藥有效嗎？）

(C) **positive** [ˋpɑzətɪv] *a.* 積極正面的；陽性的
例: Try to be more positive. Everything is going to be OK.
（設法積極正面一點。一切都會沒事的。）

(D) **sensitive** [ˋsɛnsətɪv] *a.* 敏感的，易被冒犯的
例: Fred is sensitive to others' remarks.
（弗瑞德對別人的話很敏感。）

2. 根據語意，(D) 項應為正選。

其他重點

sweet [swit] *n.* 甜食（常用複數）& *a.* 甜的；甜美的；體貼的
例: If you continue to eat sweets, you will wind up getting really fat.
（假如你繼續吃甜食，總有一天會肥死你。）

C 8.

Amy's proposal to get funding from the school did not meet any ______, so she got all the money she needed for her project.

(A) appreciation (B) gratitude (C) resistance (D) sympathy

艾咪向學校申請資助的提案未遇到任何反對，所以她得到她專案所需的全部資金。

解析

1. (A) **appreciation** [ə,priʃɪ`eʃən] *n.* 感激；欣賞（不可數）

例: The company presented Jack with a gold watch in appreciation of his faithful service.
（公司頒贈傑克一只金錶，以感謝他忠誠的服務。）

(B) **gratitude** [`grætə,t(j)ud] *n.* 感激（不可數）

例: How can I express my gratitude for your help?
（對於您的幫助，我該如何表達我的謝意呢？）

(C) **resistance** [rɪ`zɪstəns] *n.* 反對；阻力（不可數）

例: The policy suffered strong resistance from the working class.
（該政策遭受勞動階級強力反彈。）

(D) **sympathy** [`sɪmpəθɪ] *n.* 同情；慰問（不可數）

例: The rich man has no sympathy for the poor.
（那位有錢人對窮人沒有一點同情心。）

2. 根據語意，(C) 項應為正選。

其他重點

1. **proposal** [prə`pozl̩] *n.* 提案；建議；求婚

例: The proposal to close the hospital was rejected.
（關閉這家醫院的提議遭到否決。）

2. **funding** [`fʌndɪŋ] *n.* 資金提供，資助（不可數）

A 9.

William's mother was seriously hurt in the car accident; she will have to stay in the hospital for a while.

(A) badly (B) cheaply (C) hardly (D) shortly

威廉的母親在車禍中受了重傷，她必須住院一陣子。

解析

1. 原句劃線的字有下列意思及用法：

seriously [`sɪrɪəslɪ] *adv.* 嚴重地；嚴肅地；認真地；非常

例: David's back was seriously injured in a car accident.
（大衛在一場車禍中背部嚴重受傷。）

2. (A) **badly** [ˋbædlɪ] *adv.* 嚴重地；壞／差地；非常
例: Johnny fell down the steps and sprained his ankle badly.
（強尼跌下臺階，腳踝嚴重扭傷。）

(B) **cheaply** [ˋtʃiplɪ] *adv.* 便宜地
例: Sam bought the house very cheaply.
（山姆用很便宜的價錢買下這間房子。）

(C) **hardly** [ˋhɑrdlɪ] *adv.* 幾乎不
例: Don't marry Paul just yet because you hardly know him.
（現在還不要嫁給保羅，因為妳幾乎不了解他。）

(D) **shortly** [ˋʃɔrtlɪ] *adv.* 不久，立刻
例: Mary successfully found a well-paid job shortly after she graduated from college.
（瑪麗大學畢業後不久，就順利地找到一份待遇不錯的工作。）

3. 根據上述，seriously 與 badly 同義，故 (A) 項應為正選。

其他重點

for a while 一段時間
例: Don't stay inside too long. Get out and exercise for a while.
（別在室內待太久。出去運動一下。）

A **10.**
I'm sorry that I don't have any <u>spare</u> money to lend you. I spent all my money buying a new cellphone for my mom.
(A) extra (B) hot (C) quick (D) soft
很抱歉我沒有<u>多餘的</u>錢借你。我花了所有的錢買新手機給我媽。

解析

1. 原句劃線的字有下列意思及用法：
spare [spɛr] *a.* 多餘的，備用的
例: I used up all my spare money, so I'm going to withdraw some money from the bank this afternoon.
（我身上已沒多餘的錢了，所以今天下午我要到銀行提款。）

2. (A) **extra** [ˋɛkstrə] *a.* 額外的，附加的
例: This extra money should lend you a helping hand.
（這筆額外的錢應該可以幫到你。）

(B) **hot** [hɑt] *a.* 熱的；辛辣的；熱門的

例: The weather's been quite hot recently.
（最近天氣很熱。）

(C) **quick** [kwɪk] *a.* 快速的；反應快的

例: The train is very quick and convenient.
（火車既快速又方便。）

(D) **soft** [sɔft] *a.* 柔軟的；（聲音）柔和的

例: This bread is soft and delicious.
（這個麵包鬆軟好吃。）

3. 根據上述，spare 與 extra 同義，故 (A) 項應為正選。

II. 對話題

D **11.**

Anita: There's a famous Chinese restaurant across the road. They serve the best Peking duck.

Sergio: Yes, I used to go there every week before I moved away from here.

Anita: I really want to try their Peking duck. ________

Sergio: Once in a long while.

(A) Is it far away from here?
(B) Does it really taste good?
(C) Have you ever been there?
(D) Do you still go there often?

安 妮 塔：對街有一家很有名的中式餐館。他們有最棒的北京烤鴨。

塞爾希奧：對，在我搬離這裡之前，每個禮拜都會去光顧。

安 妮 塔：我真想嚐嚐他們的北京烤鴨。________

塞爾希奧：久久一次。

(A) 餐館離這裡很遠嗎？
(B) 烤鴨真的很好吃嗎？
(C) 你曾經去過嗎？
(D) 你仍然常去那裡嗎？

解析

空格後，塞爾希奧說到 "Once in a long while."（久久一次。），得知安妮塔應問他有關頻率的問題，因此 (D) 項應為正選。

其他重點

1. **famous** [ˋfeməs] *a.* 出名的

be famous for...　　以……聞名

例: This restaurant is famous for its terrific steaks.
（這家餐廳以絕佳的牛排聞名。）

2. **across** [əˋkrɔs] *prep.* 在……對面；越過
3. **serve** [sɝv] *vt.* & *vi.* 供應（餐點）

例: A waitress will serve your food in just a few minutes.
（過幾分鐘就會有女服務生過來為您上菜了。）

4. **used to V** 過去經常……

例: I used to listen to music when I studied.
（我以前讀書時都會聽音樂。）

5. **while** [(h)waɪl] *n.* 一段時間

once in a while 偶爾

A **12.**

Betty: Hello. I'm calling about your ad for the five-room rental apartment. Is it still available?

Manager: Yes, it is. ________________

Betty: Yes. I'd like to. Can you tell me the address?

(A) Would you like to see it? (B) Where did you see the ad?

(C) When do you want to see it? (D) Will your friend come with you?

貝　蒂：哈囉。我要詢問你們廣告上的五房出租公寓。請問租出去了嗎？

經　理：還沒，還在租。________________

貝　蒂：是的，我想看一看。你可以告訴我地址嗎？

(A) 請問您想要看房嗎？ (B) 請問您在哪裡看到廣告的？

(C) 請問您什麼時候想要看房？ (D) 請問您的朋友會跟您一起來嗎？

解析

空格後，貝蒂說到 "Yes. I'd like to. Can you tell me the address?"（是的，我想看一看。你可以告訴我地址嗎？），得知管理員應問她有關意願的問題，因此 (A) 項應為正選。

其他重點

1. **advertisement** [ˌædvəˋtaɪzmənt] *n.* 廣告（可數，常縮寫成 ad [æd]）
2. **rental** [ˋrɛntḷ] *n.* 出租；可出租的物品 & *a.* 可出租的
3. **available** [əˋveləbḷ] *a.* 可得到的，可用的；（人）有空的
4. **address** [ˋædrɛs / əˋdrɛs] *n.* 地址

C **13.**

Alex: I'm interested in buying an electric car.

Sales: Good choice. They cause less pollution, and there are lots of places in the city where you can charge your car.

Alex: What if I want to leave the city? How far can I go before I need to charge the car?
Sales: ________________
(A) It has gone too far. (B) You have no choice.
(C) It has a range of 200 kilometers. (D) As far as I know, there's no charge.

艾力克斯：我有興趣買輛電動車。
業 務 員：明智的選擇。電動車造成的汙染比較少，而且你在市區裡有很多地方可以充電。
艾力克斯：萬一我要去外地呢？我可以開多遠才要充電？
業 務 員：________________
(A) 它已經跑很遠了／這事太過份了。 (B) 你別無選擇。
(C) 它的里程範圍是兩百公里。 (D) 就我所知，不用收費。

解析

空格前，艾力克斯問到 "How far can I go before I need to charge the car?"（我可以開多遠才要充電？），得知業務員應表示有關距離的回應，因此 (C) 項應為正選。

其他重點

1. **electric** [ɪˋlɛktrɪk] *a.* 電的
   an electric light / car / blanket 電燈／電動車／電熱毯
2. **cause** [kɔz] *vt.* 引起；導致
   例: Ron's carelessness caused the accident.
   （榮恩的粗心大意釀成了這起意外。）
3. **pollution** [pəˋluʃən] *n.* 汙染（不可數）
   air / noise / water pollution 空氣／噪音／水汙染
4. **charge** [tʃardʒ] *vt.* & *vi.* 充電；收費 & *n.* 收費
   例: Did you charge the battery for the digital camera?
   （數位相機的電池你充電了嗎？）
   The company charged me NT$500 for fixing the television.
   （那家公司幫我修電視收了新臺幣五百元。）
5. **kilometer** [kɪˋlɑmətɚ / ˋkɪlə͵mitɚ] *n.*（長度單位）公里

B **14.**

Jane: Guess what I saw during my trip to Paris last month?
Roy: I bet you saw the Eiffel Tower (艾菲爾鐵塔), right?
Jane: Of course I saw that. And I also saw the Mona Lisa.
Roy: You mean da Vinci's (達文西) Mona Lisa?
Jane: ________________ I saw it at the Louvre (羅浮宮).
(A) No way! (B) That's the one.
(C) You're lucky! (D) Don't mention it.

珍：你猜上個月我去巴黎旅行的時候看了什麼？
羅伊：妳肯定有看到艾菲爾鐵塔，對吧？
珍：當然有看到。而且我還看了蒙娜麗莎。
羅伊：妳是指達文西的蒙娜麗莎？
珍：＿＿＿＿＿＿＿ 我在羅浮宮看到的。

(A) 怎麼可能！　(B) 就是那個。
(C) 你真幸運！　(D) 不客氣。

解析

空格前，羅伊問到 "You mean da Vinci's (達文西) Mona Lisa?"（妳是指達文西的蒙娜麗莎？），空格後，珍說到 "I saw it at the Louvre (羅浮宮)."（我在羅浮宮看到的。），得知珍應針對問題表達肯定的回應，因此 (B) 項應為正選。

C **15.**

David: Do you like watching judo (柔道) competitions?
Annie: No, not at all. But, I'm a big fan of Drangadrang (楊勇緯).
David: Really? You know him? ＿＿＿＿＿＿＿
Annie: He's talented, strong and of course, very cute. He's even won an Olympic medal!
David: Wow! You really know him, huh?

(A) How did you meet him?　(B) What does he really like?
(C) What do you like about him?　(D) How did he know about judo?

大衛：妳喜歡看柔道比賽嗎？
安妮：一點都不喜歡。但我是楊勇緯的忠實粉絲。
大衛：真的假的？妳知道他？＿＿＿＿＿＿＿
安妮：他很有天分、壯壯的，而且很有吸引力。他甚至還拿過奧運獎牌呢！
大衛：哇！妳真的很了解他，對不？

(A) 妳怎麼認識他的？　(B) 他真正喜歡什麼？
(C) 妳喜歡他哪點？　(D) 他是怎麼知道柔道的？

解析

空格後，安妮說到 "He's talented, strong and of course, very cute. He's even won an Olympic medal!"（他很有天分、壯壯的，而且很有吸引力。他甚至還拿過奧運獎牌呢！），得知大衛應詢問安妮喜歡他什麼，因此 (C) 項應為正選。

其他重點

1. **competition** [ˌkɑmpəˋtɪʃən] *n.* 比賽（可數）；競爭（不可數）

2. **talented** [ˋtæləntɪd] *a.* 有天分的
3. **medal** [ˋmɛdḷ] *n.* 獎牌；獎章

B **16.**

Jimmy: I need to find a part-time job, Ms. King.
Ms. King: May I know the reason?
Jimmy: I need to support myself through school.
Ms. King: I see. ________
Jimmy: I can type pretty fast.

(A) How soon do you need the job? (B) What kind of skills do you have?
(C) What kind of support do you need? (D) What do you know about the school?

吉　米：金女士，我需要找份兼職的工作。
金女士：可以告訴我原因嗎？
吉　米：我得負擔自己所有的學費。
金女士：原來如此。________
吉　米：我打字速度非常快。

(A) 你有多急迫想要工作？ (B) 你有什麼技能？
(C) 你需要什麼樣的協助？ (D) 你對學校了解多少？

解析

空格後，吉米說到 "I can type pretty fast."（我打字非常快。），得知金女士應詢問吉米有關能力的問題，因此 (B) 項應為正選。

其他重點

1. **part-time** [ˌpartˋtaɪm] *a.* 兼職的 & *adv.* 兼職地
   a part-time job　兼職工作
2. **support** [səˋpɔrt] *vt.* & *n.* 養活；支持
   support sb by + N/V-ing　靠……來養活／撫養某人
   support sb/sth　支持某人／某事物
   例: Duke supports his family by working as a food delivery man.
   （杜克靠做食物外送員來養家。）
3. **skill** [skɪl] *n.* 技能，技巧

D **17.**

Secretary: Hello, Dean's office, may I help you?
Jack: Good morning, Sir. I'm looking for Dr. Huang.
Secretary: ________

Jack: OK. Could you let him know that Jack, his student, would like to make an appointment with him?

Secretary: Sure, let me check his schedule.

(A) I'm sorry there's no such person here.

(B) I'm sorry you dialed the wrong number.

(C) I'm afraid he doesn't work here anymore.

(D) I'm afraid he's not in the office right now.

祕書：您好，院長辦公室，請問有什麼事？

傑克：早安，先生。我想找黃博士。

祕書：________

傑克：好的。可以轉告說他的學生傑克想要跟他約時間嗎？

祕書：好，我看一下他的行程表。

(A) 很抱歉，這裡沒有這個人。　(B) 很抱歉，您打錯號碼了。

(C) 他已不在這裡工作了唷。　(D) 他目前不在辦公室。

解析

空格前，傑克說到 "I'm looking for Dr. Huang."（我想找黃博士。），空格後，傑克則說到 "OK. Could you let him know that Jack, his student, would like to make an appointment with him?"（好的。可以轉告說他的學生傑克想要跟他約時間嗎？），得知黃博士目前不在，因此 (D) 項應為正選。

其他重點

1. **look for...** 尋找……

   例: Steve looked for his phone for more than an hour.
   （史蒂夫找他的手機找了一個多小時。）

2. **appointment** [əˋpɔɪntmənt] *n.*（公務上的）約時間見面
   make an appointment with sb　與某人約時間

   例: I already made an appointment with my doctor for seven this evening.
   （我已經和醫師約好今晚七點看診。）

3. **schedule** [ˋskɛdʒʊl] *n.* 日程 / 計畫表

4. **dial** [ˋdaɪəl] *vt.* 撥 / 按（電話號碼）
   dial a number　撥電話號碼

B 18.

Ms. Lin: Ms. Ting, Stella's ballet show yesterday was terrific. She is great.

____

Ms. Ting: Since she was seven.

Ms. Lin: I can't believe it. She must be a genius.

(A) How often did she practice ballet?
(B) How long has she been learning ballet?
(C) How old do people start learning ballet?
(D) How much will you pay for a ballet show?

林小姐：丁小姐，史黛拉昨晚的芭蕾舞表演真精彩。她好厲害喔。＿＿＿＿＿
丁小姐：從她七歲的時候起。
林小姐：我真不敢相信。她一定是個天才。
(A) 她多常練習芭蕾舞？ (B) 她學芭蕾舞多久了？
(C) 一般人幾歲開始學芭蕾舞？ (D) 妳願意花多少錢看芭蕾舞表演？

解析

空格後，丁小姐說到 "Since she was seven."（從她七歲的時候起。），得知林小姐應詢問有關史黛拉學芭蕾舞的時間，因此 (B) 項應為正選。

其他重點

1. **ballet** [bæˋle / ˋbæle] *n.* 芭蕾舞
2. **genius** [ˋdʒinjəs] *n.* 天才；天賦，天分
3. **practice** [ˋpræktɪs] *vt.* & *vi.* & *n.* 練習
例: This trip is a great opportunity to practice your English.
（這趟旅行是個練習英文的好機會。）

A **19.**
Angel: Have you ever met new friends online?
Teddy: Yes, I have. We still keep in touch now.
Angel: How did you meet them?
Teddy: ＿＿＿＿＿＿＿＿
(A) I joined an online group. (B) We never talked on the Net.
(C) They met new friends on the street. (D) He continued to play online games.

安琪兒：你曾經在網路上結交過新朋友嗎？
泰　迪：有。我們現在都還有聯絡。
安琪兒：你是怎麼認識他們的？
泰　迪：＿＿＿＿＿＿＿＿
(A) 我加入了一個線上群組。 (B) 我們從不在線上聊天。
(C) 他們在街頭結交新朋友。 (D) 他持續在玩網路遊戲。

解析

空格前，安琪兒問到 "How did you meet them?"（你是怎麼認識他們的？），得知泰迪應回答有關結交新朋友的方式，因此 (A) 項應為正選。

其他重點

1. **keep in touch (with sb)**　（與某人）保持聯絡

例: Though John rarely sees Peter, they keep in touch by email.
（雖然約翰很少見到彼得，但他們仍藉電子郵件保持聯絡。）

2. **continue** [kənˋtɪnjʊ] *vt.* & *vi.* 繼續

continue + V-ing　繼續做……
= continue to V

例: Although it started to rain, Dennis continued jogging.
= Although it started to rain, Dennis continued to jog.
（雖然開始下雨了，丹尼斯還是繼續慢跑。）

B **20.**

Nancy: Let's go out and play badminton. Do you know where the badminton gears[註1] and equipment are?
Danny: Aren't they in the closet next to you?
Nancy: ______________
Danny: Why not go check the garage?

(A) Yes, here they are.　(B) I don't see them here.
(C) They sound closer to you.　(D) No, we threw them away.

南希：咱們出去打羽球吧。你知道羽球的球具用品在哪裡嗎？
丹尼：不就在妳旁邊的衣櫃裡？
南希：______________
丹尼：去車庫找找看好了。
(A) 對，它們在這兒。　(B) 它們沒有在這裡喔。
(C) 它們聽起來離你比較近。　(D) 沒有，我們把它們丟掉了。

解析

空格前，丹尼問到 "Aren't they in the closet next to you?"（不就在妳旁邊的衣櫃裡？），空格後，丹尼又提到 "Why not go check the garage?"（去車庫找找看好了。），得知南希沒有在衣櫃裡找到球具，因此 (B) 項應為正選。

註1：gear 若表示設備、用品時，應為不可數，故此處宜改為 gear。

其他重點

1. **badminton** [ˋbædmɪntən] *n.* 羽毛球
   play badminton　打羽毛球
2. **gear** [gɪr] *n.* 裝備（集合名詞，不可數）；齒輪（可數）
   例: Uncle George spent a lot of money on his fishing gear.
   （喬治叔叔花了很多錢在釣魚的裝備上。）
3. **equipment** [ɪˋkwɪpmənt] *n.* 裝備（集合名詞，不可數）
   a piece of equipment　一件裝備
4. **garage** [gəˋrɑʒ] *n.* 車庫
5. **throw sth away / throw away sth**　將某物扔掉
   例: You need to throw away those stinky sneakers.
   （你應該把那些臭哄哄的球鞋扔掉。）

III. 綜合測驗

◎ 21 - 25

Taiwan's east coast offers marvelous views of ocean wildlife. The chances of seeing a whale are very high in summer. It's rather easy to spot whales, __21__ whales swim past Taiwan's east coast every year between April and October. Today, whale watching __22__ a popular activity. The best time for whale watching is from June to August __23__ the sea is calm. Whale watching makes up a major part of the tourism industry in Yilan, Taitung and Hualien counties. Whale watching tours have been __24__ since 1997, and boat trips have been increasing. Tour operators are expected to follow regulations governing the activity. For example, to get a closer look at the whales, boats should __25__ the animals from behind. A list of responsible whale watching principles is included in an official guide to reduce the impact of tourism on the behavior of the world's biggest animals.

21. (A) for (B) nor (C) so (D) yet
22. (A) became (B) become (C) has become (D) will become
23. (A) why (B) when (C) how (D) which
24. (A) around (B) against (C) off (D) over
25. (A) accept (B) admit (C) affect (D) approach

臺灣東海岸坐擁海洋野生動物的奇觀。在夏季有相當大的機會看到鯨魚。很容易看到鯨魚是因為牠們每年四月至十月間會游經臺灣東海岸。如今賞鯨已成為很受歡迎的活動。賞鯨的最佳時機是海面風平浪靜的六月至八月。賞鯨是宜蘭、臺東和花蓮三縣觀光業的重要一環。賞鯨旅遊在 1997 年時出現，搭船的遊覽行程一直在增加當中。經營此種行程的旅遊業者被要求遵守相關規範。例如若要更近距離地觀察鯨魚，船隻必須從後方靠近牠們。官方指南中列出一份良心賞鯨的守則清單，以期減少觀光業對這種世界最大動物的行為的衝擊。

A **21.**

解析

1. 空格前後為兩個句構完整的子句，得知空格應置連接詞以連接兩子句。
2. 四個選項皆可作連接詞，惟 (B) nor（也不）、(C) so（所以）、(D) yet（然而）置入後不符語意，僅 (A) for（因為）置入後符合語意，可知 (A) 項應為正選。

C **22.**

解析

1. 空格本句前三句提到臺灣東海岸可以看到鯨魚的機會很大，因為每年四月至十月間鯨魚會游經臺灣東海岸，又空格本句後兩句提到賞鯨的最佳時機是六月至八月，而賞鯨已是宜蘭等三縣觀光業重要的一環，可知本句句意為：如今賞鯨「已成為」很受歡迎的活動。因此空格應置現在完成式 has become。
2. 根據上述，(C) 項應為正選。

B **23.**

解析

1. 空格前為表時間的名詞 June to August（六月至八月），且空格後為一完整子句，故得知空格應置關係副詞 when，使其引導的形容詞子句可用以修飾 June to August。
2. 根據上述，(B) 項應為正選。
3. (A) why 亦可作關係副詞，但其所引導的形容詞子句只用於修飾表原因的名詞；(C) how（如何）為疑問副詞，置入後不符語意；(D) which 為關係代名詞，若要代替描述時間長度的先行詞，須加上 during 成為 during which，但此處無 during，故上述三項皆不可選。

A **24.**

解析

1. 本題測試以下固定用法：

have been around 已經存在／有（一段時間了）

例: The debate about the abolition of the death penalty has been around for many years.

（關於死刑存廢的問題已爭辯多年。）

2. 根據上述，(A) 項應為正選。

D **25.**

解析

1. (A) **accept** [ək`sɛpt] *vt.* 接受

例: Cindy decided to accept that job offer.

（辛蒂決定接受那份工作邀約。）

(B) **admit** [əd`mɪt ] *vt.* & *vi.* 承認（三態為：admit, admitted [ əd`mɪtɪd], admitted）

例: Ken admitted that he told a lie to his mother.

（肯承認他對母親撒了謊。）

(C) **affect** [ə`fɛkt] *vt.* 影響

例: Using lots of plastic bags badly affects the environment.

（使用大量塑膠袋會嚴重影響環境。）

(D) **approach** [ə`protʃ] *vt.* & *vi.* & *n.* 接／靠近

例: When the unpopular boy approached Linda and her friend, the two girls immediately walked away.

（當那個不受歡迎的男孩走近琳達和她朋友時，這兩個女孩立刻就走開了。）

2. 根據語意，(D) 項應為正選。

重要單字片語

1. **marvelous** [`mɑrvələs] *a.* 極好的
2. **wildlife** [`waɪld,laɪf] *n.* 野生動／生物（不可數）
3. **A make up B** A 組成／構成 B

例: International students make up one-third of the class.

（國際學生占本班人數的三分之一。）

4. **tourism** [`turɪzəm] *n.* 觀光／旅遊業（不可數）
5. **county** [`kauntɪ ] *n.* 縣（複數為 counties [ `kauntɪz]）
6. **regulation** [,rɛgjə`leʃən] *n.* 規定，法規
7. **govern** [`gʌvən] *vt.* 控制
8. **reduce** [rɪ`d(j)us] *vt.* & *vi.* 減少

例: Having a healthy diet can reduce the risk of developing serious diseases.

（健康飲食可降低罹患重病的風險。）

9. **behavior** [bɪˋhevjɚ] *n.* 行為，舉止

10. **impact** [ˋɪmpækt] *n.* 影響，作用 & [ɪmˋpækt] *vi.* & *vt.*（對……）產生影響

◎ 26 - 30

People take different actions when seeing a stranger who needs help. In psychology, there are two theories about the way people act in that situation, __26__ the bystander effect and the Good Samaritan effect[註1]. A bystander is a person who sees a problem but just stands and watches, and a Good Samaritan refers to the one who helps a stranger in trouble. The bystander doesn't __27__ to help, whereas the Good Samaritan jumps in to lend a hand. A bystander does not help because he or she does not want to look foolish by making a mistake when trying to help out. __28__, a Good Samaritan helps because he or she wants others to see how helpful he or she is. In addition, a Good Samaritan pays close attention __29__ other Good Samaritans. His or her action is based on what others are doing. If he or she sees others helping, he or she is more likely to help __30__. So, when you see a stranger in need, will you be a bystander or a Good Samaritan?

26. (A) called (B) calling (C) and called (D) while calling

27. (A) cross out (B) hand in (C) step in (D) throw out

28. (A) As a result (B) To sum up (C) In the first place (D) On the other hand

29. (A) at (B) in (C) of (D) to

30. (A) neither (B) otherwise (C) as well (D) so far

當看到需要幫助的陌生人時，人們會採取不同的行動。在心理學中，關於人們在那種情況下會採取的作為有兩種理論，稱為旁觀者效應和善心撒瑪利亞人（見義勇為者）效應。旁觀者是看到問題卻只是站在一旁觀看的人，而善心撒瑪利亞人是指會幫助有困難的陌生人的人。旁觀者不會插手幫忙，然而善心撒瑪利亞人則會馬上伸出援手。旁觀者不提供幫助是因為他們不想在想幫忙時因幫倒忙而出醜。話說回來，善心撒瑪利亞人助人是因為他們想要其他人目睹他們的樂於助人。此外，善心撒瑪利亞人還會密切注意其他善心撒瑪利亞人的行為。他們的行為是看別人的行動而定。如果他們看到其他人在幫忙，他們更有可能也去幫忙。說到這裡，如果是你看到一個需要幫助的陌生人，你會當旁觀者還是善心撒瑪利亞人呢？

註1：本句其實為空格前省略了 which are 留下 called 的非限定形容詞子句用法，若要將 "which are called..." 置於句中作為插入句使用（前後必須用逗點隔開）時可省略 which are，句子改寫為 "In psychology, there are two theories, called the bystander effect and the Good Samaritan effect, about the way people act in that situation."。但 "which are called..." 擺在句尾時不宜省略 which are，因會被誤解成另一個（漏寫主詞的）獨立子句。若硬要省略，可移除子句前的逗點成為限定修飾用法的形容詞子句，成為 "...that situation called the..."。

A **26.**

解析

1. 本題測試形容詞片語化簡為分詞片語的用法，原句原為：
   In psychology, there are two theories about the way people act in that situation, which are called the bystander effect and the Good Samaritan effect.
2. 此時可將關係代名詞 which 省略，之後的動詞改為現在分詞，若該動詞為 be 動詞則改為 being，且 being 可予以省略。故原句可改寫為：In psychology, there are two theories about the way people act in that situation, called the bystander effect and the Good Samaritan effect.
3. 根據上述，(A) 項應為正選。

C **27.**

解析

1. (A) **cross out sth / cross sth out...** 刪去某物
   例: The teacher crossed out three words in my paper because they weren't appropriate.
   （老師刪去我作業裡的三個字，因為它們並不恰當。）

   (B) **hand in sth / hand sth in** 繳交某物
   例: Jason handed in his final report to the professor at the last minute.
   （傑森在最後一刻將期末報告交給了教授。）

   (C) **step in** 介入，干涉
   例: The father stepped in to prevent his children from fighting.
   （那位父親出面干涉以防止他的孩子們打架。）

   (D) **throw out sth / throw sth out** 扔掉某物
   例: Jennifer threw out her old clothes to make some room in her closet.
   （珍妮佛把她的舊衣服扔掉，讓衣櫥騰出點空間。）
2. 根據語意，(C) 項應為正選。

D **28.**

解析

1. (A) **As a result, S + V** 結果／因此，……

例: A hurricane struck the country. As a result, all schools were closed for the day.
（颶風侵襲本國，因此所有學校停課一天。）

(B) **To sum up, S + V** 總之，……

例: To sum up, Bruce is a man who can be trusted.
（總之，布魯斯是一位可以信任的人。）

(C) **In the first place, S + V** 首先，……

例: Nobody likes Kelly. In the first place, she is too selfish. In the second place, she is too stingy.
（沒人喜歡凱莉。首先，她太自私了。再者，她太小氣了。）

(D) **On the other hand, S + V** 另一方面／話說回來，……

例: Jeff is bad at singing. On the other hand, he plays the guitar very well.
（傑夫歌唱得很爛。話說回來，他吉他彈得很好。）

2. 根據語意，(D) 項應為正選。

D **29.**

解析

1. 本題測試下列固定用法：
pay attention to... 注意……
例: Nobody was paying attention to what the guest speaker was saying.
（沒有人注意聽演講來賓在說什麼。）
2. 根據上述用法，(D) 項應為正選。

C **30.**

解析

1. (A) **neither** [ˋniðɚ / ˋnaɪðɚ] *adv.* 既不（與 nor 並用）& *pron.*（兩者之中）無一個
neither...nor... 既不……也不……

例: Neither the director nor the manager is able to handle the problem immediately.
（主任及經理兩人都無法立即處理這個問題。）
Monica invited two friends to the party. Neither of them showed up.
（莫妮卡邀請了兩個朋友來派對。他們都沒現身。）

(B) **otherwise** [ˋʌðɚˏwaɪz] *adv.* 否則，要不然的話

例: Paul has to work over the weekend. Otherwise, he won't make his deadline.
（保羅這個週末得要加班。不然他會趕不上他的完成期限。）

(C) **as well** 也，還

例: Living in the countryside means you have more space and cleaner air as well.
（住在鄉下意味著你擁有更多的空間而且還有更乾淨的空氣。）

(D) **so far** 到目前為止

例: We haven't had any problems with the new company rule so far.
（到目前為止，我們對公司的新規定沒有任何反彈。）

2. 根據語意，(C) 項應為正選。

重要單字片語

1. **psychology** [saɪˋkɑlədʒɪ] *n.* 心理學
2. **theory** [ˋθiərɪ] *n.* 理論

   in theory 理論上

   例: This proposal sounds perfect in theory, but it won't work at all in practice.
   （這項提議在理論上聽起來很完美，但實際上會完全行不通。）
3. **bystander** [ˋbaɪˏstændɚ] *n.* 旁觀者
4. **effect** [ɪˋfɛkt] *n.* 效應，影響（與介詞 on 並用）

   例: The medicine may have a bad effect on your kidneys.
   （這種藥也許會對你的腎臟有不良影響。）
5. **refer to...** 指的是⋯⋯

   例: These figures in the table refer to the money we've made this year.
   （圖表裡的數據指的是我們今年的收益。）
6. **whereas** [(h)wɛrˋæz] *conj.* 但是，然而

   例: Dad likes to stay up late, whereas Mom likes to go to bed early.
   （爸爸喜歡當夜貓子，而媽媽則喜歡早早上床睡覺。）
7. **in addition** 此外

   例: Linda is a good wife. In addition, she is a successful career woman.
   （琳達是個好太太。此外，她還是個成功的職業婦女。）
8. **be based on / upon...** 以⋯⋯為基礎

   例: David's opinion was based on what his teacher had taught him.
   （大衛的意見立基於老師所教給他的東西。）
9. **likely** [ˋlaɪklɪ] *a.* 可能的

   be likely to... 很可能⋯⋯

   例: The baby is likely to fall off the chair if you don't hold him.
   （要不是你抱住他的話，這小寶寶很可能會從椅子上掉下來。）

IV. 閱讀測驗

◎ 31 - 32

The following graph shows how Mary, Sam, David and Linda spend their pocket money every month. Answer the questions based on the given information.

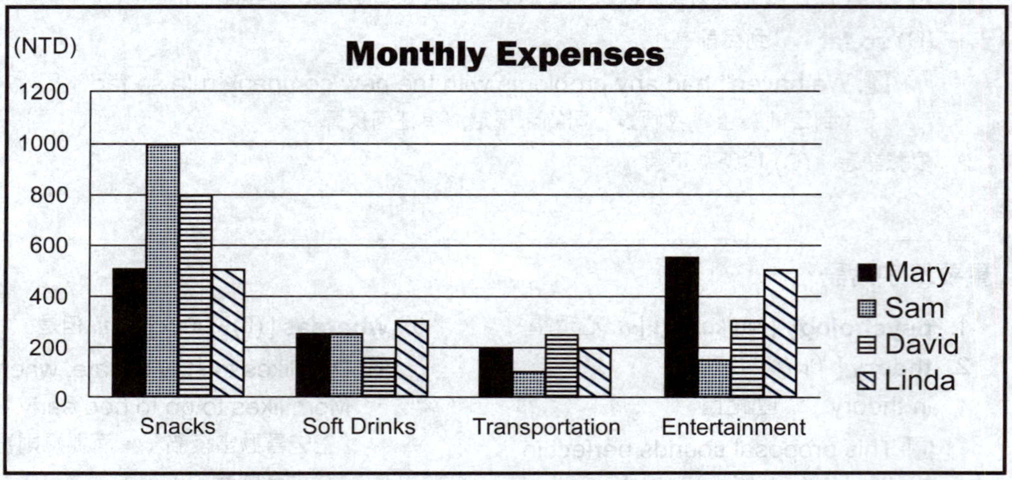

此圖表顯示瑪麗、山姆、大衛和琳達每月如何花零用錢。根據所提供的資訊回答以下問題。

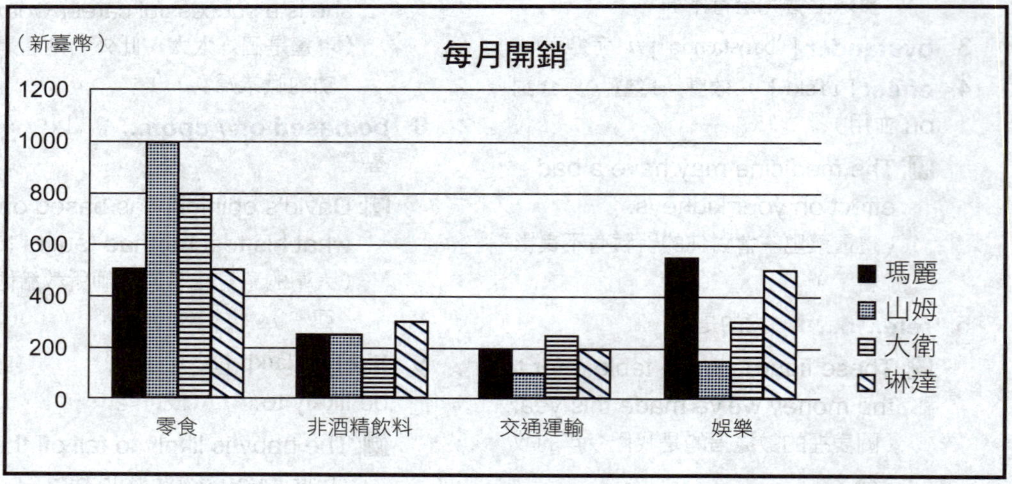

D **31.**

How much does David spend on soft drinks every month?
(A) About NT$800.
(B) More than NT$500.
(C) Exactly NT$400.
(D) Less than NT$200.

大衛每月花多少錢買非酒精飲料？
(A) 大約新臺幣 800 元。
(B) 超過新臺幣 500 元。
(C) 正好新臺幣 400 元。
(D) 低於新臺幣 200 元。

理由:
圖表中的橫軸顯示四大項目（零食、非酒精飲料、交通運輸、娛樂），縱軸顯示消費金額，在非酒精飲料項目中，大衛的消費金額直條圖高度顯示低於新臺幣 200 元，得知 (D) 項應為正選。

B **32.**

Which of the following is true?
(A) Mary spends the most money on transportation.
(B) Sam spends more money on snacks than Linda.
(C) Linda spends as much money as Mary on soft drinks.
(D) David spends less money on entertainment than Sam.

下列敘述何者為真？
(A) 瑪麗花費最多的項目是交通運輸。
(B) 山姆的零食消費高於琳達。
(C) 琳達和瑪麗在非酒精飲料部分的消費額相等。
(D) 大衛花在娛樂上面的錢低於山姆。

理由:
根據本圖表：(A) 瑪麗花費最多的項目是娛樂。(B) 山姆的零食消費直條圖高於琳達，得知 (B) 項應為正選。(C) 琳達和瑪麗的零食消費一樣多。(D) 大衛的娛樂部分開銷高於山姆。

重要單字片語

1. **graph** [græf] *n.*（直線或曲線表示的）圖表
2. **spend** [spɛnd] *vt.* 花費（金錢、時間）（三態為：spend, spent [spɛnt], spent）
   sb + spend + 金錢 / 時間 + on sth / V-ing　某人花費金錢 / 時間在……上 / 做……
   例: Emma spent one week on this novel.
   = Emma spent one week reading this novel.
   （艾瑪花了一個星期看這本小說。）
3. **pocket money**　零用錢
4. **base** [bes] *vt.* 以……為基礎
   be based on...　以……為依據
   例: The movie was based on a true story.
   （這部電影是根據真實故事所拍攝的。）

5. **monthly** [ˋmʌnθlɪ] *a.* 每月的 & *adv.* 每月地
6. **expense** [ɪkˋspɛns] *n.* 花錢；代價
7. **soft drink** 非酒精飲料
8. **transportation** [ˏtrænspɚˋteʃən] *n.* 交通運輸（工具）（不可數）
9. **entertainment** [ˏɛntɚˋtenmənt] *n.* 娛樂，樂趣（不可數）；娛樂節目（可數）
10. **exactly** [ɪgˋzæktlɪ] *adv.* 正好地
11. **as much + 不可數名詞 + as...** 與……一樣多的……
    as many + 可數名詞複數形 + as... 與……一樣多的……

◎ **33 - 35**

Read the label below and answer the questions that follow.

Drug Facts

Uses

Temporarily relieves these symptoms

- sneezing
- runny nose
- watery, itchy eyes

Warnings

Ask a doctor before use if you have

- glaucoma
- breathing problems

When using this product

- you may get drowsy
- avoid alcoholic drinks
- be careful when driving a motor vehicle or operating machinery

If pregnant or breastfeeding, ask a doctor before use.

Directions

Adults and children 12 years and over	Take 2 tablets every 4 to 6 hours; not more than 12 tablets in 24 hours
Children under 12 years	Ask a doctor

Other information

Store in a cool, dry place

閱讀以下標籤並回答以下問題。

藥物資訊

用途

暫時緩解以下症狀

■ 打噴嚏　■ 流鼻涕　■ 眼睛流淚、發癢

警示

若有以下病症，使用前請先諮詢醫師

■ 青光眼
■ 呼吸困難

使用本藥品時

■ 可能會昏昏欲睡　■ 避免飲酒
■ 開車或操作機械時要小心

若懷孕或正在哺乳，使用前請先諮詢醫師。

用法

成人及十二歲以上孩童	每四至六小時服用兩粒； 二十四小時內不能服用超過十二粒
十二歲以下孩童	請諮詢醫師

其他資訊

存放於陰涼乾燥處

C **33.**

Which part should you check to find out how to take the medicine?

(A) Uses
(B) Warnings
(C) Directions
(D) Other information

如何服用此藥物應要看哪個部分？

(A) 用途
(B) 警示
(C) 用法
(D) 其他資訊

理由:

根據小標題「Directions（用法）」的下文提到 "Adults and children 12 years and over"（成人及十二歲以上孩童），其用法為 "Take 2 tablets every 4 to 6 hours; not more than 12 tablets in 24 hours"（每四至六小時服用兩粒；二十四小時內不能服用超過十二粒），而 "Children under 12 years"（十二歲以下孩童），則要 "Ask a doctor"（請諮詢醫師），得知 (C) 項應為正選。

B **34.**

Which effect should you be aware of if you want to take the medicine?

(A) You may feel cool and have dry skin.

(B) You may feel sleepy and cannot think clearly.

(C) You may have watery eyes and a runny nose.

(D) You may have itchy eyes and cannot breathe well.

若你想服用此藥，應該注意哪些副作用？

(A) 你可能會感到涼快，皮膚可能會乾燥。

(B) 你可能會想睡覺且無法清晰思考。

(C) 你可能會流眼淚、流鼻涕。

(D) 你可能會眼睛發癢、呼吸困難。

理由:

根據小標題「When using this product（使用本藥品時）」的第一點 "you may get drowsy"（可能會昏昏欲睡），得知 (B) 項應為正選。

A **35.**

According to the label, which of the following is true?

(A) A 13-year-old child can take ten tablets in a day.

(B) Adults should take the medicine with alcoholic drinks.

(C) A patient can take two tablets every six hours to treat glaucoma.

(D) A 30-year-old pregnant woman should take the medicine without asking a doctor.

根據本標籤，下列敘述何者為真？

(A) 一個十三歲的小孩一天可服用十粒。

(B) 成人應搭著酒精飲料一起服藥。

(C) 患者可以每六小時服用兩粒來治療青光眼。

(D) 一位三十歲的孕婦無須諮詢醫師即可服用此藥。

理由:

根據小標題「Directions（用法）」的下文提到 "Adults and children 12 years and over"（成人及十二歲以上孩童），其用法為 "Take 2 tablets every 4 to 6 hours; not more than 12 tablets in 24 hours"（每四至六小時服用兩粒；二十四小時內不能服用超過十二粒），得知 (A) 項應為正選。

重要單字片語

1. **relieve** [rɪˋliv] *vt.* 緩解

   例: Take this medicine, and it can relieve your pain.

   （吃這藥，它可以緩解你的疼痛。）
2. **symptom** [ˋsɪmptəm] *n.* 症狀
3. **sneeze** [sniz] *vi.* 打噴嚏

   例: I keep sneezing. Maybe I've got the flu.

   （我一直在打噴嚏。也許我得了流感。）
4. **runny** [ˋrʌnɪ] *a.* 流鼻涕的
5. **watery** [ˋwɔt(ə)rɪ] *a.* 含水的
6. **itchy** [ˋɪtʃɪ] *a.* 發癢的
7. **glaucoma** [glauˋkomə / glɔˋkomə] *n.* 青光眼
8. **drowsy** [ˋdrauzɪ] *a.* 昏昏欲睡的
9. **alcoholic** [ˏælkəˋhɔlɪk] *a.* 酒精的
10. **machinery** [məˋʃɪnərɪ] *n.*（總稱）機器（不可數）
11. **pregnant** [ˋprɛgnənt] *a.* 懷孕的
12. **breastfeed** [ˋbrɛstˏfid] *vi.* & *vt.* 哺乳

◎ 36 - 37

The following notice is posted by a high school before the summer vacation. Answer the questions based on the given information.

How to protect yourself from job scams

A scam is a way of tricking people into giving money or personal details to criminals. In a job scam, criminals pose as employers to cheat you of your money[註1] or your personal information by offering you a job. Very often, they offer large sums of money for little skill, effort or experience. Here are the common job scams and tips to help you avoid them.

Common job scams

A type of job scams asks you to use your bank account to receive and pass on payments for others. They will pay you a fee for helping to transfer the money.

Some scammers might ask you to deposit money into their account. Or, they will ask you for your bank details before they've even offered you the job.

In another instance, the fake employer wants to set up an interview. But first, they ask you to provide your bank details, a scan of your identity card or other personal information.

If a company is asking you to buy the products before you sell them, beware!

Things to watch out for

Unclear job description: Very little information about the job is provided and no skills or experience is required.

Unbelievably high pay: The job requires very little effort for high returns.

Requesting personal information: If you provide your bank account details, the scammer may use them to commit crimes.

Remember: If a job offer seems too good to be true, it's probably a scam.

How can I protect myself?

Do background check[註2] on the company and the person who claims to be hiring you. If a job offer doesn't feel right, feel free to contact the school staff for help.

以下公告是由某所高中在暑假前發布的。請根據得到的資訊回答問題。

如何防止自己遭到求職詐騙

詐騙是誘騙人們把金錢或個人詳細資料提供給罪犯的一種方式。罪犯在進行求職詐騙時會冒充僱主，藉由提供你工作機會來騙取你的金錢或個資。他們常會在不要求技能、努力或經驗的前提下就提供高薪。以下是常見的求職詐騙手法以及幫助你避免被詐騙的幾個祕訣。

常見的求職詐騙

有一種求職詐騙會要你用你的銀行帳戶幫他人收款及轉帳。他們會支付你一筆幫忙轉帳的費用。

有些詐欺犯可能會要求你把錢存入他們的帳戶。或者他們會在還沒答應要給你工作之前就先詢問你的銀行詳細資料。

還有一種情況是，假僱主要安排面試。但首先他們會要求你提供銀行詳細資料、你的身份證掃描檔案或其他個人資料。

如果有公司要求你在銷售他們的產品之前得先自己購買，那麼當心了！

該小心的情況

不明確的工作內容敘述：提供的工作內容資訊很少，而且不要求任何工作技能或經驗。

不合理的高薪：這份工作不需要努力就能獲得高回報。

索取個人資料：如果你提供你的銀行帳戶詳細資料，詐欺犯可能會利用它們進行犯罪。

記住：如果有份工作機會看來好到不真實的地步，那它很可能是騙局。

我該如何保護自己？

對該公司和聲稱要僱用你的人進行背景調查。如果你覺得這個工作機會不對勁，隨時聯繫學校教職員尋求幫助。

註1：此處的片語 cheat sb out of sth（騙取某人某物）為固定用法，故宜改為 cheat you out of your money。
註2：check 當名詞表「檢查」時為可數名詞，故此處應改為 Do a background check。

A **36.**

Which is NOT mentioned as how job scams work?
(A) Applicants have to give their cellphones to the employer.
(B) Applicants are asked to send in money before they get hired.
(C) Applicants have to pay for products before they sell the items.
(D) Applicants may be paid to use their bank accounts for money transfers.

文中沒有提到下列哪一項求職詐騙方式？
(A) 求職者必須將手機交給僱主。
(B) 要求求職者先匯款才錄用。
(C) 求職者必須先買產品然後才能進行產品銷售。
(D) 求職者可能用自己的銀行帳戶進行資金轉移以獲得報酬。

理由:
根據本公告 Common job scams（常見的求職詐騙）中的第二段第二句 "Or, they will ask you for your bank details before they've even offered you the job."（或者他們會在還沒答應要給你工作之前就先詢問你的銀行詳細資料。）及第三段第二句 "But first, they ask you to provide your bank details, ..."（但首先他們會要求你提供銀行詳細資料……），得知詐欺犯是要求求職者提供個人資料而非手機，故 (A) 項應為正選。

C **37.**

Which of the following is true?
(A) Scammers are people who help to look for criminals.
(B) The notice gives a list of common job scam websites.
(C) Job applicants should find out more about the employers.
(D) The school staff helps employers feel good about job ads.

下列敘述何者為真？
(A) 詐欺犯是幫助找出罪犯的人。
(B) 本公告提供了一份常見的求職詐騙網站清單。
(C) 求職者應多了解僱主。
(D) 學校工作人員協助僱主對求才廣告滿意。

理由:
根據本公告 How can I protect myself?（我該如何保護自己？）的第一句 "Do background check on the company and the person who claims to be hiring you."（對該公司和聲稱要僱用你的人進行背景調查。），得知 (C) 項應為正選。

重要單字片語

1. **scam** [skæm] *n.* 詐欺
2. **trick sb into + V-ing**
騙某人去做……
例: Jenny tricked her brother into doing the laundry for her.
（珍妮騙她弟弟替她洗衣服。）
3. **criminal** [ˋkrɪmən̩l] *n.* 罪犯
4. **employer** [ɪmˋplɔɪɚ] *n.* 僱主，老闆
5. **pose as...** 冒充 / 喬裝成……
例: David was caught posing as a police officer.
（大衛被逮到冒充警察。）
6. **sum** [sʌm] *n.* 金額；總額
a large / small sum of money
巨額 / 小額金錢
例: Kevin had a large sum of money in a bank account in Switzerland.
（凱文在瑞士某家銀行存有大筆金錢。）
7. **transfer** [trænsˋfɝ] *vt.* & *vi.* & *n.*
轉帳；調離；移轉（三態為：transfer, transferred [trænsˋfɝd / ˋtrænsfɝd], transferred）
例: Can you transfer the fee into my account by Friday?
（你能否在週五前把費用匯到我的帳戶？）
8. **deposit** [dɪˋpazɪt] *vt.* 存入 & *n.* 存款
例: Sam always deposits half of his salary into his savings account.
（山姆總是把一半的薪水存進儲蓄帳戶裡。）
9. **fake** [fek] *a.* 假的，冒牌的
例: This clothes shop was forced to close down as it sold fake products.
（因為這家服飾店賣假貨，所以被迫關門。）
10. **scan** [skæn] *n.* 掃描（檔案）*vt.* 掃描；粗略地看（三態為：scan, scanned [skænd], scanned）
scan sth into the computer
將某物掃描至電腦中
例: Could you help me scan these documents into the computer?
（你能不能幫我把這些文件掃描進電腦裡？）
11. **beware** [bɪˋwɛr] *vi.* 留神，當心
（只用於命令句中）
beware of + N/V-ing 小心提防……
例: Beware of that mad dog! It might bite you.
（小心那隻瘋狗！牠可能會咬你。）
12. **unbelievably** [ˏʌnbəˋlivəblɪ] *adv.*
不可置信地
13. **request** [rɪˋkwɛst] *vt.* & *n.* 要求，請求
例: Bruce requested permission to take photographs in the museum.
（布魯斯請求准許在博物館內拍照。）
14. **commit** [kəˋmɪt] *vt.* 犯（罪）
（三態為：commit, committed [kəˋmɪtɪd], committed）
commit a crime 犯罪
例: If you commit a crime, you'd better be ready to go to jail.
（你要是犯法，就要有坐牢的準備。）
15. **background** [ˋbækˏgraund] *n.* 背景
16. **hire** [haɪr] *vt.* 僱用
例: Our department is going to hire a new secretary to replace Linda.
（我們部門將僱用一名新祕書來接琳達的缺。）
17. **staff** [stæf] *n.*（全體）職員（集合名詞，不可數）

◎ 38 - 42

Technology is continuously changing the sports industry for the better. Electronic devices known as sensors can detect changes and provide instant information about the health and movements of the athlete. Technology has changed the way some athletes train by **live tracking** the athlete's performances, perfecting the athlete's movements, and preventing sports injuries.

Using sensors worn by the athlete, sports trainers can measure and track performance in real time. Nearly everything about the athlete can be measured, from breathing and heart rate, to sweat and temperature. The real-time information can help the trainer determine what aspects each athlete needs to focus on more. During practice, the trainer can read the data and decide when it's time to rest, stretch or train harder. In the past, however, the practice session would be recorded, and the athlete's performance would be judged later after the practice.

Technological tools also provide a lot of information about the athlete's movements. These tools can measure the exact position, distance, and speed of the athlete. The sensors on a swimmer's body, for example, provide data on movements like dive angle and leg movement. Observing these movements allows the trainer to help athletes perfect their performance.

The most important effect of technology on sports training is that injuries have been sharply reduced. Training software can assist trainers to keep watch on all aspects of training, including diet, energy, and sleep. This helps prevent fatigue and self-created injuries during practice.

Technology allows athletes to not only get the most out of their training but also stay injury free. Sports technology will undoubtedly increase the athlete's potential.

科技正在不斷改變與精進運動產業。被稱作感應器的電子裝置能夠偵測變化，提供運動員健康狀況和動作的即時資訊。透過**即時追蹤**運動員表現、精進其動作以及防止運動傷害，科技已改變了某些運動員的訓練方式。

體育訓練員透過佩戴在運動員身上的感應器，可以即時測量和追蹤他們的表現。運動員的所有數據幾乎都可以測量，包括呼吸、心率、流汗及體溫等等。即時資訊可以幫助訓練員判定每個運動員需要加強的層面。在練習時訓練員可以透過數據判讀來決定何時該休息、伸展或加強訓練。然而在從前，練習過程需要錄影下來，運動員的表現只能在練習結束後進行評估。

科技工具還可以提供關於運動員動作的大量資訊。這些工具可以測量運動員確切的姿勢、距離和速度。例如游泳選手身上的感應器可以提供跳水角度和腿部動作等動作數據。觀察這些動作能幫助訓練員完善運動員的表現。

科技對運動訓練最重要的影響是大幅減少了運動傷害。訓練軟體可以協助訓練員監督訓練的各個面向，包括飲食、體力狀況和睡眠。這有助於預防練習過程中的過勞以及由運動員自身造成的傷病。

科技不僅讓運動員的訓練效果最大化，而且還能保持不受傷。運動科技無疑將可以提升運動員的潛能。

B **38.**

What is the passage mainly about?
(A) Tracking the performance of trainers.
(B) Training athletes with technological tools.
(C) Perfecting the body movements of trainers.
(D) Preventing the damage of technological tools.

本文的主旨是什麼？
(A) 追蹤訓練員的表現。
(B) 使用科技工具訓練運動員。
(C) 完善訓練員的身體動作。
(D) 預防科技工具損壞。

理由:
本文主要談論科技如何改變運動產業，並且為訓練員及運動員提供更多即時資訊和測量數據，幫助運動員改善表現、預防受傷。故 (B) 項應為正選。

D **39.**

Which is closest in meaning to the phrase "**live tracking**" in paragraph 1?
(A) Checking an activity after it is over
(B) Discussing an activity that may happen
(C) Following an activity before it happens
(D) Observing an activity when it is taking place

哪一項與第一段的片語 "**live tracking**" 意思最相近？
(A) 在活動結束之後檢查它
(B) 討論可能舉辦的活動
(C) 在活動舉辦前關注它
(D) 在活動發生當下觀察它

理由:
本句片語的 live [laɪv] 為副詞，意為「即時地」，track 為動詞「追蹤」的意思，合在一起為「即時追蹤」之意，故 (D) 項應為正選。

D **40.**

According to the passage, how has technology changed sports training?

(A) The athlete and the trainer can have a healthy diet.

(B) The athlete and the trainer can stop during practice.

(C) The trainer can understand the athlete's performance only after practice.

(D) The trainer can find out at once how the athlete performs during practice.

根據本文，科技如何改變運動訓練？

(A) 運動員及訓練員能享有健康的飲食。

(B) 運動員及訓練員能在練習期間喊停。

(C) 訓練員只能在練習結束後了解運動員的表現。

(D) 訓練員能立即得知運動員在練習期間的表現。

理由:

由第二段第一句 "Using sensors worn by the athlete, sports trainers can measure and track performance in real time."（體育訓練員透過佩戴在運動員身上的感應器，可以即時測量和追蹤他們的表現。）得知，(D) 項應為正選。

A **41.**

In the writer's opinion, what is the best benefit of using technology in sports training?

(A) Avoiding sports injuries.

(B) Watching a performance.

(C) Recording the sports practice.

(D) Making the movements perfect.

依作者之見，使用科技幫助運動訓練最大的好處是什麼？

(A) 避免運動傷害。

(B) 監看表現。

(C) 記錄運動訓練過程。

(D) 讓動作臻於完美。

理由:

由第四段第一句 "The most important effect of technology on sports training is that injuries have been sharply reduced."（科技對運動訓練最重要的影響是大幅減少了運動傷害。）得知，(A) 項應為正選。

D **42.**

Which of the following statements is true?
(A) An athlete can detect the movements of sensor devices.
(B) Technological tools measure only the athlete's heart rate.
(C) Trainers dive at a perfect angle when swimmers wear sensors.
(D) Technological tools can show detailed movements of an athlete.

下列敘述何者為真？
(A) 運動員能察覺感應器具的移動。
(B) 科技工具只測量運動員的心率。
(C) 游泳選手穿戴感應器時，訓練員就能以完美的角度跳入水中。
(D) 科技工具能記錄運動員的細部動作。

理由:
由第三段第二句 "These tools can measure the exact position, distance, and speed of the athlete."（這些工具可以測量運動員確切的姿勢、距離和速度。）得知，(D) 項應為正選。

重要單字片語

1. **continuously** [kən`tɪnjuəslɪ] *adv.* 連續不斷地
2. **for the better** 改善（常與 change 搭配）
   例: Kelly decided to change her eating habits for the better and eat more fruits and vegetables.
   （凱莉決定要改善她的飲食習慣並多吃蔬菜水果。）
3. **an electronic device** 電子裝置
   electronic [ɪ͵lɛk`trɑnɪk] *a.* 電子的
   device [dɪ`vaɪs] *n.* 裝置；設計
4. **sensor** [`sɛnsɚ] *n.* 感應器
5. **perfect** [pɚ`fɛkt ] *vt.* 使完美，改善 & [ `pɝfɪkt] *a.* 完美的；完全的
   例: Raymond perfected his Chinese by living in Taiwan for years.
   （雷蒙透過在臺灣居住多年來精進自己的中文。）
6. **in real time** 即時地
   例: The GPS app on my phone provides my location in real time as I walk.
   （我手機上的 GPS 應用程式會在我走路時即時提供我的定位。）
7. **aspect** [`æspɛkt] *n.* 方面
8. **session** [`sɛʃən] *n.*（從事某項活動的）一段時間；講習會；開會
9. **technological** [͵tɛknə`lɑdʒɪkl̩] *a.* 科技的
10. **fatigue** [fə`tig] *n.* 疲勞（不可數）
11. **free** [fri] *a.* 沒有（不想要或令人不快之物）的；不受限制的 & *adv.* 免費地；自由地 & *vt.* 釋放
    例: John felt like a free bird after graduating from high school.
    （約翰高中畢業後感覺像飛鳥一樣自由。）
12. **undoubtedly** [ʌn`daʊtɪdlɪ] *adv.* 無庸置疑地

第二部分：非選擇題（第 I 題，每格 2 分，共 4 分；第 II 題 6 分；第 III 題 6 分；共 16 分）

I. 填充

1. 在洗衣服的時候，你應該把白色和深色的衣服分開。

When doing the l___①___, you should s___②___ white and dark clothes.

① laundry　② separate

解析

1. 本題空格 ① 的對照譯詞為『衣服』，且空格為 l 開頭，故空格應置名詞 laundry。
   laundry [ˋlɔndrɪ] *n.* 待洗衣物（集合名詞，不可數）
   do the laundry　洗衣服
   例: I used to do the laundry once a week when I lived in a dormitory.
   （我以前住宿舍時一星期洗一次衣服。）
2. 本題空格 ② 的對照譯詞為『分開』，且空格為 s 開頭，故空格應置動詞 separate。
   separate [ˋsɛpəˏret] *vt.* & *vi.*（使事物）分開；（使人）分開 / 散
   例: The woman separated the two fighting dogs.
   （這名婦女把這兩隻正在打架的狗分開。）

其他重點

1. When doing the laundry, you should separate white and dark clothes.
   此題為簡化副詞子句的分詞構句，目的為避免前後主詞重複。使用時機為：當兩個子句主詞相同時，可將副詞子句的主詞刪除並將動詞改為分詞。以下為其原始句子：
   When you do the laundry, you should separate white and dark clothes.
2. **separate A from B**　把 A 與 B 分開來
   例: We separated the salad forks from the dinner forks.
   （我們將沙拉叉與餐叉分別開來。）

II. 句子重組

2. how to deal with / was formed to / the high inflation rate / The research team / find out

The research team was formed to find out how to deal with the high inflation rate.
（這個研究團隊組建的目的是要尋覓處理高通膨的對策。）

解析

1. 先找出開頭為大寫的詞組 The research team（這個研究團隊）作為句首。

2. 主詞 The research team 之後應接動詞或動詞詞組。重組部分中，was formed to（被組成以求……）及 find out（找出）為動詞詞組，因主詞的詞組為單數形式，故應選擇 was formed to（被組成以求……），形成 "The research team was formed to..."。
3. was formed to 的 to 為不定詞，其後須加動詞原形或原形動詞片語，用以表被組成的目的。find out（找出）為動詞片語，因此可接在 was formed to（被組成以求……）其後作為目的。由上得知，可形成 "The research team was formed to find out..."。
4. 剩下的詞組中，how to deal with（如何處理）為名詞片語詞組，之後應接 the high inflation rate（高通膨率）作受詞，形成 how to deal with the high inflation rate 並置於 find out 之後作其受詞使句子完整。故可得出答案：The research team was formed to find out how to deal with the high inflation rate.

其他重點

1. **research** [ˋrisɝtʃ / rɪˋsɝtʃ] *n.* 研究（不可數）& [rɪˋsɝtʃ] *vt.* 研究
2. **form** [fɔrm] *vt.* 形成 & *n.* 表格；形狀；形式

   例: We formed a circle and danced around the campfire.
   （我們圍成一個圓圈，繞著營火跳舞。）
3. **find out...** 找到……

   例: You have to find out the answer by yourself.
   （你必須自己找出答案。）
4. **deal with...** 處理……；與……交易

   例: This week I have a lot of work to deal with.
   （這個星期我有很多工作要處理。）
5. **inflation** [ɪnˋfleʃən] *n.* 通貨膨脹，物價上漲（不可數）

III. 中譯英

3. 很多社團鼓勵他們的成員回收塑膠袋。

Many clubs encourage their members to recycle plastic bags.

或：A lot of clubs encourage their members to recycle plastic bags.

或：Lots of clubs encourage their members to recycle plastic bags.

解析

1. 『很多社團』可譯成 Many clubs、A lot of clubs 或 Lots of clubs。
2. 『鼓勵』可譯成 encourage。通常有下列用法：

   encourage sb to V 鼓勵某人做……

   例: The teacher encouraged us to try again.
   （老師鼓勵我們再試一次。）
3. 『他們的成員』可譯為 their members。

4. 『回收』可譯為 recycle。
5. 『塑膠袋』可譯為 plastic bags。
6. 由上得知，本句可譯為：
   Many clubs encourage their members to recycle plastic bags.
   或：A lot of clubs encourage their members to recycle plastic bags.
   或：Lots of clubs encourage their members to recycle plastic bags.

111

四技二專統一入學測驗－詳解

111 年統測
試題講解

第一部分：選擇題

I. 字彙題 (111 年-2～10)

II. 對話題 (111 年-10～19)

III. 綜合測驗 (111 年-20～26)

IV. 閱讀測驗 (111 年-26～39)

第二部分：非選擇題

I. 填充 (111 年-40)

II. 句子重組 (111 年-41)

III. 中譯英 (111 年-41)

選擇題解答

1	2	3	4	5	6	7	8	9	10
A	A	D	D	B	C	A	C	B	D
11	12	13	14	15	16	17	18	19	20
B	C	A	A	B	A	D	B	A	D
21	22	23	24	25	26	27	28	29	30
B	D	C	A	B	D	B	C	C	D
31	32	33	34	35	36	37	38	39	40
A	D	C	D	C	C	A	A	A	C
41	42								
B	B								

111 年四技二專統一入學測驗詳解

第一部分：選擇題（84 分）

I. 字彙題

A **1.**

We had better leave early to ______ the heavy traffic to get home on time.

(A) avoid (B) drop (C) invite (D) mind

為了能避開壅塞的交通準時到家，我們最好早一點離開。

解析

1. (A) **avoid** [əˋvɔɪd] *vt.* 避免，防止

   avoid + N/V-ing 預防／避免……

   例: Keep in mind that you should always try to avoid making the same mistake again.

   （記住你一定要想辦法避免再犯同樣的錯誤。）

   (B) **drop** [drɑp] *vt.* & *vi.*（使）掉落 & *vi.* 下降（三態為：drop, dropped [drɑpt], dropped）

   例: Erin dropped her spoon into the bowl and splashed soup onto her skirt.

   （艾琳的湯匙掉進碗裡，湯濺到了她的裙子上。）

   (C) **invite** [ɪnˋvaɪt] *vt.* 邀請

   invite sb to + 活動／地點 邀請某人去某活動／地點

   例: My husband invited Will and his girlfriend to the ball.

   （我先生邀請威爾和他女友參加舞會。）

   (D) **mind** [maɪnd] *vt.* & *vi.* 介意 & *n.* 頭腦

   mind (sb) + V-ing 介意（某人）做……

   例: Would you mind turning off the radio for a while?

   （你介不介意把收音機關掉一會兒？）

2. 根據語意，(A) 項應為正選。

其他重點

had better V 最好……

例: Now that it is raining hard outside, you had better stay here.

（既然外頭雨下得那麼大，你最好留在這裡。）

A **2.**

Anny's grandson is always full of ______ and wants to go to the park every day.

(A) energy (B) hurry (C) identity (D) safety

安妮的孫子總是充滿活力，每天都想去公園。

解析

1. (A) **energy** [ˋɛnədʒɪ] *n.* 精力，能量；能源

例: Mandy devoted most of her energy to caring for her two children.
（曼蒂將大部分精力都用在照顧她的兩個孩子。）

(B) **hurry** [ˋhɝɪ] *n.* 匆忙

in a hurry　匆忙地，倉促地

例: Anna typed the report in a hurry and made a lot of spelling errors.
（安娜的報告打得匆忙，因此有不少拼字錯誤。）

(C) **identity** [aɪˋdɛntətɪ] *n.* 身分

例: Jason suffered an injury to the head and couldn't remember his identity.
（傑森頭部受傷，想不起來自己的身分。）

(D) **safety** [ˋseftɪ] *n.* 安全

例: Tour buses are required to play safety videos at the start of each ride.
（遊覽車依規定在每趟旅程開始時都要播放安全逃生影片。）

2. 根據語意，(A) 項應為正選。

其他重點

be full of...　充滿……
= be filled with...

例: Cathy's room is full of stuffed animals and dolls.
（凱西的房間裡全都是填充動物玩具和娃娃。）

D **3.**

I've put on so much weight recently that these jeans are too ______ for me to wear now.

(A) loose　(B) ripe　(C) swift　(D) tight

我最近變胖很多以致於現在這些牛仔褲對我來說都太緊而穿不下。

解析

1. (A) **loose** [lus] *a.* 鬆的，鬆動的

例: Jessica's bracelet fell off because it was loose.
（潔西卡的手鐲因為鬆掉而脫落。）

(B) **ripe** [raɪp] *a.*（水果、農作物）成熟的

例: I dislike eating bananas that are too ripe.
（我不喜歡吃過熟的香蕉。）

(C) **swift** [swɪft] *a.* 迅速的

例: The swift current carried the little boat down the river.
（這道急流將這艘小船沖向河流的下游。）

(D) **tight** [taɪt] *a.* 緊的；緊湊的

例: The tight T-shirt shows off Al's muscles.
（那件緊身T恤展現出艾爾的肌肉。）

2. 根據語意，(D) 項應為正選。

其他重點

1. **put on weight** 體重增加
= gain weight

例: If you eat junk food regularly, you are likely to put on weight.
（如果你常態性地吃垃圾食物，你就會變胖。）

2. **too + 形容詞 / 副詞 + (for sb) to + V** （對某人來說）太……而不能……

例: The story is too hard for a kid to understand.
（這個故事對一個小孩來說太難懂了。）

D **4.**

My boss totally accepted my suggestion and kept nodding to ______ his full agreement.

(A) deny (B) excuse (C) forget (D) indicate

我的老闆全然接受我的建議並不斷點頭表示完全同意。

解析

1. (A) **deny** [dɪˋnaɪ] *vt.* 否認；拒絕（三態為：deny, denied [dɪˋnaɪd], denied）
deny + V-ing 否認做……
= deny that...

例: Catherine denied stealing money from her parents.
= Catherine denied that she had stolen money from her parents.
（凱薩琳否認從爸媽那裡偷錢。）

(B) **excuse** [ɪkˋskjuz] *vt.* 原諒；使免除 & [ɪkˋskjus] *n.* 藉口

例: Please excuse me for not coming to the wedding last week.
（請原諒我上星期沒有去參加婚禮。）

(C) **forget** [fɚˋgɛt] *vt.* & *vi.* 忘記（三態為：forget, forgot [fɚˋgɑt], forgot / forgotten [fɚˋgɑtn̩]）
forget to V 忘了要做……
forget + V-ing 忘了曾做……

例: Isabella often forgets to punch out when she leaves the office.
（伊莎貝拉下班時常常忘記打卡。）
＊punch in / out 打卡上 / 下班

(D) **indicate** [ˋɪndəˏket] *vt.* 表明，表示（常與 that 並用）

例: The medical study indicated that a proper diet can prevent many diseases.
（那項醫學研究顯示，恰當的飲食能預防許多疾病。）

2. 根據語意，(D) 項應為正選。

其他重點

1. **totally** [ˋtotḷɪ] *adv.* 完全地
= completely

例: The movie's ending was totally unexpected.
（這部電影的結局完全出乎意料之外。）

2. **full** [fʊl] *a.* 完全的

B **5.**

To protect your head, when you ride a motorcycle, you must wear a ______.

(A) beard (B) helmet (C) necklace (D) tie

為了保護你的頭部，騎摩托車時一定要戴安全帽。

解析

1. (A) **beard** [bɪrd] *n.* 下巴及兩耳下方的鬍鬚

例: Vincent looks younger after he shaved his beard.
（文森把他的鬍子刮掉後，看起來比較年輕。）

(B) **helmet** [ˋhɛlmɪt] *n.* 安全帽

例: Will my helmet fit in your locker?
（我的安全帽放得進你的置物櫃嗎？）

(C) **necklace** [ˋnɛklɪs] *n.* 項鍊

例: The necklace was exactly what Shelly wanted.
（這條項鍊正是雪莉想要的。）

(D) **tie** [taɪ] *n.* 領帶（= necktie）；關係（此意常用複數）

例: Is this tie suitable for tonight's party?
（這條領帶適合今晚的派對嗎？）
There are close economic ties between Taiwan and Japan.
（臺灣和日本的經濟關係很緊密。）

2. 根據語意，(B) 項應為正選。

其他重點

(in order) to + V 為了……（可放句首，需用逗點與後面的子句隔開）
= so as to + V（不可放句首）

例: To earn more money, Grace got two part-time jobs.
= Grace got two part-time jobs so as to earn more money.
（葛蕾絲做兩份兼差好多賺一些錢。）

C **6.**

David's ______ hair color is brown, but he recently dyed it purple.

(A) ancient (B) historical (C) natural (D) opposite

大衛的天然髮色是棕色的，但他最近把它染成紫色。

解析

1. (A) **ancient** [ˋenʃənt] *a.* 古老的；古代的

   例: Ancient people used rocks to make tools.
   （古代人用石頭做成工具。）

   (B) **historical** [hɪsˋtɔrɪkḷ] *a.* 歷史的，有關歷史的

   例: As time goes by, people forget some historical events.
   （隨著時光消逝，人們忘卻了一些歷史事件。）

   比較:
   historic [hɪsˋtɔrɪk] *a.* 有重大歷史意義的
   The historic invention of the computer has changed our lives.
   （電腦這個歷史性的發明改變了我們的生活。）

   (C) **natural** [ˋnætʃərəl] *a.* 天然的；自然的

   例: The natural disaster caused great damage to the country.
   （這場天災對該國造成極大的損失。）

   (D) **opposite** [ˋɑpəzɪt] *a.* 相反的；相對的

   例: I thought this medicine would help me sleep, but it had the opposite effect.
   （我以為這種藥會幫助我入睡，但效果卻完全相反。）

2. 根據語意，(C) 項應為正選。

其他重點

dye [daɪ] *vt.*（用染料）染

例: Eve wanted a new look, so she dyed her hair red.
（依芙想換個新造型，所以她把頭髮染紅了。）

A **7.**

We got train seats for the Lunar New Year season as we planned ______ and made our reservation once tickets went on sale.

(A) ahead (B) almost (C) either (D) even

我們買到了農曆新年期間的火車票，因為我們提前準備，在車票一開賣時就去訂票。

解析

1. (A) **ahead** [əˋhɛd] *adv.*（較預定時間）提前，事先（= ahead of time）

   例: The police couldn't trace the serial killer because he seemed to be always one step ahead of them.
   （警方無法追蹤到那個連續殺人犯，因為他似乎總是先警察一步。）
   ＊serial [ˋsɪrɪəl] *a.* 連續的

   (B) **almost** [ˋɔl͵most] *adv.* 幾乎，差不多

   例: Though Joey is very busy, he exercises almost every day.
   （雖然喬伊很忙，但他還是幾乎每天運動。）

   (C) **either** [ˋiðɚ / ˋaɪðɚ] *adv.* 也（不）（與 not 並用）

   例: If you aren't going to the party, then I'm not, either.
   （如果你不去那個派對，那我也不要去。）

   (D) **even** [ˋivən] *adv.* 甚至

   例: We're not friends. I don't even know his name.
   （我們不是朋友。我甚至不知道他叫什麼名字。）

2. 根據語意，(A) 項應為正選。

其他重點

1. **Lunar New Year** 農曆新年
2. **reservation** [͵rɛzɚˋveʃən] *n.* 預訂
   make a reservation 預訂／約

   例: I would like to make a reservation for two at 7 p.m. tonight.
   （我想預訂今晚七點兩個人用餐。）

C **8.**

To ease his pressure, Mr. Hung decided to listen to bedtime music for ______.

(A) presentation (B) publication (C) relaxation (D) reputation

為了減緩壓力，洪先生決定聽睡前音樂來放鬆。

解析

1. (A) **presentation** [͵prɛzənˋteʃən] *n.* 簡報，報告
   make a presentation 做介紹／口頭報告

例: Jerry will make a short presentation on the product later.
（稍後傑瑞會對產品做簡短的介紹。）

(B) **publication** [ˌpʌblɪˋkeʃən] *n.* 出版（不可數）；出版物（可數）

例: Tom edited the manuscripts for publication.
（湯姆編輯這些手稿準備出版。）

＊manuscript [ˋmænjəˌskrɪpt] *n.* 手稿

(C) **relaxation** [ˌrilækˋseʃən] *n.* 放鬆

例: Bali is an ideal destination for relaxation and fun in the sun.
（峇里島是個在陽光下放鬆和遊玩的理想地點。）

(D) **reputation** [ˌrɛpjəˋteʃən] *n.* 名聲，名望

例: Wulai has a reputation for great hot springs.
（烏來的溫泉頗負盛名。）

2. 根據語意，(C) 項應為正選。

其他重點

ease [iz] *vt.* 減輕，緩和

例: This medicine can ease your headache.
（這個藥能減輕你的頭痛。）

B **9.**

The police pursued the bank robber through the streets last night.

(A) begged (B) chased (C) praised (D) treated

昨晚警方在大街上追捕銀行搶匪。

解析

1. 原句劃線的字有下列意思及用法：

pursue [pɚˋsu] *vt.* 追趕，追捕

例: The hunters spent much time pursuing the bear.
（獵人們花了許多時間追捕這隻熊。）

2. (A) **beg** [bɛg] *vt.* & *vi.* 懇求；行乞（三態為：beg, begged [bɛgd], begged）

例: Sam got down on his knees and begged for forgiveness.
（山姆跪下來請求原諒。）
A homeless man is begging for food in front of the church.
（一個流浪漢在教堂前乞討食物。）

(B) **chase** [tʃes] *vt.* & *vi.* 追趕，追捕

例: The cat chased the mouse around the house.
（貓追著老鼠滿屋子跑。）

(C) **praise** [prez] *vt.* 稱讚，讚揚

例: Jeremy should be praised for his honesty.
（傑瑞米的誠實應該受到讚揚。）

(D) **treat** [trit] *vt.* 對待；治療

例: James was furious at the way his boss treated him.
（詹姆士對他老闆待他的方式感到很生氣。）
Depression can be treated with medicine or counseling.
（憂鬱症可以用藥物或心理諮商來治療。）

3. 根據上述，pursue 與 chase 同義，故 (B) 項應為正選。

其他重點

robber [ˋrɑbɚ] *n.* 搶匪，強盜

D **10.**

I have looked through the records extensively, but couldn't find anything about the person you mentioned.

(A) eventually (B) marginally (C) occasionally (D) thoroughly

我已全面地瀏覽這些紀錄，但無法找到你提到的那號人物。

解析

1. 原句劃線的字有下列意思及用法：
extensively [ɪkˋstɛnsɪvlɪ] *adv.* 廣泛地
例: Jane plans to travel extensively when she finishes college.
（珍計劃在完成大學學業後四處旅遊。）

2. (A) **eventually** [ɪˋvɛntʃuəlɪ] *adv.* 最後
例: After being delayed for nine hours, the plane eventually took off.
（班機延誤了九小時後，終於起飛了。）

(B) **marginally** [ˋmɑrdʒənl̩ɪ] *adv.* 稍微地
例: The manager was worried because the sales record only increased marginally last month.
（上個月的銷售紀錄只有些許成長，因此經理很擔心。）

(C) **occasionally** [əˋkeʒənl̩ɪ] *adv.* 偶爾
例: Tim occasionally goes jogging with his friends.
（提姆偶爾會和他的朋友一起去慢跑。）

(D) **thoroughly** [ˋθɝolɪ] *adv.* 全面地，徹底地；仔細地
例: I helped Emily clean her room thoroughly.
（我幫艾蜜莉徹底地打掃了她的房間。）

3. 根據上述，extensively 與 thoroughly 同義，故 (D) 項應為正選。

其他重點

look through sth 瀏覽某物

例: Joe looked through his notes before the exam.

（喬在考試前瀏覽他的筆記。）

II. 對話題

B **11.**

Father: OK! We are ready to start baking a cake. We need to find some things first.

Son: So, what should I get?

Father: Well, ________________

Son: Oh! Sorry, I drank the whole bottle yesterday!

(A) the cake is baking now.
(B) I need two cups of milk.
(C) go get some flour for me.
(D) we need 50 grams of butter.

父親：好！我們準備開始烤蛋糕吧。我們得先找到原料。

兒子：好，要我去拿什麼？

父親：嗯，________________

兒子：喔！對不起，我昨天把整瓶喝光光了！

(A) 蛋糕現在正在烤。
(B) 我需要兩杯牛奶。
(C) 幫我拿些麵粉過來。
(D) 我們需要五十公克奶油。

解析

空格前，兒子問父親 "So, what should I get?"（好，要我去拿什麼？），空格後，兒子回答 "Oh! Sorry, I drank the whole bottle yesterday!"（喔！對不起，我昨天把整瓶喝光光了！），得知父親要兒子去拿某種飲料，因此 (B) 項應為正選。

其他重點

1. **bake** [bek] *vt.* & *vi.*（用烤箱）烤，烘

   例: It took Holly two hours to bake those cookies.

   （荷莉花了兩個小時烤那些餅乾。）

2. **flour** [flaʊr] *n.* 麵粉（不可數）& *vt.* 把麵粉撒在……

   例: To make a cake, you need flour and eggs.

   （做蛋糕需要麵粉和雞蛋。）

   Flour the bottom of the bowl before you put the meat in.

   （先將麵粉撒在碗底，再把肉放進去。）

3. **gram** [græm] *n.* 公克（重量單位，縮寫為 g）

C **12.**

Judy: OK, here's your tea. But no snacks, as you wanted.

Tina: Oh, thanks.

Judy: ________________ I have some homemade cookies left. My mom made them.

Tina: Oh, no thanks. I'm fine. I'm really full.

(A) Are you sure I cannot eat any cookies?

(B) Do you know you shouldn't eat too much?

(C) Are you sure you don't want anything to eat?

(D) Do you know you should buy something for me?

茱　蒂：好，妳的茶來了。沒有點心喔，照妳說的。

提　娜：哦，謝謝。

茱　蒂：________________ 我還有剩一些自製餅乾。是我媽做的。

提　娜：喔，不用了，謝謝。我吃太飽了。

(A) 妳確定我不能吃任何餅乾嗎？　(B) 妳知道妳不該吃太多嗎？

(C) 妳確定妳不想吃點兒什麼嗎？　(D) 妳知道妳該幫我買點東西嗎？

解析

空格前，茱蒂說到 "But no snacks, as you wanted."（沒有點心喔，照妳說的。），空格後，茱蒂又提及她有一些她媽媽做的自製餅乾，提娜回答 "Oh, no thanks. I'm fine. I'm really full."（喔，不用了，謝謝。我吃太飽了。），得知茱蒂在問提娜是否真的不想再吃任何東西了，因此 (C) 項應為正選。

其他重點

1. **snack** [snæk] *n.* 點心，零食 & *vi.* 吃點心

例: After class, we ate some snacks.
（下課後我們吃了一些點心。）
Jenny cannot snack between meals because she's on a diet.
（珍妮不能在兩餐之間吃點心，因為她在節食。）

2. **homemade** [ˋhom,med] *a.* 自製的，家常的

例: I'd like to buy some homemade soap from that store.
（我想在那家店買幾塊手工肥皂。）

3. **full** [fʊl] *a.* 飽的；完整的

例: I'm too full to eat anything else.
（我很飽，再也吃不下其他東西了。）
The man was asked to write down his full name.
（那名男子被要求寫下他的全名。）

A **13.**

Ann: What do you want to see at the computer exhibition?

Ken: I want to find the booth that has the virtual reality setup.

Ann: Virtual reality? ______________

Ken: You have to put on a headset, and when the game is turned on, you feel like you are actually in the game.

(A) How does it work? (B) What did you see?

(C) When was it set up? (D) Where have you been?

安：你想在電腦展裡看些什麼？

肯：我想找有虛擬實境裝置的攤位。

安：虛擬實境？______________

肯：妳必須戴上一副顯示裝置，遊戲啟動後，妳會覺得自己彷彿置身於遊戲中。

(A) 要怎麼玩？ (B) 你看到什麼？

(C) 它是何時設定的？ (D) 你去哪裡了？

解析

空格前，安問到 "Virtual reality?"（虛擬實境？），空格後，肯說到 "You have to put on a headset, and when the game is turned on, you feel like you are actually in the game."（妳必須戴上一副顯示裝置，遊戲啟動後，妳會覺得自己彷彿置身於遊戲中。），得知安在問虛擬實境是怎麼一回事，因此 (A) 項應為正選。

其他重點

1. **exhibition** [ˌɛksəˋbɪʃən] *n.* 展覽（會）
2. **booth** [buθ] *n.* 攤位；亭子
3. **virtual reality** [ˋvɝtʃuəl riˋælətɪ] 虛擬實境
4. **setup** [ˋsɛtˌʌp] *n.* 裝置；陷阱
5. **headset** [ˋhɛdˌsɛt] *n.* 頭戴顯示裝置；（有麥克風的）頭戴式耳機
6. **actually** [ˋæktʃuəlɪ] *adv.* 事實上，實際上（= in fact）

   例: Nick likes to act like a teenager, but actually he's more than 30 years old.
   （尼克喜歡裝作青少年的樣子，但他事實上已經三十多歲了。）

A **14.**

Ted: Do you want to jog around the track one more time?

Sue: Sure, I think I can make it.

Ted: If you're tired, you can wait here for me. I know you haven't been jogging for a while.

Sue: ______________ Come on, let's go.

(A) Don't worry about me.
(B) Please cover your tracks.
(C) No, I'll be waiting here.
(D) Yes, you're tired of jogging.

泰　德：妳想再繞著跑道慢跑一趟嗎？
蘇：當然，我想我可以辦到。
泰　德：如果妳累了，可以在這裡等我。我知道妳有一陣子沒慢跑了。
蘇：＿＿＿＿＿＿＿ 來吧，一起跑。
(A) 別擔心我。
(B) 請掩藏你的行蹤。
(C) 不，我會在這裡等著。
(D) 對，你厭倦慢跑了。

解析

空格前，泰德說到 "I know you haven't been jogging for a while."（我知道妳有一陣子沒慢跑了。），空格後，蘇說到 "Come on, let's go."（來吧，一起跑。），得知蘇確認自己可以繼續慢跑而要泰德別擔心，因此 (A) 項應為正選。

其他重點

1. **jog** [dʒɑg] *vi.* 慢跑（三態為：jog, jogged [dʒɑgd], jogged）
   例: Edward has been jogging every morning for the past 10 years.
   （愛德華過去十年來每天早上慢跑。）
2. **make it** 成功；及時趕上
   例: Linda made it as an actress at the age of 18.
   （琳達十八歲時就成功成為一名女演員。）
   If we run, we should make it on time.
   （如果我們用跑的，應該可以準時趕上。）
3. **cover one's tracks** 掩蓋行蹤，湮滅證據
   例: The accountant destroyed documents to cover her tracks.
   （會計師把文件銷毀以湮滅證據。）

B **15.**

Tour agent: Welcome to Fun Travel, ma'am. My name is Willy. How may I help you?
Alice: I'm here to get more information about your travel special.
Tour agent: Good. ＿＿＿＿＿＿＿
Alice: I'd like to go in June, I think.

(A) What do you want to see?
(B) When do you plan to travel?
(C) How is the weather in June?
(D) Where would you like to go?

旅行社人員：小姐，歡迎光臨歡樂旅遊。我是威利。需要幫忙嗎？
愛　麗　絲：我來是想多了解一下你們旅遊特別方案的資訊。
旅行社人員：好的。＿＿＿＿＿＿＿＿
愛　麗　絲：我想我應該會在六月去。
(A) 您想參觀什麼？　(B) 您打算何時去旅遊？
(C) 六月的天氣如何？　(D) 您想去哪裡？

解析

空格前，愛麗絲說到 "I'm here to get more information about your travel special."（我來是想多了解一下你們旅遊特別方案的資訊。），空格後，愛麗絲回答 "I'd like to go in June, I think."（我想我應該會在六月去。），得知旅行社人員應是在詢問愛麗絲何時要去旅遊，因此 (B) 項應為正選。

其他重點

1. **a tour agent** [ˋtʊr ˋedʒənt]　旅行社人員（travel agent 較為常用）
2. **ma'am** [mæm] *n.* 女士（是 madam [ˋmædəm] 的口語說法）
3. **information** [ˏɪnfɚˋmeʃən] *n.* 消息，資料（不可數，有時縮寫成 info [ˋɪnfo]）

A **16.**
Ann: Do you want to see a movie? There's a terrific animated movie at the theater.
Dan: Animation? You mean like a cartoon? ＿＿＿＿＿＿＿＿
Ann: Not at all. Many adults also enjoy animation, just like children do.
Dan: Really? I guess I should go and see if I like it.
Ann: Great. The movie starts at 7 p.m. Do you want me to pick you up?
(A) Isn't that just for children?　(B) Isn't it nice to see it again?
(C) Do the children go with us? 註1　(D) Do you get the tickets now? 註2

安：想不想看電影？電影院正在演一部很棒的動畫片。
丹：動畫片？妳是說卡通嗎？＿＿＿＿＿＿＿＿
安：才不是呢。許多大人也跟小孩一樣喜歡看動畫片。
丹：真假？也許我該去看看我會不會喜歡。
安：太好了。電影晚上七點開演。要我去接你嗎？
(A) 那不是小孩子在看的嗎？　(B) 再看一次不是很不錯嗎？
(C) 要帶孩子們去嗎？　(D) 妳現在要買票了嗎？

解析

本則對話中，一開始安問丹是否想去電影院看動畫片，空格前丹問到 "Animation? You mean like a cartoon?"（動畫片？妳是說卡通嗎？），空格後，安說到 "Not at all. Many adults also enjoy animation, just like children do."（才不是呢。許多大人也跟小孩一樣喜歡看動畫片。），得知丹應是在質疑動畫片只是給小孩子看的，因此 (A) 項應為正選。

註1：此句時態錯誤，宜改成 Will the children go with us?

註2：此句時態錯誤，宜改成 Will you get the tickets now?

其他重點

1. **terrific** [tə`rɪfɪk] *a.* 很棒的

   例: The restaurant on the corner serves terrific food.

   （轉角那家餐廳的東西非常好吃。）

2. **animated** [`ænə͵metɪd] *a.* 動畫的

   animation [͵ænə`meʃən] *n.* 動畫片

   例: Disney is going to launch a series of animated movies.

   = Disney is going to launch a series of animations.

   （迪士尼準備要推出一系列動畫電影。）

3. **cartoon** [kɑr`tun] *n.* 卡通

4. **adult** [`ædʌlt / ə`dʌlt] *n.* 成人

D **17.**

Bank clerk: May I help you?

Simon: Yes, where should I go to ask for a loan?

Bank clerk: ______________ He's on the second floor.

Simon: Thank you.

(A) How much do you plan to ask for?

(B) What is the interest rate next year?

(C) I'm afraid that we don't offer any loans this year.

(D) The manager in the loan department can help you.

銀行職員：需要幫忙嗎？

賽　　門：嗯，我該去哪裡申請貸款？

銀行職員：______________ 他在二樓。

賽　　門：謝謝。

(A) 您打算申請多少貸款？　(B) 明年的利率是多少？

(C) 恐怕我們今年不提供任何貸款。　(D) 貸款部的經理可以幫您處理。

解析

空格前，賽門問到 "Yes, where should I go to ask for a loan?"（嗯，我該去哪裡申請貸款？），空格後，銀行職員說到 "He's on the second floor."（他在二樓。），得知銀行職員應是告知賽門可以上二樓找負責貸款的人員幫忙，因此 (D) 項應為正選。

其他重點

1. **loan** [lon] *n.* 貸款 & *vt.* 借給（= lend）
   loan sb sth　把某物借給某人
   例: How soon can you pay off the loan?
   （你的貸款多久才能還清？）
   Could you loan me your car for the weekend?
   （你的車週末可以借我用嗎？）
2. **rate** [ret] *n.* 率；比率
   interest rate　利率
   例: The interest rate will be increased by 0.5 percentage points, effective on July 1.
   （利率將調升 0.5 個百分點，自七月一日生效。）

B **18.**

Wife: So, which apartment do you like?
Husband: I like the one near the post office. The best thing is it has a free parking space.
Wife: ________________ I think the one near the train station is better. We can take the train to the office. And the rent is a lot cheaper!
Husband: Yeah, you're right. Let's take it.

(A) We can rest in the park.　(B) But we don't have a car.
(C) It's the best choice to make.　(D) But it's not cheap to park there.

妻　子：那麼，你喜歡哪一間公寓？
丈　夫：我喜歡郵局附近那一間。它最好的是有附一個免費停車位。
妻　子：______________ 我覺得靠近火車站的那一間比較好。我們可以搭火車去公司。而且房租便宜很多！
丈　夫：是的，妳說得沒錯。我們就租這一間吧。

(A) 我們可以在公園裡休息。　(B) 但是我們沒有車。
(C) 這樣選擇是最好的。　(D) 但在那裡停車並不便宜。

解析

對話中一對夫妻在討論要租哪一間公寓，空格前，丈夫說到 "I like the one near the post office. The best thing is it has a free parking space."（我喜歡郵局附近那一間。它最好的是有附一個免費停車位。），空格後妻子說到 "I think the one near the train station is better. We can take the train to the office."（我覺得靠近火車站的那一間比較好。我們可以搭火車去公司。），得知可推論他們其實沒有交通工具而得利用大眾運輸通勤，因此 (B) 項應為正選。

其他重點

1. **a post office** 郵局
2. **rent** [rɛnt] *n.* 租金 & *vt.* & *vi.* 租借

   例: How much is your monthly rent for your apartment?
   （你每月公寓租金是多少錢？）
   Becky is still considering whether to buy or rent an apartment in this city.
   （貝琪還在考慮要在這城市買還是租公寓。）

A **19.**

Tim: What kind of vacation do you like the best?[註3]

Kelly: ________________ I'm dog-tired. I need a break! I just want to go to the beach, and do absolutely nothing.

Tim: Sounds good. But, I like doing things. I like to see places and go to museums.

(A) A lazy vacation, of course. (B) A shopping vacation is great.
(C) I like to go on business trips. (D) I like to work and save money.

提　姆：妳最喜歡怎樣的假期？
凱　莉：________________ 我累斃了。我需要休息！我只想去海邊然後啥事都不做。
提　姆：聽起來不錯。不過我喜歡有事做。我想要到處看看，還要去參觀博物館。
(A) 當然是躺平的假期。 (B) 購物的假期超棒。
(C) 我喜歡出差。 (D) 我喜歡工作並存錢。

解析

空格前，提姆問到 "What kind of vacation do you like the best?"（妳最喜歡怎樣的假期？），空格後，凱莉說到 "I just want to go to the beach, and do absolutely nothing." (我只想去海邊然後啥事都不做。），得知凱莉最喜歡不做任何事情的慵懶假期，因此 (A) 項應為正選。

註3：本句建議改為 "What kind of vacation would you prefer this time?"（這次妳想要度哪種假？）較佳，因空格後的回答是針對當下狀況而言，而非指一般的喜好。

其他重點

1. **vacation** [veˋkeʃən] *n.* 假期 & *vi.* 去度假
be on vacation in + 地方　在某地度假
= be vacationing in + 地方
例: Christine is on vacation in Europe.
= Christine is vacationing in Europe.
（克莉絲汀在歐洲度假。）

2. **dog-tired** [ˋdɔg͵taɪrd] *a.* 非常疲累的，累壞了
例: After the long hike, I was dog-tired.
（長途健行後，我累壞了。）

3. **absolutely** [ˋæbsə͵lutlɪ] *adv.* 絕對地，完全地
例: It is absolutely impossible to swim across the ocean.
（想要游過那片海洋是絕對不可能的。）

D **20.**

Manager: Lin's steak house[註4]. How may I help you?
Mr. White: Hi, ________________
Manager: Just a minute... Yes, I have your booking here. It's 6:30 p.m.
Mr. White: That's right. Unfortunately, our trip got delayed. Is it possible that I[註5] change the reservation to Friday?
Manager: Sure. No problem.

(A) I heard that you've just updated the menu.
(B) I just want to check if you are open this Friday.
(C) I'd like to book a table for two by the window.
(D) I made a reservation under James White tonight[註6].

經　　理：林家牛排館，您好。請問需要幫忙嗎？
懷特先生：嗨，________________
經　　理：請稍等一下……對，我這裡有看到您的訂位紀錄。是晚上六點半。
懷特先生：沒錯。但很不幸的我們的行程被耽誤了。我能不能把訂位改到星期五？
經　　理：當然。沒問題。

(A) 聽說你們剛更新菜單。
(B) 我只是想問一下你們這禮拜五有沒有開。
(C) 我想訂靠窗的位子，兩位。
(D) 我用詹姆士．懷特的名字訂了今晚的位子。

解析

空格前懷特先生致電牛排館，空格後經理回答 "Yes, I have your booking here. It's 6:30 p.m."（對，我這裡有看到您的訂位紀錄。是晚上六點半。），得知懷特先生應在提供訂位資訊做確認，因此 (D) 項應為正選。

註4：此處應為完整的餐廳名稱，第一個字母均應大寫，故宜改為 Lin's Steak House。

註5：Is it possible + that 子句表詢問「某事發生的可能性」，而 Is it possible to V 表詢問「能否做到或達成某事」，根據語意，本句改以後者開頭較佳。

註6：根據上下文，懷特先生的訂位時間是今晚六點半，tonight 前加上介詞 for 較明確。

其他重點

1. **unfortunately** [ʌnˋfɔrtʃənɪtlɪ] *adv.* 遺憾地；不幸地

例: Unfortunately, John didn't show up on time.
（遺憾的是，約翰並未準時出現。）
Unfortunately, there's no one to take care of the sick old man.
（很不幸地，沒有人照顧那個生病的老先生。）

2. **delay** [dɪˋle] *vt.* & *vi.* & *n.*（使）延誤／延期
delay + N/V-ing　延誤／期⋯⋯
a delay in + N/V-ing　⋯⋯延誤／期

例: Don't delay paying the bill.
（不要延誤繳帳單的時間。）
The release date of the movie has been delayed until the end of this month.
（這部電影的上映日期已延到本月底。）
We're trying to figure out what caused the delay in payment.
（我們正在努力找出導致付款延遲的原因。）

3. **reservation** [ˏrɛzɚˋveʃən] *n.* 預訂
make a reservation for...　預訂⋯⋯

例: Kevin made a last-minute reservation for a hotel room.
（凱文臨時訂了飯店房間。）

4. **update** [ʌpˋdet] *vt.* 使更新；為⋯⋯提供最新消息 & [ˋʌpdet] *n.* 更新
update sb on sth　告知某人某事的最新消息

例: We're going to update our computer software next month.
（我們將於下個月更新我們的電腦軟體。）
We'll update you on the latest developments in the murder trial.
（我們會隨時向你報告這起謀殺案審判的最新發展。）
Coming up next on this station is our news update.
（本臺接下來進行的是即時新聞。）

III. 綜合測驗

◎ 21 - 25

When should a child start to learn to use a computer? The answer depends on __21__ you ask. Some early childhood educators feel that "the earlier, the better." They believe that in modern society, computer skills are essential for every child, just like reading and counting. __22__, children should start using and playing with computers before elementary school. However, other educators believe that computers could have a negative effect __23__ the mental development of children. They say that children who play alone with a computer do not learn how to share or interact with others. Furthermore, children do not use their imagination enough __24__ the computer screen shows everything. Perhaps the best way for children to use computers __25__ to use them only for a short period of time each day. If a child uses a computer for only thirty minutes each day, she or he still has plenty of time to learn and play away from the computer.

21. (A) which (B) whom (C) whose (D) how

22. (A) Instead (B) Nonetheless (C) Otherwise (D) Therefore

23. (A) near (B) from (C) on (D) at

24. (A) because (B) or (C) so that (D) rather than

25. (A) are (B) is (C) have (D) has

兒童應該何時開始學習使用電腦？答案因人而異。有些幼兒教育學家認為「越早越好」。他們相信在現今的社會中，電腦技能對每個兒童來說就如同閱讀與計算能力一樣不可或缺，因此該在上小學之前就開始使用電腦與玩電腦遊戲。然而有其他教育學家認為電腦對兒童的心理發展可能造成負面影響。他們表示獨自玩電腦遊戲的兒童沒有學到如何與他人分享或互動。再者，由於電腦螢幕上可見鉅細靡遺的影像，兒童無法盡情發揮他們的想像力。也許讓兒童使用電腦的最佳方式就是每天僅使用一小段時間。如果兒童每天僅使用電腦三十分鐘，那麼她或他還會有很多時間遠離電腦去學習與玩耍。

B **21.**

解析

1. 空格前為及物片語動詞 depend on，後方應接受詞，而空格後為主詞 + 及物動詞，可知 depend on 的受詞為一名詞子句，而此名詞子句尚欠缺及物動詞 ask 的受詞。後句提到

"Some early childhood educators feel that..."（有些幼兒教育學家認為……），可推測空格內應選代表「人」且可作為 ask 受詞的疑問詞 whom。

2. 根據上述，(B) 項應為正選。

D 22.

解析

1. (A) **instead** [ɪnˋstɛd] *adv.* 作為替代，反而

   例: I don't want an apple. Instead, I want a peach.
   （我不想要蘋果，而是想要水蜜桃。）

   (B) **nonetheless** [ˌnʌnðəˋlɛs] *adv.* 然而

   例: John had a bad cold. Nonetheless, he came to work.
   （約翰得了重感冒。儘管如此，他還是來上班。）

   (C) **otherwise** [ˋʌðɚˌwaɪz] *adv.* 否則；以相反的方式

   例: You'd better come clean. Otherwise, you'll make things worse.
   （你最好從實招來，否則會讓事情更糟。）

   (D) **therefore** [ˋðɛrˌfɔr] *adv.* 因此

   例: When the cat's away, the mice will play. Therefore, I won't leave Dan at home alone.
   （大人不在，小孩就要造反。所以我不會讓丹獨自在家。）

2. 根據語意，(D) 項應為正選。

C 23.

解析

1. 本題測試以下固定用法：

   have an effect / influence on... 對……有影響

   例: Scientists proved that too much coffee has bad effects on people.
   （科學家證實飲用咖啡過量對人們有不良影響。）

2. 根據上述用法，(C) 項應為正選。

A 24.

解析

1. 空格前後皆為完整子句，故知空格應置連接詞連接前後子句。

2. 四個選項皆可作連接詞，惟 (B) or（否則）、(C) so that（因此）、(D) rather than（而不是）置入後不符合語意，僅 (A) because（因為）置入後符合語意，可知 (A) 項應為正選。
3. **rather than...** 而不是……

例: David chose a brown tie rather than a black belt as his father's birthday gift.
（大衛選了一條棕色領帶當作他父親的生日禮物，而沒選黑色皮帶。）

B **25.**

解析

1. 本題測試以下固定用法：

the way for sb to V_1 is to V_2... 對某人來說要……的方法就是……

例: One of the best ways for children to learn to be independent is to let them do some housework.
（對孩子來說要學習獨立最好的方法之一就是讓他們做點家事。）

2. 根據上述用法，得知 (B) 項應為正選。

重要單字片語

1. **depend on...** 取決於……

例: I'm not sure if we can go camping. It depends on the weather.
（我不確定我們是否可以去露營。要視天氣而定。）

2. **educator** [ˋɛdʒə͵ketɚ] *n.* 教育學家

educate [ˋɛdʒə͵ket] *vt.* 教育，栽培

3. **essential** [ɪˋsɛnʃəl] *a.* 必要的，不可或缺的

be essential to / for... 對……是不可或缺的

例: Nutrition and exercise are essential to our health.
（營養和運動對我們的健康來說很重要。）

4. **elementary** [͵ɛləˋmɛntərɪ] *a.* 基本的；初級的，基礎的

an elementary school 小學

5. **mental** [ˋmɛntḷ] *a.* 心理的

例: It is said that the old lady living in the house alone has some mental problems.
（據說那棟房子裡的獨居老婦人有些精神方面的問題。）

6. **interact** [͵ɪntɚˋækt] *vi.* 互動

interact with... 與……互動

例: Bruce seldom interacts with his co-workers.
（布魯斯很少跟他同事互動。）

7. **furthermore** [ˋfɝðɚ͵mɔr] *adv.* 而且

例: This movie is long and boring. Furthermore, no one understands the ending.
（這部電影既冗長又無趣。再者，沒人看得懂它的結局。）

8. **imagination** [ɪ͵mædʒəˋneʃən] *n.* 想像力

9. **plenty** [ˋplɛntɪ] *pron.* 充分（與介詞 of 並用）
plenty of + 複數可數名詞 / 不可數名詞 很多……

例: Getting plenty of sleep improves your memory.
（充足的睡眠會增強你的記憶力。）

◎ 26 - 30

Two government projects in Taiwan provide funds for children of foreign-born parents[註1] to understand more about their parents'[註2] cultural background. The projects aim to help young people connect ___26___ their parents'[註3] home countries. These places are mostly located in Southeast Asia, where about 180,000 foreign persons ___27___ to Taiwanese citizens come from. One of the projects pays for participants to visit their immigrant parents' home countries. The purpose is to learn more about the local culture and language. ___28___ project organizes trips to Taiwanese-owned companies in Southeast Asia. Vietnam, ___29___, receives the largest Taiwanese investment. These Taiwanese-owned companies provide employment for 60,000 Taiwanese. When they hire a new employee from Taiwan, they ___30___ the person's ability to adapt to the Vietnamese culture.[註4] For many young Taiwanese with parents[註5] of Vietnamese origin, this offers an opportunity to work in their parents'[註6] home country.

26. (A) into (B) onto (C) from (D) with
27. (A) marry (B) married (C) will marry (D) are married
28. (A) Any (B) Other (C) The other (D) The only
29. (A) however (B) similarly (C) for example (D) in addition
30. (A) get off (B) get over (C) look after (D) look for

臺灣政府有兩項計畫，提供資金讓父親或母親為外籍人士的孩子更了解爸爸或媽媽的文化背景。這些計畫旨在幫助青少年與父親或母親的母國建立聯結。這些國家大多位於東南亞，大約十八萬名與臺灣公民結婚的外籍人士來自這個地區。計畫之一是資助參與者造訪其新移民父母的母國。目的是要加強了解當地文化與語言。另一項計畫則安排造訪臺商位於東南亞的公司。例如臺灣在越南的投資為最大宗。這些臺灣人經營的公司提供六萬名臺人就業。這些公司從臺灣僱用新員工時，會看重員工適應越南文化的能力。對於許多父親或母親來自越南的臺灣青年而言，這提供他們在父親或母親的母國工作的機會。

註1：因外籍配偶有可能是父母其中一人是外籍而已，所以在此 foreign-born parents 應改為單數 a foreign-born parent 較適宜。

註2：their parents' 應改為單數 their parent's，理由同上。

註3：their parents' 應改為單數 their parent's，理由同上。

註4：根據本句語意，片語 look for 後應接「人」較為合適，故本句應改為 "When they hire a new employee from Taiwan, they look for people with the ability to adapt to the Vietnamese culture."。

註5：parents 應改為單數 a parent，理由同上。

註6：their parents' 應改為單數 their parent's，理由同上。

D **26.**

解析

1. 本題測試以下固定用法：

connect with... 和……建立／形成聯結，和……產生共鳴

例: The Indian women really connected with the feminist lawyer after her speech.
（印度女性在這位女權律師的演說結束之後，和她產生很大的共鳴。）

2. 根據上述，(D) 項應為正選。

B **27.**

解析

1. 本題測試形容詞片語化簡為分詞片語的用法，原句原為：
..., where about 180,000 foreign persons who / that are married to Taiwanese citizens come from.
2. 此時可將關係代名詞 who / that 省略，之後的動詞改為現在分詞，若該動詞為 be 動詞則改為 being，且 being 可予以省略。故原句可改寫為：
..., where about 180,000 foreign persons married to Taiwanese citizens come from.
3. 根據上述，(B) 項應為正選。

C **28.**

解析

1. 本題測試以下用於表示限定兩者的固定用法：

one... the other... 一個……另一個……

例: Paul has two older brothers. One is a teacher, and the other is a chef.
（保羅有兩個哥哥。一個是老師，另一個是大廚。）

2. 本文第一句表示臺灣政府有兩項計畫，且第四句提及 One of the projects（計畫之一），得知空格應置 The other。
3. 根據上述，(C) 項應為正選。

C 29.

解析

1. (A) **however** [haʊˋɛvɚ] *adv.* 然而

   例: Penguins are birds; however, they don't fly.
   = Penguins are birds. However, they don't fly.
   （企鵝是鳥類，然而牠們不會飛。）

   (B) **similarly** [ˋsɪmələlɪ] *adv.* 同樣地

   例: The boss respects his workers. Similarly, his workers respect him.
   （這位老闆尊重他的員工。同樣地，他的員工也尊重他。）

   (C) **for example** 舉例來說

   例: Ethan has many talents. For example, he can play the piano.
   （伊森才華洋溢。舉例來說，他會彈鋼琴。）

   (D) **in addition** 此外

   例: John has a heart of gold. In addition, he is very clever.
   （約翰心地善良。此外，他又很聰明。）
2. 根據語意，(C) 項應為正選。

D 30.

解析

1. (A) **get off...** 下（公車、火車等）

   例: I bumped into a passenger as I got off the train.
   （我下火車時撞到一名乘客。）

   (B) **get over...** 從……恢復過來

   例: It took me a long time to get over the shock.
   （我花了很長的時間才從驚嚇中恢復過來。）

   (C) **look after...** 看管……；照顧……

   例: Never ask a stranger to look after your luggage.
   （絕對不要請陌生人幫你看管行李。）

   (D) **look for...** 尋找……

   例: The manager is looking for someone that has a passion for fashion.
   （這名主管在找對時尚有熱忱的人。）
2. 根據語意，(D) 項應為正選。

重要單字片語

1. **funds** [fʌndz] *n.* 資金（恆用複數）
2. **locate** [ˋloket / loˋket] *vt.* 位於（常用於被動語態）；找到……的位置
   be located in / on / at... 位於……
   例: Our school is located in the center of the town.
   （我們學校位於小鎮的中央。）
3. **citizen** [ˋsɪtəzn̩] *n.* 公民；市民
4. **participant** [pɑrˋtɪsəpənt] *n.* 參加者
5. **immigrant** [ˋɪməgrənt] *n.*（由外移入的）移民者
6. **investment** [ɪnˋvɛstmənt] *n.* 投資
7. **hire** [haɪr] *vt.* 僱用 & *n.* 新僱員
   例: We hired a gardener to take care of the flowers.
   （我們僱用一位園丁來照顧這些花。）
8. **adapt** [əˋdæpt] *vi.* & *vt.*（使）適應
   adapt (oneself) to + N/V-ing 使（自己）適應於……
   例: It took the new student about a month to adapt to the new environment.
   （這名新同學花了一個月左右的時間去適應新環境。）

IV. 閱讀測驗

◎ 31 - 32

The Diamond Hotel is a quarantine hotel. It has seventy rooms for guests. Every room can only have one guest. This line graph shows how many of the rooms were occupied during 2020 and 2021.

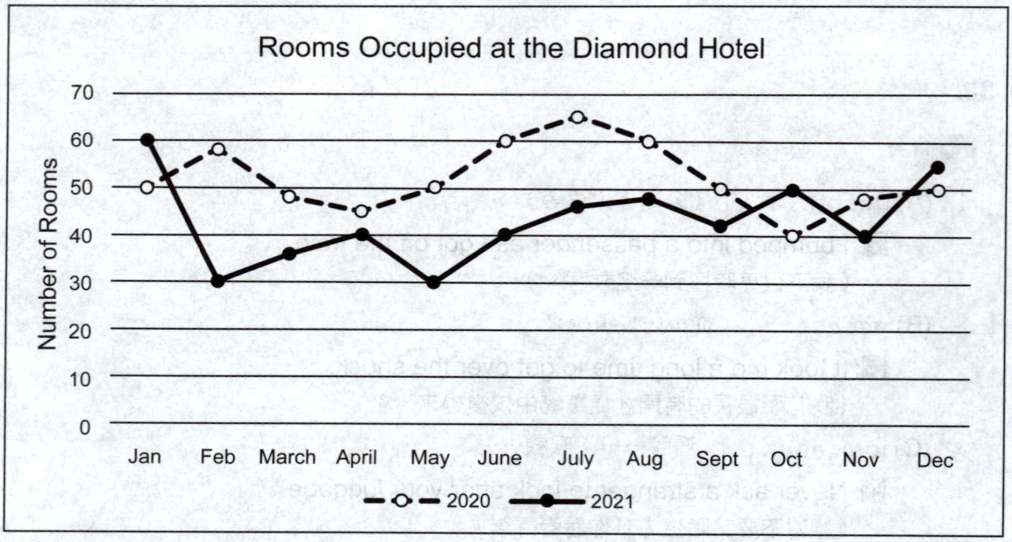

鑽石旅館是間防疫旅館。它有七十間客房。每個房間只能容納一位客人。本折線圖顯示在 2020、2021 年間被使用的房間數。

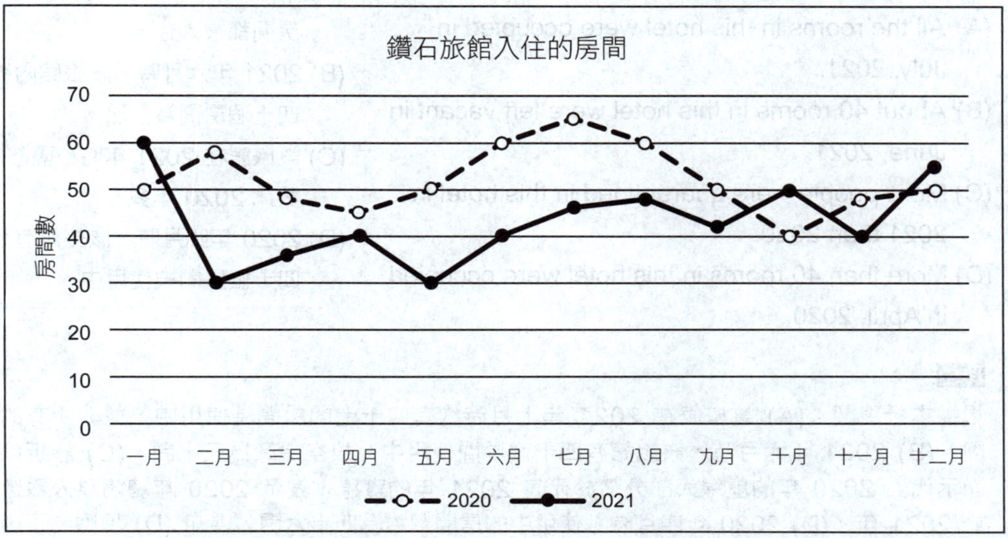

A **31.**

Since every room only had one guest, how many guests stayed at this hotel in May, 2021?

(A) 30

(B) 40

(C) 50

(D) 60

既然每個房間只能容納一位客人，那麼在 2021 年五月有多少客人住進這間旅館？

(A) 30

(B) 40

(C) 50

(D) 60

理由:

折線圖內的實線顯示 2021 年的住宿房數、虛線顯示 2020 年的住宿房數，縱軸表示房間數、橫軸表示月分，可知 2021 年的五月共有三十位客人住在這間旅館，得知 (A) 項應為正選。

D **32.**

According to the line graph, which of the following is true?

(A) All the rooms in this hotel were occupied in July, 2021.

(B) About 40 rooms in this hotel were left vacant in June, 2021.

(C) More people were quarantined in this hotel in 2021 than 2020.

(D) More than 40 rooms in this hotel were occupied in April, 2020.

根據本折線圖，下列敘述何者為真？

(A) 該旅館在 2021 年七月時所有的房間都被入住。

(B) 2021 年六月時，該旅館內約有四十個房間為空房。

(C) 該旅館在 2021 年時被隔離的人數比 2020 年多。

(D) 2020 年四月時，該旅館有超過四十個房間被使用中。

理由:

根據本折線圖：(A) 該旅館在 2021 年七月時約有四十七間房間為使用中，並非所有的房間。(B) 2021 年六月時，該旅館有四十個房間使用中，故空房應為三十間。(C) 該折線圖顯示代表 2020 年的虛線大部分高於代表 2021 年的實線，表示 2020 年總隔離人數應多於 2021 年。(D) 2020 年四月時，使用中的房間數約為四十六間，得知 (D) 項應為正選。

重要單字片語

1. **quarantine** [ˋkwɔrən͵tin] *n.* 隔離 & *vt.* 使隔離
   a quarantine hotel　防疫旅館
   in quarantine　隔離
   例: The traveler was kept in quarantine for 14 days after he was confirmed positive.
   （這名旅客被確認陽性後隔離了十四天。）

2. **a line graph**　折線圖，線狀圖
   a bar graph　柱狀圖
   graph [græf] *n.*（直線或曲線表示的）圖表

3. **occupied** [ˋɑkjə͵paɪd] *a.* 使用中的；被占據的；忙碌的
   occupy [ˋɑkjə͵paɪ] *vt.* 擁有（某職務）；占據；使忙碌（三態為：occupy, occupied [ˋɑkjə͵paɪd], occupied）

4. **vacant** [ˋvekənt] *a.* 空缺的，未被占用的

◎ 33 - 34

Karano High School Video Competition

Competition Rules

ENTRY GUIDELINES

1. General
   - Participation is open only to students who are now studying in Karano High School.
   - Only one video is allowed per student / team.
   - Submit your video by September 30th, 2022.
2. Video Production
   - Videos must be one minute in length.
   - Videos must be original; use of material must be permitted by law.
3. Content
   - Must address the theme, "Karano High School – A Special Place!" describing what you love about this school and what it is like to be a student here.
   - Must be suitable for all audiences.

JUDGING CRITERIA

Judges will give points based on creativity, production quality, and how well the theme is presented.

PRIZES

Results will be announced on December 1st, 2022 during the School Anniversary Celebration, and three cash prizes totaling NT$10,000 will be awarded.

卡拉諾高中短片競賽

競賽規則

參賽規則

1. 一般規則
   - 僅卡拉諾高中在學學生具備參賽資格。
   - 每名學生／每組團隊限繳一支參賽影片。
   - 繳件期限為 2022 年九月三十日。
2. 影片製作
   - 影片必須長一分鐘。
   - 影片必須為原創作品；必須使用合法素材。
3. 內容
   - 主題須為「卡拉諾高中 —— 一個特別的地方！」描述你愛這所學校的理由，以及在這裡當學生的感受。
   - 必須適合所有觀眾觀賞。

評判標準

評審會依創意、製作品質以及主題貼合度來評分。

獎金

2022 年十二月一日校慶時公布結果，並頒發三項總計現金新臺幣一萬元的獎金。

C **33.**

What is the competition about?

(A) Producing a video about student life and special education.

(B) Creating a video specially for students who love the school.

(C) Making a short video on how the school is special to oneself.

(D) Filming a one-minute video of the Anniversary Celebration day.

此競賽是關於什麼？

(A) 製作關於學生生活和特教的影片。

(B) 專門為熱愛該校的學生製作的影片。

(C) 製作一部短片，講述該校對製作者的特別之處。

(D) 拍攝一分鐘的校慶影片。

理由:

根據小標題「3. Content（內容）」的第一點 "Must address the theme, 'Karano High School – A Special Place!' describing what you love about this school..."（主題須為「卡拉諾高中 —— 一個特別的地方！」描述你愛這所學校的理由……）得知，(C) 項應為正選。

D **34.**

According to the competition rules, which of the following is true?

(A) Videos must be entries from former Karano students.

(B) Judges can only get points for creativity and quality.

(C) Students must hand in videos by December 1st, 2022.

(D) Participants can only use material as allowed by law.

根據競賽規則，下列哪一項是正確的？

(A) 參賽影片必須是由卡拉諾高中校友所製作。

(B) 評審只能根據創意和品質來得分。

(C) 學生必須在 2022 年十二月一日前繳件。

(D) 參賽者只能用合法的素材。

理由:

根據小標題「2. Video Production（影片製作）」的最後一點 "... use of material must be permitted by law."（……必須使用合法素材。）得知，(D) 項應為正選。

重要單字片語

1. **competition** [ˌkɑmpəˋtɪʃən] *n.* 競賽

   例: Kelly is the youngest contestant in the piano competition.
   （凱莉是這場鋼琴比賽最年輕的參賽者。）

2. **entry** [ˋɛntrɪ] *n.* 參賽（作品）；進入
3. **participation** [pɑrˌtɪsəˋpeʃən] *n.* 參加
4. **original** [əˋrɪdʒənl̩] *a.* 原創的；原作的
5. **permit** [pɚˋmɪt] *vt.* 允許（三態為：permit, permitted [pɚˋmɪtɪd], permitted）

   例: You are not permitted to set up a stall here.
   （你們不可以在此擺攤。）

6. **audience** [ˋɔdɪəns] *n.* 觀眾
7. **criterion** [kraɪˋtɪrɪən] *n.* 標準（複數為 criteria [kraɪˋtɪrɪə]）

   例: A good educational background is one of our criteria for selecting new employees.
   （好的學歷是我們挑選新進員工的標準之一。）

8. **creativity** [ˌkrieˋtɪvətɪ] *n.* 創造力（不可數）
9. **theme** [θim] *n.* 主題
10. **announce** [əˋnaʊns] *vt.* 公布，宣布

    例: Robin will announce who will play the main characters in the play.
    （羅賓會公布該戲劇的主要角色由哪些人來擔綱。）

11. **anniversary** [ˌænəˈvɝsərɪ] *n.* 週年紀念（日）

例: My parents invited their friends to their 20th wedding anniversary celebration.
（我父母親邀請朋友來參加他倆的結婚二十週年紀念慶祝會。）

12. **celebration** [ˌsɛləˈbreʃən] *n.* 慶祝會

◎ 35 - 37

To: Molly
From: Jim<jim888@gmailer.com>
Subject: My volunteer trip

16th, July Sat. 12:55 P.M.

Hi Molly,

We arrived in Cuzco last Friday. Can you imagine? This city sits at 3,400 meters above sea level and has a population of 350,000. It's near the Andes Mountains, and about three hours by train to Machu Picchu. At the end of the four-week volunteer trip, we're going to visit Machu Picchu. I can't wait to see the mysterious Inca city!

Here, we all stay with local families. My host family is wonderful. I eat meals with them and speak Spanish with them. I also help them around the house. From Monday to Saturday, we go to a local school to work with the teachers and help them with anything they need. We teach English, and help with art, music, and sports. Also, we help repair the school, such as putting in new windows and painting the classrooms. I feel exhausted sometimes. However, when I see the children's happy faces, I know that I have made the right decision. How's your trip?

Jim

收件者： 茉莉　　七月十六日，星期六，中午 12:55
寄件者： 吉姆 <jim888@gmailer.com>
主　旨： 我的志工之旅

嗨，茉莉：

我們上週五抵達庫斯科。妳能想像嗎？這座城市的海拔高度有三千四百公尺，而且有三十五萬人口。庫斯科位於安地斯山脈附近，從這裡搭火車約三小時就可以到馬丘比丘。在這趟為期四週的志工之旅尾聲，我們將走訪馬丘比丘。我好想親眼看看這座神祕的印加古城！

在此地，我們都住當地人家裡。我的寄宿家庭很好。我和他們一起吃飯、用西班牙話交談。我也幫他們做家事。我們星期一到星期六都會去當地的學校和老師一起工作，提供他們需要的任何幫助。我們教英文並協助美術、音樂及體育科的教學。此外，我們也幫忙整修學校，例如安裝新窗戶和油漆教室。有時候我覺得很累，但當我看到孩子們快樂的臉龐時，我知道我做了對的決定。妳的旅遊如何呢？

吉姆

To: Jim<jim888@gmailer.com> 17th, July Sun. 10:00 A.M.
From: Molly
Subject: Re: My volunteer trip

Hi Jim,

It's good to hear that you enjoy what you are doing there. I was worried that you wouldn't get used to the weather and the hard work in Cuzco. My art trip starts from Louvre museum, Paris. We are now here to see the art display of Leonardo da Vinci, an Italian artist. His paintings are great. Tomorrow, we'll leave for the British Museum in London. Talk to you then.
BTW, don't forget to share pictures of Machu Picchu. Take care!

Molly

收件者： 吉姆 <jim888@gmailer.com> 七月十七日，星期日，早上 10:00
寄件者： 茉莉
主 旨： Re: 我的志工之旅

嗨，吉姆：

聽你說喜歡那裡的活動真是高興。我本來很擔心你會適應不來庫斯科的天氣和辛苦的工作。我的藝術之旅從巴黎的羅浮宮開始。我們此刻正在欣賞義大利籍藝術家李奧納多・達文西的作品。他的畫作非常棒。我們明天會去倫敦的大英博物館。到時再聯絡。
對了，別忘了分享馬丘比丘的照片。保重！

茉莉

C **35.**

According to Jim's email, which of the following is true?
(A) There are 3,400 people living in Cuzco.
(B) Jim goes to help at school 7 days a week.
(C) Jim is staying in Cuzco for about 4 weeks.
(D) Cuzco is about 3 hours on foot to Machu Picchu.

根據吉姆的電子郵件，下列何者為真？
(A) 有三千四百人住在庫斯科。
(B) 吉姆一週七天都去學校幫忙。
(C) 吉姆將待在庫斯科約四週。
(D) 從庫斯科走路到馬丘比丘大約要三小時。

理由:
根據吉姆的電子郵件第一段倒數第二句 "At the end of the four-week volunteer trip, ..."（在這趟為期四週的志工之旅尾聲，……），得知 (C) 項應為正選。

C **36.**

Where was Molly when she wrote the email to Jim?
(A) Cuzco
(B) London
(C) Paris
(D) Machu Picchu

茉莉寫電子郵件給吉姆時身處何處？
(A) 庫斯科
(B) 倫敦
(C) 巴黎
(D) 馬丘比丘

理由:
根據茉莉的電子郵件第一段第三、四句 "... Louvre museum, Paris. We are now here..."（……巴黎的羅浮宮。我們現在就在這裡……），可推測 here 即指巴黎的羅浮宮，故 (C) 項應為正選。

A **37.**

Which of the following could be inferred from these emails?
(A) Jim can speak both Spanish and English.
(B) Jim is good at art and likes da Vinci's paintings.
(C) Molly knew that Jim would like the volunteer work.
(D) Molly likes the Louvre better than the British Museum.

從這兩封電子郵件中可推論出下列何事？
(A) 吉姆會說西班牙語和英語。
(B) 吉姆擅長藝術並且喜歡達文西的畫作。
(C) 茉莉早就知道吉姆會喜歡志工工作。
(D) 茉莉喜歡羅浮宮勝過大英博物館。

理由:
根據吉姆的電子郵件第二段第三句 "... and speak Spanish with them."（……用西班牙話交談）及第二段第六句 "We teach English, ..."（我們教英文……），可推測吉姆會說西班牙語和英語，故 (A) 項應為正選。

重要單字片語

1. **volunteer** [ˌvɑlənˋtɪr] *n.* 志工，義工
2. **sit** [sɪt] *vi.* 位於

例: Quinn went to a small village that sits on a hilltop.
（昆恩去了位於山頂的小村莊。）

3. **sea level** 海平面
 數字 + above / below sea level
 海拔…… / 海面下……
4. **population** [ˌpɑpjəˋleʃən] *n.* 人口
5. **mysterious** [mɪsˋtɪrɪəs] *a.* 神祕的
6. **exhausted** [ɪgˋzɔstɪd] *a.* 疲憊的
7. **get used to + N/V-ing** 習慣……

 例: It seemed that Jason couldn't get used to army life.
 （傑森似乎無法適應軍隊生活。）

8. **display** [dɪˋsple] *n.* 陳列，展示
9. **leave for + 地點** 出發前往某地

 例: Jim left for Peru last Friday.
 （吉姆上週五出發前往秘魯。）

10. **BTW** 順帶一提（為 by the way 的縮寫）

◎ 38 - 42

Carbon dioxide (CO_2) is good at holding in heat from the Sun, and even a small increase of the gas in the atmosphere can cause Earth to get even warmer. Carbon capture, usage and storage (CCUS)[註1] is about different technologies that can keep CO_2 produced by factories and power plants from causing global warming. The idea is simple, and there are only a few main steps in the process. The first step is about trapping carbon emissions from factory chimneys. For instance, a filter can be placed in the chimney, so that the carbon is trapped and it cannot go out into the atmosphere. Then, the gas is piped to places where it can be stored or used. If stored underground, it cannot contribute to the climate crisis. If used, for instance, it can help grow greenhouse plants or make soda drinks.

While CCUS projects can clearly benefit the environment, these projects are not straightforward as there are many issues to be dealt with, such as maintaining the storage site, which have slowed start-ups of CCUS projects worldwide. Thus, with only a few CCUS projects operating now, there still aren't enough to seriously help with the world's carbon emissions. Early forerunners in this technology are the US, Canada, and Norway. The good news is that CCUS has now gained momentum in other countries, where 30 new projects have begun in the past three years. The International Energy Agency says there must be many more to keep carbon emissions from heating the world too much.

二氧化碳（CO_2）很會儲存來自太陽的熱能，在大氣中的這種氣體就算僅少量增加，也會造成地球變得更熱。碳捕集、利用與封存（CCUS）是幾種不同的技術，能防止工廠和發電廠製造的二氧化碳造成全球暖化。概念很簡單，而此過程只有幾個主要步驟。第一步是捕捉工廠煙囪的碳排放物。例如在煙囪內放置過濾器，藉此將碳排放攔截下來而不會進入大氣。然後二氧化碳氣體透過管路輸送到可封存或利用的所在。如果封存在地底下，它就不會造成氣候危機。如果要利用的話，舉個例子，它可以幫助溫室植物栽培或生產碳酸飲料。

雖然 CCUS 計畫顯然對環境有益，但這些計畫並沒有順利推動，因為有許多問題需要處理，像是封存場的維護等，這減緩了全球 CCUS 計畫的啟動。所以現在只有幾個 CCUS 計畫正在運作，這樣仍不足以幫助解決全球碳排放。美國、加拿大和挪威是此技術起步階段的領先者。好消息是 CCUS 現在在其他國家聲勢漸增，過去三年中已有三十個新計畫被啟動。國際能源署表示必須要有更多的響應計畫，才能防止碳排放造成世界過度暖化。

註1：CCUS 應為 Carbon Capture, Utilization and Storage 的縮寫。

A **38.**

What is the purpose of this article?

(A) It informs us about CCUS.

(B) It advises us against CCUS.

(C) It introduces new CCUS projects.

(D) It shows CCUS impact on technology.[註2]

這篇文章的目的為何？

(A) 告訴我們 CCUS 的資訊。

(B) 勸我們不要執行 CCUS。

(C) 介紹新的 CCUS 計畫。

(D) 說明 CCUS 對科技的影響。

理由:

本文第一段簡介 CCUS 這項技術的使用與作用，第二段說明這項計畫執行上的問題與現況，得知 (A) 項應為正選。

註2：應改為 It shows CCUS' impact on technology.

A **39.**

What is the process of CCUS?

(A) To trap the CO_2, and then either keep it or use it.

(B) To use the CO_2, and then store it in greenhouse plants.

(C) To pipe the CO_2, and then trap it to cause the climate crisis.

(D) To store the CO_2 underground, and then pipe it to the chimneys.

CCUS 的步驟為何？

(A) 捕捉二氧化碳，然後封存或利用它。

(B) 利用二氧化碳，再將它儲存在溫室植物中。

(C) 用管路輸送二氧化碳，再捕捉它來造成氣候危機。

(D) 將二氧化碳封存在地底下，再將它用管路輸送到煙囪。

理由:
根據本文第一段第四句 "The first step is about trapping carbon emissions from factory chimneys."（第一步是捕捉工廠煙囪的碳排放物。）以及第六句 "Then, the gas is piped to places where it can be stored or used."（然後二氧化碳氣體透過管路輸送到可封存或利用的所在。），得知 (A) 項應為正選。

C **40.**

Why is carbon dioxide put underground?

(A) To light up greenhouses.

(B) To cool down soda drinks.

(C) To limit global warming.

(D) To worsen climate change.

為何要將二氧化碳放在地底下？

(A) 為提供溫室照明。

(B) 為冷卻碳酸飲料。

(C) 為抑制全球暖化。

(D) 為使氣候變遷惡化。

理由:
根據本文第一段倒數第二句 "If stored underground, it cannot contribute to the climate crisis."（如果封存在地底下，它就不會造成氣候危機。），得知 (C) 項應為正選。

B **41.**

Which of the following is closest in meaning to "**momentum**" in paragraph 2?

(A) decrease

(B) progress

(C) wealth

(D) fortune

下列哪一項意思最貼近第二段中的「力道」？

(A) 減少

(B) 進展

(C) 財富

(D) 運氣

理由:
根據本文第二段倒數第二句 "..., where 30 new projects have begun in the past three years."（……，過去三年中已有三十個新計畫被啟動。），可推知此計畫很有「進展」，得知 (B) 項應為正選。

B **42.**

What can be concluded from paragraph 2?

(A) CCUS will be stopped from now on to save money.

(B) The number of countries using CCUS may increase.

(C) CCUS benefits problems such as storage site maintenance.

(D) There are enough CCUS projects to stop heating the world.

從第二段可得出何種結論？

(A) 為了省錢，CCUS 必須從現在開始中斷。

(B) 使用 CCUS 計畫的國家數量可能增加。

(C) CCUS 有益於處理封存場維護之類的問題。

(D) CCUS 計畫的數量足以阻止地球暖化。

理由:

根據本文第二段最後兩句，"The good news is that CCUS has now gained momentum in other countries, where 30 new projects have begun in the past three years. The International Energy Agency says there must be many more to keep carbon emissions from heating the world too much."（好消息是 CCUS 現在在其他國家聲勢漸增，過去三年中已有三十個新計畫被啟動。國際能源署表示必須要有更多的響應計畫，才能防止碳排放造成世界過度暖化。），得知 (B) 項應為正選。

重要單字片語

1. **carbon dioxide** [ˋkɑrbən daɪˋɑksaɪd] *n.* 二氧化碳（不可數）（= CO_2）
2. **atmosphere** [ˋætməsˏfɪr] *n.* 大氣；空氣
   the atmosphere 大氣，大氣層
3. **storage** [ˋstɔrɪdʒ] *n.* 儲藏（空間）（不可數）
4. **a power plant** 發電廠
   plant [plænt] *n.* 工廠
5. **emission** [ɪˋmɪʃən] *n.* 排放物（可數）；（氣體、光線等）排放（不可數）
   carbon emissions 碳排放
6. **filter** [ˋfɪltɚ] *n.* 過濾器 & *vt.* 過濾
7. **pipe** [paɪp] *vt.* 以管路輸送（常用被動）
   例: Natural gas in Europe is piped in from Russia.
   （歐洲的天然氣是從俄羅斯輸入的。）
8. **contribute** [kənˋtrɪbjut] *vi.* 促成，導致（與介詞 to 並用）
   contribute to... 導致……
   例: Hard work alone does not necessarily contribute to success.
   （光靠努力不一定就會成功。）
9. **straightforward** [ˏstretˋfɔrwɚd] *a.* 簡單的，易懂的
10. **issue** [ˋɪʃu] *n.* 問題；議題
11. **forerunner** [ˋfɔrˏrʌnɚ] *n.* 先驅
12. **agency** [ˋedʒənsɪ] *n.* 署、局、部等；機關
13. **impact** [ˋɪmpækt] *n.* 影響 & [ɪmˋpækt] *vt.* 對……產生影響
    例: Many experts believe the new policy will greatly impact the society.
    （許多專家都認為那項新政策會對社會帶來巨大衝擊。）
14. **maintenance** [ˋmentənəns] *n.* 維護，保養（不可數）

第二部分：非選擇題（第 I 題，每格 2 分，共 4 分；第 II 到 III 題，每題 6 分，共 16 分）

I. 填充

1. 這項任務指派給對挑戰有正向態度的人。

This m ___①___ is assigned to people who have a p ___②___ attitude toward challenges.

① mission　② positive

解析

1. 本題空格 ① 的對照譯詞為『任務』，且空格為 m 開頭，故空格應置名詞 mission。
mission [ˋmɪʃən] *n.* 任務
例: The rescuers pulled off a dangerous mission.
（搜救人員成功地完成一項危險的任務。）

2. 本題空格 ② 的對照譯詞為『正向』，且空格為 p 開頭，故空格應置形容詞 positive。
positive [ˋpɑzətɪv] *a.* 積極正面的；有把握的；（化驗／檢驗等結果）陽性的
例: My roommate tested positive for COVID-19. Now I have to be kept in quarantine.
（我的室友冠狀病毒的檢驗結果為陽性。現在我得被隔離了。）

其他重點

1. **assign** [əˋsaɪn] *vt.* 指派；分配
sth be assigned to sb　某事被指派給某人處理
例: A different task was assigned to each man according to his skills.
（每個人視其專長而被賦予不同的任務。）
sb be assigned to V　某人被指派處理……
例: Kevin was assigned to oversee the project.
（凱文被指派來監督這個專案的進行。）

2. **attitude** [ˋætət(j)ud] *n.* 態度
an attitude to / toward(s)...　對……的態度
例: Mark's sloppy attitude towards work was the reason he got fired.
（馬克對工作懶散的態度是他被資遣的原因。）

3. **challenge** [ˋtʃæləndʒ] *n.* 挑戰 & *vt.* 向……挑戰
face a challenge (of...)　面臨（……的）挑戰
例: The president is facing the toughest challenge of his career.
（這位總統正面臨他職涯中最艱困的挑戰。）

II. 句子重組

2. are conducting research / fatal diseases / to stop / Many scientists / the spread of

Many scientists are conducting research to stop the spread of fatal diseases.
（許多科學家正進行研究來阻止致命疾病的傳播。）

解析

1. 先找出開頭為大寫的詞組 Many scientists（許多科學家）作為句首。
2. 主詞 Many scientists 之後應接動詞。重組部分中，are conducting research 為動詞詞組，表『正在進行研究』，故形成 "Many scientists are conducting research..."。
3. 其後應接 to stop...（來阻止……）用以補充說明動詞詞組 are conducting research 的目的。
4. 剩下的詞組中，the spread of（的傳播）為介詞詞組，之後應接 fatal diseases（致命疾病）作受詞，形成 the spread of fatal diseases 並置於 stop 之後作其受詞。故可得出答案：Many scientists are conducting research to stop the spread of fatal diseases.

其他重點

1. **conduct** [kən\`dʌkt] *vt.* 進行（研究等）；處理

conduct { research 進行研究
　　　　{ a survey / an investigation / an experiment 進行調查 / 實驗

例: Allen conducted a survey on consumer behavior for his marketing assignment.
（艾倫為他的市調作業進行消費者行為調查。）

2. **research** [\`risɝtʃ ] *n.* 研究（不可數）& [ rɪ\`sɝtʃ] *vt.* 研究
3. **fatal** [\`fetl̩] *a.* 致命的；無可挽回的

III. 中譯英

3. 健行和露營是兩項非常受歡迎的戶外活動。

Hiking and camping are two very popular outdoor activities.

解析

1. 『健行』可譯成 hiking。『露營』可譯成 camping。兩者為句子的主詞。
2. 『兩項』可譯成 two。
3. 『非常受歡迎的』可譯為 very popular。
4. 『戶外活動』可譯為 outdoor activities。
5. 由上得知，本句可譯為：
Hiking and camping are two very popular outdoor activities.

110

四技二專統一入學測驗－詳解

110 年統測
試題講解

第一部分：選擇題

I. 字彙題 (110 年-2～10)

II. 對話題 (110 年-10～20)

III. 綜合測驗 (110 年-20～26)

IV. 閱讀測驗 (110 年-27～38)

第二部分：非選擇題

I. 填充 (110 年-39)

II. 句子重組 (110 年-39～40)

III. 中譯英 (110 年-40)

選擇題解答

1	2	3	4	5	6	7	8	9	10
D	A	D	A	A	A	A	C	B	C
11	12	13	14	15	16	17	18	19	20
A	B	B	A	A	B	B	C	C	D
21	22	23	24	25	26	27	28	29	30
C	C	B	D	D	A	B	C	D	D
31	32	33	34	35	36	37	38	39	40
A	A	C	B	B	B	D	C	D	D
41									
B									

110 年四技二專統一入學測驗詳解

第一部分：選擇題（82 分）

I. 字彙題

D **1.**

The shy little boy spoke so ______ that I had a hard time hearing what he said.

(A) bravely (B) clearly (C) openly (D) softly

這個害羞的小男孩講話太輕聲細語以致於我很難聽到他說了什麼。

解析

1. (A) **bravely** [ˋbrevlɪ] *adv.* 勇敢地
   例: Some people bravely skated on the thin ice of the frozen pond.
   （有些人很勇敢地在結薄冰的池塘上溜冰。）
   (B) **clearly** [ˋklɪrlɪ] *adv.* 清楚地
   例: George used a chart to present the figures more clearly.
   （喬治用圖表來更清楚地呈現數據。）
   (C) **openly** [ˋopənlɪ] *adv.* 公開地
   例: Openly criticizing your coworkers at the workplace is not acceptable.
   （在辦公場所公然批評自己的同事是不能被接受的。）
   (D) **softly** [ˋsɔftlɪ] *adv.* 輕柔地
   例: The mother softly touched the baby's cheek.
   （這位母親溫柔地碰觸小寶寶的臉頰。）
2. 根據語意，(D) 項應為正選。

其他重點

1. **so... that...** 如此……以致於……
   例: Kevin runs so fast that no one can catch him.
   （凱文跑得真快，沒有人追得上。）
2. **have a hard time + V-ing** 做……有困難
   = have difficulty + V-ing
   例: Tim had a hard time calming down the crying baby.
   = Tim had difficulty calming down the crying baby.
   （提姆無法安撫哭泣的小嬰兒。）

A **2.**

I am terribly sorry. Please ______ my sincere apology.

(A) accept (B) ignore (C) propose (D) refuse

我非常抱歉。請接受我誠摯的道歉。

解析

1. (A) **accept** [ək`sɛpt] *vt.* 接受

例: Our manager is open-minded and willing to accept other people's opinions.
（我們的經理很開明，願意接納大家的看法。）

(B) **ignore** [ɪg`nor] *vt.* 忽略，忽視

例: Sally chooses to ignore the bad things people say about her.
（莎莉選擇忽視別人對她的批評。）

(C) **propose** [prə`poz] *vt.* 提議，建議

例: Peter proposed hiring a band for the company's year-end celebration.
（彼得提議找一個樂團到公司的尾牙上表演。）

(D) **refuse** [rɪ`fjuz] *vt.* & *vi.* 拒絕

例: Johnny was upset because Lisa refused his invitation to dinner.
（強尼很難過，因為莉莎拒絕了他的晚餐邀約。）

2. 根據語意，(A) 項應為正選。

其他重點

1. **terribly** [`tɛrəblɪ] *adv.* 非常，極度

例: Jason missed his girlfriend terribly, so he flew to England to see her.
（傑森非常想念他的女友，所以他搭飛機去英國看她。）

2. **sincere** [sɪn`sɪr] *a.* 由衷的，真誠的
3. **apology** [ə`pɑlədʒɪ] *n.* 道歉，認錯

D **3.**

I am a ______ customer at that restaurant. I eat there at least four or five times a week.

(A) delicious (B) former (C) negative (D) regular

我是那間餐廳的常客。我一週到那裡用餐至少四、五次。

解析

1. (A) **delicious** [dɪ`lɪʃəs] *a.* 美味的，可口的

例: Taiwan is known for its delicious snacks.
（臺灣以美味小吃聞名。）

(B) **former** [`fɔrmɚ] *a.* 前任的

例: Mr. Lin was the former principal of our school.
（林先生是我們學校的前任校長。）

(C) **negative** [`nɛgətɪv] *a.* 負面的，消極的

例: Lack of sleep can have a negative impact on your performance at school.
（缺乏睡眠會對你的在校表現有負面影響。）

(D) **regular** [ˋrɛgjələ] *a.* 經常去的；定期的

例: The professional athlete is a regular guest on the TV show.
（這名職業運動員是這個電視節目的常客。）

2. 根據語意，(D) 項應為正選。

其他重點

at least 至少

例: Katie swims at least three times a week to stay fit.
（凱蒂一週至少游泳三次來保持健康。）

A **4.**

Eating too many potato chips makes you thirsty because chips ______ a large amount of salt.

(A) contain (B) control (C) contract (D) contact

吃太多洋芋片會讓你口很乾，因為洋芋片含有大量鹽分。

解析

1. (A) **contain** [kənˋten] *vt.* 包含

例: The cardboard box contains fragile items, so you have to handle it with care.
（紙箱裡裝有易碎品，因此你必須小心處理。）

(B) **control** [kənˋtrol] *vt.* 控制

例: Amy refuses to let her parents control her life.
（艾咪拒絕讓父母控制她的人生。）

(C) **contract** [kənˋtrækt] *vt.* 感染 & *vi.* & *vt.*（使）收縮 & [ˋkɑntrækt] *n.* 契約

例: Nearly half of the adult population there has contracted malaria.
（那一帶有近半數的成年人染上瘧疾。）
＊malaria [məˋlɛrɪə] *n.* 瘧疾

(D) **contact** [ˋkɑntækt] *vt.* & *n.* 聯繫，聯絡

例: If you need more details, please contact me directly.
（如果你需要更多詳情，請直接跟我聯絡。）

2. 根據語意，(A) 項應為正選。

其他重點

amount [əˋmaʊnt] *n.* 數量

a small / large amount of + 不可數名詞 少量／大量的⋯⋯

比較: a small / large number of + 可數複數名詞 少數／許多⋯⋯

例: A large amount of money was stolen from the bank.
（此銀行遭竊取一筆鉅款。）

A **5.**

The weather is very hot in summer, while in winter it is really ______.

(A) chilly (B) previous (C) tropical (D) visible

夏天天氣很熱，而冬天非常冷。

解析

1. (A) **chilly** [ˋtʃɪlɪ] *a.* 寒冷的

 例: A chilly and cloudy day always makes Lucy feel down.
 （陰冷的天氣總讓露西心情低落。）

 (B) **previous** [ˋprivɪəs] *a.* 先前的

 例: Miranda worked as an accountant in her previous job, but now she is a secretary.
 （米蘭達的前一份工作是會計，但現在是祕書。）

 (C) **tropical** [ˋtrɑpɪkl̩] *a.* 熱帶的

 例: Bananas, durians, and mangos are tropical fruits.
 （香蕉、榴槤和芒果都是熱帶水果。）

 (D) **visible** [ˋvɪzəbl̩] *a.* 顯而易見的；看得見的

 例: The stain on your white shirt is visible ten feet away.
 （你白襯衫上的汙漬在十英尺外都看得到。）

2. 根據語意，(A) 項應為正選。

其他重點

while [(h)waɪl] *conj.*（然）而

例: Some people like tennis, while some like basketball.
（有些人喜歡網球，而另一些人則喜歡籃球。）

A **6.**

Hand washing is one of the best ways to keep healthy and stop the spread of ______ and viruses.

(A) bacteria (B) fever (C) moisture (D) sweat

洗手是保持健康和阻止細菌、病毒傳播的最佳方式之一。

解析

1. (A) **bacteria** [bækˋtɪrɪə] *n.* 細菌（複數；單數形為 bacterium [bækˋtɪrɪəm]）

 例: Besides making clothes whiter, bleach can be used to kill harmful bacteria, too.
 （除了讓衣服更白之外，漂白水也可用來殺菌。）

(B) **fever** [ˋfivɚ] *n.* 發燒

例: Coughing and fever are typical symptoms of the flu.
（咳嗽和發燒是流感的典型症狀。）

(C) **moisture** [ˋmɔɪstʃɚ] *n.* 水氣，溼氣

例: Moisture in the air damages old paintings.
（空氣中的溼氣會毀損古畫。）

(D) **sweat** [swɛt] *n.* 汗水 & *vi.* 流汗，冒汗

例: Sweat dripped from the farmer's forehead while he was working in the field.
（這個農夫在田裡工作時，汗水順著他的額頭滴落。）
*drip [drɪp] *vi.* 滴下，瀝下

2. 根據語意，(A) 項應為正選。

其他重點

1. **spread** [sprɛd] *n.* 擴散，蔓延 & *vt.* & *vi.* 散布，散播（三態同形）

例: The authorities are doing their best to stop the spread of the disease.
（當局正傾全力阻止疾病蔓延。）

2. **virus** [ˋvaɪrəs] *n.* 病毒

A **7.**

In the admission interview, the ______ are often asked to explain why they want to enter the university.

(A) applicants (B) associates (C) receptionists (D) relatives

在入學面試時，申請者常被要求解釋他們想進入該大學的理由。

解析

1. (A) **applicant** [ˋæpləkənt] *n.* 申請人；應徵者

例: The job opening at the huge company attracted many applicants.
（這間大型公司的職缺吸引了許多應徵者。）

(B) **associate** [əˋsoʃɪət] *n.* 合夥人 & *vt.* [əˋsoʃɪˌet] 使有關聯

例: Jason is one of my business associates.
（傑森是我的事業夥伴之一。）

(C) **receptionist** [rɪˋsɛpʃənɪst] *n.* 櫃檯人員

例: We'd better go down to the lobby and ask the receptionist why there's no power in our room.
（我們最好下去大廳問問櫃檯人員為什麼我們房間沒有電。）

(D) **relative** [ˋrɛlətɪv] *n.* 親戚

例: Those people talking to the bride are my distant relatives from Australia.
（跟新娘講話的那些人是我在澳洲的遠房親戚。）

2. 根據語意，(A) 項應為正選。

其他重點

1. **admission** [ədˋmɪʃən] *n.* 允許進入；入場費

例: Admission is ten dollars, and you can sit anywhere you want.
（入場費十美元，你可以隨便找位子坐。）

2. **interview** [ˋɪntə͵vju] *n.* 面試，面談 & *vt.* 訪問；採訪

例: You should dress formally for interviews.
（參加面試時應穿著正式服裝。）

C **8.**

Pets, such as cats and dogs, are humans' favorite companions.

(A) listeners (B) directors (C) partners (D) strangers

寵物如貓狗是人類最愛的同伴。

解析

1. 原句劃線的字有下列意思及用法：
companion [kəmˋpænjən] *n.* 同伴；朋友

例: Life is better when shared with a companion.
（生活有伴同享，才會更美好。）

2. (A) **listener** [ˋlɪsn̩ə] *n.* 聽眾

例: Paul's song has touched the hearts of listeners around the world.
（保羅的歌曲感動了全世界聽眾的心。）

(B) **director** [dəˋrɛktə] *n.* 導演

例: The director's latest project is a film about firemen.
（這位導演的最新企畫是講消防隊員的電影。）

(C) **partner** [ˋpɑrtnə] *n.* 夥伴

例: Gary chatted with his business partner over a cup of coffee.
（蓋瑞和他的生意夥伴邊喝咖啡邊聊天。）

(D) **stranger** [ˋstrendʒə] *n.* 陌生人

例: The mother always tells her children to stay away from strangers.
（這位母親總是告誡她的小孩要遠離陌生人。）

3. 根據上述，companion 與 partner 同義，故 (C) 項應為正選。

其他重點

such as... 像……，例如……

例: I can't eat seafood such as fish, shrimps, crabs, and so on.
（我不能吃海鮮，像是魚、蝦、螃蟹等等。）

B **9.**

The weather forecast said the temperature would dip from 20 degrees during the day to 12 degrees at night.

(A) dim (B) drop (C) fail (D) leak

天氣預報說氣溫將從白天的 20 度降到晚上的 12 度。

解析

1. 原句劃線的字有下列意思及用法：

   dip [dɪp] *vi.* 下沉，下降

   例: The prices of airline tickets dipped when the low season came.
   （機票價格在淡季開始時下跌。）

2. (A) **dim** [dɪm] *vi.* & *vt.*（使）變暗

   例: The light in the living room was dimmed to create a romantic mood.
   （客廳的燈被調暗以營造浪漫的氣氛。）

   (B) **drop** [drɑp] *vi.* 下降

   例: Our volume of trade with Italy has recently dropped.
   （最近我們和義大利的貿易量下滑。）
   *volume [ˋvɑljəm] *n.*（總）量

   (C) **fail** [fel] *vi.* 失敗，未成功

   例: Unfortunately, Zack's plan failed in the end.
   （不幸的是，柴克的計畫終告失敗。）

   (D) **leak** [lik] *vi.* & *vt.* 漏，滲

   例: The roof sometimes leaks when it rains.
   （下雨天時，屋頂有時會漏水。）

3. 根據上述，dip 與 drop 同義，故 (B) 項應為正選。

其他重點

1. **forecast** [ˋfɔrˏkæst] *n.* 預報
2. **temperature** [ˋtɛmprətʃɚ] *n.* 氣溫
3. **degree** [dɪˋgri] *n.* 度

C **10.**

Many early American Indians preferred hunting, so they lived primarily on buffalo meat.

(A) barely (B) frequently (C) mainly (D) scarcely

許多早期的美國印第安人偏好打獵，所以他們主要吃水牛肉。

解析

1. 原句劃線的字有下列意思及用法：

   primarily [praɪˋmɛrəlɪ] *adv.* 主要地

   例: Football is primarily a man's sport.

   （美式橄欖球是以男性為主的運動。）

2. (A) **barely** [ˋbɛrlɪ] *adv.* 僅僅；幾乎沒有

   例: I could barely recognize Holly after she put on that stunning dress.

   （荷莉穿上那件令人驚豔的洋裝後，我幾乎認不出她來。）

   * stunning [ˋstʌnɪŋ] *a.* 極美的，令人目瞪口呆的

   (B) **frequently** [ˋfrikwəntlɪ] *adv.* 經常地，頻繁地

   例: Cindy frequently goes hiking in the woods because she loves being outdoors.

   （辛蒂經常去森林裡健行，因為她熱愛戶外。）

   (C) **mainly** [ˋmenlɪ] *adv.* 主要地

   例: The group is made up of mainly young people.

   （這個團體主要是由年輕人組成。）

   (D) **scarcely** [ˋskɛrslɪ] *adv.* 幾乎不，幾乎沒有

   例: Rita could scarcely see anything in the dark room.

   （莉塔在這陰暗的房間內幾乎看不到任何東西。）

3. 根據上述，primarily 與 mainly 同義，故 (C) 項應為正選。

其他重點

1. **live on sth** 以……為食；靠……生存
2. **buffalo** [ˋbʌfl̩ˏo] *n.* 水牛（複數為 buffalo 或 buffaloes）

A **11.**

Marie Curie（居禮夫人）was a magnificent scientist who was the first woman to win the Nobel Prize.

(A) brilliant (B) believable (C) critical (D) commercial

居禮夫人是一位非凡的科學家，她是第一位贏得諾貝爾獎的女性。

解析

1. 原句劃線的字有下列意思及用法：
magnificent [mæg`nɪfəsn̩t] *a.* 極好的；壯觀的
例: We were impressed with the dancer's magnificent performance at the end of the opening ceremony.
（此舞者在開幕典禮結尾的優秀演出讓我們驚艷不已。）
2. (A) **brilliant** [`brɪljənt] *a.* 優秀的；絕妙的；聰明的
例: The brilliant writer has written several award-winning books.
（這位才華洋溢的作家寫了幾本得獎的書。）
(B) **believable** [bɪ`livəbl̩] *a.* 可信的
例: I didn't find Matthew's explanation believable.
（我覺得馬修的解釋並不可信。）
(C) **critical** [`krɪtɪkl̩] *a.* 挑剔的，批判的（常與介詞 of 並用）；關鍵性的
例: Josh is always critical of his wife's cooking.
（喬許老愛挑剔他老婆的廚藝。）
(D) **commercial** [kə`mɝʃəl] *a.* 商業的
例: This image is used for commercial purposes.
（這張照片被用於商業用途。）
3. 根據上述，magnificent 與 brilliant 同義，故 (A) 項應為正選。

其他重點

Nobel Prize 諾貝爾獎
例: The Nobel Prize winner was quite modest about what he had achieved.
（這位諾貝爾獎得主對他的成就相當謙虛。）

II. 對話題

B **12.**

Anderson: Why are you studying English?
Wan-Ting: I hope to study abroad one day, so I need good English.
Anderson: Then what is the most difficult part of learning English?
Wan-Ting: ______________ Native speakers talk so fast that I have problems understanding them.

(A) No problem at all. (B) Probably listening.
(C) The difficulties of living alone. (D) Speaking in my native language.

安德森：妳為何學英文？
婉　婷：我希望有一天能出國念書，所以英文要很好。
安德森：那妳覺得學英文最困難的部分是什麼？
婉　婷：________________ 英文的母語人士講話太快，我沒辦法聽懂。

(A) 一點都不困難。　(B) 可能是聽力吧。
(C) 獨自生活的困難。　(D) 說我的母語。

解析

空格前，安德森詢問 "Then what is the most difficult part of learning English?"（那妳覺得學英文最困難的部分是什麼？），空格後，婉婷回答 "Native speakers talk so fast that I have problems understanding them."（英文的母語人士講話太快，我沒辦法聽懂。），得知婉婷覺得聽力部分最困難，因此 (B) 項應為正選。

其他重點

1. **abroad** [əˋbrɔd] *adv.* 國外地

例: My dream is to study abroad.
（我的夢想是出國念書。）

2. **a native speaker** 母語人士
3. **so... that...** 太……以致於……

例: John was so tired that he could not concentrate on his work.
（約翰太累以致於無法專心工作。）

4. **probably** [ˋprɑbəblɪ] *adv.* 很可能，或許

例: We'll probably be 30 minutes late when we get there.
（我們很可能會晚三十分鐘到那邊。）

B **13.**

Waitress: Lotus Chinese Restaurant.
Customer: Hi, could I order some take-out, please?
Waitress: Sure, what do you want to order?
Customer: Sweet and sour pork, please.
Waitress: ________________
Customer: Um, then I'll have the barbecued duck.

(A) Sure, here you are.　(B) Sorry, we've run out of pork.
(C) Oh no, we don't have any duck.　(D) OK, I'll place the order.

女服務生：蓮花中餐廳。
顧　　客：嗨，請問我可以叫外賣嗎？
女服務生：當然，您想要點什麼？
顧　　客：我要點糖醋排骨，麻煩一下。
女服務生：＿＿＿＿＿＿＿＿
顧　　客：嗯，那我點烤鴨。
(A) 好，這個是您的。　(B) 抱歉，我們豬肉賣完了。
(C) 喔糟糕，我們沒有鴨肉。　(D) 好的，我會為您下單。

解析

空格前，顧客說 "Sweet and sour pork, please."（我要點糖醋排骨，麻煩一下。），空格後，顧客又說 "Um, then I'll have the barbecued duck."（嗯，那我點烤鴨。），得知應該是糖醋排骨賣完了，所以顧客換點別道菜，因此 (B) 項應為正選。

其他重點

1. **lotus** [ˋlotəs] *n.* 蓮花
2. **order** [ˋɔrdɚ] *vt.* 點菜，訂購
   例: I'd like to order some French fries and a Coke.
   （我想要點薯條和一杯可樂。）
3. **take-out** [ˋtekˌaut] *n.* 外賣食物（= takeout）
   例: We'll have take-out for dinner tonight.
   （今晚我們會叫外賣來吃。）
4. **sweet and sour pork**　糖醋排骨
5. **run out of...**　用光……，耗完……
   例: We have run out of gas.
   （我們沒有汽油了。）
6. **place an order**　訂購，下訂單
   例: I'd like to place an order for a bouquet of flowers.
   （我想要訂購一束花。）

A **14.**

Husband: Do you like my new coat?
Wife: It looks great!
Husband: I'm glad you like it.
Wife: ＿＿＿＿＿＿＿＿
Husband: It was on sale, 50% off.
(A) Was it a good deal?　(B) Would you go with me?
(C) What was it made of?　(D) Where will you buy it?

丈夫：妳喜歡我的新外套嗎？
妻子：很好看！
丈夫：很高興妳喜歡。
妻子：＿＿＿＿＿＿＿＿
丈夫：它在特價，打五折。
(A) 價錢划算嗎？　(B) 你要和我一起去嗎？
(C) 這是用什麼做的？　(D) 你要在哪裡買？

解析

空格後，丈夫回答 "It was on sale, 50% off."（它在特價，打五折。），得知妻子在詢問外套的價錢，因此 (A) 項應為正選。

其他重點

1. **on sale**　特價出售

例: The shirt is on sale now. It's 20% off.
（這件襯衫現在特價。打八折。）

比較:
for sale　供出售，待售

例: All of the paintings on display at the exhibit are not for sale.
（畫展上所有展示的畫作都是非賣品。）

2. **數字 + % + off**　打……折
30% off　打七折
60% off　打四折

3. **be a good deal**　是划算的買賣

例: You should buy that guitar because it's a good deal.
（你應該買下那把吉他，因為很划算。）

A **15.**
Ken: Is there a drugstore nearby?
Ann: Just around the corner. Why?
Ken: ＿＿＿＿＿＿＿＿
Ann: Oh, no! What's wrong?
(A) I don't feel well.　(B) I need a birthday cake.
(C) It's not too far, though.　(D) You can pay me later.

肯：這附近有藥妝店嗎？

安：就在轉角。幹嘛？

肯：________

安：喔，糟糕！你怎麼了嗎？

(A) 我不太舒服。 (B) 我要買一個生日蛋糕。

(C) 不過沒有很遠。 (D) 你可以晚點再付錢給我。

解析

本則對話中，一開始肯詢問 "Is there a drugstore nearby?"（這附近有藥妝店嗎？），空格後，安說 "Oh, no! What's wrong?"（喔，糟糕！你怎麼了嗎？），得知肯應該是不太舒服，因此 (A) 項應為正選。

其他重點

1. **drugstore** [ˋdrʌɡˏstɔr] *n.* 藥妝店

   例: The drugstore is open 24 hours a day.
   （這間藥妝店二十四小時營業。）

2. **nearby** [ˋnɪrˏbaɪ] *adv.* 在附近

   例: Is there an ATM nearby where I can withdraw some money?
   （這附近有沒有提款機可以讓我提點錢？）

3. **around the corner** 在轉角處；附近

   例: Hannah likes to go to the coffee shop around the corner.
   （漢娜喜歡去轉角的那家咖啡廳。）

B **16.**

Peter: I'd like to rent a car.

Clerk: Sure. What kind of car do you want?

Peter: Small, 2-door.

Clerk: Here are some 2-door small cars.

Peter: ________

Clerk: It's NT$5,000.

(A) How is the condition? (B) What's the weekly rate?

(C) How many people does it take? (D) Are 2-door cars more powerful?

彼得：我想要租車。

店員：好的。您想要哪種車？

彼得：兩門小型車。

店員：這一邊是兩門小型車。

彼得：________

店員：新臺幣五千元。

(A) 車況如何？　　(B) 每週租金多少？

(C) 可以載多少人？　　(D) 兩門車是否更有力？

解析

空格後，店員回答 "It's NT$5,000."（新臺幣五千元。），得知彼得在詢問費用，因此 (B) 項應為正選。

其他重點

1. **rent** [rɛnt] *vt.* 租借；出租

例: I rent an apartment from Mr. Wang at NT$26,000 a month.
（我向王先生租了一間公寓，每月新臺幣兩萬六千元。）

2. **condition** [kənˋdɪʃən] *n.* 狀況；條件

be in good / poor condition　　情況不錯 / 不佳

例: The second-hand car is still in good condition.
（這臺二手車的車況仍維持得不錯。）

3. **rate** [ret] *n.* 費用，價格

例: What is the rate for the honeymoon package?
（蜜月套裝行程的價格是多少？）

B **17.**

Ling: Do you want me to send you some pineapple cakes? They're terrific desserts.

Holly: That's great. I really like pineapple cakes.

Ling: ________

Holly: I agree. So, why don't you send me two bags of Oolong tea as well?

(A) I prefer coffee to tea.　　(B) It goes very well with tea.

(C) When is pineapple season?　　(D) Do you need any other desserts?

玲：妳要我寄點鳳梨酥給妳嗎？它們是很棒的甜點唷。
荷莉：太好了。我很喜歡鳳梨酥。
玲：＿＿＿＿＿＿＿
荷莉：我同意。那妳何不也寄兩包烏龍茶給我？
(A) 我喜歡咖啡勝過茶。　(B) 它配茶很好。
(C) 鳳梨季是何時？　(D) 妳需要其他甜點嗎？

解析

空格後，荷莉回答 "I agree. So, why don't you send me two bags of Oolong tea as well?"（我同意。那妳何不也寄兩包烏龍茶給我？），得知玲提到關於茶的事情，(A)、(B) 項皆與茶有關，惟置入 (A) 項後語意不連貫，因此 (B) 項應為正選。

其他重點

1. **a pineapple cake**　鳳梨酥
2. **terrific** [təˋrɪfɪk] *a.* 很棒的
   例: The restaurant on the corner serves terrific food.
   （轉角那間餐廳的餐點棒極了。）
3. **dessert** [dɪˋzɝt] *n.* 甜點
   例: What are we having for dessert?
   （我們甜點要吃什麼？）
4. **Oolong tea**　烏龍茶
5. **as well**　也；還有
   例: Japanese food is not only delicious, but it has visual appeal as well.
   （日本食物不但好吃，視覺上也同樣誘人。）
6. **prefer A to B**　喜歡 A 勝過 B
   例: Jack prefers playing the guitar to playing the drums.
   （傑克喜歡彈吉他勝過打鼓。）
7. **go with...**　與……相配
   例: I'm looking for a pair of heels to go with this dress.
   （我在找一雙和這件洋裝搭配的高跟鞋。）

C **18.**
Ms. Chen: Pam, ＿＿＿＿＿＿＿＿?
Pam: I work for Smart Computers. I'm a sales representative for Japan and Singapore.
Ms. Chen: Oh, international sales representative. How do you like that?
Pam: It's a great job. I like to travel, and like to work with people from other countries.
(A) are you looking for a local job　(B) did you compute your travel cost
(C) would you tell us about what you do　(D) can you tell me when you got the job

陳小姐：潘，________？

潘：我在智慧電腦工作。我是日本和新加坡地區的業務員。

陳小姐：喔，跨國業務員。你喜歡嗎？

潘：這是個很不錯的工作。我喜歡旅行，也喜歡和其他國家的人一起工作。

(A) 你在找當地的工作嗎　　(B) 你算過你的旅費了嗎

(C) 可以告訴我們你的工作嗎　　(D) 可以告訴我你何時得到這工作的嗎

解析

空格後，潘回答 "I work for Smart Computers. I'm a sales representative for Japan and Singapore."（我在智慧電腦工作。我是日本和新加坡地區的業務員。），得知陳小姐在詢問潘的工作內容，因此 (C) 項應為正選。

其他重點

1. **representative** [ˌrɛprɪˋzɛntətɪv] *n.* 代表者
   a sales representative　業務員，銷售代表
2. **look for...**　尋找……
   例: Andy has spent an hour looking for the pen he had lost.
   （安迪已經花了一個小時尋找他弄丟的筆。）
3. **compute** [kəmˋpjut] *vt.*（用電腦）計算
   例: Make sure these figures are accurately computed, or we could invite trouble.
   （這些數據務必要精確計算，否則我們可能會招來麻煩。）
4. **cost** [kɔst] *n.* 費用
   at a cost of + 金錢　成本……錢
   例: Harry bought that book at a cost of NT$300.
   （哈利花了新臺幣三百元買那本書。）

C **19.**

Peter: Fanny, I got it!
Fanny: What?
Peter: The jewelry job!
Fanny: Oh my God! I'm talking with a jewelry designer! Congratulations!
Peter: ________ Pick a restaurant. It's my treat.

(A) Are you kidding?　　(B) It's so easy for you.

(C) Let's go celebrate.　　(D) How did you make it?

彼得：芬妮，我中了！
芬妮：什麼？
彼得：那個珠寶的工作！
芬妮：喔天啊！我在跟珠寶設計師說話耶！恭喜！
彼得：＿＿＿＿＿＿＿＿ 餐廳妳選。我請客。
(A) 妳在開玩笑嗎？ (B) 對妳來說太簡單了。
(C) 我們去慶祝一下吧。 (D) 妳怎麼做到的？

解析

空格後，彼得說 "Pick a restaurant. It's my treat."（餐廳妳選。我請客。），得知彼得要找芬妮一起慶祝，因此 (C) 項應為正選。

其他重點

1. **jewelry** [ˋdʒuəlrɪ] *n.* 珠寶（不可數）
2. **my treat** 我請客
   例: It's my treat today.
   （今天我請客。）
3. **make it** 成功
   例: You'll make it as long as you keep working hard.
   （只要你不斷努力，就會成功。）

D **20.**

Doctor: Good morning, Mr. Lee. How are you feeling today?
Mr. Lee: Not very well. I always feel tired, but when I go to bed, I can't sleep.
Doctor: That's too bad. How long have you had this problem for?
Mr. Lee: ＿＿＿＿＿＿＿＿ I am in advertising, and work about 80 hours a week.
Doctor: You are overworked! You need to relax.
(A) Many times. (B) Once in a while.
(C) As long as you help me. (D) Since I started my new job.

醫　生：早安，李先生。今天感覺還好嗎？
李先生：不太好。我一直覺得累，但當我要睡覺時又睡不著。
醫　生：真糟糕。這個問題持續多久了？
李先生：＿＿＿＿＿＿＿＿ 我在廣告業工作，一個禮拜大概工作八十個小時。
醫　生：你工作過度了！你需要休息。
(A) 很多次。 (B) 偶爾。
(C) 只要你幫我。 (D) 自從我開始了新的工作。

解析

空格前，醫生詢問 "How long have you had this problem for?"（這個問題持續多久了？），空格後，李先生回答 "I am in advertising, and work about 80 hours a week."（我在廣告業工作，一個禮拜大概工作八十個小時。），得知空格應置能呼應醫生的問題，並需與空格後提及的工作相呼應，因此 (D) 項應為正選。

其他重點

1. **advertising** [ˋædvɚˏtaɪzɪŋ] *n.* 廣告業
2. **overworked** [ˏovɚˋwɝkt] *a.* 工作過度的

   例: They are overworked because the company is understaffed.
   （他們工作超量，因為公司缺人。）
3. **once in a while** 偶爾

   例: Once in a while, my brother goes to the movies with us.
   （我哥偶爾和我們去看電影。）
4. **as long as...** 只要……

   例: As long as you perform well at the company, you'll have a lot of opportunities for promotion.
   （只要你在公司表現良好，你會有很多升遷的機會。）

C **21.**

Teacher: Why are your class scores always so bad?

Johnny: Because... I always sleep in class, Sir.

Teacher: ______________

Johnny: That's right, Sir. This is something I won't do again.

(A) Maybe you should sleep more at home.

(B) You should try and fail the next test, too.

(C) Do you stay up playing games every night?

(D) Why don't you try to study more at home?

老師：為何你在班上的成績總是那麼糟？

強尼：因為……我上課時老是睡著，老師。

老師：______________

強尼：是的，老師。我不會再這樣了。

(A) 也許你在家裡應該多睡一點。　(B) 你應該試試下一次考試也考不及格。

(C) 你是不是每晚都熬夜打電動？　(D) 你為什麼不試著在家多念點書？

解析

空格前，強尼說 "I always sleep in class,..."（我上課時老是睡著，……），空格後，強尼回答 "That's right, Sir. This is something I won't do again."（是的，老師。我不會再這樣了。），得知老師是在詢問強尼是否做了某件負面的事，因此 (C) 項應為正選。

其他重點

1. **score** [skɔr] *n.* 成績，分數

   例: Do you know what your TOEFL score is?
   （你知道自己托福的成績嗎？）

2. **stay up + V-ing** 熬夜
   = stay up to V

   例: James stayed up all night studying English.
   （詹姆士整晚熬夜讀英文。）

III. 綜合測驗

◎ 22 - 26

When traveling abroad, it is always important to follow the local customs. Here are some tips to make sure you don't upset someone on your travels. For example, if you have dinner at a friend's house in Germany, be polite enough to eat everything, __22__ the host will think you didn't enjoy the meal. In Korea, while taking public transport, passengers should always keep quiet. Being noisy __23__ to be very rude. When visiting Saudi Arabia, be sure to eat with your right hand because most people there use their left hand for the bathroom. In Pakistan, you don't want to be __24__. This is because guests are expected to be fifteen minutes late for a meal. __25__, if you are visiting a friend's house in Denmark, don't be late. People in Denmark think it is impolite to be late. With so many different customs __26__ the world, it is impossible to know them all. If you mistakenly upset someone, make sure to say sorry.

22. (A) and (B) but (C) or (D) so

23. (A) considers (B) is considered (C) has considered (D) had been considering

24. (A) at a time (B) for all time (C) in time (D) on time

25. (A) Consequently (B) Similarly (C) By far (D) In contrast

26. (A) around (B) beyond (C) during (D) under

到國外旅遊時，遵循當地習俗向來是很重要的。這裡提供一些小祕訣，確保你在旅程中不會惹毛某些人。例如到德國的朋友家吃晚餐時，要把所有東西吃光才算誠意滿點，否則主人會認為你不喜歡那頓飯。在韓國搭乘大眾運輸時，乘客應保持安靜，吵鬧會被視為非常沒規矩。到沙烏地阿拉伯旅遊時，務必用右手吃東西，因為大多數當地人的左手是上廁所時用的。在巴基斯坦，建議你不要準時，因為飯局時客人們被預期要遲到十五分鐘。相對地，如果你到丹麥的朋友家拜訪，切勿遲到。丹麥人認為遲到是不禮貌的。由於世界各地有各式各樣的習俗，要全部都了解是不可能的。如果你弄錯而惹毛了別人，請務必道歉。

C **22.**

解析

1. 空格前後為兩個句構完整的子句，得知空格應置連接詞以連接兩子句。
2. 四個選項皆可作連接詞，惟 (A) and（和）、(B) but（但是）、(D) so（因此）置入後不符語意，僅 (C) or（否則）置入後符合語意，可知 (C) 項應為正選。

B **23.**

解析

1. 本題測試以下固定用法：

   A be considered (to be) B A 被認為是 B

   consider [kənˋsɪdɚ] *vt.* 把……視為……；考慮

   例: The Taj Mahal is considered to be one of the greatest wonders of the world.
   （泰姬瑪哈陵被視為世界上最偉大的奇蹟之一。）
2. 由文章內容敘述到各國應遵循的習俗，可知本題時態應使用現在式描述一般事實。
3. 根據上述，(B) 項應為正選。

D **24.**

解析

1. (A) **at a time** 一次

   例: The waiter can deliver six plates of food at a time.
   （那名侍者可以一次端出六盤菜。）

   (B) **for all time** 一直，總是

   例: Michael Jackson will be the King of Pop for all time.
   （麥可．傑克森將永遠是流行樂之王。）

   (C) **in time** 及時

   例: My father usually comes home in time to cook dinner for us.
   （我爸通常會及時回家給我們做晚飯。）

   (D) **on time** 準時

   例: The team members labored through the night trying to finish the project on time.
   （團隊成員連夜趕工，想準時完成專案。）

2. 根據語意，(D) 項應為正選。

D **25.**

解析

1. (A) **consequently** [ˋkɑnsə͵kwɛntlɪ] *adv.* 因此，所以

   例: Connie works late every day. Consequently, she is always exhausted when she gets home.
   （康妮每天都工作到很晚。因此她回到家時總是精疲力竭。）

   (B) **similarly** [ˋsɪmɪlɚlɪ] *adv.* 同樣地

   例: John wore red and white yesterday, and his girlfriend was similarly dressed.
   （約翰昨天穿紅白色系，而他的女友也穿得很類似。）

   (C) **by far** [͵baɪ ˋfɑr] 大幅度地（強調語氣用，常修飾比較級或最高級形容詞或副詞）

   例: Man is by far the most dangerous animal that has ever walked the earth.
   （人類是歷來生存在地球上最最危險的動物。）

   (D) **in contrast** [͵ɪn ˋkɑntræst] 相形之下，相對地
   in contrast to... 與……形成對比

   例: The North is cool and wet. In contrast, the South is hot and dry.
   （北部涼爽而潮溼。相對地，南部炎熱而乾燥。）

In contrast to the past, people nowadays are less willing to get married and have children.
（與過去形成明顯對比的是，現在的人比較不願結婚生子。）

2. 根據語意，(D) 項應為正選。

A **26.**

解析

1. 本題測試以下固定用法：

around the world 在世界各地
= all over the world

例: Wikipedia is an online encyclopedia completely written and edited by people around the world.
（維基百科是線上百科全書，由世界各地的人編寫而成。）

2. 根據上述用法，(A) 項應為正選。

重要單字片語

1. **upset** [ʌpˋsɛt] *vt.* 使難過，使生氣 & *a.* 難過的，生氣的

   例: The fact that Tim's company is going to shut down really upsets him.
   （提姆的公司即將倒閉一事讓他心煩意亂。）

2. **travels** [ˋtrævl̩z] *n.*（到遠方的）旅行（恆為複數）

   例: Tony entertained his guests with stories of his travels abroad.
   （東尼講述他到海外旅遊的見聞以娛佳賓。）

3. **public transport** [ˋpʌblɪk ˋtræns͵pɔrt] 大眾運輸

4. **passenger** [ˋpæsn̩dʒɚ] *n.* 乘客

   例: Several passengers were injured during the bumpy flight.
   （好幾名乘客在顛簸的飛行途中受傷。）

5. **be expected to + V** 被預期／計……

   例: The mayor is expected to resign due to the financial scandal.
   （市長被預期因此財務醜聞而辭職。）

6. **mistakenly** [mɪsˋtekənlɪ] *adv.* 錯誤地

   例: In the story, the hunter mistakenly took the dog for a fox and almost shot it.
   （故事中，這個獵人誤把這隻狗當成狐狸而差點射殺牠。）

◎ 27 - 31

The eastern part of Taiwan is a place of natural beauty. However, it is also an area __27__ earthquakes occur very often. The government has recently completed work on an undersea cable system to detect earthquakes and tsunamis. The system makes it possible for people __28__ about 10 seconds before an earthquake strikes. The purpose is to reduce __29__ and injuries. Starting in 2011, cables were put under the sea on the east coast. The location was chosen __30__ most of the earthquakes happen there. The undersea cable system stretches for 735 km, with nine points __31__ its entire length to detect the quakes. The deepest detection point lies 5,554 m under the sea.

27. (A) when (B) where (C) which (D) whose

28. (A) are warned (B) to warn (C) to be warned (D) will be warned

29. (A) dies (B) dead (C) deadly (D) deaths

30. (A) if (B) till (C) unless (D) because

31. (A) along (B) during (C) except (D) since

臺灣東部是擁有自然美景的地方，但也是經常發生地震的區域。政府最近完成了海底電纜系統的建置，以偵測地震和海嘯。這個系統讓人們得以在地震發生前十秒左右得到預警。其目的為降低傷亡人數。自 2011 年開始，電纜被布建於東海岸的海底。選擇這個地點是因為大部分的地震發生在這裡。此海底電纜系統長達七百三十五公里，沿線設有九個觀測點來偵測地震。最深的觀測點位於海底五千五百五十四公尺處。

B **27.**

解析

1. 空格前為表地方的名詞 area（區域），且空格後為一完整子句，故得知空格應置關係副詞 where，使其引導的形容詞子句可用以修飾 area。
2. 根據上述，得知 (B) 項應為正選。
3. (A) when 亦可作關係副詞，但其所引導的形容詞子句只用於修飾表時間的名詞；(C) which 為關係代名詞，若置空格，需在其前加上介詞 in；(D) whose 為關係代名詞所有格，故上述三項皆不可選。

C 28.

解析

1. 本題測試下列固定用法：
   make it possible for sb/sth to V 讓某人／某事物可以……
   例: Your timely help made it possible for me to finish the work on time.
   （你及時的幫助讓我得以準時完工。）
2. 再根據語意，空格處應使用被動語態，故得知 (C) 項應為正選。

D 29.

解析

1. 空格後有對等連接詞 and 及複數名詞 injuries（傷害），得知空格應置名詞，使 and 連接的是兩個對等名詞。
2. (A) **die** [daɪ] *vi.* 死亡（三態為：die, died [daɪd], died）
   die of... 死於（疾病等）
   例: Our dog died of cancer and was buried in the backyard.
   （我們的狗死於癌症，被埋在後院。）
   (B) **dead** [dɛd] *a.* 死亡的 & *adv.* 完全地 & *n.* 死者
   the dead 死者（視為複數）
   例: After the water receded, Ron found a dead whale on the beach.
   （退潮之後，榮恩發現海灘上有一隻死鯨魚。）
   You are dead wrong to think that Eric doesn't care about you.
   （你若認為艾瑞克不關心你，那就大錯特錯了。）
   (C) **deadly** [ˋdɛdlɪ] *a.* 致命的 & *adv.* 非常，極其
   例: After the outbreak of COVID-19, millions of people fell victim to the deadly virus.
   （新冠疫情爆發後，數百萬人成為此致命病毒的犧牲者。）
   Lillian found the party deadly boring and wanted to leave.
   （莉莉安覺得這場派對無聊極了，想要離開。）
   (D) **death** [dɛθ] *n.* 死亡
   例: I felt sad over the death of my pet dog.
   （我的寵物狗死掉後，我很難過。）
3. 根據上述，(D) 項應為正選。

D **30.**

解析

1. 空格前為一完整子句，空格後亦為一完整子句，故知空格應置連接詞連接兩個完整子句。
2. 四個選項皆可作連接詞。(A) if 表「如果；是否」；(B) till 表「直到」；(C) unless 表「除非」；(D) because 表「因為」，根據語意，得知 (D) 項應為正選。

A **31.**

解析

1. 空格應置介詞來表明 nine points（九個觀測點）與 its entire length（沿線）之間的關係。
2. 四個選項皆可作介詞。(A) along 表「沿著」；(B) during 表「在……期間」；(C) except 表「除……之外」；(D) since 表「自從（某時間點）以來」，根據語意，得知 (A) 項應為正選。

重要單字片語

1. **undersea** [ˌʌndɚˋsi] *a.* 海底的
2. **cable** [ˋkebl̩] *n.* 纜線；電纜
3. **detect** [dɪˋtɛkt] *vt.* 發現，察覺
   例: Once the sensors detect any poisonous gas, they will set off the alarm automatically.
   （感應器一旦偵測到任何有毒氣體，就會自動啟動警報器。）
4. **tsunami** [tsuˋnɑmi] *n.* 海嘯
5. **strike** [straɪk] *vi.* & *vt.*（災難、疾病等）突然發生／侵襲
   例: Disasters often strike when you least expect them.
   （災難常在你最意想不到的時候來襲。）
6. **reduce** [rɪˋd(j)us] *vt.* & *vi.* 降低，減少
   例: We should avoid using disposable tableware to reduce waste.
   （我們應避免使用拋棄式餐具以減少垃圾量。）
7. **location** [loˋkeʃən] *n.* 地點，位置
8. **stretch** [strɛtʃ] *vi.*（距離）延伸
   例: The iceberg stretched a few hundred kilometers.
   （這座冰山綿延數百公里。）
9. **quake** [kwek] *n.* 地震
   （= earthquake [ˋɝθˌkwek]）
10. **detection** [dɪˋtɛkʃən] *n.* 發覺，偵測（不可數）

IV. 閱讀測驗

◎ 32 - 33

The notice below is a guideline for tourists in a national park — "Leave No Trace". Read the notice and answer the following questions.

LEAVE NO TRACE Travel Principles	
	PLAN AHEAD Know the regulations of the places you're visiting
	RESPECT WILDLIFE Do not approach wildlife
	LOOK WITH YOUR EYES, NOT WITH YOUR HANDS Admire cultural / historic objects at a distance and follow paths
	WHAT YOU FIND STAYS BEHIND Shells and sand stay on the beach; fruit, wood, and seeds should be left to keep trees healthy
	WASTE & RECYCLING Learn local recycling and waste laws, ask if unsure
	BE CONSIDERATE OF OTHER VISITORS Keep noise to a minimum; allow everyone a turn to admire the sights at viewing points or platforms

以下告示為造訪國家公園的遊客必須遵循的準則 ——「無痕運動」。請閱讀告示並回答以下問題。

無痕運動 旅遊準則	
	事前規劃 了解你即將造訪之場所的規範
	尊重野生動物 勿靠近野生動物
	動眼不動手 觀賞文物／史蹟時保持距離，並遵循步道路線
	發現的物品請勿帶走 貝殼及沙請留沙灘上；水果、木頭及種子都應留置以保護樹木健康
	丟棄及回收 了解當地的回收及廢棄物處理法，不確定者可詢問
	體貼其他遊客 將噪音音量降到最低；讓每個人都有機會在景點或觀景平臺上欣賞美景

A **32.**

Which of the following is **NOT** encouraged by the travel principles?

(A) Collect shells on the beach.

(B) Speak quietly to your friends.

(C) Understand the rules and regulations.

(D) Take pictures of birds from far away.

旅遊準則不鼓勵下列何種行為？

(A) 拿走沙灘上的貝殼。

(B) 跟朋友輕聲說話。

(C) 了解規則及規範。

(D) 從遠處拍攝鳥兒照片。

理由:

由第四項："Shells and sand stay on the beach; fruit, wood, and seeds should be left to keep trees healthy"（貝殼及沙請留沙灘上；水果、木頭及種子都應留置以保護樹木健康）得知，(A) 項應為正選。

C **33.**

What do the travel principles probably want visitors to do?

(A) To study law in order to reach wildlife

(B) To allow everyone to express their views

(C) To keep nature the same as much as possible

(D) To clean their hands before touching anything

旅遊準則可能希望遊客怎麼做？

(A) 研讀法律以便接觸野生動物

(B) 讓每個人表達自己的觀點

(C) 盡可能維護大自然原貌

(D) 碰觸任何東西前先洗手

理由:

本告示中的第三至第五項之準則意指遊客遊玩大自然時，如何能夠做到不破壞大自然，故 (C) 項應為正選。

重要單字片語

1. **guideline** [ˋgaɪd͵laɪn] *n.* 行動綱領；指導原則（常用複數）

   例: The guidelines will give you a good idea of what you're supposed to do.
   （這些指導方針可以讓你清楚知道該怎麼做。）

2. **tourist** [ˋturɪst] *n.* 遊客
3. **trace** [tres] *n.* 蹤跡

   without a trace　　無影無蹤

   例: The plane flew into the Bermuda Triangle and disappeared without a trace.
   （這架飛機飛進百慕達三角洲，然後就消失無蹤。）

4. **regulation** [͵rɛgjəˋleʃən] *n.* 規定，法規

   例: A good student should obey school regulations.
   （好學生應遵守校規。）

5. **wildlife** [ˋwaɪld͵laɪf] *n.* 野生動物
6. **admire** [ədˋmaɪr] *vt.* 欣賞；欽佩

   admire sb for + N/V-ing　　欽佩某人……

   例: I admire Alison for her confidence and charm.
   （我很欣賞艾莉森的自信與魅力。）

7. **historic** [hɪsˋtɔrɪk] *a.* 歷史上著名的

   似: historical [hɪsˋtɔrɪkḷ] *a.* 有關歷史的

   例: The fall of the Berlin Wall was a historic moment.
   （柏林圍牆的倒場是歷史性的一刻。）
   Many historical documents were destroyed during the war.
   （許多歷史紀錄都在戰爭中被摧毀了。）

8. **recycling** [͵riˋsaɪklɪŋ] *n.* 回收（物）（不可數）
9. **considerate** [kənˋsɪdərɪt] *a.* 體貼的

   It is considerate of sb to V　某人體貼地（做某事）

   例: It is considerate of you to turn down the volume of the TV at night.
   （你在晚上調低電視的音量真是善體人意。）

10. **minimum** [ˋmɪnəməm] *n.* 最少量

    反: maximum [ˋmæksəməm] *n.* 最大量

    a minimum / maximum of + 數字　至少 / 最多……

    例: This type of rum contains a minimum of 50 percent alcohol by volume.
    （這款蘭姆酒包含最少百分之五十的酒精含量。）

◎ 34 - 35

Read the following job advertisements from the classified section of the website. Then answer the questions based on the given information.

(A) Auto Mechanic	(B) Hiring dependable helper
Goodcar dealership has openings for certified mechanics. Pay based on ability. Range from $160 to $200 per hour. Benefits include uniforms, health care, paid vacations. Call 06-5893642	Mature capable person to work on standard bred horse farm. General maintenance & farm work. Health care & housing provided. Call 08-7769521
(C) Want a career in real estate?	**(D) Food delivery on wheels**
No experience needed. We offer a training program for employees on how to sell land and buildings. Come in person to the main office of Royal Estate, 33 Lily Rd., Taipei. Come between 11 a.m. & 5 p.m.	No experience needed. Have motorcycle with driver license. $160/hr. Health care provided. Email: foodonwheels111@mail2.com

請閱讀以下網站分類廣告版面上的徵人廣告。並根據內容回答問題。

(A) 汽車技師	(B) 招募可靠助手
好車經銷商正招募有證照的技師。依能力計酬。時薪一百六十元至兩百元。福利含制服、健保、有薪假等。 請電 06-5893642	幹練的成年人，於標準的種馬場工作。一般維護工作與牧場日常工作。供健保及住宿。請電 08-7769521
(C) 想找不動產工作嗎？	**(D) 機車送餐服務**
無經驗可。我們提供員工銷售土地與房產的訓練課程。請親洽臺北市百合路 33 號皇家不動產總部。請於上午十一點至下午五點間前來。	無經驗可。有機車及駕照。時薪一百六十元。供健保。 電子郵件： foodonwheels111@mail2.com

B **34.**

Ju-Yi is graduating from the Animal Science Department. She wants to find a job with a place to stay. Which job advertisement is she most likely to be interested in?

(A) A
(B) B
(C) C
(D) D

朱依將從動物科學系畢業。她想要找份有地方住的工作。她最有興趣的可能是哪一則徵人廣告？

(A) A
(B) B
(C) C
(D) D

理由:
根據第二項廣告的第三句 "Health care & housing provided."（供健保住宿。）得知，(B) 項應為正選。

B **35.**

Ming-Hua is interested in becoming a house seller. What should he do to apply for the job?

(A) Call 06-5893642.
(B) Visit Royal Estate.
(C) Email foodonwheels111@mail2.com.
(D) Mail the resume to 33 Lily Rd., Taipei.

明華有意成為房屋銷售員。他應該做什麼來應徵該職務？

(A) 致電 06-5893642。
(B) 親至皇家不動產。
(C) 寄電子郵件至 foodonwheels111@mail2.com。
(D) 郵寄履歷至臺北市百合路 33 號。

理由:
根據第三項廣告的第三句 "Come in person to the main office of Royal Estate, 33 Lily Rd., Taipei."（請親洽臺北市百合路 33 號皇家不動產總部。）得知，(B) 項應為正選。

重要單字片語

1. **advertisement** [ˌædvɚˋtaɪzmənt] *n.* 廣告，宣傳（通常縮寫為 ad [æd]）
2. **classified** [ˋklæsɪˌfaɪd] *a.* 分類的
   a classified catalogue　分類產品目錄
3. **dealership** [ˋdilɚˌʃɪp] *n.*（尤指汽車的）經銷商／店
4. **certified** [ˋsɝtɪˌfaɪd] *a.* 有證書的；合格的
   a certified nurse　有執照的護士
5. **mature** [məˋtjʊr] *a.* 成熟的
   immature [ˌɪməˋtjʊr] *a.* 不成熟的
   例: Susan is mature physically, but she is still immature mentally.
   （蘇珊生理上雖已成熟，但心理仍未成熟。）

6. **maintenance** [ˋmentənəns] *n.* 維護，保養（不可數）
7. **real estate** [ˋriəl ɪˏstet] *n.* 不動產
8. **in person** 親自

例: I'd like to speak with you in person about your son.
（我想親自和你談一談關於你兒子的事。）

9. **graduate** [ˋgrædʒuˏet] *vi.* 畢業
graduate from... 從……畢業

例: Lisa found a job soon after she graduated from college.
（麗莎大學畢業後沒多久就找到工作。）

10. **apply** [əˋplaɪ] *vi.* 申請
apply for + 事物 申請（入學許可、護照、簽證、獎學金等）

例: I'd like to apply for a job. Do you have any openings here?
（我想求職。您這裡有職缺嗎？）

◎ 36 - 38

In 2020, the United Nations World Food Program (WFP) was awarded the Nobel Peace Prize for its efforts to fight hunger, to help bring about peace, and to prevent the use of hunger as a weapon of war. The WFP focuses its work on hunger and food security issues. In 1962, the organization shipped wheat, sugar and tea to Iran after an earthquake killed 12,000 people. Since then, it has been helping victims of natural disasters.

Other areas of work include the school meals program which covered about 17 million children in 2019. The WFP believes that food security and peace **go hand in hand**. The world cannot end hunger without putting an end to conflict. In 2010, the WFP successfully resolved a conflict situation in Central Asia. Several villages on the border of two countries were quarreling over water resources. The WFP helped to rebuild water supply systems which were shared across borders and provided food for people who joined in the construction.

In 2017, millions of people in the Arab country of Yemen were close to starving in the war between rival groups. Some of these groups cut off food supplies to cause fear in the population. However, WFP workers managed to bring wheat flour to people in need, preventing the use of hunger as a weapon of war. About 100 million people received WFP food assistance in 2020. By winning the Nobel Prize, the WFP hopes that it will draw attention to the problem of hunger.

在 2020 年，聯合國世界糧食計畫署（WFP）獲得諾貝爾和平獎，以表彰其對抗飢餓、協助帶來和平，以及防止將飢餓作為戰爭手段的努力。世界糧食計畫署的工作重點在於飢餓和糧食安全問題。1962 年，伊朗發生地震造成一萬兩千人死亡，該組織運送了小麥、糖和茶葉到伊朗。自此該組織就一直在幫助天災受害者。

其他工作範圍包括光在 2019 年就造福了約一千七百萬名孩童的學校供餐計畫。世界糧食計畫署認為糧食安全與和平是息息相關的。這世界若不終止衝突，就無法消除飢餓。2010 年，它成功化解了中亞的衝突局勢。中亞某兩國邊境的幾個村莊當時正為了水源而爭執。世界糧食計畫署幫忙重建跨境共用的供水系統，還為參與建設的人提供了食物。

在 2017 年，阿拉伯國家葉門的敵對團體之間交戰，致使數百萬人瀕臨餓死。其中某些組織切斷糧食補給以製造民眾恐懼。但世界糧食計畫署的工作人員成功將小麥麵粉帶給有需要的人，防止飢餓成為戰爭的手段。在 2020 年，大約有一億人接受了世界糧食計畫署的糧食援助。世界糧食計畫署希望能藉由贏得諾貝爾獎，來讓大家關注飢餓問題。

B **36.**

Why was the 2020 Nobel Peace Prize given to the WFP?

(A) For putting an end to war and natural disasters
(B) For protecting people from hunger and conflicts
(C) For preventing the use of hunger and weapons in war
(D) For persuading people to welcome food aid and conflicts

為什麼 2020 年的諾貝爾和平獎頒給世界糧食計畫署？

(A) 因為它終結了戰爭和天災
(B) 因為它保護人們免受飢餓和衝突
(C) 因為它防止在戰爭中使用飢餓與武器
(D) 因為它說服人們歡迎糧食援助和衝突

理由:
根據本文第一段第一句 "In 2020, the United Nations World Food Program (WFP) was awarded the Nobel Peace Prize for its efforts to fight hunger, to help bring about peace, and to prevent the use of hunger as a weapon of war."（在 2020 年，聯合國世界糧食計畫署（WFP）獲得諾貝爾和平獎，以表彰其對抗飢餓、協助帶來和平，以及防止將飢餓作為戰爭手段的努力。）得知，(B) 項應為正選。

D **37.**

Which of the following is closest in meaning to "**go hand in hand**" in the second paragraph?

(A) need hard work
(B) need real action
(C) are available
(D) are connected

下列哪一項意思最貼近第二段中的「息息相關」？
(A) 需要努力工作
(B) 需要實際行動
(C) 可以取得
(D) 有關聯

理由:
根據本文第二段第三句 "The world cannot end hunger without putting an end to conflict."（這世界若不終止衝突，就無法消除飢餓。），可推知世界糧食計畫署認為糧食安全與和平是「有關聯的」，故 (D) 項應為正選。

C **38.**

According to the passage, which statement is true?

(A) About 17 million children worked for their school meals.
(B) Groups fighting in Yemen managed to receive wheat flour.
(C) In Central Asia, the WFP ended a conflict through cooperation.
(D) The WFP donated food to 12,000 victims in the Iran earthquake.

根據本文，哪一項陳述為真？
(A) 大約有一千七百萬名孩童為了要付學校的膳食費而去工作。
(B) 在葉門打仗的數個團體成功獲得小麥麵粉。
(C) 在中亞，世界糧食計畫署透過合作而終止了一場衝突。
(D) 世界糧食計畫署捐贈糧食給一萬兩千名伊朗地震災民。

理由:
根據本文第二段最後三句 "In 2010, the WFP successfully resolved a conflict situation in Central Asia. Several villages on the border of two countries were quarreling over water resources. The WFP helped to rebuild water supply systems which were shared across borders and provided food for people who joined in the construction."(2010 年，它成功化解了中亞的衝突局勢。中亞某兩國邊境的幾個村莊當時正為了水源而爭執。世界糧食計畫署幫忙重建跨境共用的供水系統，還為參與建設的人提供了食物。）得知，(C) 項應為正選。

重要單字片語

1. **award** [ə`wɔrd] *vt.* 頒發 & *n.* 獎（金／品）
   award sb sth　頒發某物給某人
   例: To Rita's amazement, the organization awarded her a scholarship.
   （此組織頒給麗塔獎學金，讓她頗為驚訝。）
2. **hunger** [`hʌŋgɚ] *n.* 飢餓
3. **bring about sth**　引起某事物
   例: Technology has brought about major changes in our lives.
   （科技為我們的生活帶來重大改變。）
4. **prevent** [prɪ`vɛnt] *vt.* 防／阻止
   prevent... from + V-ing　防／阻止……做……
   例: Drinking ginger tea every day could prevent you from feeling cold.
   （每天喝薑茶可以預防身體感到寒冷。）
5. **weapon** [`wɛpən] *n.* 武器
6. **security** [sɪ`kjurətɪ] *n.* 安全
7. **issue** [`ɪʃu] *n.* 問題，議題
8. **victim** [`vɪktəm] *n.* 受害者
9. **disaster** [dɪ`zæstɚ] *n.* 災難，災禍
10. **go hand in hand**　息息相關的
    例: Crime and poverty go hand in hand.
    （犯罪與貧窮是息息相關的。）
11. **put an end to sth**　終止某事物
    例: After work, Walter liked to have a massage because he thought it would put an end to his tiredness.
    （下班後，華特喜歡去按摩，因為他認為這樣可以消除疲勞。）
12. **resolve** [rɪ`zalv] *vt.* 消除，解決
    resolve a conflict　消弭／解決衝突
13. **quarrel** [`kwɔrəl] *vi.* & *n.* 爭吵
    quarrel over...　為……爭吵
    例: Teddy told me his parents always quarreled over money.
    （泰迪告訴我，他的父母總是為了錢爭吵。）
14. **rival** [`raɪvl̩] *n.* 敵手
15. **supplies** [sə`plaɪz] *n.* 補給（品），生活必需品（恆用複數）
16. **in need**　有困難的，貧困的
17. **assistance** [ə`sɪstəns] *n.* 援助
18. **draw attention to sth**　吸引人關注某事物
    例: The movie was well received and drew attention to the problem of child abuse.
    （這部電影廣受歡迎，也讓大家關注到虐童的問題。）
19. **persuade** [pɚ`swed] *vt.* 說服
20. **paragraph** [`pærə͵græf] *n.* 段落
21. **cooperation** [ko͵apə`reʃən] *n.* 合作
22. **donate** [`donet / do`net] *vt.* & *vi.* 捐助
    donate A to B　捐 A 給 B
    例: Natasha donated some money to the local charity every month.
    （娜塔莎每月都會捐一些錢給當地的慈善機構。）

◎ 39 - 41

Imagine getting into your car, speaking a location into your car's computer, and then letting it drive you to your destination. The idea behind self-driving cars is fairly simple: build a car with a computer that is connected with[註3] many cameras which can track all the objects close to it, give the computer all the driving rules and routes, and then the computer should be able to drive to the destination.

There are many benefits of self-driving cars. Research shows that using self-driving cars can greatly reduce the number of cars on the street because 80% only have one person driving alone in a car. Self-driving cars can also lower the cost of transportation, which is 18% of a person's income in the U.S.A. Besides, "These cars won't get drunk, drive too fast, or take risks," said the CEO of Fastcar, John Smith.

Early estimates suggested that self-driving cars would be the standard in 2020, but instead there were only a few research vehicles on the road in 2020. As the technology is currently under research and being improved, it is likely in the near future that we will see self-driving cars move safely on public roads among traditional cars. When they arrive, their cost, safety and convenience will make them part of our daily lives. Companies that research self-driving cars which plan ahead, adjust the quickest, and imagine the most will succeed.

想像一下你上了車，對著車子的電腦講一個地點，然後就讓車子載你到達目的地。自動駕駛汽車背後的想法相當簡單：建造一輛配備電腦的車，該電腦連接許多臺相機，可以追蹤靠近車子的所有物體；對電腦下達所有駕駛規則和路線；然後電腦便應該能駕駛車輛至目的地。

自駕車有許多好處。研究顯示，使用自駕車可以大幅減少路上的汽車數量，因為 80% 的車都只有一人獨自駕駛。自駕車也可以降低交通費，在美國，交通費占個人收入的 18%。此外，Fastcar 公司執行長約翰・史密斯表示：「這些車不會喝醉、開快車或冒險。」

早期的評估指出自駕車在 2020 年將會是常態，但其實在那年僅有一些研究用車輛上路而已。由於這項科技目前正在研究、改善之中，在不久的將來，我們就可能在公共道路上看到自駕車安全行駛在傳統汽車之間。自駕車問世後，它們的價格、安全和便利將讓它們成為我們日常生活的一部分。研究自駕車的公司中，那些能夠超前部署、最快調整適應和最富想像力的公司將獲致成功。

註3：A be connected with B 之意為「A 和 B 有關聯」，而 A be connected to B 指「A 和 B（實體地）連接在一起」或「A 和 B 有關聯」。由本句判斷應將介詞改為 to 較符合語意。

D **39.**

What is the main idea of this article?

(A) Setting up self-driving car companies

(B) Driving rules for self-driving cars

(C) The costing of self-driving cars

(D) The coming of self-driving cars

這篇文章的主旨為何？

(A) 創辦自駕車公司

(B) 自駕車的駕駛規範

(C) 自駕車的成本估算

(D) 自駕車的到來

理由:

本文第一段簡介自駕車背後的想法，第二段說明自駕車的好處，第三段則說明自駕車的發展現況，得知 (D) 項應為正選。

D **40.**

What are the key things a self-driving car needs in order to get to your destination?

(A) Objects next to the car, a camera, and a road map.

(B) Speakers, a computer, and objects next to the car.

(C) Cameras, speakers, driving rules and a road map.

(D) Cameras, a computer, driving rules, and a road map.

自駕車需要哪些關鍵事物才能到達目的地？

(A) 車子旁邊的物體、一臺相機和一份道路地圖。

(B) 喇叭、一臺電腦和車子旁邊的物體。

(C) 相機、喇叭、駕駛規則和一份道路地圖。

(D) 相機、一臺電腦、駕駛規則和一份道路地圖。

理由:

根據本文第一段第二句 "... build a car with a computer that is connected with many cameras which can track all the objects close to it, give the computer all the driving rules and routes,..."（……建造一輛配備電腦的車，該電腦連接許多臺相機，可以追蹤靠近車子的所有物體；對電腦下達所有駕駛規則和路線，……），得知 (D) 項應為正選。

B **41.**

Which of the following is true about self-driving cars in 2020?

(A) Self-driving cars were everywhere.

(B) Self-driving cars were at the research stage.

(C) Self-driving cars replaced all traditional cars.

(D) Self-driving car technology was fully developed.

關於 2020 年的自駕車，下列敘述何者為真？

(A) 自駕車到處都是。

(B) 自駕車仍處在研究階段。

(C) 自駕車取代了所有傳統汽車。

(D) 自駕車科技已完善發展。

理由:

根據本文第三段第二句 "As the technology is currently under research and being improved,..."（由於這項科技目前正在研究、改善之中，……），得知 (B) 項應為正選。

重要單字片語

1. **destination** [ˌdɛstəˋneʃən] *n.* 目的地
2. **a self-driving car** 自駕車
3. **connected** [kəˋnɛktɪd] *a.* 連接的
   be connected to... 和……連接
   例: This computer is connected to the building's fire alarm system.
   （這臺電腦連接大樓的火警系統。）
4. **track** [træk] *vt.* 追蹤（……的動向）
   例: Scientists have been tracking this bird species since the 1990s.
   （自一九九〇年代以來，科學家就一直在追蹤這種鳥類。）
5. **route** [rut] *n.* 路線
6. **benefit** [ˋbɛnəfɪt] *n.* 好處，優勢
7. **research** [ˋrisɝtʃ] *n.* 研究（不可數）
   & [rɪˋsɝtʃ] *vt.* & *vi.* 研究
   例: The professor asked the students to research the works of Tagore.
   （教授叫學生去研究泰戈爾的作品。）
8. **transportation** [ˌtrænspɚˋteʃən] *n.* 交通運輸（不可數）
9. **take a risk** 冒險（行事）
   例: Don't take any risk. Just do exactly what I tell you.
   （不要冒任何風險。就照我告訴你的去做。）
10. **estimate** [ˋɛstəmət] *n.* 估計
11. **vehicle** [ˋviɪkḷ] *n.* 車輛
12. **currently** [ˋkɝəntlɪ] *adv.* 目前，現在
13. **convenience** [kənˋvinjəns] *n.* 便利，方便（不可數）
14. **adjust** [əˋdʒʌst] *vi.* & *vt.* （使）適應
    adjust (oneself) to + N/V-ing 適應……
    例: It took Steve some time to adjust to his new job.
    （史蒂夫花了一些時間適應新工作。）
15. **replace** [rɪˋples] *vt.* 代替
    replace A with B 用 B 代替 A
    例: Emily decided to replace her old oven with a new one.
    （艾蜜莉決定將烤箱汰舊換新。）

第二部分：非選擇題（第 I 至 III 題，每題 6 分，共 18 分）

I. 填充

1. 為保持健康，均衡的飲食、充足的運動及避免過多的壓力是有必要的。

To stay healthy, it is necessary to have a balanced diet and s ___①___ exercise, and to avoid too much p ___②___.

① sufficient ② pressure

解析

1. 本題空格 ① 的對照譯詞為『充足的』，且空格為 s 開頭，故空格應置形容詞 sufficient。
   sufficient [sə`fɪʃənt] *a.* 充足的
   例: This money will be sufficient for our living expenses for the next two months.
   （這筆錢將足夠應付我們下兩個月的生活開銷。）
2. 本題空格 ② 的對照譯詞為『壓力』，且空格為 p 開頭，故空格應置名詞 pressure。
   pressure [`prɛʃɚ] *n.* 壓力

其他重點

1. **stay healthy** 保持健康
2. **it is necessary (for sb) to V** （某人）做……是有必要的
   例: It's necessary for people to find proper outlets for negative emotions.
   （人們需要找到宣洩負面情緒的適當出口。）
3. **balanced** [`bælənst] *a.* 均衡的，平衡的
   a balanced diet 均衡的飲食

II. 句子重組

2. in the economy / All governments / due to / predicted a decline / the COVID-19 pandemic

All governments predicted a decline in the economy due to the COVID-19 pandemic.
（由於新冠肺炎，所有的政府都預測經濟會衰退。）

解析

1. 先找出開頭為大寫的詞組 All governments（所有政府）作為句首。
2. 主詞詞組 All governments 之後應接動詞。重組部分中，predicted a decline 為動詞詞組，predicted 為及物動詞，表『預測』，decline 為名詞，表『衰退』，作 predicted 的受詞，故形成 "All governments predicted a decline..."，如此形成一個完整的句子結構：主詞 + 動詞 + 受詞。

3. decline 作名詞，其後可接介詞 in 引導的介詞片語，形成 a decline in...，表『在……方面的衰退』，故將重組部分中的介詞片語 in the economy（在經濟中）接在 decline 後。
4. 剩下的詞組中，due to 表『由於，因為』，為介詞片語，後須接名詞或動名詞，引出導致某事物發生的原因，可置句首或句中，故將 due to 與最後剩下的詞組 the COVID-19 pandemic 合併後，得出答案：

   All governments predicted a decline in the economy due to the COVID-19 pandemic.

其他重點

1. **predict** [prɪˋdɪkt] *vt.* 預測，預料

   predict + (that)...　　預測／預料……

   例: The fortune-teller predicted that Terry would make a lot of money this year.
   （算命師預言泰瑞今年會賺大錢。）
2. **decline** [dɪˋklaɪn] *n.* 衰退；下降

   a decline in...　　在……方面的衰退／下降
3. **economy** [ɪˋkɑnəmɪ] *n.* 經濟
4. **pandemic** [pænˋdɛmɪk] *n.*（大規模蔓延的）流行病

Ⅲ. 中譯英

3. 有些學校將會帶他們的學生去動物園。

   Some schools will take their students to the zoo.

   或：Some of the schools will take their students to the zoo.

解析

1. 『有些學校』可譯成 Some schools，此時 some 為形容詞；亦可譯成 Some of the schools，此時 some 為代名詞。
2. 『將會』表未來，翻譯時使用未來式的助動詞 will。
3. 『帶（某人）去（某地）』可譯成 take sb to + 地點。
4. 『他們的學生』可譯成 their students。
5. 『動物園』可譯成 the zoo。
6. 由上得知，本句可譯為：

   Some schools will take their students to the zoo.

或: Some of the schools will take their students to the zoo.

109

四技二專統一入學測驗－詳解

109 年統測
試題講解

第一部分：選擇題

第二部分：非選擇題

選擇題解答

1	2	3	4	5	6	7	8	9	10
A	D	B	C	B	A	A	C	A	C
11	12	13	14	15	16	17	18	19	20
A	C	A	A	D	D	B	B	C	D
21	22	23	24	25	26	27	28	29	30
C	C	B	D	D	B	D	B	D	C
31	32	33	34	35	36	37	38	39	40
B	D	D	C	A	B	C	A	C	C
41									
A									

109 年四技二專統一入學測驗詳解

第一部分：選擇題（82 分）

I. 字彙題

A **1.**

You can wear sunglasses if you think the sunlight is too ______ outside.

(A) bright (B) gray (C) large (D) weak

如果你覺得外面的陽光太亮的話，你可以戴上太陽眼鏡。

解析

1. (A) **bright** [braɪt] *a.* 明亮的

   例: This room is not bright enough. Can we turn on another lamp?
   （這房間不夠亮。我們可以打開另一盞燈嗎？）

   (B) **gray** [gre] *a.* 灰色的

   例: Gary usually wears a gray shirt to work.
   （蓋瑞常穿灰色襯衫去上班。）

   (C) **large** [lɑrdʒ] *a.* 大的

   例: Jerry moved to a large apartment after he got married.
   （傑瑞婚後搬去一間大公寓。）

   (D) **weak** [wik] *a.* 虛弱的；很弱的；差勁的

   例: The weak boy could not lift the rock.
   （虛弱的男孩無法舉起這石塊。）

2. 根據語意，(A) 項應為正選。

D **2.**

Every Saturday, the library holds talks on various ______ that include friendship, career[註1], photography and health.

(A) jobs (B) hobbies (C) products (D) topics

每週六，圖書館會舉辦有關各種主題的講座，包括交友、事業、攝影及健康。

註1：career 為可數名詞，故此處應更改為 careers。

解析

1. (A) **job** [dʒab] *n.* 職業；工作（可數）

   例: John has already spent six months looking for a job.
   （約翰已經花了六個月找工作。）

(B) **hobby** [ˋhɑbɪ] *n.* 嗜好

例: Listening to music is a hobby you can enjoy all your life.
（聽音樂是一個你可以終身享受的嗜好。）

(C) **product** [ˋprɑdʌkt] *n.* 產品；產物

例: The company introduced a new product recently.
（這家公司最近推出了一項新產品。）

(D) **topic** [ˋtɑpɪk] *n.* 主題

例: Have you chosen a topic for your speech?
（你選好演講題目了嗎？）

2. 根據語意，(D) 項應為正選。

其他重點

1. **various** [ˋvɛrɪəs] *a.* 各式各樣的
例: Our company publishes various kinds of books.
（我們公司出版各式各樣的書籍。）
2. **career** [kəˋrɪr] *n.* 職業（尤指終身的職業）
3. **photography** [fəˋtɑgrəfɪ] *n.* 攝影

B **3.**

I don't feel ______ gossiping about Michael's life because it is wrong to discuss other people's private lives.

(A) annoyed (B) comfortable (C) embarrassed (D) fearful

八卦麥可的生活讓我覺得不舒服，因為討論別人的私生活是不對的。

解析

1. (A) **annoyed** [əˋnɔɪd] *a.* 感到氣惱的

be annoyed by sth 被某事物所激怒

例: The teacher was annoyed by the noise some students were making outside her classroom.
（這老師被教室外學生製造的噪音弄得很煩。）

(B) **comfortable** [ˋkʌmfɚtəbl̩] *a.* 自在的；舒服的

例: Richard is not comfortable with public speeches.
（理查對於在眾人面前講話感覺不自在。）

(C) **embarrassed** [ɪmˋbærəst] *a.* 感到尷尬的，感到難為情的

例: The bride was too embarrassed to kiss the groom in front of so many people.
（新娘不好意思在那麼多人面前吻新郎。）

(D) **fearful** [ˋfɪrfəl] *a.* 害怕的
be fearful of...　害怕……
例: The little boy is fearful of strangers.
（小男孩很怕陌生人。）

2. 根據語意，(B) 項應為正選。

其他重點

gossip [ˋgɑsəp] *vi.* 說閒話，說長道短（與介詞 about 並用）& *n.* 閒話（不可數）
例: Nora loves to gossip about her coworkers.
（諾拉喜歡聊同事的八卦。）

C **4.**

Computer technology ______ people to work at home effectively[註2] without having to go to the office.

(A) attacks　(B) confuses　(C) enables　(D) reduces

電腦科技可以讓人可以不用進公司就能有效率地在家上班。

註2：effectively 表「有效地」，在本句中較不符語意，應改成 efficiently（有效率地；高效能地）較佳。

解析

1. (A) **attack** [əˋtæk] *vt.* 攻擊，襲擊
例: The dog is trained to attack strangers.
（那隻狗受過訓練會攻擊陌生人。）

(B) **confuse** [kənˋfjuz] *vt.* 使困惑；混淆
例: Please slow down—you are confusing me.
（請說慢一點 —— 你把我搞糊塗了。）

(C) **enable** [ɪnˋebl̩] *vt.* 使（某人）能夠
enable sb to V　使某人能夠從事……
例: Knowledge enables humans to solve problems.
（知識使人類有能力解決難題。）

(D) **reduce** [rɪˋdjus] *vt.* 減少；降低
例: The boss will do anything to reduce costs.
（老闆將不擇手段來減低成本。）

2. 根據語意，(C) 項應為正選。

其他重點

effectively [əˋfɛktɪvlɪ] *adv.* 有效地
例: We've solved the problem effectively.
（我們有效地解決了問題。）

B **5.**

The shoes usually cost a lot, but now they are ______ cheap after[註3] discount.

(A) regionally (B) relatively (C) reluctantly (D) respectfully

這雙鞋子通常很貴，但是打折後現在比較便宜了。

註3：由於此處的 discount 特指鞋子的折扣，故宜在其前加上 the。

解析

1. (A) **regionally** [ˋridʒənlɪ] *adv.* 地方地，區域性地

例: The central government's new housing policy doesn't seem to work well regionally.

（中央政府的新住屋政策，似乎在地方不太奏效。）

(B) **relatively** [ˋrɛlətɪvlɪ] *adv.* 比較，相對地

例: It was cold yesterday, and it is relatively warm today.

（昨天很冷，今天就比較溫暖。）

(C) **reluctantly** [rɪˋlʌktəntlɪ] *adv.* 不情願地

例: Little Johnny reluctantly shared his French fries with his brother.

（小強尼很勉強地與哥哥分享薯條。）

(D) **respectfully** [rɪˋspɛktfəlɪ] *adv.* 恭敬地；有禮地

例: Sarah always treats others respectfully.

（莎拉總是以禮待人。）

2. 根據語意，(B) 項應為正選。

其他重點

discount [ˋdɪskaʊnt] *n.* 折扣

A **6.**

Mozart（莫札特）was a great musician who started to ______ music when he was very young.

(A) compose (B) lighten (C) monitor (D) reject

莫札特是一位偉大的音樂家，他在很小的時候就開始作曲了。

解析

1. (A) **compose** [kəmˋpoz] *vt.* & *vi.* 作（曲、詩等）

例: John is very good at composing songs.

（約翰很擅長創作歌曲。）

(B) **lighten** [ˋlaɪtn̩] *vt.* 照亮，使明亮；減輕 & *vi.* 變亮

例: Dad painted the walls white to lighten the room.

（老爸把牆壁漆成白色好讓房間明亮起來。）

(C) **monitor** [ˋmɑnətɚ] *vt.* 監視，監控

例: The hidden cameras helped the manager monitor his staff.
（隱藏式攝影機幫助經理監視員工。）

(D) **reject** [rɪˋdʒɛkt] *vt.* 拒絕；否決

例: Our plans were rejected by the boss.
（我們的計畫被老闆否決了。）

2. 根據語意，(A) 項應為正選。

其他重點

musician [mjuˋzɪʃən] *n.* 音樂家

A **7.**

A(n) _______ face is essential to dramatic acting because it is good at showing all kinds of emotions.

(A) expressive (B) identical (C) protective (D) reasonable

有豐富表情的臉龐對戲劇表演是不可或缺的，因為它有助於表現各種情緒。

解析

1. (A) **expressive** [ɪkˋsprɛsɪv] *a.* 表情豐富的；表達清楚的

例: People can be trained to be more expressive when giving speeches.
（人們可以被訓練在演講時表達更清楚。）

(B) **identical** [aɪˋdɛntɪkl̩] *a.* 完全相同的；極為相似的

例: The houses in that area were all identical.
（那個地區的房子全都是一個樣。）

(C) **protective** [prəˋtɛktɪv] *a.* 防護的，保護的；愛護的

例: You need to wear protective clothing to get the honey from the beehive.
（你需要穿防護衣來取蜂巢裡的蜂蜜。）

(D) **reasonable** [ˋrizənəbl̩] *a.* 價格公道的，合理的

例: The rent of the apartment was pretty reasonable, so I decided to take it.
（這間公寓的租金還挺合理的，所以我決定租下來。）

2. 根據語意，(A) 項應為正選。

其他重點

1. **essential** [ɪˋsɛnʃəl] *a.* 不可或缺的，必要的

例: The book has all the essential elements of a good romantic novel.
（這本書具有好的言情小說必備的所有元素。）

2. **dramatic** [drəˋmætɪk] *a.* 戲劇的

例: Angela studied dramatic arts in graduate school.
（安琪拉在研究所念的是戲劇藝術。）

C 8.

Henry has been very busy looking for a new job lately, so he hasn't contacted his family for almost two weeks.

(A) fairly (B) nearly (C) recently (D) shortly

亨利最近一直忙著找新工作，所以他將近兩個禮拜沒有和家人聯絡。

解析

1. 原句劃線的字有下列意思及用法：

lately [ˋletlɪ] *adv.* 最近，近來（常與現在完成式或現在完成進行式並用）

= recently [ˋrisn̩tlɪ]

例: Cindy hasn't had much sleep lately because she's been busy with both work and family.

（辛蒂最近睡得很少，因為她同時忙工作和家務。）

2. (A) **fairly** [ˋfɛrlɪ] *adv.* 公平地；相當地

例: The boss treats every employee fairly.

（老闆很公平對待每位員工。）

(B) **nearly** [ˋnɪrlɪ] *adv.* 幾乎

例: When I arrived at the theater, the show was nearly over.

（當我抵達戲院時，表演差不多快結束了。）

(C) **recently** [ˋrisn̩tlɪ] *adv.* 最近，近來

例: There is a big difference between the artist's early works and what she's done recently.

（這個藝術家的早期作品和她的近作差別甚大。）

(D) **shortly** [ˋʃɔrtlɪ] *adv.* 不久；立刻

例: Adam said that he would be back shortly, but he left me waiting for almost an hour.

（亞當說他不久就會回來，但是他讓我等了將近一個小時。）

3. 根據上述，lately 與 recently 同義，故 (C) 項應為正選。

其他重點

contact [ˋkɑntækt] *vt.* 聯繫，聯絡

例: I check my email regularly, so you can contact me anytime.

（我定期檢查我的電子信箱，所以你隨時可以跟我聯絡。）

A 9.

Mary broke up with her boyfriend because she felt he had no regard for her feelings.

(A) concern (B) fortune (C) silence (D) temper

瑪麗跟她男友分手了，因為她覺得他都不關心她的感受。

解析

1. 原句劃線的字有下列意思及用法：

regard [rɪˋgɑrd] *n.* 關心，關注

little / no regard (for...)　（對……）不大 / 不關心

例: Ella has no regard for her classmates.

（艾拉並不關心她的同學。）

2. (A) **concern** [kənˋsɝn] *n.* 關心；擔憂

例: There is growing concern about violence on television.

（世人對電視上的暴力日漸感到憂心。）

(B) **fortune** [ˋfɔrtʃən] *n.* 運氣；命運；財富

good / bad fortune　好 / 壞運氣

例: Eddy had the good fortune to win the NT$1,000,000 lottery.

（艾迪很好運中了百萬樂透。）

(C) **silence** [ˋsaɪləns] *n.* 安靜，寂靜

例: The silence in the room made me very nervous.

（房間裡鴉雀無聲，讓我很緊張。）

(D) **temper** [ˋtɛmpɚ] *n.* 脾氣

lose one's temper　發脾氣

例: I've never seen Victoria lose her temper.

（我從來沒看過維多莉亞發脾氣。）

3. 根據上述，regard 與 concern 同義，故 (A) 項應為正選。

其他重點

feelings [ˋfilɪŋz] *n.*（尤指易受傷的）情感（恆用複數）

C **10.**

A medical report indicates that there is an association between high levels of stress and skin problems.

(A) an exchange　(B) an obstacle　(C) a relationship　(D) a similarity

一份醫學報告指出高度壓力與皮膚疾病之間有關聯。

解析

1. 原句劃線的字有下列意思及用法：

association [əˌsosɪˋeʃən] *n.* 關聯 / 係（常與介詞 with 並用）

例: The mayor denied any association with that land development company.

（市長否認與那家土地開發商有任何關係。）

2. (A) **exchange** [ɪksˋtʃendʒ] *n.* 交換
in exchange for... 以交換……
例: I gave Beth some cake in exchange for her homemade cookies.
（我送貝絲一些蛋糕，以交換她的手工餅乾。）
(B) **obstacle** [ˋɑbstəkḷ] *n.* 障礙（物）
例: The research team hit an obstacle and couldn't go on with the experiments.
（研究團隊遇到阻礙，無法繼續做實驗。）
(C) **relationship** [rɪˋleʃən͵ʃɪp] *n.* 關係
例: Morris has a difficult relationship with his parents.
（莫瑞斯和他父母之間的關係不好。）
(D) **similarity** [͵sɪməˋlærətɪ] *n.* 相似處，相同點
例: There are a few similarities between the two products.
（這兩種產品有些相似之處。）
3. 根據上述，association 與 relationship 同義，故 (C) 項應為正選。

其他重點

1. **indicate** [ˋɪndə͵ket] *vt.* 顯示；指出
例: The study indicates that a proper diet can prevent many diseases.
（那項研究顯示，適當的飲食能預防許多疾病。）
2. **stress** [strɛs] *n.* 壓力

A **11.**
The government declared that the new city hall would be open to the public this summer.
(A) announced (B) discovered (C) imagined (D) predicted
政府宣布今年夏天新的市政府大樓將會對大眾開放。

解析

1. 原句劃線的字有下列意思及用法：
declare [dɪˋklɛr] *vt.* 宣布；宣稱
declare + that 子句 宣布／宣稱……
例: The woman declared that she was able to communicate with dead people.
（那名女子宣稱她能與死者溝通。）
2. (A) **announce** [əˋnaʊns] *vt.* 宣布
例: Brad and Lily announced that they are going to get married this year.
（布萊德和莉莉宣布他們將在今年完婚。）
(B) **discover** [dɪsˋkʌvɚ] *vt.* 發現
例: When Grace got to the door, she discovered that she had lost her key.
（葛瑞絲到門口時才發現她的鑰匙不見了。）

(C) **imagine** [ɪˋmædʒɪn] *vt.* 想像

例: Can you imagine that this store was once a church 25 years ago?

（你能想像這間商店二十五年前曾是教堂嗎？）

(D) **predict** [prɪˋdɪkt] *vt.* 預測，預料

例: I predict that Teddy will be bald before he turns 30.

（我預測泰迪三十歲前就會禿頭。）

3. 根據上述，declare 與 announce 同義，故 (A) 項應為正選。

其他重點

1. **city hall** [ˋsɪtɪ ˌhɔl] *n.* 市政府（大樓），市政廳
2. **be open to the public / visitors** 開放給大眾 / 參觀者

   be open to... 對……開放

   例: The library is open to the public from Monday to Friday.

   （該圖書館星期一至星期五對大眾開放。）

II. 對話題

C **12.**

Rose: Hey, let's go to Mama's Kitchen for some food.

Jane: Sounds great. ________________

Rose: No, it's next to the bank.

Jane: Oh, it's quite far from here. But never mind. Let's go!

(A) Is the food there really good? (B) Can you say it one more time?

(C) Is it across from the Internet cafe? (D) Are you sure you want to go there?

蘿絲：嘿，咱們去「媽媽廚房」吃點東西吧。

阿珍：聽起來很棒。________________

蘿絲：不，它在銀行隔壁。

阿珍：喔，那離這兒還蠻遠的。但沒關係。咱們走吧！

(A) 那裡的食物真的很棒嗎？ (B) 妳能再說一遍嗎？

(C) 它在網咖對面嗎？ (D) 妳確定想去那裡嗎？

解析

空格後，蘿絲回答 "No, it's next to the bank."（不，它在銀行隔壁。），得知阿珍詢問蘿絲要確認「媽媽廚房」的位置，因此 (C) 項應為正選。

其他重點

1. **never mind** 算了；沒關係

例: A: I can visit my grandmother some other night if you want.
B: Never mind. I'll find someone else to go to the party with me.
（甲：如果你想的話，我可以在別天晚上再去看我奶奶。）
（乙：沒關係。我找別人陪我去派對好了。）

2. **across** [əˋkrɔs] **from** 在……對面（= opposite [ˋɑpəzɪt]）

例: Henry lives across from the train station.
（亨利住在火車站對面。）

3. **Internet cafe** 網咖

例: Mary had a great time playing online games at the Internet cafe.
（瑪莉在那間網咖玩線上遊戲玩得很開心。）

A **13.**

Alan: I've been looking for that book! Where did you get it?

Betty: ________________ I just did a search on the Web and found it. It's not that difficult, you know.

Alan: Really? I must try my hand at it. Can you show me how to do it?

(A) I bought it online.
(B) I paid by credit card.
(C) I left it in the drawer.
(D) I finished it in one night.

艾倫：我一直在找那本書！妳在哪裡弄到的？
貝蒂：________________ 我只是在網路上搜尋便找到的。你知道那並不難。
艾倫：真的嗎？我一定要自己試一次。妳可以示範怎麼做嗎？
(A) 我在網路上買的。
(B) 我用信用卡付款。
(C) 我把它留在抽屜裡了。
(D) 我一個晚上就看完了。

解析

空格前，艾倫問到 "Where did you get it?"（妳在哪裡弄到的？），得知艾倫想要知道貝蒂在哪個地方找到那本書，因此 (A) 項應為正選。

其他重點

1. **search** [sɝtʃ] *n.* 搜尋

do a search for... （在電腦、網路上）搜尋……

例: Tom did a search for apartments for rent in his neighborhood.
（湯姆在他的社區搜尋可租的公寓。）

2. **try one's hand at sth** 初次嘗試做……

例: I thought I'd try my hand at fishing.
（我想嘗試一下釣魚。）

3. **online** [ˋɑn,laɪn] *adv.* 在線上

例: Brian likes to shop online because it's very convenient.
（布萊恩喜歡線上購物，因為很方便。）

4. **leave** [liv] *vt.* 留下；離開

例: Cindy left her keys in her office.
（辛蒂把鑰匙留在她辦公室裡了。）
As soon as Ella left the room, her baby began to cry.
（艾拉一離開房間，她的寶寶就哭了起來。）

A **14.**

Steve: So, have you made up your mind about a career?
Becky: Pretty much. It's going to be something with either dancing or singing. I mean it.
Steve: ________ You've always been the musical type.

(A) It makes sense to me. (B) It will never come true.
(C) I'm pretty good at music. (D) Neither of them will work.

史蒂夫：那麼，妳已打定主意要從事什麼工作了嗎？
貝　姬：差不多了。我的工作將要跟跳舞或唱歌有關。我說真的。
史蒂夫：________ 妳一直都是熱愛音樂的。

(A) 我覺得有道理。 (B) 那不會成真。
(C) 我相當擅長音樂。 (D) 兩者都行不通。

解析

空格前，貝姬說到 "It's going to be something with either dancing or singing. I mean it."（我的工作將要跟跳舞或唱歌有關。我說真的。），空格後，史蒂夫說到 "You've always been the musical type."（妳一直都是熱愛音樂的。），得知史蒂夫認同貝姬的說法，因此 (A) 項應為正選。

其他重點

1. **make up one's mind** 下定決心

例: Peter made up his mind to become a doctor when he was thirteen.
（彼得在十三歲時決定當醫生。）

2. **career** [kəˋrɪr] *n.* 職業（尤指終身職業）

3. **either... or...** 不是……就是……
（此對等連接詞可接兩單字、片語及子句。連接兩主詞時，動詞按較接近的主詞作變化。）

例: We can either take the train or the bus to Hualien.
（我們可以搭火車或巴士去花蓮。）
Either Sue or the girls are going to cook lunch.
（不是蘇就是女孩們要煮午餐。）

4. **make sense** （言之）有理
5. **neither** [ˋniðɚ] *pron.* 兩者皆不

例: Neither of the two boys was absent.
（這兩個男孩都沒缺席。）

6. **work** [wɝk] *vi.* 起作用

例: Jack knew that the plan would not work.
（傑克知道該計畫會行不通。）

D **15.**

Mom: I think you have too much junk in your room. Why don't you clean up right now?
Mark: Junk? There is no junk. ________
Mom: How about these empty boxes and broken mugs?
Mark: They are for my art class.

(A) We can ask for help. (B) You can say that again.
(C) It's too late to clean up. (D) I keep things for a reason.

媽媽：我認為你房間有太多垃圾。現在清理乾淨好不好？
馬克：垃圾？沒有垃圾。________
媽媽：那這些空盒子和破馬克杯呢？
馬克：它們是美術課要用的。

(A) 我們可以尋求幫助。 (B) 一點都沒錯。
(C) 時間太晚無法做打掃工作。 (D) 我留著東西是有理由的。

解析

空格前，馬克說到 "There's no junk."（沒有垃圾。），空格後，媽媽質問 "How about these empty boxes and broken mugs?"（那這些空盒子和破馬克杯呢？），得知馬克要解釋他留下媽媽認為是垃圾的東西的理由，因此 (D) 項應為正選。

其他重點

1. **junk** [dʒʌŋk] *n.*（用不到的）廢棄物；垃圾（集合名詞，不可數）

例: The zipper on the jacket that I just bought is not working. What a piece of junk!
（我剛買的夾克拉鍊是壞的。真是爛貨！）

2. **clean up** 清理乾淨
3. **mug** [mʌg] *n.* 馬克杯
4. **ask for** 請求

例: You can ask for a refund if the DVD player is faulty.
（若 DVD 播放器有問題可以退錢。）
＊faulty [ˋfɔltɪ] *a.* 有缺點的

D **16.**

Ken: Hello. This is Ken Wang. I bought a jacket on your website a month ago. I haven't received it. Why?

Joy: Hi, Mr. Wang. Let me check. Ah! ________ Our records show a delay in delivery.

Ken: Well, you should have called me about it.

Joy: I'm truly sorry. I'll try my best to send it out to you today.

(A) I could not find any records of your order.
(B) I phoned you last week about that order.
(C) There was no order placed for the jacket.
(D) There has been a problem with that order.

肯：你好。我是王肯。我一個月前在你們的網站上買了一件夾克。我一直沒有收到。這是怎麼回事？

喬伊：王先生，您好。讓我查一下。啊！________ 我們的紀錄顯示延遲出貨。

肯：你們應該打電話給我說明這情形。

喬伊：我真的很抱歉。我會盡力今天把它寄出給您。

(A) 我找不到您任何訂單的紀錄。 (B) 我上週打過電話給您，說明那張訂單的問題。
(C) 這件夾克沒有下訂紀錄。 (D) 那張訂單是有問題。

解析

對話中王先生打電話詢問未收到訂貨的問題，空格後，客服喬伊回答 "Our records show a delay in delivery."（我們的紀錄顯示延遲出貨。），得知喬伊說明該訂單有問題的地方，因此 (D) 項應為正選。

其他重點

1. **receive** [rɪˋsiv] *vt.* 收到，接收

例: Doris received a certificate after she completed the course.
（朵瑞絲上完這門課後獲得一份證書。）
＊certificate [sɚˋtɪfəkɪt] *n.* 證書

2. **record** [ˋrɛkɚd] *n.* 紀錄

例: Not only did Roy win the race, but he set a new record.
（羅伊不僅贏得比賽，更創下新紀錄。）

3. **delay** [dɪˋle] *n.* & *vt.* 延誤

例: The spokesman explained that the delay was a result of bad weather.
（發言人解釋延誤是惡劣天氣造成的。）
Don't delay paying the bill.
（不要延誤繳納帳單的時間。）

4. **delivery** [dɪˋlɪvərɪ] *n.* 遞送

例: There is no postal delivery on Sundays.
（星期天郵差不送信。）
＊postal [ˋpostḷ] *a.* 郵政的

5. **truly** [ˋtrulɪ] *adv.* 真正地

例: Your opinion is truly important to me.
（你的意見對我來說真的很重要。）

6. **place an order** 下訂單

例: Jerry couldn't place an order online because he didn't have a credit card.
（因為傑瑞沒有信用卡，所以他不能在網路上下訂單。）

B **17.**

Jennifer: That was an interesting speech. I learned a lot!
Shu-hua: Yes, although the topic was hard to follow for a foreigner like me!
Jennifer: ________________
Shu-hua: Thank you. It's very kind of you.

(A) The speaker is from Canada. (B) But your English is excellent.
(C) I've followed the speaker for a while. (D) And the topic was about foreign cultures.

珍妮佛：那場演講真有意思。我學到好多！
淑　華：對啊，不過這個主題對像我這樣的外國人來說很難懂！
珍妮佛：________________
淑　華：謝謝妳。妳人真好。

(A) 演說者是加拿大人。 (B) 但妳的英文很棒。
(C) 我已追蹤這演說者有一陣子了。 (D) 而且這個主題是有關外國文化。

解析

此對話為珍妮佛和淑華在討論一場英文演說，空格前，淑華說到 "Yes, although the topic was hard to follow for a foreigner like me!"（對啊，不過這主題對像我這樣的外國人來說很難懂！)，空格後淑華表達對珍妮佛的感謝，得知可推論是因為珍妮佛稱讚淑華的英文能力，因此 (B) 項應為正選。

其他重點

1. **follow** [ˋfɑlo] *vt.* 明白（事物）；（在社群網路上）追蹤或跟進
2. **foreigner** [ˋfɔrɪnɚ] *n.* 外國人
   foreign [ˋfɔrɪn] *a.* 外國的
   例: Many foreigners in Taiwan are afraid to try stinky tofu.
   （許多在臺灣的外國人很害怕吃臭豆腐。）
   We have a foreign visitor today.
   （我們今天會有一位外賓來訪。）
3. **It is / was kind of sb to V** 某人（做）……是體貼的
   例: It was kind of you to give me a hand.
   （你真好，助我一臂之力。）
4. **for a while** 一陣子
   例: Henry hasn't gone swimming for a while.
   （亨利已經好一陣子沒去游泳了。）

B **18.**

Interviewer: Have you always worked in the service line[註1]?
Tim: Yes. Ever since I graduated from college.
Interviewer: I see. ________________
Tim: Well. I think I am very hardworking but a little impatient sometimes.

(A) How do you spend your free time?
(B) What are your strong and weak points?
(C) Please tell us about your educational background.
(D) Please say something about your work experience.

面試官：你一直都從事服務業嗎？
提　姆：是的。從我大學畢業起都是。
面試官：好的。________________
提　姆：嗯。我認為我很認真工作，但有時有些沒耐心。
(A) 你如何運用你的閒暇時間？　(B) 你的優缺點是什麼？
(C) 請告訴我們你的教育背景。　(D) 請談談你的工作經驗。

解析

空格後，提姆說到 "I think I am very hardworking but a little impatient sometimes."（我認為我很認真工作，但有時有些沒耐心。），得知面試官想了解提姆的優缺點，所以提出請他分享他個人優缺點的問題，因此 (B) 項應為正選。

註1：原文 line 宜改為 industry（產業）。

其他重點

1. **interviewer** [ˋɪntɚˌvjuɚ] *n.* 面試官

例: It's not necessary to try to guess what the interviewer might ask.
（沒有必要去猜測面試官可能會問什麼問題。）

2. **educational** [ˌɛdʒʊˋkeʃənl̩] *a.* 教育的；教育性的

例: The educational system in the U.S. is different from that in Taiwan.
（美國的教育制度和臺灣不同。）
The movie was not only entertaining but very educational.
（這部電影不僅有娛樂性，而且還非常具有教育性。）
*entertaining [ˌɛntɚˋtenɪŋ] *a.* 有娛樂性的

3. **impatient** [ɪmˋpeʃənt] *a.* 不耐煩的

例: Tess became very impatient because Ray kept asking her similar questions.
（因為雷不停問黛絲類似的問題，所以她變得非常不耐煩。）

C **19.**

Mike: My brother has really gone crazy. He says he wants to take up skydiving. Can you believe that?
Lily: What? ________________
Mike: I'm not. He's dead serious.
Lily: Well, you have to stop him. It's really dangerous.

(A) Am I crazy?
(B) I believe he's dangerous.
(C) You've got to be kidding.
(D) Have you talked to him seriously?

麥克：我弟弟真的瘋了。他說他想玩高空跳傘。你會相信嗎？
莉莉：什麼？________________
麥克：我沒有。他是玩真的。
莉莉：那麼，你一定要阻止他。那真的很危險。

(A) 我瘋了嗎？
(B) 我相信他是危險人物。
(C) 你一定是在開玩笑吧。
(D) 你有認真跟他談過嗎？

解析

空格前麥克說到，"He says he wants to take up skydiving."（他說他想玩高空跳傘。），空格後麥克回答，"I'm not. He's dead serious."（我沒有。他是玩真的。），得知莉莉當時懷疑麥克是否在開玩笑而推論說出該句子，因此 (C) 項應為正選。

其他重點

1. **go crazy** 陷入瘋狂，發瘋
= go nuts

例: On seeing the huge pile of gifts under the Christmas tree, the kids went crazy.
（孩子們一看到耶誕樹下一大堆禮物就高興得發狂。）

2. **take up...** （因有興趣而）開始從事……

例: Jonathan took up painting two months ago, but he quickly lost interest.
（強納森兩個月前開始從事繪畫，但他很快就失去興趣。）

3. **skydiving** [ˋskaɪˏdaɪvɪŋ] *n.* 高空跳傘

例: To help me overcome my fear of heights, David encouraged me to go skydiving.
（為了幫我克服懼高症，大衛鼓勵我去玩高空跳傘。）

4. **dead serious** 極為認真的
serious [ˋsɪrɪəs] *a.* 認真的；嚴重的

5. **seriously** [ˋsɪrɪəslɪ] *adv.* 認真地；嚴重地

例: Wendy is seriously thinking of quitting her job.
（溫蒂認真地思考要離職。）
Frank's back was seriously injured in a car accident.
（法蘭克在一場車禍中背部受重傷。）

D **20.**

Bill: Nina, ____________
Nina: Not really. I'd like to check out this city. But I need to learn how to take the MRT first.
Bill: I'm going to the station. If you want, we can go together. You'll find it easy.
Nina: That would be great! Thanks.

(A) where are you from? (B) do you have a check?
(C) how do you like this city? (D) do you have any plans?

比爾：妮娜，____________
妮娜：並沒有。我想看看這座城市。但我先需要學如何搭捷運。
比爾：我正要去車站。如果妳想要的話，我們可以一起前往。妳會發現那很容易。
妮娜：那就太棒了！謝謝。
(A) 妳來自哪一個國家？ (B) 妳有一張支票嗎？
(C) 妳覺得這座城市如何？ (D) 妳有任何計畫嗎？

解析

空格後，妮娜回答，"Not really. I'd like to check out this city."（並沒有。我想看看這座城市。），得知妮娜接下來打算去參觀該城市，可推論比爾想詢問妮娜是否有其他計畫行程，因此 (D) 項應為正選。

其他重點

check out... 看一看／瞧一瞧……
= take a look at...

例: Why don't we go and check out that store? I think they have shoes in your size.
（我們何不去那家店看一看？我想他們有符合你尺寸的鞋子。）

C **21.**

Peter: Did you hear that band Mayday（五月天）is having two shows here this summer?

Leo: Yes. And tickets are on sale this Friday. But fan club members like us can buy tickets right now. Let's see what we can get.

Peter: There are different kinds of seating in the stadium—floor, lower level, and upper level.

Leo: ______________ I want to sit near the stage.

(A) Isn't it far from the stadium?　(B) How much is the fan club fee?
(C) Why don't we go with floor seats?　(D) Can we sell tickets on[註2] the upper level?

彼得：你聽說了五月天樂團今年夏天要在這裡辦兩場演出嗎？

里歐：沒錯。門票這週五開賣。但像我們粉絲俱樂部的會員現在就可以購票了。咱們來看看可以買到什麼票。

彼得：體育場內有不同的座位安排 —— 地面層、低層和高層。

里歐：______________ 我想要坐靠近舞臺。

(A) 它不是離體育場很遠嗎？　(B) 粉絲俱樂部的會費多少錢？
(C) 我們選擇地面層的座位如何？　(D) 我們能賣高層座位的票嗎？

解析

空格前彼得說到體育場內包含不同階層的座位，空格後里歐表示 "I want to sit near the stage."（我想要坐靠近舞臺。），得知里歐提議選擇地面層的座位，因此 (C) 項應為正選。

註2：介詞 on 宜改為 for。

其他重點

1. **seating** [ˋsitɪŋ] *n.*（某處的全部）座位

例: The sports center has a seating capacity of 2,000.
（此運動中心看臺可以容納二千人。）

＊capacity [kəˋpæsətɪ] *n.* 容量

2. **stadium** [ˋstedɪəm] *n.* 運動場，體育場

例: The stadium will be packed on the day of the concert.
（這個體育場在演唱會當天會爆滿。）

3. **upper** [ˋʌpɚ] *a.* 上面的，較高的

例: Linda bites on her upper lip when she's nervous.

（琳達緊張時會咬上嘴唇。）

4. **fee** [fi] *n.* 費用

例: School fees have gone up in recent years.

（近幾年學費已經上漲了。）

5. **go with...** 選擇／接受……

例: I think I'll go with plan B.

（我想我會選擇 B 計畫。）

III. 綜合測驗

◎ 22 - 26

Rainforests are the Earth's oldest living ecosystems. They __22__ only a small part of the Earth's surface, about six percent, but they are very important to us. For example, they provide us with __23__ of the Earth's oxygen and fresh water. A lot of medicines we use today to treat cancer or heart disease __24__ from the plants that grow only in rainforests. Many items we use in our own homes come from the rainforest as well. __25__, rainforests are disappearing at an alarmingly fast pace, largely due to human development over the past few centuries. Problems __26__ from the decrease of rainforests include more pollutions[註1], less oxygen, and fewer species of animals. To keep rainforests from disappearing and save the Earth for our children, we must do something immediately.

22. (A) call off (B) look into (C) make up (D) turn down

23. (A) many (B) much (C) several (D) a few

24. (A) manufacture (B) manufactured (C) are manufacturing (D) are manufactured

25. (A) In addition (B) Luckily (C) To conclude (D) Unfortunately

26. (A) result (B) resulting (C) have resulted (D) that resulting

熱帶雨林是地球上現存最古老的生態系統。它們只占地球表面的一小部分，大約 6%，但它們對我們來說非常重要。例如，熱帶雨林為我們提供了地球上大部分的氧氣和淡水。很多我們今日用來治療癌症或心臟病的藥物，都是由只能生長在熱帶雨林中的植物所製成。我們在自己家中所使用的許多物品也來自熱帶雨林。不幸的是，熱帶雨林正以驚人的速度消失，這主要

是因為過去幾世紀以來人類的開發。熱帶雨林減少所帶來的問題包括：汙染變多、氧氣變少以及動物種類變少。為了防止熱帶雨林消失，也為了我們的孩子來拯救地球，我們必須立即採取行動。

註1：pollution（汙染）為不可數名詞，因此本空格後的 more pollutions 實應改為 more pollution。

C **22.**

解析

1. (A) **call off...** 取消……

   例: The concert was called off because of the typhoon.
   （那演唱會因颱風來而取消了。）

   (B) **look into...** 調查……

   例: The police are looking into the robbery case.
   （警方正在調查這起搶劫案。）

   (C) **make up...** 組 / 構成……；編造……

   例: Foreign workers make up about 20% of the labor force in this country.
   （外籍勞工約占該國勞動力的 20%。）

   (D) **turn down... / turn...down** 拒絕……；降低（音量，亮度等）

   例: John invited Lisa to his birthday party, but she turned him down because she was sick.
   （約翰邀請麗莎參加他的生日派對，但麗莎因為生病而拒絕了他。）

2. 根據語意，(C) 項應為正選。

B **23.**

解析

1. (A) **many of + 可數名詞** 很多……

   例: At this museum, you can see many of the famous artist's sculptures displayed outdoors.
   （在這博物館，你可以在館外看到許多這位著名藝術家的雕塑作品。）

   (B) **much of + 不可數名詞** 很多……

   例: Much of Jane's salary went into her hobby—painting.
   （珍大部分的薪水都花在了她的愛好上 —— 繪畫。）

(C) **several of + 可數名詞**　幾／數個……

例: Several of my friends are studying abroad, and I only meet them about once a year.
（我有幾個朋友出國留學，而我大約每年只見他們一次。）

(D) **a few of + 可數名詞**　一些……

例: We should buy a few of these special wooden dolls for our coworkers.
（我們應該買一些這款特別的木製娃娃給我們的同事。）

2. 空格後的 the Earth's oxygen and fresh water（地球的氧氣和淡水）皆為不可數名詞，所以根據上述用法，(B) 項應為正選。

D **24.**

解析

1. A lot of medicines（很多藥物）應是「被製作」的，因此空格應使用被動語態：be + p.p.。
2. 根據上述，(D) 項應為正選。

D **25.**

解析

1. (A) **in addition**　除此之外

   例: These chocolate cookies are tasty. In addition, they're very cheap.
   （這些巧克力餅乾很好吃。此外，它們非常便宜。）

   (B) **luckily** [ˋlʌkəlɪ] *adv.* 幸好

   例: Luckily, no one was injured in the factory fire.
   （所幸沒人在這場工廠火災中受傷。）

   (C) **to conclude**　總之

   例: To conclude, this building project will have a harmful effect on the environment.
   （總之，此建築工程將對環境有害。）

   (D) **unfortunately** [ʌnˋfɔrtʃənətlɪ] *adv.* 不幸地

   例: Unfortunately, Linda can't join us tonight because she caught a cold.
   （不幸的是，琳達今晚不能加入我們，因為她感冒了。）

2. 根據語意，(D) 項應為正選。

B **26.**

解析

1. 本題測試形容詞子句化簡為分詞片語的用法，原句原為：
Problems that / which result from the decrease of rainforests include more pollutions...
2. 此時可將關係代名詞 that / which 省略，之後的動詞改成現在分詞，若該動詞為 be 動詞則改為 being，且 being 可予以省略。故原句可改寫為：
Problems resulting from the decrease of rainforests include more pollutions...
3. 根據上述，(B) 項應為正選。

重要單字片語

1. **rainforest** [ˋrenˏfɔrɪst] *n.* 熱帶雨林
2. **ecosystem** [ˋikoˏsɪstəm] *n.* 生態系統
3. **percent** [pɚˋsɛnt] *n.* 百分比
例: You can get a 10 percent discount on these books from July 4 to August 5.
（從七月四日到八月五日，這些書有九折優惠。）
4. **oxygen** [ˋɑksədʒən] *n.* 氧氣
5. **disease** [dɪˋziz] *n.* 疾病
例: No one knew what kind of disease the little boy had.
（沒人知道那小男孩得了哪種病。）
6. **manufacture** [ˏmænjəˋfæktʃɚ] *vt.* 製造
例: How many face masks can this factory manufacture in a day?
（這家工廠一天可以生產幾個口罩？）
7. **alarmingly** [əˋlɑrmɪŋlɪ] *adv.* 令人驚恐地，令人擔心地
例: Alarmingly, plastic waste has been threatening more and more sea creatures.
（令人震驚的是，塑膠廢棄物已經威脅到越來越多的海洋生物。）
8. **pace** [pes] *n.* 速度
at a fast / slow pace
以很快 / 慢的速度
例: Tom walked through the park at a slow pace in order to enjoy the pleasant sunshine.
（湯姆慢慢地散步穿過公園，以享受宜人的陽光。）
9. **due to...** 因為
同: because of...
例: The picnic was canceled due to the heavy rain.
（由於雨下得很大，所以野餐取消了。）
10. **pollution** [pəˋluʃən] *n.* 汙染
例: One way to reduce air pollution is to take public transportation, rather than drive.
（一種減少空氣汙染的方法是乘坐大眾交通工具，而非開車。）
11. **species** [ˋspiʃiz] *n.* 物種（單複數同形）
例: We have to protect endangered species such as pandas and blue whales.
（我們必須保護熊貓和藍鯨等瀕臨滅絕的物種。）

12. **immediately** [ɪˋmidɪɪtlɪ] *adv.* 立即，馬上
同: at once
= instantly
= right away

例: Jeff left the party immediately after his girlfriend called him.
（傑夫在他女朋友打電話給他後，就立刻離開了派對。）

◎ 27 - 31

In 1275, Marco Polo（馬可波羅）arrived in China. During this journey, he came close to losing his life a few times, __27__ he kept going and finally succeeded in reaching his goal. At about the same time, Polynesians（玻里尼西亞人）were exploring the islands of the South Pacific. __28__ the great dangers of sailing long distance[註2] in open canoes, they managed to explore and occupy all the major islands. About 200 years later, Christopher Columbus（哥倫布）left Europe to find a new way to Asia. __29__ the earth to be flat, many people at that time were afraid that he would fall off the edge of the world. Columbus did not reach his original goal to find treasures in Asia; __30__, he opened up a vast new world, the Americas. Every explorer needs a vision. But what __31__ explorers to leave the security of the known world to face the dangers of the unknown? For many of them, it is simply the love of adventure.

27. (A) for (B) or (C) so (D) yet

28. (A) Compared to (B) Despite (C) Rather than (D) Unlike

29. (A) Been believed (B) Being believing (C) Believed (D) Believing

30. (A) as usual (B) for instance (C) instead (D) moreover

31. (A) drive (B) drives (C) have driven (D) is driven

西元 1275 年時，馬可波羅抵達中國。他在這趟旅程中好幾次差點丟了性命，然而他勇往直前，最後終於成功達成目標。約在同一時間，玻里尼西亞人正在探索南太平洋的島嶼。儘管乘著無頂獨木舟航行長遠距離是危險重重，他們仍成功探索並占領所有大島。大約兩百年後，哥倫布從歐洲出發去尋找一條前往亞洲的新路線。當時有許多人認為地球是平的，因而擔心他會從世界的邊緣墜下。哥倫布並沒有達成原本要在亞洲尋找寶藏的目的，然而他開啟了一個巨大的新世界 —— 美洲。每一位探險家都需要有個夢想。但驅使探險家離開已知的安全世界而迎向未知的危險的動力是什麼呢？對他們許多人來說，不過就是對冒險的熱愛罷了。

註2：本句中的 distance 建議改為複數 distances。

D 27.

解析

1. 空格前後為兩個句構完整的子句，得知空格應置連接詞以連接兩子句。
2. 四個選項皆可作連接詞，惟 (A) for（因為）、(B) or（否則）、(C) so（因此）置入後不符語意，僅 (D) yet（然而）置入後符合語意，可知 (D) 項應為正選。

B 28.

解析

1. (A) **compared to + N/V-ing** 與……相較之下

   例: Compared to those from Hollywood, independent films have more original plots.
   （相較於好萊塢電影，獨立製片的情節較富原創性。）

   (B) **despite + N/V-ing** 儘管／不論……
   = regardless of + N/V-ing
   = in spite of + N/V-ing

   例: The explorers pressed on despite the bad weather.
   （儘管天氣狀況不佳，探險家們仍繼續前進。）

   (C) **rather than...** 而非……

   例: David chose a brown tie rather than a black belt as his father's birthday gift.
   （大衛選了一條棕色領帶當作他父親的生日禮物，而不是黑色腰帶。）

   (D) **unlike + N/V-ing** 不像……

   例: Unlike his brother, Gary likes to listen to classical music.
   （不像他哥哥，蓋瑞喜歡聽古典音樂。）
2. 根據語意，可知 (B) 項應為正選。

D 29.

解析

1. 原句實為：
   Many people believed the earth to be flat, many people at that time were afraid that he would fall off the edge of the world.
   上句包含兩個句構完整的子句，但兩個子句之間並無連接詞連接，不合乎文法；因兩子句共用主詞 many people，可將第一句的主詞省略，再將動詞 believed 改為現在分詞 believing，形成分詞構句。
2. 根據上述用法，可知 (D) 項應為正選。

C 30.

解析

1. (A) **as usual** 一如往常

例: As usual, I had an omelet and black coffee for breakfast today.
（我今天一如往常吃煎蛋捲、喝黑咖啡當早餐。）

(B) **for instance** 舉例來說
= for example

例: Ted is a responsible worker. For instance, he always completes his work on time.
（泰德是個負責任的員工。舉例來說，他總是準時完成工作。）

(C) **instead** [ɪnˋstɛd] *adv.* 相反地；取而代之

例: Jeff didn't hide from the questions. Instead, he explained everything as clearly as he could.
（傑夫並沒有逃避問題。相反地，他盡量把每一件事情解釋清楚。）

(D) **moreover** [mɔrˋovɚ] *adv.* 並且；此外
= in addition

例: Ms. Yang is knowledgeable. Moreover, she is very patient with students.
（楊老師知識淵博。此外，她對學生很有耐心。）

2. 根據語意，可知 (C) 項應為正選。

B 31.

解析

1. 空格前為本問句的主詞 what，空格後為名詞 explorers（探險家），得知空格應置本句主要動詞，以接 explorers 作受詞。本句為敘述不變的事實，須用現在式，而疑問代名詞 what 作問句的主詞時，視為單數，故動詞應使用第三人稱單數動詞，且依語意應使用主動語態。
2. 根據上述及語意，可知 (B) 項應為正選。

重要單字片語

1. **journey** [ˋdʒɝnɪ] *n.* 旅行（尤指長途旅行）& *vi.* 旅行
2. **come close to + N/V-ing**
差一點……

例: The stray dog came close to being run over by a car.
（那隻流浪狗差點被一輛車輾過。）

3. **succeed in + N/V-ing**
成功（做）……

例: Danny succeeded in convincing the seller to lower the price.
（丹尼成功說服賣方降價。）

4. **explore** [ɪkˋsplɔr] *vt.* 探索，探尋
explorer [ɪkˋsplɔrɚ] *n.* 探險家
例: Ricky enjoys exploring haunted houses.
（瑞奇喜歡到鬼屋探險。）

5. **canoe** [kəˋnu] *n.* 獨木舟

6. **manage** [ˋmænɪdʒ] *vi.* 搞定 & *vt.* 搞定；經營，管理
manage to V 成功完成……，設法做到……
例: Seth managed to bring up his kids without any help after his wife passed away.
（賽斯在妻子過世後設法不靠任何幫助而獨力將孩子撫養長大。）

7. **occupy** [ˋɑkjə͵paɪ] *vt.* 擁有；占據；使忙碌
例: The bed occupied most of Henry's bedroom.
（這張床占掉了亨利臥房中大半的空間。）

8. **major** [ˋmedʒɚ] *a.* 主要的；重要的

9. **original** [əˋrɪdʒənl̩] *a.* 原來的；原創的

10. **open up sth** 開啟某物；開拓／開闢某地方
例: This job might open up a whole new world for you.
（這份工作可能會為你開啟一個全新的世界。）

11. **vast** [væst] *a.* 巨大的

12. **vision** [ˋvɪʒən] *n.* 幻想，憧憬；視力；遠見

13. **drive** [draɪv] *vt.* 驅使；駕駛（汽車等）& *vi.* 開車

14. **security** [sɪˋkjurətɪ] *n.* 安全

15. **the unknown** 未知的事物
unknown [ʌnˋnon] *a.* 未知的
注意: "the + 形容詞" 視為名詞，表所有具該形容詞特性的人／事／物。
例: the elderly 年長者
the rich 有錢人

16. **adventure** [ədˋvɛntʃɚ] *n.* 冒險，奇遇

IV. 閱讀測驗

◎ 32 - 33

Kelly, Linda, Vivian, and Wendy are at a night market in Tainan. They are looking at the menu and talking about what they would like to eat. Everyone will order only one portion of any item she likes for herself.

Menu

Item	**Price** (for one portion)
Oyster omelet	NT$ 80
Danzai noodles	NT$ 70
Taiwanese Meatball[註1]	NT$ 50
Milkfish soup	NT$ 90
Coffin bread	NT$ 70
Bubble tea	NT$ 50

Kelly: I am hungry. I can[註2] eat a horse.

Linda: Me, too. Let's get something good to eat. I'd like to have Danzai noodles first.

Wendy: I'll get Oyster omelet[註3]. My cousin said that's a must-try. And, I also want to try Taiwanese meatball[註4]. I want to see how different it is[註5] from American meatballs.

Vivian: I'm hungry and thirsty. I'll get bubble tea and coffin bread.

Kelly: The most famous dish in Tainan is milkfish; I must try it. Besides, eating fish makes you smart!

凱莉、琳達、薇薇安和溫蒂在臺南的夜市裡。她們正看著菜單討論想吃的東西。每個人都只會點自己想吃的一客小吃。

菜單

品項	價格（一份）
蚵仔煎	臺幣 80 元
擔仔麵	臺幣 70 元
肉圓	臺幣 50 元
虱目魚湯	臺幣 90 元
棺材板	臺幣 70 元
珍珠奶茶	臺幣 50 元

凱　莉：我好餓，我可以吃下很多東西。

琳　達：我也是。我們來吃點好吃的吧。我想先吃擔仔麵。

溫　蒂：我要吃蚵仔煎，我表妹説一定要試試看這一味。還有，我也想吃肉圓，我想知道它跟美國的肉丸子有多不一樣。

薇薇安：我又餓又渴，所以我要喝珍珠奶茶還要吃棺材板。

凱　莉：臺南最有名的就是虱目魚，我一定要嚐嚐看。而且吃魚會變聰明喔！

註1：為與其他品項寫法一致，此處 Meatball 宜改為小寫開頭並為複數 meatballs。

註2：助動詞 can 應改為過去式的助動詞 could，以表與現在事實相反的假設語氣。

註3：此處 Oyster omelet 因非專有名詞，故宜改為小寫，且此為可數名詞，故前宜加 an，寫為 an oyster omelet。

註4：meatball 常為 meatballs，故宜改為 Taiwanese meatballs。

註5：這裡的 it 代替的是前句的 Taiwanese meatball，但 Taiwanese meatball 應改為複數較合理，故此處亦應改為複數寫法 they are。

D **32.**

What is Kelly going to order?

(A) A horse
(B) Bubble tea
(C) Coffin bread
(D) Milkfish soup

凱莉將會點哪道菜？
(A) 一匹馬
(B) 珍珠奶茶
(C) 棺材板
(D) 虱目魚湯

理由:
根據對話最後一句凱莉說 "The most famous dish in Tainan is milkfish; I must try it."（臺南最有名的就是虱目魚，我一定要嚐嚐看。）得知凱莉想吃虱目魚，可推測她將會點虱目魚湯，故 (D) 項應為正選。

D **33.**

According to the menu and the conversation, who will have to pay the most if everyone orders only one portion of each item she wants to eat?

(A) Kelly
(B) Linda
(C) Vivian
(D) Wendy

根據菜單及對話內容，如果每個人只點一份她想吃的東西，誰將付最多錢？
(A) 凱莉
(B) 琳達
(C) 薇薇安
(D) 溫蒂

理由:
根據對話可知凱莉想吃的是虱目魚湯，需付 90 元；琳達想吃的是擔仔麵，需付 70 元；薇薇安想吃的是珍珠奶茶（50 元）跟棺材板（70 元），需付 120 元；溫蒂想吃的是蚵仔煎（80 元）跟肉圓（50 元），需付 130 元。可知溫蒂將會付最多錢，因此 (D) 項應為正選。

重要單字片語

1. **portion** [ˋpɔrʃən] *n.*（食物）一客／份；部分
   a small / good / large portion of...
   一小／大部分的……
   例: The police recovered a good portion of the stolen goods.
   （警方找回大部分的遺失物。）
2. **item** [ˋaɪtəm] *n.* 品項；物品
3. **for oneself** 為某人自己
   例: You will be allowed to decide things for yourself when you are old enough.
   （等你夠大了就准你替自己決定事情。）

4. **I can eat a horse.** 我吃得下一匹馬。引申為某人餓到可以吃下很多東西的意思。
註：can 應改為 could。
eat like a horse / bird 食量很大 / 小

例: When John is stressed out, he tends to eat like a horse.
（當約翰壓力很大時，他就會暴食。）

5. **must-try** [ˋmʌsˌtraɪ] *n.* 一定要嘗試的東西

◎ 34 - 37

Cocoa trees were first brought to Taiwan from Indonesia by the Japanese when they ruled the island. But, the Japanese could not overcome the difficulties in growing the crop. It was not until about 20 years ago that Taiwanese farmers succeeded in growing the tropical plant.

Thanks to modern techniques, local farmers in Pingtung（屏東）are able to produce better-quality beans that can be made into fine chocolate. In order to promote chocolate industry[註6], local chocolate makers have also created new flavors of chocolate such as tea, fruit, and pepper for the past few years. Starting in 2016, this newly emerging cocoa industry in Pingtung went on to win international fame. In years 2018 and 2019, Taiwanese chocolate makers won numerous top prizes in the International Chocolate Award (ICA)'s World Finals. The rise of Taiwan's chocolate industry and its wonderful results even gave the country the honor of hosting the ICA's Asia-Pacific competition in 2019.

Even then, the industry is facing a problem. Not many chocolate eaters in Taiwan go for local products. To meet local taste, chocolate makers have come up with a variety of fine chocolates. They hope that as more people learn to appreciate and buy fine chocolate, the domestic market will **take off**. Encouraged by their success in global competitions, the chocolate makers are also targeting at the global market[註7]. They are eager to win over chocolate lovers worldwide with the delicate flavors of Taiwanese chocolate.

日本人統治臺灣時，他們首次把可可樹從印尼引進臺灣。但日本人無法克服種植這種作物的種種困難。直到大約二十年前，臺灣的農夫才成功種植這種熱帶植物。

由於現代技術，屏東當地的農夫得以產出品質更好的可可豆，這些豆子可以用來做成優質巧克力。為了要提倡巧克力產業，當地巧克力製造商在過去幾年來也研發新的巧克力口味，例如：茶、水果和胡椒口味。這個在屏東興起的可可產業始於 2016 年，隨後該產業便揚名國際。在 2018、2019 年，臺灣巧克力製造商在世界巧克力大賽的全球決賽中贏得了多項首獎。臺灣巧克力產業的的崛起及其令人驚歎的成果，甚至讓該國有幸主辦 2019 年世界巧克力大賽的亞太區競賽。

儘管如此，該產業正面臨一個問題。在臺灣，吃巧克力的人不太喜歡在地產品。為了符合本地人的口味，巧克力製造商推出了多種優質巧克力。他們希望隨著更多人懂得欣賞與購買優質巧克力，國內市場能一飛沖天。巧克力製造商受到國際比賽成功的激勵，也要進軍國際市場。他們渴望用臺灣巧克力的細緻風味擄獲全世界巧克力愛好者的芳心。

註6：原文的 chocolate industry 宜改為 the chocolate industry，因在此特指臺灣的巧克力產業。

註7：原文使用 are also targeting at，惟因 target 為及物動詞，故此處不宜在 targeting 後接 at，若要保留 at，則應把 targeting 改為 aiming。

C **34.**

What is the contribution of the Japanese to Taiwan's chocolate industry?

(A) They knew how to produce chocolate.
(B) They moved from Indonesia to Taiwan.
(C) They introduced cocoa trees to Taiwan.
(D) They succeeded in growing cocoa trees.

日本人對臺灣巧克力產業的貢獻是什麼？

(A) 他們知道如何生產巧克力。
(B) 他們從印尼搬遷至臺灣。
(C) 他們把可可樹引進臺灣。
(D) 他們成功種植了可可樹。

理由:

根據本文第一段第一句："Cocoa trees were first brought to Taiwan from Indonesia by the Japanese when they ruled the island."（日本人統治臺灣時，他們首次把可可樹從印尼引進臺灣。），得知 (C) 項應為正選。

A **35.**

According to the passage, which of the following statements is true?

(A) Taiwan-made chocolate is gaining world attention.
(B) Taiwan's chocolate makers produce a single flavor.
(C) Many Taiwanese chocolate eaters like local products.
(D) Indonesia farmers planted cocoa trees in Taiwan 20 years ago.

根據本文，下列哪一項敘述是正確的？

(A) 臺灣製的巧克力正獲得世界的關注。
(B) 臺灣的巧克力製造商只出產單一口味。
(C) 許多吃巧克力的臺灣人喜歡在地產品。
(D) 印尼的農夫二十年前在臺灣種植了可可樹。

理由:

根據本文第二段第三句："Starting in 2016, this newly emerging cocoa industry in Pingtung went on to win international fame."（這個在屏東興起的可可產業始於 2016 年，隨後該產業便揚名國際。）得知，(A) 項應為正選。

B **36.**

What does the phrase "**take off**" in paragraph 3 mean?

(A) Remove its obstacles

(B) Become successful

(C) Appear competitive

(D) Present its challenges

第三段中的片語 "**take off**" 是什麼意思？

(A) 移除障礙

(B) 變成功

(C) 看來很有競爭力

(D) 提出質疑

理由:

take off 本身即有「迅速成功」的意思，若不知道該片語，亦可從文章的上下文推測，本文第三段的前三句提及臺灣巧克力產業面臨的問題及解決方法，第四句則描述他們對於這種解決方法的期待，故得知 (B) 項為正選。

C **37.**

What is the main purpose of the passage?

(A) To discuss Taiwan's problems of planting cocoa trees.

(B) To introduce different flavors of Taiwanese chocolate.

(C) To show the development in Taiwan's chocolate industry.

(D) To describe Taiwan's success in selling chocolate worldwide.

本文的主旨為何？

(A) 討論臺灣種植可可樹的問題。

(B) 介紹臺灣不同風味的巧克力。

(C) 說明臺灣巧克力產業的發展。

(D) 描述臺灣在全球販售巧克力的成功經驗。

理由:

本文第一段簡介臺灣引進可可樹的由來，第二段介紹臺灣的巧克力產業如何開始發跡並獲得國際關注，第三段則說明臺灣巧克力產業的現況，通篇文章說明臺灣巧克力產業的發展，故 (C) 項應為正選。

重要單字片語

1. **rule** [rul] *vt.* & *vi.* 統治

   例: The king has ruled this kingdom for forty years.
   （國王統治這個國家四十年了。）

2. **overcome** [ˌovɚˋkʌm] *vt.* 克服
   （三態為：overcome, overcame, overcome）

   例: We have to overcome many hurdles in order to be successful.
   （為了成功，我們必須克服許多障礙。）

3. **crop** [krɑp] *n.* 作物

4. **succeed** [səkˋsid] *vi.* 成功
succeed in + N/V-ing　成功做……
例: The doctor succeeded in finding a cure for the disease.
（這位醫生成功發現治療該疾病的方法。）

5. **tropical** [ˋtrɑpɪkḷ] *a.* 熱帶的

6. **technique** [tɛkˋnik] *n.* 技巧，手法

7. **fine** [faɪn] *a.* 優良的，水準很高的

8. **promote** [prəˋmot] *vt.* 促進，提倡
例: The company promotes education by offering scholarships to the poor.
（該公司提供清寒獎學金來推廣教育。）

9. **industry** [ˋɪndəstrɪ] *n.* 產業；行業；工業
the travel / fashion industry
旅遊業／時裝業

10. **flavor** [ˋflevɚ] *n.* 口／風味

11. **fame** [fem] *n.* 名聲，名氣
win fame　贏得名聲

12. **rise** [raɪz] *n.* 興起，崛起；上升
the rise of...　……的興起／崛起

13. **go for sth**　喜歡／支持某物
例: I don't really go for Italian food.
（我不太喜歡吃義大利菜。）

14. **appreciate** [əˋpriʃɪ͵et] *vt.* 欣賞；感激
例: Nora respects those who can appreciate art or music.
（諾拉尊敬懂得欣賞藝術或音樂的人。）

15. **domestic** [dəˋmɛstɪk] *a.* 國內的，本國的

16. **take off**　迅速成功；很快走紅
例: The writer's novel took off soon after it was published.
（該作家的小說出版不久後便快速竄紅了。）

17. **target** [ˋtɑrgɪt] *vt.* 以……（某消費族群等）為目標
target A at B　A 以 B 為目標
例: This new store is targeted at female customers.
（這間新開的店以女性顧客為目標。）

18. **eager** [ˋigɚ] *a.* 渴望的
be eager to V　渴望做……

19. **delicate** [ˋdɛləkət] *a.*（口味）細緻的

◎ 38 - 41

Early this year, a new coronavirus（新冠狀病毒）caused the rapid spread of the Coronavirus Disease 2019 (COVID-19). Many countries began practicing "social distancing" to prevent infection spread by increasing the space between people. All over the world, social distancing brought about changes in people's ways of living, learning, and working.

Lifestyle changes due to social distancing affected almost everyone. People avoided crowded places and unnecessary traveling. In Italy, for example, church leaders spoke to followers online. Elsewhere, online shopping in Taiwan and home entertainment in China rose significantly in February.

Social distancing also had an effect on learning. In Australia, when schools were still open, teachers tried not to let students mix in common areas that included the classroom, café and library. As the crisis worsened, schools closed **one** after another. By early April, over 90% of the world's students were not attending school. In some places, such as Italy and Hong Kong, students turned to learning from home through Internet connection.

To lower the risk of infection, companies put distance between employees in the workplace and told sick employees to stay home. Offices were generally flexible in the time and place of work. Furthermore, to keep the workplace safe, the United States passed a law to provide paid sick leave for all employees. This was to make sure that workers who fell ill with the coronavirus would stay home without fear of losing their income.

In the fight against the coronavirus, people stayed apart to stay healthy. However, they all stayed connected to feel a sense of togetherness.

今年初，一種新的冠狀病毒造成了 2019 冠狀病毒疾病（COVID-19）迅速地傳播。許多國家開始實行「保持社交距離運動」，好藉由增加人與人之間的距離，以防止傳染的擴散。保持社交距離運動帶來了全球民眾在生活、學習、以及工作方式上的改變。

因為保持社交距離運動而對生活方式帶來的改變，影響了幾乎每個人。民眾會避開擁擠的地方，以及避免不必要的旅行。舉例來說，在義大利，教會的領袖會在線上與教友對話。而在其他地方，臺灣的線上購物以及中國大陸的家庭娛樂方面，二月時有大幅度的增加。

保持社交距離運動在學習上也有影響。在澳洲，當學校還是開放的時候，教師都會試圖不讓學生在包含教室、咖啡廳與圖書館等公共場所裡群聚在一起。當疫情更加嚴重時，學校一間接著一間關閉。直至四月初，全世界超過 90% 的學生沒有去上學。在某些地方，譬如說在義大利及香港，學生開始轉向在家透過網路連線來學習。

為了要降低感染的風險，許多公司在工作場所要求員工之間要保持距離，並且要求生病的員工要待在家。許多公司在工作時間與工作地點上，一般都保有彈性。此外，為了保持工作場所的安全，美國通過了一條法律，好提供所有的員工支薪的病假。這是為了確保得了冠狀病毒的員工待在家時，可以不必害怕失去他們的收入。

在與冠狀病毒對抗的過程中，民眾為了保持健康而保持距離。然而，民眾仍又保持交流，好感到某種凝聚感。

A **38.**

What is the best title for this passage?

(A) Less Human Contact for Good Health

(B) Better Learning with Internet Connection

(C) Flexible Time and Place for Employment

(D) Safe Homes with Popular Entertainments

本文章最適合的標題是什麼？

(A) 減少與人接觸以保持健康

(B) 用網路連線能學得較好

(C) 彈性的工作時間與工作地點

(D) 安全的住家並具備受歡迎的娛樂活動

理由:

根據本文第一段指出，為了防止傳染的擴散，許多國家紛紛實行「保持社交距離運動」，並接著解釋在生活、學習、以及工作方式上所帶來的影響。故 (A) 項應為正選。

C **39.**

What does the word **"one"** in paragraph 3 refer to?

(A) classroom

(B) crisis

(C) school

(D) student

本文第三段的 **"one"** 一字指的是什麼？

(A) 教室

(B) 疫情

(C) 學校

(D) 學生

理由:

本文第三段第三句 "As the crisis worsened, schools closed one after another." 中，代名詞 one 意指前面的 school（學校）。而 one after another 則表「一個接著一個」。故 (C) 項應為正選。

C **40.**

According to the passage, which of the following statements is true?

(A) About 90% of the students stayed at home to learn to use the Internet.

(B) Social distancing measured how fast the coronavirus spreads in a country.

(C) Schools stopped students from gathering in large groups to prevent infection.

(D) A new US law stated that sick employees would be paid if they worked at the office.

根據本文，下列哪一項敘述是正確的？

(A) 大約 90% 的學生待在家學習使用網路。

(B) 保持社交距離運動測量出一個國家裡冠狀病毒散播得有多快。

(C) 學校制止學生群聚在一起以防止感染。

(D) 美國的一條新法律明定，如果生病的員工在辦公室上班，就會被支薪。

理由:
根據本文第三段第二句 "In Australia, when schools were still open, teachers tried not to let students mix in common areas that included the classroom, café and library."（在澳洲，當學校還是開放的時候，教師都會試圖不讓學生在包含教室、咖啡廳與圖書館等公共場所裡群聚在一起。）得知，(C) 項應為正選。

A **41.**

According to the passage, which of the following is **NOT** an act of social distancing?
(A) Attending a live concert filled with people.
(B) Reducing the number of workers in the office.
(C) Holding online church meetings with followers.
(D) Watching videos at home instead of going to the movies.

根據本文，下列哪一項不是保持社交距離運動的表現？
(A) 參加擁擠的現場演唱會。
(B) 減少辦公室裡的員工人數。
(C) 與教友在線上舉行教會聚會。
(D) 在家看影片，而不是去看電影。

理由:
根據本文第二段第二句 "People avoided crowded places and unnecessary traveling."（民眾會避開擁擠的地方，以及避免不必要的旅行。）得知，(A) 項應為正選。

重要單字片語

1. **corona** [kəˋronə] *n.* 日冕（此字源自拉丁文，表「冠」）
2. **virus** [ˋvaɪrəs] *n.* 病毒
3. **rapid** [ˋræpɪd] *a.* 迅速的
4. **disease** [dɪˋziz] *n.* 疾病
   a common / rare disease
   常見 / 罕見疾病
5. **practice** [ˋpræktɪs] *vt.* 實施，實行
   例: My mother taught me to practice good manners.
   （我媽媽教我要表現好的禮貌。）
6. **prevent** [prɪˋvɛnt] *vt.* 阻止
   prevent sb/sth from + N/V-ing
   避免……；阻止……
   例: We should do something to prevent our child from lying again.
   （我們應採取作為防止我們的孩子再度說謊。）
7. **infection** [ɪnˋfɛkʃən] *n.* 感染
   例: White blood cells help the body defend itself against infection.
   （白血球會幫助我們的身體抵禦感染。）
8. **bring about...** 導致……
   = lead to...
   例: What brought about the crisis?
   （是什麼導致這危機的？）
9. **avoid** [əˋvɔɪd] *vt.* 避免
   avoid + V-ing 避免……
   例: You should avoid taking in too much fat.
   （你應避免攝取過多的脂肪。）
10. **entertainment** [ˌɛntəˋtenmənt] *n.* 娛樂，樂趣

11. **mix** [mɪks] *vi.* 相處，打交道
例: Mary mixes well in social situations.
（瑪莉在社交場合與人相處得很融洽。）

12. **crisis** [ˋkraɪsɪs] *n.*（疾病的）危險期；危機
the oil crisis　　石油危機

13. **turn to...**　　改做 / 用……
例: John sang rock music before turning to the blues.
（約翰在改唱藍調前是唱搖滾樂的。）

14. **flexible** [ˋflɛksəbl̩] *a.* 有彈性的
例: I prefer to keep my schedule flexible when I travel abroad.
（我出國旅行時比較喜歡有彈性的行程。）

15. **leave** [liv] *n.* 休假（不可數）
be on leave　　休假中
be on annual / maternity / sick leave　　休年假 / 產假 / 病假中
paid / unpaid leave　　有薪 / 無薪假
例: Our manager is on maternity leave.
（我們經理在休產假。）

16. **ill** [ɪl] *a.* 生病的
fall ill　　生病了
例: John fell ill and had to ask for leave.
（約翰生病了所以得請假。）

17. **income** [ˋɪnkʌm] *n.* 收入
例: Sam has had a stable income for several years.
（山姆這幾年來收入穩定。）

18. **togetherness** [təˋgɛðɚnɪs] *n.* 團聚；和睦

19. **measure** [ˋmɛʒɚ] *vt.* 測量，評估
例: It's difficult to measure the importance of these campaigns.
（要評斷這些活動的重要性很難。）

20. **go to the movies**　　看電影
例: I go to the movies on weekends to relax.
（週末我會看電影輕鬆一下。）

第二部分：非選擇題（第 I 至 III 題，每題 6 分，共 18 分）

I. 填充

1. 這炸雞很美味，但對我來說有點太鹹了！

The fried c__①__ is tasty, but a little bit too s__②__ for me.

① chicken　　② salty

解析

1. 本題空格 ① 的對照譯句為『雞（肉）』，且空格為 c 開頭，後接單數 be 動詞 is，故空格應置不可數名詞 chicken。
2. 本題空格 ② 的對照譯句為『鹹（的）』，且空格為 s 開頭，故該空格應置 salty。

其他重點

1. **fried** [fraɪd] *a.* 油炸的；油煎的
2. **tasty** [ˋtestɪ] *a.* 美味的（= delicious = yummy）
3. **a little bit** 稍微地（= a little = a bit = somewhat）

例: My grandfather feels a little bit under the weather today.
（我爺爺今天身體有點不舒服。）

II. 句子重組

2. stared at / who was talking loudly / the boy / on his cellphone / People on the bus

People on the bus stared at the boy who was talking loudly on his cellphone.
（公車上的人都瞪著那個講手機很大聲的男生。）

解析

1. 先找出開頭為大寫的詞組 People on the bus 作為句首。
2. 主詞詞組 People on the bus（公車上的人）之後應接動詞。重組部分中，stared at 為動詞詞組，表『瞪／怒視』，故形成 "People on the bus stared at..."。
3. at 之後應接表『被瞪的人或物』的名詞詞組 the boy（那個男生），形成句子結構：主詞 + 動詞 + 受詞。
4. 剩下的詞組部分，who was talking loudly（講話很大聲）為形容詞子句的開頭，可用以修飾先行詞 the boy，後接剩下的介詞片語 on his cellphone（講手機）以形成一個完整的形容詞子句。
5. 由上可得答案：
People on the bus stared at the boy who was talking loudly on his cellphone.

其他重點

stare [stɛr] *vi.* 瞪；凝視
stare at... 瞪／凝視……

例: Everyone was staring at the strange man.
（大家都盯著那名怪怪的男人。）

III. 中譯英

3. 我表姊邀請我去參加她的婚禮。
My cousin invited me to her wedding.
或：My cousin invited me to attend her wedding.

解析

1. 『我表姊』可譯成 My cousin。cousin 可代表堂 / 表兄弟姊妹。
2. 『邀請我去參加』可譯成 invited me to (attend)...。
3. 『她的婚禮』可譯成 her wedding。
4. 由上得知，本句可譯為：
   My cousin invited me to her wedding.
   或：My cousin invited me to attend her wedding.
5. 請注意：與中文『參加』對應的英文還有 join, take part (in), participate (in)，但本處並不合用。原因是 join 以『加入群體、團隊、活動』的意思為主；take part in, participate in 則是『參加比賽、討論』等。婚禮（wedding）與這兩個用法的受詞性質不太一樣，且婚禮是當事人兩人的事情，你不能『加入』，只能『到場』，所以不適用。

   例: I will join my best friend's wedding party this Sunday.
   （我這個禮拜天要去參加好友的婚禮派對。）
   Do you take part in extra-curricular activities at school?
   = Do you participate in extra-curricular activities at school?
   （你有參加學校的課外活動嗎？）

其他重點

1. **invite sb to N** 邀請某人（去）……
   invite sb to V 邀請某人（做）……

   例: Lauren invited me to dine with her parents.
   （蘿倫邀請我跟她的父母一起用餐。）
2. **wedding** [ˋwɛdɪŋ] *n.* 婚禮

國家圖書館出版品預行編目（CIP）資料

四技二專統測歷屆英文試題完全解析詳解本.
114 年版／賴世雄作. -- 初版. -- 臺北市：
常春藤數位出版股份有限公司, 2025.06
面； 公分.
--（常春藤升科大四技二專系列；IA02-114）
ISBN 978-626-7225-93-6（平裝）
1. CST：英語 2. CST：問題集
805.189 114006798

填讀者問卷
送熊贈點

常春藤升科大四技二專系列【IA02－114】

四技二專統測歷屆英文試題完全解析－詳解本（114 年版）

總 編 審 賴世雄
終 審 梁民康
執行編輯 許嘉華
編輯小組 常春藤中外編輯群
設計組長 王玥琦
封面設計 王穎緁
排版設計 王穎緁・林桂旭
錄 音 林政偉
播音老師 賴世雄・奚永慧
法律顧問 北辰著作權事務所蕭雄淋律師
出 版 者 常春藤數位出版股份有限公司
地 址 臺北市忠孝西路一段 33 號 5 樓
電 話 (02) 2331-7600
傳 真 (02) 2381-0918
網 址 www.ivy.com.tw
電子信箱 service@ivy.com.tw
郵政劃撥 50463568
戶 名 常春藤數位出版股份有限公司
定 價 320 元（2 書）
出版日期 2025 年 6 月 初版／一刷

114

四技二專 統測

試題本

歷屆英文試題**完全解析**

序

我們出版本書的目的，就是要**從根本出發，協助所有高職同學培養對英文的熱愛及答題的技巧**，使他們對未來的四技二專入學測驗不再畏懼，甚至以超高分通過這個令許多高職學生頭痛的英文科測驗。

早年（1980 年代初）我曾在升大學補習班所謂的『台大醫科班』教授英文。這是許多在補習班任教的老師競相爭取的班級，只要能在此班任教就被視作『王牌名師』。相對的，在『職校班』任教的老師多被視為『二線老師』。我覺得這是很不妥的想法。於是，我自願撥出時間教職校班，認為**這些學生只要肯用功一樣能考上理想的大學**。

第一次接觸職校班時令我印象深刻。這些職校的同學個個老實又樂天知命。他們滿腔熱忱，對人生抱持樂觀的態度。比較起來，醫科班的學生聰明又較理性，而職校班的學生則謙虛且有人情味，因此**我教職校班的時候，心情總是很愉快**。

不可諱言，職校的學生英文程度平均較差，有些連國中的程度都不及。深知這點，我就以極慢的速度教學，教材內容就選定歷屆試題。每次上課一個半小時，我最多只能講解兩三行。我慢慢地教，耐心地教，把每一個字詞的用法做最清晰完整的解說，一年的時間才講解不到兩份試卷，但卻也見到他們顯著的進步。**那年，班上有一半的同學考上了與普通高中生同時競爭的『大學聯考』**。這些同學中不乏現在事業有成的名人（如電視界的主持名人**于美人**及臺灣網通董事長**謝效家**），其中**謝效家**在當年的大學聯考英文科甚至考了 85 分（當時全臺灣 90 分以上的同學不到 10 位），這個分數贏過了不少從明星高中畢業的高材生！

有感於坊間專為高職生出版的升學用書，多為簡答且解析又不夠完整的參考書，我很感念當年與職校班的一段淵源，遂決定出版《四技二專統測歷屆英文試題完全解析》，希望能夠助職校同學一臂之力。本書蒐集歷屆試題 6 回，書中的內容鋪陳，百分百是我當年教導職校班的縮影——**題題詳解，並將重要字詞一一陳述其用法並輔以簡單例句，以引導讀者掌握考試重點**。

我深知職校同學對英文的苦惱，因此與常春藤合作多年的資深講解老師奚永慧（Wesley）老師合作，特地將此 6 回試題講解**錄製成音檔**，每一回試題均為 2~3 小時左右的長度，為的是讓讀者一方面細閱書中的講解，一方面聽著解說，**這種視聽雙管齊下的方式最能在短時間之內迅速培養職校同學的英文功力**。並且為了讓同學能夠隨時隨地學習，我們特地將音檔都上傳本公司專屬的音檔收聽櫃，同學只要掃瞄 QR Code，就能馬上用手機播放音檔，學習不設限，好用又方便。

這樣的編輯方針及態度，當然能讓讀者立刻明白這本書是道道地地的好書，也看出常春藤編輯群的用心。不過，我們並不以此為傲，我們關心的是你是否能配合本書用心學習。如果能的話，你當可輕易奪取高分，進入理想的大學，這也是我們最大的期望！

目錄 CONTENTS

114 四技二專統一入學測驗－試題

第一部分：選擇題

- I. 字彙題
- II. 對話題
- III. 綜合測驗
- IV. 閱讀測驗

第二部分：非選擇題

- I. 填充
- II. 句子重組
- III. 中譯英

第一部分：選擇題（第 1 至 42 題，每題 2 分，共 84 分）

Ⅰ. 字彙題：

第 1 至 8 題，每題均有一空格字詞，請選擇最適合的答案，以完成該英文句子。第 9 至 10 題，每題均有一個劃底線的字詞，請在四個選項中，選擇一個與劃底線的字詞意義最接近的答案。

1. This child is using colored chalks to ______ pictures on a blank piece of paper.
(A) draw (B) heat (C) mail (D) type

2. The room was so ______ that I couldn't even find space for these new chairs.
(A) available (B) crowded (C) empty (D) positive

3. Many people have climbed the main ______ of Mount Jade in Taiwan, which is the highest point on the island.
(A) base (B) peak (C) shore (D) valley

4. After looking at his grandfather's ______ on the wall, John was happy to discover that his grandfather and he really looked alike.
(A) cattle (B) jewelry (C) portrait (D) whistle

5. It is risky for people to touch plants in rainforests because some plants can be ______ to humans.
(A) fashionable (B) jealous (C) poisonous (D) reasonable

6. Governments have the ______ to punish people who drink and drive.
(A) authority (B) bargain (C) courtesy (D) infection

7. During the night, the sensor lights in the park will ______ turn on by themselves when someone is passing by.
(A) automatically (B) organically (C) productively (D) selfishly

8. Chen Chieh-hsien (陳傑憲) ______ the WBSC Premier12 2024 MVP (Most Valuable Player) due to his magnificent performance.
(A) was named after (B) made fun of
(C) was in charge of (D) stood out as

9. Mary came to me and introduced herself again. Apparently, she thought that I had forgotten her name.
(A) actively (B) entirely (C) internally (D) obviously

10. My sister decided to abandon her old habits and start a fresh chapter in her life.
(A) bring about (B) carry on (C) give up (D) run into

II. 對話題：

第 11 至 20 題，請依對話內容選出一個最適合的答案，使其成為有意義的對話。

11. Dad: Hey, you're always on your phone!
Son: I know. I just like playing games and watching videos.
Dad: But if you use the phone too much, you might hurt your eyes.
Son: ________
Dad: Yeah, let's go jogging. It's more fun.
(A) Then I should use it less.
(B) Should I use a new phone?
(C) Do you like to watch videos, too?
(D) So you should play online games.

12. Lucy: Do you know that plastics can take 20 years to break down?
John: That's awful! We really need to use less plastic.
Lucy: I agree. ________
John: Great idea! I'll try that, too.
(A) No wonder I prefer buying plastic containers.
(B) So I keep using plastic straws for all my drinks.
(C) That's why I always carry my own water bottle.
(D) And I make sure to throw away everything I buy.

13. Vendor: These vegetables are chemical free.
Customer: They look great. But what about the eggs? ________
Vendor: Of course! We get them straight from the farm every morning. They are the best.
(A) Are they fresh? (B) How much are they?
(C) Do you plant them? (D) How do you cook them?

14. Ken: The line is too long! Let's cut in line, so we can get into the theater in time.
July: No way. ________________
Ken: OK. Let's go to the back of the line.
(A) Which theater do you prefer?
(B) Which movie are we going to see?
(C) How much do you pay for two adults?
(D) How can you even think of doing that?

15. Dave: I'm going to a job interview this Thursday. What should I prepare?
Nancy: A good first impression is important. ________________
Dave: For example?
Nancy: A suit or something formal that looks professional.
(A) You have to dress properly.
(B) You need to speak carefully.
(C) You ought to show interest in the pay.
(D) You should ask questions about the job.

16. Anna: Hey Terry, do you know that Lee Yang (李洋) and Wang Chi-lin (王齊麟) won a gold medal at the Paris Olympics?
Terry: Yeah! That makes two gold medals, including the one from the Tokyo Olympics.
Anna: Their skills are incredible. And their teamwork is super impressive, too!
Terry: ________________
Anna: Exactly! That's why badminton is getting more popular in Taiwan these days.
(A) They have decided not to work together.
(B) Some people say their success was just luck.
(C) I believe they don't need to practice anymore.
(D) I think their success has motivated many people.

17. Mom: Guess what? A high school student offered his seat to me on the bus today. He's so sweet!
Son: ________________
Mom: That's true, because I'd been working all day and I could hardly keep my eyes open.
(A) Did you say anything?
(B) Maybe you looked tired.
(C) Surely he liked standing.
(D) Was he getting off the bus?

18. Housekeeping: May I help you?

Mrs. Liu: Yes. I'm Mrs. Liu. We've just changed rooms, from 706 to 1012. I think I lost my scarf during the move.

Housekeeping: I'm sorry. ______________

Mrs. Liu: It's blue and green, made of silk. Very expensive!

(A) Where did you lose the scarf?
(B) Which room do you like better?
(C) What does your scarf look like?
(D) Why did you move to another room?

19. Ms. Lee: Are you an art lover, Johnson?

Johnson: I'm passionate about art. I majored in art history and modern sculpture.

Ms. Lee: Impressive! ______________

Johnson: Your focus on modern art matches my background and interests. I'm excited to use what I've learned at this job.

Ms. Lee: That's great to hear. We'll let you know the outcome as soon as possible.

(A) Have you heard the outcome yet?
(B) Are you majoring in modern history?
(C) What's your educational background?
(D) Why do you want to work at my gallery?

20. Paul: I read an article online. It said Thomas Edison (湯瑪斯・愛迪生) didn't actually invent the light bulb. What he did was make it work for homes.

Jack: Really? ______________

Paul: The article said it's Humphry Davy, a scientist. He created the first electric light.

(A) But who finally switched it off?
(B) Then who came up with it first?
(C) Who bought the first light bulb anyway?
(D) So who did he really invite to his home?

III. 綜合測驗：

以下兩篇短文，共有 8 個空格，為第 21 至 28 題，每題有四個選項，請依各篇短文文意，選出一個最適合該空格的答案。

◎下篇短文共有 4 個空格，為第 21-24 題，請依短文文意，選出一個最適合該空格的答案。

Taiwan won 43 awards, including two golds, at the 47th WorldSkills Competition hosted by France in September 2024. About 1,400 students competed in over 60 skill categories __21__ robotics, carpentry, and refrigeration and air conditioning. Taiwan's competitors Tsai Yun-rong (蔡昀融) and Chen Sz-yuan (陳思源) won the top awards in cabinetmaking, and refrigeration and air conditioning, respectively. Tsai said he dedicated many hours of study and practice to his skills. Encouraged __22__ his father, Tsai tried woodworking in kindergarten. Since junior high school, he has spent 12 hours every day in the carpentry workshop to improve his skills. As for Chen, he emphasized the importance of hands-on training. Chen joined a training program in refrigeration and air conditioning at the age of 15, and __23__ the six-month course when most people dropped out. The two winners are clear examples of learning by doing. They develop their skills through direct experience and __24__ over a long period of time. The competition, also known as "Skills Olympics," provides a global stage for young people to demonstrate their talents.

21. (A) compared with (B) except for (C) such as (D) rather than

22. (A) at (B) by (C) from (D) with

23. (A) complete (B) completed (C) completing (D) will complete

24. (A) constant practice (B) giving awards (C) robotics talents (D) speech training

◎下篇短文共有 4 個空格，為第 25-28 題，請依短文文意，選出一個最適合該空格的答案。

E-cigarettes were once advertised as a healthier choice than regular cigarettes. Their sweet flavors and cool designs have made the public believe they are harmless. __25__, the truth is e-cigarettes contain nicotine (尼古丁), which can lead to addiction and lung damage. According to an expert at the Einstein Medical Center in Philadelphia, __26__ a teaspoonful of liquid nicotine could kill a person weighing 91 kilograms. Despite the risks, the number of high school students who smoke e-cigarettes __27__ worldwide in the past five years. In Taiwan, more and more teenagers are smoking e-cigarettes. A 2021 survey found that 3.9% of junior high and 8.8% of high school students used e-cigarettes. One possible reason for this trend is the ease of buying e-cigarettes online. Sellers even deliver them to convenience stores. ___28___, Taiwan's government banned e-cigarettes starting in 2023. They also reminded teenagers to follow the "Three No's Policy": no trying, no buying, and no recommending e-cigarettes. Otherwise, there would be a fine of up to NT$10,000.

25. (A) However (B) Therefore (C) At last (D) By chance

26. (A) as far as (B) as tall as (C) as little as (D) as many as

27. (A) double (B) has doubled (C) will double (D) have doubled

28. (A) To stop this rise (B) Due to the price (C) With regard to fashion (D) Instead of taking action

Ⅳ. **閱讀測驗：**

以下有五篇短文，共有 14 個題目，為第 29 至 42 題，請於閱讀短文後，選出最適當的答案。

◎閱讀下文，回答第 29-30 題

Answer the questions based on the poster below.

Dorothy Hodgkin: an outstanding chemist who won a Nobel Prize in 1964 for her studies in vitamins.

Grace Hopper: a mathematician who was a pioneer in developing computer technology. She served in the U.S. Navy during World War II.

Maria Mayer: a scientist who won a Nobel Prize in 1963 for her work in atomic science.

Maria Mitchell: a famous astronomer who discovered a new comet in 1847. She was the first woman ever to be voted into the American Academy of Arts and Sciences.

Nancy Roman: an astronomer who worked with rockets and space exploration. She was called a "wizard in math" while in college.

Chien-Shiung Wu: a nuclear physicist who was regarded as the "top woman experimental physicist in the world" by Princeton University in 1958. She came to the United States from China.

29. What is the best title for the poster?

(A) The power of women
(B) Wizards in World War II
(C) The Nobel Prize winners
(D) Women chemists in the world

30. According to the poster, which of the following statements is **NOT** true?

(A) Maria Mitchell was an astronomer who found a new comet.
(B) Dorothy Hodgkin and Maria Mayer were Nobel Prize winners.
(C) Grace Hopper and Nancy Roman were good at mathematics.
(D) Chien-Shiung Wu was a scientist born in the United States.

◎ 閱讀下文，回答第 31-32 題

Dave is seeking Betty's advice on choosing a mobile data plan. Answer the questions based on the conversation and the table below.

Dave: Hey Betty, I need your advice on choosing a cell phone plan.
Betty: Of course. What's the most important to you in a data plan?
Dave: I need a lot of data since I play online games and watch tons of videos online.
Betty: Me too. How much data are you thinking of?
Dave: My plan with Horizon offers 10 GB at NT$399. I'm considering upgrading to 20 GB.
Betty: If you watch videos very often, you might need unlimited data.
Dave: Unlimited? Isn't that super expensive?
Betty: Not necessarily. My plan is NT$699 per month with unlimited data, calls and texts.
Dave: Really? I'll switch to the same plan then. Thanks a lot!
Betty: You're welcome!

Horizon Mobile Data Plans		
Plan	***Fee / Month***	***Data / Month***
A*	NT$399	10 GB
B	NT$599	20 GB
C*	NT$699	unlimited
D	NT$999	unlimited

* Special discounts for students only

31. According to the conversation and the table, which of the following statements is <u>**NOT**</u> true?
(A) Both Dave and Betty play games and watch videos online.
(B) Horizon offers two different types of discounts to students.
(C) Dave's current data plan includes 10 GB of data per month.
(D) Betty wants to upgrade her data plan to include 20 GB of data.

32. According to the conversation, which data plan will Dave choose in the end?
(A) Plan A (B) Plan B (C) Plan C (D) Plan D

◎根據以下圖表，回答第 33-35 題

The table below contains data on typhoons that hit Taiwan in 2021, 2022, and 2023. Answer the questions based on the table below.

Year	Typhoon Name	Warning Period (Dates)	Intensity near Taiwan
2023	KOINU	2023-10-02 ~ 2023-10-06	Moderate Intensity
2023	HAIKUI	2023-09-01 ~ 2023-09-05	Moderate Intensity
2023	SAOLA	2023-08-28 ~ 2023-08-31	Intense Intensity
2023	KHANUN	2023-08-01 ~ 2023-08-04	Moderate Intensity
2023	DOKSURI	2023-07-24 ~ 2023-07-28	Moderate Intensity
2023	MAWAR	2023-05-29 ~ 2023-05-31	Moderate Intensity
2022	NESAT	2022-10-15 ~ 2022-10-16	Moderate Intensity
2022	MUIFA	2022-09-11 ~ 2022-09-13	Moderate Intensity
2022	HINNAMNOR	2022-09-02 ~ 2022-09-04	Intense Intensity
2021	KOMPASU	2021-10-10 ~ 2021-10-12	Severe tropical storm
2021	CHANTHU	2021-09-10 ~ 2021-09-13	Intense Intensity
2021	LUPIT	2021-08-04 ~ 2021-08-05	Severe tropical storm
2021	IN-FA	2021-07-21 ~ 2021-07-24	Moderate Intensity
2021	CHOI-WAN	2021-06-03 ~ 2021-06-04	Severe tropical storm

33. Which month has the most typhoons in 2023?
(A) July (B) August (C) September (D) October

34. Which of the following statements is true?
(A) There were a total of six typhoons in 2021.
(B) There were more typhoons in 2022 than in 2021.
(C) Both typhoons MUIFA and LUPIT hit Taiwan in 2022.
(D) Most typhoons were of Moderate Intensity during the three years.

35. Which of the following charts shows the data on the table correctly?

(A)
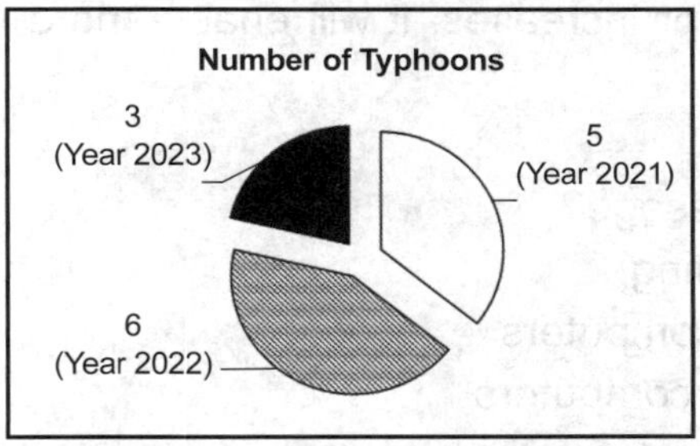

(B)
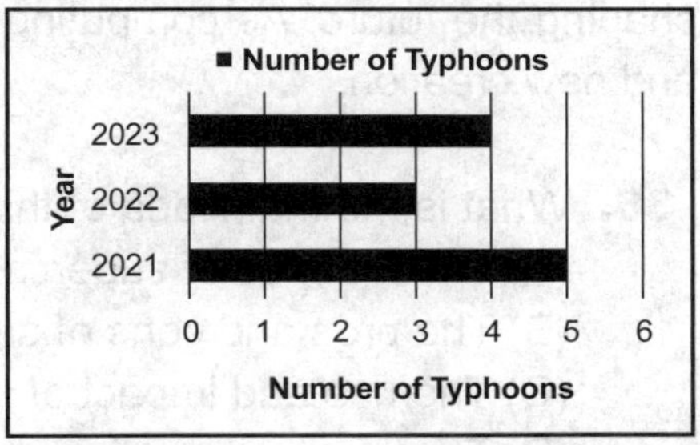

(C)
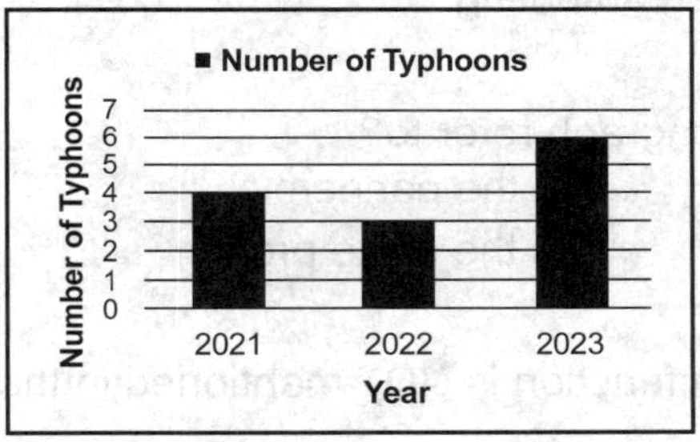

(D)
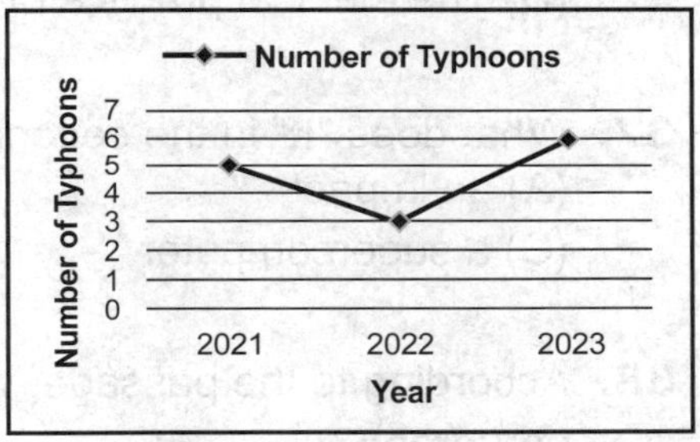

◎閱讀下文，回答第 36-38 題

With the rise of AI, supercomputers have become more important than ever. These powerful machines can process large amounts of data quickly. They help drive innovation and improve efficiency in the modern economy. Increasingly, governments and companies are building advanced supercomputing systems.

Around the world, supercomputers have already made an impact in various fields. During the pandemic, a supercomputer helped scientists isolate and identify the spike protein (棘蛋白) in COVID-19 virus. **It** analyzed and compared samples from different countries to better understand the spike protein. Hopefully, supercomputers will also contribute to developing cures for cancers that have remained challenging for years. Another area supercomputers can be used in is wind power production. They can help predict climate factors and improve the efficiency of wind farm performance.

In Taiwan, supercomputers have been providing services that benefit both businesses and the public. For instance, the Taiwan Computing Cloud (臺灣 AI 雲) supercomputer helps pig farmers select healthy young pigs and predict the growth of these pigs. The selection starts when the pigs are just seven days old.

In this way, it saves time, reduces costs, and enhances livestock quality. Another supercomputer system, the Central Weather Bureau's supercomputer, improves the accuracy of weather forecasting and strengthens Taiwan's earthquake early warning system. It is worth mentioning that the powerful supercomputer at the National Health Research Institutes supports advanced biotechnology and pharmaceutical projects. This contributes to better health of the population.

In conclusion, supercomputing is not just about technology; it is also about shaping the future. As computing power increases, it will enable more innovation and new creation.

36. What is the main idea of this passage?
(A) The theories of supercomputing
(B) The pros and cons of supercomputers
(C) The use and impact of supercomputers
(D) The medical practice of supercomputing

37. What does "**It**" in the second paragraph refer to?
(A) an impact (B) the pandemic
(C) a supercomputer (D) the spike protein

38. According to the passage, which function is **NOT** mentioned in the third paragraph?
(A) Helping people become healthier
(B) Enhancing wind power performance
(C) Improving Taiwan's livestock quality
(D) Providing more accurate weather forecasts

◎閱讀下文，回答第 39-42 題

Taiwan supplies a third of the world's orchids. As Taiwan's top flower exports, orchids brought in export earnings of NT$ 7 billion in 2023. The most popular export variety is Taiwan's unique moth orchids (蝴蝶蘭). Often used as gifts or for displays, moth orchids come in different shapes and colors.

Taiwan's orchid industry emerged in the 1980s. It has flourished with the use of greenhouse farming. In fact, flower exports increased tenfold between 1995 and 2008. In 2007, Taiwan lost its top position in the global flower market to the Netherlands. To cope with this challenge, Taiwan growers worked hard to make themselves different from their competitors. They began focusing on the export of orchid seedlings, young orchid plants that have just grown from seeds. In 2018, Taiwan exported about NT$ 4.5 billion worth of moth orchid seedlings to over 80 countries. The large diversity of native orchids on the island enables the creation of many commercial varieties. Growers mix different native species to develop a new variety. Taiwan has the largest concentration of orchid greenhouse growing and related services in the world.

Taiwan growers' achievements have gained worldwide recognition. In 2024, Taiwan hosted the World Orchid Conference for the first time. The main topics centered on Orchid Technology and Conservation & Preservation. The orchid industry in Taiwan uses high-tech farming and advanced technology. On the other hand, more needs to be done in conservation and preservation. The source of moth orchids for creating new varieties is decreasing. Native species have gradually disappeared from the wild. The orchid industry realized that ecological protection goes hand in hand with economic growth. This was the aim of a volunteer program that began in 2018 to replant native species in nature. Given time, orchids may not only decorate homes but also enrich Taiwan's forest ecosystem.

39. What is the topic of the passage?
(A) An introduction to Taiwan's orchid industry
(B) The development of the global orchid market
(C) Varieties created by Taiwan's orchid industry
(D) Activities of the 2024 World Orchid Conference

40. What is the main idea of the third paragraph?
(A) The differences between native plant species and new varieties
(B) The report of the World Orchid Conference on orchid exports
(C) The operations of high-tech farming in Taiwan's orchid industry
(D) The balance between industry growth and orchid species protection

41. According to the passage, which of the following statements is true?
(A) Moth orchids are the largest item of Taiwan's flower imports.
(B) Taiwan growers mix native species to produce new orchid varieties.
(C) The Netherlands has the world's largest greenhouse orchid industry.
(D) Volunteers removed native orchid plants from the wild in 2018.

42. Arrange the following events according to the historical timeline of Taiwan's orchid industry.
a. Taiwan's orchid export earnings were NT$ 7 billion.
b. Taiwan lost its top position in the global orchid market.
c. Taiwan exported moth orchid seedlings to over 80 countries.
d. Taiwan hosted the World Orchid Conference.
(A) b → d → c → a (B) b → c → a → d
(C) c → a → b → d (D) c → d → b → a

第二部分：非選擇題（第 I 題，每格 2 分，共 4 分；第 II 題 6 分；第 III 題 6 分；共 16 分）

I. 填充

說明：▲ 請依據中文提示，將試題內空格 ①、② 答案之完整單字（含提示之字首），分別作答於答案卷之作答欄 ①、② 之指定範圍內以完成句子。
▲ 請勿抄題，每格限填一字，超過一字者視為錯誤，不予計分。

1. 這位巨星在台北三場演唱會的所有門票在五分鐘內全部售完。
All tickets for the superstar's three c ① in Taipei were s ② out in just five minutes.
① __________ ② __________

II. 句子重組

說明：▲ 請將題中 5 段提示字詞重組成一完整句子，並於句尾加上適當標點符號。
▲ 請將重組後的句子寫在答案卷之「非選擇題作答區」指定範圍內，答案中不能增減字詞或修改變化字詞，請勿抄題。

2. are a bad gift choice / the cutting of / Knives or scissors / as they symbolize / a solid friendship

____

____

III. 中譯英

說明：▲ 請將以下中文句子譯成正確、通順、達意的英文，並將答案寫在「非選擇題作答區」之指定範圍內，請勿抄題。

3. 如果你接獲不明來電，未經確認前不要接聽。

____

____

113 四技二專統一入學測驗－試題

第一部分：選擇題

- I. 字彙題
- II. 對話題
- III. 綜合測驗
- IV. 閱讀測驗

第二部分：非選擇題

- I. 填充
- II. 句子重組
- III. 中譯英

第一部分：選擇題（第 1 至 42 題，每題 2 分，共 84 分）

Ⅰ. 字彙題：

第 1 至 7 題，每題均有一空格字詞，請選擇最適合的答案，以完成該英文句子。第 8 至 10 題，每題均有一個劃底線的字詞，請在四個選項中，選擇一個與劃底線的字詞意義最接近的答案。

1. Johnny is wearing a very ______ hat that looks different from those of other people.
(A) common (B) general (C) regular (D) special

2. Loud noises can make it hard for me to ______, so I always find a quiet place to study with full attention.
(A) bend (B) focus (C) panic (D) wander

3. Here is a helpful ______ for cooking chicken soup: add a little salt. It will make the soup tasty.
(A) lip (B) gap (C) tip (D) nap

4. My grandpa sleeps at ______ the same time every day. He goes to bed at about 9 pm.
(A) briefly (B) fluently (C) gently (D) roughly

5. Being friendly with your roommates can help you stay away from ______ with them.
(A) dialogues (B) conflicts (C) personality (D) relationship

6. Jack is a very ______ person. He will never change his decisions no matter how hard you try to persuade him.
(A) easy-going (B) democratic (C) obedient (D) stubborn

7. Kuo, Hsing-chun (郭婞淳) won a gold medal in the 2020 Tokyo Olympics. I ______ her a lot and want to be like her one day.
(A) admire (B) frighten (C) impress (D) suspect

8. Though she hurt her arm last week, Amy could still play the violin as <u>skillfully</u> as before.
(A) casually (B) cruelly (C) smoothly (D) strictly

9. May has to <u>conquer</u> her fear of flying if she wants to travel by airplane.
(A) beat (B) hunt (C) recover (D) select

10. It is <u>against the law</u> for drivers not to stop at the crosswalk and allow walkers to cross first. If drivers do so, they will be fined.
(A) illegal (B) national (C) political (D) unusual

II. 對話題：

第 11 至 20 題，請依對話內容選出一個最適合的答案，使其成為有意義的對話。

11. Customer: I'd like to have one oyster omelette and fried noodles, please.
Stall owner: Ok. Your order will be ready in five minutes.
Customer: I can't use chopsticks. Can I have a fork, please?
Stall owner: ______________
Customer: Thank you.
(A) You're very welcome. (B) Of course, here you go.
(C) Oyster is also delicious. (D) Sure, we have instant noodles.

12. Tina: An old friend is coming to visit me tomorrow. I haven't seen him for ten years.
Mike: An old friend? ______________
Tina: He wants to tell me something about his girlfriend. They broke up!
Mike: Sorry for him.
(A) How old is he? (B) Why is he coming?
(C) When will you see him? (D) Who was he looking for?

13. Mrs. Chen: I heard that the new neighbors moved in yesterday.
Mr. Chen: ______________
Mrs. Chen: No, not yet. What do they look like?
Mr. Chen: The lady is tall and thin and the man is kind of chubby.
(A) I'm glad I just met them. (B) The neighbors have two cats.
(C) They ran a small business here. (D) I thought you've met them already.

14. Adam: We all know that the Wright brothers (萊特兄弟) flew the first airplane in 1903. But do you know which one of them flew the airplane?

Jacky: The older brother did.

Adam: I'm surprised you know that. OK. ______________

Jacky: Only about 12 seconds.

Adam: Wow, you really know a lot!

(A) How long was the flight?

(B) How old was his brother?

(C) How many times had he tried before?

(D) How far did the airplane actually fly?

15. Amy: Did you finish your report for the Performing Arts class?

Janet: Yes. ______________

Amy: Like what?

Janet: For example, women were not allowed to act on stage in the past.

Amy: That was really unfair, wasn't it?

(A) But I haven't given it to Professor Johnson.

(B) And I've read many books about famous artists.

(C) But I'm not sure if my mom allows me to act on stage.

(D) And I've gathered a lot of information about the theater.

16. Rita: Why did you apply for this position?

Ben: I'd like to work for a large company. Your company is the perfect fit for me.

Rita: In this position, you'll have to lead a small team. How have you shown leadership at your other jobs?

Ben: ______________

Rita: That's good.

(A) I worked for my team leader in the past ten years.

(B) I'd like to apply for a perfect job in a smaller team.

(C) From now on, I'll lead a team in this large company.

(D) At my current position, I manage a team of ten workers.

17. Sue: How's the project going?

Eric: It's going well.

Sue: Oh, good. ______________

Eric: They are great, and they have a lot of creative ideas.

Sue: I'm happy to hear that.

(A) But who is not feeling well?

(B) But how did they come to the office?

(C) And what are the new colleagues like?

(D) And when will the project be created?

18. Jason: Where are you? The presentation is about to begin.
Susan: I'm almost there. The traffic is terrible this morning.
Jason: ________________
Susan: Yes, please. You can make a start, and I can handle the rest of the slides myself.
(A) Do you want me to cancel the presentation?
(B) Would you like me to order snacks and drinks?
(C) Do you want me to introduce the first few pages?
(D) Would you like me to turn off the audio equipment?

19. Student: Sir, we are raising money to help save the rainforest. Would you like to donate some money?
Man: Are you kidding? ________________ It doesn't affect me!
Student: Well, sir, rainforests are very important to us. Many things we use are made from rainforest plants, such as the clothes we wear.
Man: Oh, I see. Young man, I'll donate NT$ 500.
(A) I'll never save the rain!
(B) I won't take your money.
(C) What is your favorite clothing style?
(D) Why do I have to save the rainforest?

20. Jack: I got a text message from the hotel. They ask us to click on a link to confirm our reservation.
Lucy: ________________ This message seems strange.
Jack: But could it be a new policy? I'm afraid our reservation would be cancelled.
Lucy: Let me call the hotel. It's better to be safe than sorry.
(A) Hey, don't do that. (B) Just click on it now.
(C) Absolutely, go ahead. (D) It's a standard procedure.

Ⅲ. 綜合測驗：

以下兩篇短文，共有 8 個空格，為第 21 至 28 題，每題有四個選項，請依各篇短文文意，選出一個最適合該空格的答案。

◎下篇短文共有 4 個空格，為第 21-24 題，請依短文文意，選出一個最適合該空格的答案。

Living on Orchid Island, the Yami (Tao) people are able to keep their traditions going. The best-known tradition is the "flying fish season" of spring and summer. Flying fish ___21___ as a gift from heaven. During the festival period, the local people have to be very careful of their actions and words in order not to break with traditions. __22__ the years, hundreds and thousands of tourists have visited Orchid Island every flying fish season. Many tourists have shown a lack of respect for local customs. Therefore, residents keep reminding tourists to avoid __23__. One thing tourists should not do is touching the fishing boats when taking pictures. Traditionally, Yami (Tao) women and outsiders are not allowed to touch the fishing boats. __24__ thing tourists should not do is entering the backyard of houses where local residents dry their flying fish. Acts of disrespect, according to local fishermen, would bring bad luck. Tourists should remember not to disturb normal life on the island.

21. (A) regard (B) regarded (C) are regarded (D) are regarding

22. (A) About (B) Below (C) Over (D) Without

23. (A) good manners (B) rude behaviors (C) spending money (D) showing consideration

24. (A) Another (B) Other (C) Any other (D) No other

◎下篇短文共有 4 個空格，為第 25-28 題，請依短文文意，選出一個最適合該空格的答案。

The 3D printer is a machine that can create three-dimensional solid objects. In the printing process, the printer adds layers upon layers of materials until a solid object is completed. __25__, 3D printers only made small, simple plastic objects. But now, 3D printer technology can help house builders know the exact amount of materials they need even before they start construction. Therefore, building 3D printed homes requires fewer resources and produces __26__ waste than the traditional way.

The 3D printer can improve the quality of the objects they create by using artificial intelligence (AI). One of the most exciting applications of AI in 3D printing __27__ generative design. Generative design is a computer-aided design technique that uses AI to improve the design process. It helps create lighter and stronger structures. This is because AI can find the best way to reduce the weight of a structure __28__ increasing its strength. In this way, better buildings can be created.

25. (A) Finally (B) Soon (C) At first (D) In summary

26. (A) last (B) less (C) least (D) little

27. (A) is (B) are (C) has (D) have

28. (A) nor (B) since (C) unless (D) while

IV. 閱讀測驗：

以下有五篇短文，共有 14 個題目，為第 29 至 42 題，請於閱讀短文後，選出最適當的答案。

◎ 根據以下圖表，回答第 29-30 題

Answer the questions based on the following timetable.

Timetable

Train No.	Operation Day	Taichung	Miaoli	Hsinchu	Taoyuan	Banqiao	Taipei	Nangang
1510	Mon ~ Fri	07:12	07:31	07:45	07:58	08:10	08:21	08:30
802	Daily	07:25	07:45	07:58	08:10	08:22	08:32	08:40
1202	Mon ~ Fri	07:21	—	—	—	—	08:07	08:15
1602	Mon ~ Fri	07:40	—	08:05	08:18	08:31	08:42	08:50
1302	Mon ~ Fri	07:53	—	—	08:27	—	08:47	08:55
204	Daily	07:48	—	—	—	08:27	08:37	08:45
606	Sat	08:00	—	08:25	08:38	08:51	09:02	09:10

29. Which of the following is **NOT** true about the timetable?

(A) Train No. 802 operates every day of the week from Monday to Sunday.

(B) Train No. 1510 takes longer to get from Taichung to Taipei than Train No. 1202.

(C) If Mr. Sakula takes Train No. 606 on Saturday, he will arrive at Taoyuan at 08:30.

(D) From Taichung to Nangang, Train No. 204 will make a stop at Banqiao and Taipei.

30. Maria is planning to take a train from Taichung to Taipei this Saturday morning. On the way, Denny will join her on the train at Hsinchu. They will be meeting Mr. Lee at Taipei station at 08:50. Which train is her best choice?

(A) No. 802　(B) No. 1202　(C) No. 1602　(D) No. 606

◎ 根據以下圖表，回答第 31-32 題

After the 2022 Asian Games, Minhua, Yating, and Fuhao are motivated to join the University Student Sports Clubs. Answer the questions based on the poster below.

CLUB	HOW TO PLAY	PRACTICE TIME
Badminton	Two or four people hit a shuttlecock over a high net.	Evening on Fridays
Basketball	Two teams score points by throwing a large ball through an open net.	Evening on Tuesdays and Saturdays
Cycling	An individual rides a bicycle.	Morning on Thursdays
Rugby	Two teams score points by carrying an oval ball across a particular line.	Evening on Saturdays
Swimming	An individual moves through water by moving the body.	Evening on Mondays
Weightlifting	An individual lifts heavy objects as a sport.	Evening on Tuesdays and Fridays

31. Minhua and Yating are interested in playing a team sport, which clubs are they likely to join?
(A) Basketball and weightlifting (B) Badminton and cycling
(C) Swimming and badminton (D) Rugby and basketball

32. Fuhao works in the evening on Mondays and Tuesdays. Which clubs is he likely to join?
(A) Badminton, Cycling, Rugby (B) Basketball, Swimming, Weightlifting
(C) Rugby, Weightlifting, Swimming (D) Cycling, Basketball, Badminton

◎根據以下圖表，回答第 33-35 題

Lina is planning a trip and comparing two hotels in a tourist spot. Answer the questions based on the information below.

Hotelcomparison ×

http://www.hotelcomparison.com

	Cruise Hotel	**Universe Hotel**
Facilities	Fitness center Indoor car parking Restaurants	Business center Outdoor pool Gift shop
Services	Free airport shuttle Laundry service Free Wi-Fi	24-hour room service Free Wi-Fi Car rental service
Distance from tourist attractions	Sunset Beach (1 km) Theme Park (6 km) Art Museum (8 km)	Art Museum (2 km) Theme Park (16 km) Sunset Beach (20 km)
Room rates	Single: NT$ 2,700 Double: NT$ 3,600 Triple: NT$ 5,200	Single: NT$ 1,800 Double: NT$ 2,400 Triple: NT$ 3,500

33. Which facility or service is provided by both hotels?
(A) Outdoor pool (B) Business center
(C) Free Wi-Fi (D) Laundry service

34. How far does Lina have to drive to the Theme Park if she stays in the hotel closer to it?
(A) 2 km (B) 6 km (C) 8 km (D) 16 km

35. Which of the following is true?
(A) If Lina likes to use the fitness center, she should choose Universe Hotel.
(B) If Lina likes to swim in the pool, she should choose Universe Hotel.
(C) Lina will have to pay NT$ 1,800 for a single room in Cruise Hotel.
(D) Lina is able to use room service anytime in Cruise Hotel.

◎閱讀下文，回答第 36-38 題

Jensen Huang (黃仁勳) is the chief executive of NVIDIA, a leading company that makes chips used in artificial intelligence (AI). In 2023, Huang was listed among the 100 most influential people in AI. An inspiration to many, Huang encourages young people to seize the opportunities that AI will present. Meanwhile, he reminds them to take a positive attitude towards challenges.

In a speech to university graduates in Taiwan last year, Huang shared two important lessons he has learned in the past three decades. The first lesson is not to be discouraged by failure. In 1996, his company nearly closed down due to rapid changes in the industry. They soon realized that they had made a mistake, and Huang humbly asked a major customer for help. With the customer's support, the company moved on to invent the chip that led to their future success. Huang's advice is to always honestly face your mistakes and seek help.

The second lesson is to keep going despite difficulties. In 2007, the company made an expensive investment on product improvements. The new products were not selling well for many years until they started being used for machine learning. The experience taught Huang and his colleagues to handle the pain and suffering needed to achieve their vision. Their continued efforts help build NVIDIA into a global leader in AI technologies.

Huang's life story is also about **pushing oneself to do better**. Born in Taiwan, Huang moved to the United States at the age of nine. He later earned two engineering degrees before working for two chip companies. In 1993, on his 30th birthday, he and two friends founded NVIDIA. Today, Huang often advises students to live a life of purpose, and to run, not walk, towards their goals.

36. What is the main idea of this passage?
(A) How to come up with a speech
(B) How to succeed in chip making
(C) How to seize opportunities in AI
(D) How to deal with difficult situations

37. According to the passage, which is <u>**NOT**</u> an example of "**pushing oneself to do better**"?
(A) Working for chip companies
(B) Reaching the age of 30 in 1993
(C) Earning two engineering degrees
(D) Founding NVIDIA with two friends

38. Based on the passage, arrange the following events in the order in which they happened.

a. New products made profits when they were used for machine learning.

b. Huang's company almost shut down because of challenges in the industry.

c. Huang became one of the most 100 influential people in artificial intelligence.

d. The company admitted their mistake and obtained help to develop a product.

(A) b → a → c → d (B) b → d → a → c

(C) c → d → b → a (D) c → a → d → b

◎閱讀下文，回答第 39-42 題

On October 9, 2023, Triton, the first weather satellite made in Taiwan successfully entered space. It is also the fourth satellite in the world to use GNSS-R instrument to collect weather data. Its purpose is to help us predict the weather more accurately.

This satellite is named after Triton, an ancient Greek god of the sea. The sea god commands the wind and waves. The satellite Triton is able to gather such data as wave heights and sea wind speeds. Triton uses a technique that collects signals **reflected** from the Earth's surface. It carries GNSS-R instrument to receive signals which are sent back from sea surfaces. The calmer the sea, the stronger the signal, indicating weaker winds. This information is valuable as wind speed data is not easy to collect. Such information improves the prediction of typhoon strengths and movements. Triton observes weather changes mainly in the Atlantic Ocean, Indian Ocean, and central Pacific Ocean.

Triton, started in 2014, is the fruitful cooperation between Taiwan Space Agency (TASA) and local companies. TASA developed GNSS-R instrument and key components such as the Onboard Computer and GPS Receiver. More than 20 local research groups and manufacturers participated in developing the ground station equipment. The satellite is 82% developed and produced in Taiwan.

Now that Triton is in space, we can expect it to provide more accurate information and support disaster prevention. The success of Triton contributes to global weather forecasting. It is also an important step forward for Taiwan's space engineering.

Triton: 獵風者氣象衛星

TASA: Taiwan Space Agency 國家太空中心

GNSS-R: Global Navigation Satellite System-Reflectometry 全球導航衛星系統反射訊號接收儀

39. What is the passage mainly about?
(A) Challenges of space engineering in Taiwan
(B) The description of the Greek sea god Triton
(C) Differences in weather forecasting techniques
(D) The introduction of a weather satellite in Taiwan

40. Which is closest in meaning to "**reflected**" in the second paragraph?
(A) looked into (B) made of (C) sent back (D) named after

41. According to the passage, which of the following is true?
(A) Triton started to collect wind speed data before 2014.
(B) All of Triton was developed and produced in Taiwan.
(C) Triton shows the improvement in Taiwan's space skills.
(D) Fewer than 20 local companies worked on the Triton project.

42. Which of the following can be inferred from the passage about the contribution of Triton?
(A) It helps reduce damage caused by bad weather.
(B) It improves the speed and strength of typhoons.
(C) It connects the Atlantic Ocean and Indian Ocean.
(D) It measures the heights of satellites from sea surfaces.

第二部分：非選擇題（第 I 題，每格 2 分，共 4 分；第 II 題 6 分；第 III 題 6 分；共 16 分）

I. 填充

說明：▲ 請依據中文提示，將試題內空格 ①、② 答案之完整單字（含提示之字首），分別作答於答案卷之作答欄 ①、② 之指定範圍內以完成句子。
▲ 請勿抄題，每格限填一字，超過一字者視為錯誤，不予計分。

1. 你比較喜歡用現金付款或是電子錢包？
Would you p___①___ to pay by cash or with an electronic w___②___?
① ________ ② ________

II. 句子重組

說明：▲ 請將題中 5 段提示字詞重組成一完整句子，並於句尾加上適當標點符號。
▲ 請將重組後的句子寫在答案卷之「非選擇題作答區」指定範圍內，答案中不能增減字詞或修改變化字詞，請勿抄題。

2. work on / to see that / It is good / solving pollution problems / more people

III. 中譯英

說明：▲ 請將以下中文句子譯成正確、通順、達意的英文，並將答案寫在「非選擇題作答區」之指定範圍內，請勿抄題。

3. 一些專家說今年將比去年更熱更潮濕。

112 四技二專統一入學測驗－試題

第一部分：選擇題

- I. 字彙題
- II. 對話題
- III. 綜合測驗
- IV. 閱讀測驗

第二部分：非選擇題

- I. 填充
- II. 句子重組
- III. 中譯英

第一部分：選擇題（84 分）

Ⅰ. 字彙題：

第 1 至 8 題，每題均有一空格字詞，請選擇最適合的答案，以完成該英文句子。第 9 至 10 題，每題均有一個劃底線的字詞，請在四個選項中，選擇一個與劃底線的字詞意義最接近的答案。

1. It is a big ______ for people in this small town to learn that the only movie theater is going to shut down next month.
(A) cable (B) shock (C) tube (D) zone

2. The animal rights group is going to ______ a party to raise money for street cats.
(A) break (B) fight (C) hold (D) spell

3. I have ______ finished writing the novel, and I'm going to complete the last chapter tonight.
(A) almost (B) already (C) always (D) altogether

4. In some countries, looking at someone in the eye for too long is considered ______, so you should avoid doing it.
(A) basic (B) classical (C) legal (D) rude

5. If you keep blowing air into the balloon, it will ______ with a loud bang.
(A) aim (B) burst (C) explore (D) shine

6. The boss agreed to increase workers' ______, so they can make more money to improve their life.
(A) permits (B) risks (C) scales (D) wages

7. Since my teeth are very ______ to sweets, I don't eat candies and cookies.
(A) attractive (B) effective (C) positive (D) sensitive

8. Amy's proposal to get funding from the school did not meet any ______, so she got all the money she needed for her project.
(A) appreciation (B) gratitude (C) resistance (D) sympathy

9. William's mother was <u>seriously</u> hurt in the car accident; she will have to stay in the hospital for a while.
(A) badly (B) cheaply (C) hardly (D) shortly

10. I'm sorry that I don't have any <u>spare</u> money to lend you. I spent all my money buying a new cellphone for my mom.
(A) extra (B) hot (C) quick (D) soft

Ⅱ. 對話題：

第 11 至 20 題，請依對話內容選出一個最適合的答案，使其成為有意義的對話。

11. Anita: There's a famous Chinese restaurant across the road. They serve the best Peking duck.
Sergio: Yes, I used to go there every week before I moved away from here.
Anita: I really want to try their Peking duck. ______
Sergio: Once in a long while.
(A) Is it far away from here? (B) Does it really taste good?
(C) Have you ever been there? (D) Do you still go there often?

12. Betty: Hello. I'm calling about your ad for the five-room rental apartment. Is it still available?
Manager: Yes, it is. ______
Betty: Yes. I'd like to. Can you tell me the address?
(A) Would you like to see it? (B) Where did you see the ad?
(C) When do you want to see it? (D) Will your friend come with you?

13. Alex: I'm interested in buying an electric car.
Sales: Good choice. They cause less pollution, and there are lots of places in the city where you can charge your car.
Alex: What if I want to leave the city? How far can I go before I need to charge the car?
Sales: ______
(A) It has gone too far. (B) You have no choice.
(C) It has a range of 200 kilometers. (D) As far as I know, there's no charge.

14. Jane: Guess what I saw during my trip to Paris last month?
Roy: I bet you saw the Eiffel Tower (艾菲爾鐵塔), right?
Jane: Of course I saw that. And I also saw the Mona Lisa.
Roy: You mean da Vinci's (達文西) Mona Lisa?
Jane: ______ I saw it at the Louvre (羅浮宮).
(A) No way! (B) That's the one.
(C) You're lucky! (D) Don't mention it.

15. David: Do you like watching judo (柔道) competitions?
Annie: No, not at all. But, I'm a big fan of Drangadrang (楊勇緯).
David: Really? You know him? ________________
Annie: He's talented, strong and of course, very cute. He's even won an Olympic medal!
David: Wow! You really know him, huh?
(A) How did you meet him? (B) What does he really like?
(C) What do you like about him? (D) How did he know about judo?

16. Jimmy: I need to find a part-time job, Ms. King.
Ms. King: May I know the reason?
Jimmy: I need to support myself through school.
Ms. King: I see. ________________
Jimmy: I can type pretty fast.
(A) How soon do you need the job?
(B) What kind of skills do you have?
(C) What kind of support do you need?
(D) What do you know about the school?

17. Secretary: Hello, Dean's office, may I help you?
Jack: Good morning, Sir. I'm looking for Dr. Huang.
Secretary: ________________
Jack: OK. Could you let him know that Jack, his student, would like to make an appointment with him?
Secretary: Sure, let me check his schedule.
(A) I'm sorry there's no such person here.
(B) I'm sorry you dialed the wrong number.
(C) I'm afraid he doesn't work here anymore.
(D) I'm afraid he's not in the office right now.

18. Ms. Lin: Ms. Ting, Stella's ballet show yesterday was terrific. She is great. ________________
Ms. Ting: Since she was seven.
Ms. Lin: I can't believe it. She must be a genius.
(A) How often did she practice ballet?
(B) How long has she been learning ballet?
(C) How old do people start learning ballet?
(D) How much will you pay for a ballet show?

19. Angel: Have you ever met new friends online?
Teddy: Yes, I have. We still keep in touch now.
Angel: How did you meet them?
Teddy: ________________
(A) I joined an online group.
(B) We never talked on the Net.
(C) They met new friends on the street.
(D) He continued to play online games.

20. Nancy: Let's go out and play badminton. Do you know where the badminton gears and equipment are?
Danny: Aren't they in the closet next to you?
Nancy: ________________
Danny: Why not go check the garage?
(A) Yes, here they are. (B) I don't see them here.
(C) They sound closer to you. (D) No, we threw them away.

III. 綜合測驗：

以下兩篇短文，共有 10 個空格，為第 21 至 30 題，每題有四個選項，請依各篇短文文意，選出一個最適合該空格的答案。

◎下篇短文共有 5 個空格，為第 21-25 題，請依短文文意，選出一個最適合該空格的答案。

Taiwan's east coast offers marvelous views of ocean wildlife. The chances of seeing a whale are very high in summer. It's rather easy to spot whales, __21__ whales swim past Taiwan's east coast every year between April and October. Today, whale watching __22__ a popular activity. The best time for whale watching is from June to August __23__ the sea is calm. Whale watching makes up a major part of the tourism industry in Yilan, Taitung and Hualien counties. Whale watching tours have been __24__ since 1997, and boat trips have been increasing. Tour operators are expected to follow regulations governing the activity. For example, to get a closer look at the whales, boats should __25__ the animals from behind. A list of responsible whale watching principles is included in an official guide to reduce the impact of tourism on the behavior of the world's biggest animals.

21. (A) for (B) nor (C) so (D) yet
22. (A) became (B) become (C) has become (D) will become
23. (A) why (B) when (C) how (D) which

24. (A) around (B) against (C) off (D) over

25. (A) accept (B) admit (C) affect (D) approach

◎下篇短文共有 5 個空格，為第 26-30 題，請依短文文意，選出一個最適合該空格的答案。

People take different actions when seeing a stranger who needs help. In psychology, there are two theories about the way people act in that situation, __26__ the bystander effect and the Good Samaritan effect. A bystander is a person who sees a problem but just stands and watches, and a Good Samaritan refers to the one who helps a stranger in trouble. The bystander doesn't __27__ to help, whereas the Good Samaritan jumps in to lend a hand. A bystander does not help because he or she does not want to look foolish by making a mistake when trying to help out. __28__, a Good Samaritan helps because he or she wants others to see how helpful he or she is. In addition, a Good Samaritan pays close attention __29__ other Good Samaritans. His or her action is based on what others are doing. If he or she sees others helping, he or she is more likely to help __30__. So, when you see a stranger in need, will you be a bystander or a Good Samaritan?

26. (A) called (B) calling (C) and called (D) while calling

27. (A) cross out (B) hand in (C) step in (D) throw out

28. (A) As a result (B) To sum up
(C) In the first place (D) On the other hand

29. (A) at (B) in (C) of (D) to

30. (A) neither (B) otherwise (C) as well (D) so far

Ⅳ. 閱讀測驗：

以下有四篇短文，共有 12 個題目，為第 31 至 42 題，請於閱讀短文後，選出最適當的答案。

◎根據以下圖表，回答第 31-32 題

The following graph shows how Mary, Sam, David and Linda spend their pocket money every month. Answer the questions based on the given information.

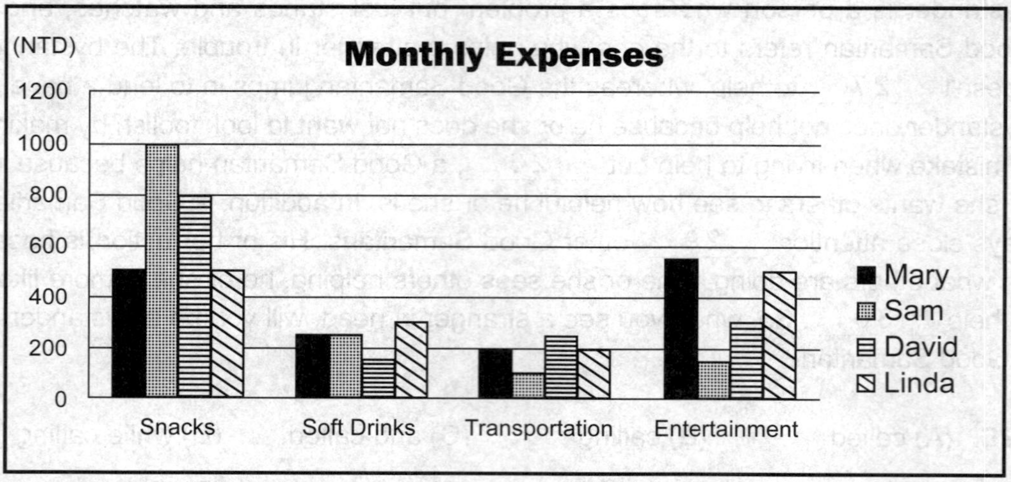

31. How much does David spend on soft drinks every month?

(A) About NT$800.　(B) More than NT$500.

(C) Exactly NT$400.　(D) Less than NT$200.

32. Which of the following is true?

(A) Mary spends the most money on transportation.

(B) Sam spends more money on snacks than Linda.

(C) Linda spends as much money as Mary on soft drinks.

(D) David spends less money on entertainment than Sam.

◎ 根據以下圖表，回答第 33-35 題

Read the label below and answer the questions that follow.

Drug Facts

Uses

Temporarily relieves these symptoms

- sneezing
- runny nose
- watery, itchy eyes

Warnings

Ask a doctor before use if you have

- glaucoma
- breathing problems

When using this product

- you may get drowsy
- avoid alcoholic drinks
- be careful when driving a motor vehicle or operating machinery

If pregnant or breastfeeding, ask a doctor before use.

Directions

Adults and children 12 years and over	Take 2 tablets every 4 to 6 hours; not more than 12 tablets in 24 hours
Children under 12 years	Ask a doctor

Other information

Store in a cool, dry place

33. Which part should you check to find out how to take the medicine?
(A) Uses (B) Warnings (C) Directions (D) Other information

34. Which effect should you be aware of if you want to take the medicine?
(A) You may feel cool and have dry skin.
(B) You may feel sleepy and cannot think clearly.
(C) You may have watery eyes and a runny nose.
(D) You may have itchy eyes and cannot breathe well.

35. According to the label, which of the following is true?
(A) A 13-year-old child can take ten tablets in a day.
(B) Adults should take the medicine with alcoholic drinks.
(C) A patient can take two tablets every six hours to treat glaucoma.
(D) A 30-year-old pregnant woman should take the medicine without asking a doctor.

◎閱讀下文，回答第 36-37 題

The following notice is posted by a high school before the summer vacation. Answer the questions based on the given information.

How to protect yourself from job scams

A scam is a way of tricking people into giving money or personal details to criminals. In a job scam, criminals pose as employers to cheat you of your money or your personal information by offering you a job. Very often, they offer large sums of money for little skill, effort or experience. Here are the common job scams and tips to help you avoid them.

Common job scams

A type of job scams asks you to use your bank account to receive and pass on payments for others. They will pay you a fee for helping to transfer the money.

Some scammers might ask you to deposit money into their account. Or, they will ask you for your bank details before they've even offered you the job.

In another instance, the fake employer wants to set up an interview. But first, they ask you to provide your bank details, a scan of your identity card or other personal information.

If a company is asking you to buy the products before you sell them, beware!

Things to watch out for

Unclear job description: Very little information about the job is provided and no skills or experience is required.

Unbelievably high pay: The job requires very little effort for high returns.

Requesting personal information: If you provide your bank account details, the scammer may use them to commit crimes.

Remember: If a job offer seems too good to be true, it's probably a scam.

How can I protect myself?

Do background check on the company and the person who claims to be hiring you. If a job offer doesn't feel right, feel free to contact the school staff for help.

36. Which is <u>NOT</u> mentioned as how job scams work?
(A) Applicants have to give their cellphones to the employer.
(B) Applicants are asked to send in money before they get hired.
(C) Applicants have to pay for products before they sell the items.
(D) Applicants may be paid to use their bank accounts for money transfers.

37. Which of the following is true?
(A) Scammers are people who help to look for criminals.
(B) The notice gives a list of common job scam websites.
(C) Job applicants should find out more about the employers.
(D) The school staff helps employers feel good about job ads.

◎閱讀下文，回答第 38-42 題

Technology is continuously changing the sports industry for the better. Electronic devices known as sensors can detect changes and provide instant information about the health and movements of the athlete. Technology has changed the way some athletes train by **live tracking** the athlete's performances, perfecting the athlete's movements, and preventing sports injuries.

Using sensors worn by the athlete, sports trainers can measure and track performance in real time. Nearly everything about the athlete can be measured, from breathing and heart rate, to sweat and temperature. The real-time information can help the trainer determine what aspects each athlete needs to focus on more. During practice, the trainer can read the data and decide when it's time to rest, stretch or train harder. In the past, however, the practice session would be recorded, and the athlete's performance would be judged later after the practice.

Technological tools also provide a lot of information about the athlete's movements. These tools can measure the exact position, distance, and speed of the athlete. The sensors on a swimmer's body, for example, provide data on movements like dive angle and leg movement. Observing these movements allows the trainer to help athletes perfect their performance.

The most important effect of technology on sports training is that injuries have been sharply reduced. Training software can assist trainers to keep watch on all aspects of training, including diet, energy, and sleep. This helps prevent fatigue and self-created injuries during practice.

Technology allows athletes to not only get the most out of their training but also stay injury free. Sports technology will undoubtedly increase the athlete's potential.

38. What is the passage mainly about?
(A) Tracking the performance of trainers.
(B) Training athletes with technological tools.
(C) Perfecting the body movements of trainers.
(D) Preventing the damage of technological tools.

39. Which is closest in meaning to the phrase "**live tracking**" in paragraph 1?
(A) Checking an activity after it is over
(B) Discussing an activity that may happen
(C) Following an activity before it happens
(D) Observing an activity when it is taking place

40. According to the passage, how has technology changed sports training?
(A) The athlete and the trainer can have a healthy diet.
(B) The athlete and the trainer can stop during practice.
(C) The trainer can understand the athlete's performance only after practice.
(D) The trainer can find out at once how the athlete performs during practice.

41. In the writer's opinion, what is the best benefit of using technology in sports training?
(A) Avoiding sports injuries.
(B) Watching a performance.
(C) Recording the sports practice.
(D) Making the movements perfect.

42. Which of the following statements is true?
(A) An athlete can detect the movements of sensor devices.
(B) Technological tools measure only the athlete's heart rate.
(C) Trainers dive at a perfect angle when swimmers wear sensors.
(D) Technological tools can show detailed movements of an athlete.

第二部分：非選擇題（第 I 題，每格 2 分，共 4 分；第 II 題 6 分；第 III 題 6 分；共 16 分）

I. 填充

說明：▲ 請依據中文提示，將試題內空格 ①、② 答案之完整單字（含提示之字首），分別作答於答案卷之作答欄 ①、② 之指定範圍內以完成句子。

▲ 請勿抄題，每格限填一字，超過一字者視為錯誤，不予計分。

1. 在洗衣服的時候，你應該把白色和深色的衣服分開。

When doing the l___①___, you should s___②___ white and dark clothes.

① __________ ② __________

II. 句子重組

說明：▲ 請將題中 5 段提示字詞重組成一完整句子，並於句尾加上適當標點符號。

▲ 請將重組後的句子寫在答案卷之「非選擇題作答區」指定範圍內，答案中不能增減字詞或修改變化字詞，請勿抄題。

2. how to deal with / was formed to / the high inflation rate / The research team / find out

____

____

III. 中譯英

說明：▲ 請將以下中文句子譯成正確、通順、達意的英文，並將答案寫在「非選擇題作答區」之指定範圍內，請勿抄題。

3. 很多社團鼓勵他們的成員回收塑膠袋。

____

____

111 四技二專統一入學測驗－試題

第一部分：選擇題

- I. 字彙題
- II. 對話題
- III. 綜合測驗
- IV. 閱讀測驗

第二部分：非選擇題

- I. 填充
- II. 句子重組
- III. 中譯英

第一部分：選擇題（84 分）

Ⅰ. 字彙題：

第 1 至 8 題，每題均有一空格字詞，請選擇最適合的答案，以完成該英文句子。第 9 至 10 題，每題均有一個劃底線的字詞，請在四個選項中，選擇一個與劃底線的字詞意義最接近的答案。

1. We had better leave early to ______ the heavy traffic to get home on time.
(A) avoid (B) drop (C) invite (D) mind

2. Anny's grandson is always full of ______ and wants to go to the park every day.
(A) energy (B) hurry (C) identity (D) safety

3. I've put on so much weight recently that these jeans are too ______ for me to wear now.
(A) loose (B) ripe (C) swift (D) tight

4. My boss totally accepted my suggestion and kept nodding to ______ his full agreement.
(A) deny (B) excuse (C) forget (D) indicate

5. To protect your head, when you ride a motorcycle, you must wear a ______.
(A) beard (B) helmet (C) necklace (D) tie

6. David's ______ hair color is brown, but he recently dyed it purple.
(A) ancient (B) historical (C) natural (D) opposite

7. We got train seats for the Lunar New Year season as we planned ______ and made our reservation once tickets went on sale.
(A) ahead (B) almost (C) either (D) even

8. To ease his pressure, Mr. Hung decided to listen to bedtime music for ______.
(A) presentation (B) publication (C) relaxation (D) reputation

9. The police pursued the bank robber through the streets last night.
(A) begged (B) chased (C) praised (D) treated

10. I have looked through the records extensively, but couldn't find anything about the person you mentioned.
(A) eventually (B) marginally (C) occasionally (D) thoroughly

II. 對話題：

第 11 至 20 題，請依對話內容選出一個最適合的答案，使其成為有意義的對話。

11. Father: OK! We are ready to start baking a cake. We need to find some things first.
Son: So, what should I get?
Father: Well, ________
Son: Oh! Sorry, I drank the whole bottle yesterday!
(A) the cake is baking now. (B) I need two cups of milk.
(C) go get some flour for me. (D) we need 50 grams of butter.

12. Judy: OK, here's your tea. But no snacks, as you wanted.
Tina: Oh, thanks.
Judy: ________ I have some homemade cookies left. My mom made them.
Tina: Oh, no thanks. I'm fine. I'm really full.
(A) Are you sure I cannot eat any cookies?
(B) Do you know you shouldn't eat too much?
(C) Are you sure you don't want anything to eat?
(D) Do you know you should buy something for me?

13. Ann: What do you want to see at the computer exhibition?
Ken: I want to find the booth that has the virtual reality setup.
Ann: Virtual reality? ________
Ken: You have to put on a headset, and when the game is turned on, you feel like you are actually in the game.
(A) How does it work? (B) What did you see?
(C) When was it set up? (D) Where have you been?

14. Ted: Do you want to jog around the track one more time?
Sue: Sure, I think I can make it.
Ted: If you're tired, you can wait here for me. I know you haven't been jogging for a while.
Sue: ________ Come on, let's go.
(A) Don't worry about me. (B) Please cover your tracks.
(C) No, I'll be waiting here. (D) Yes, you're tired of jogging.

15. Tour agent: Welcome to Fun Travel, ma'am. My name is Willy. How may I help you?
Alice: I'm here to get more information about your travel special.
Tour agent: Good. ________
Alice: I'd like to go in June, I think.
(A) What do you want to see? (B) When do you plan to travel?
(C) How is the weather in June? (D) Where would you like to go?

16. Ann: Do you want to see a movie? There's a terrific animated movie at the theater.
Dan: Animation? You mean like a cartoon? ________
Ann: Not at all. Many adults also enjoy animation, just like children do.
Dan: Really? I guess I should go and see if I like it.
Ann: Great. The movie starts at 7 p.m. Do you want me to pick you up?
(A) Isn't that just for children? (B) Isn't it nice to see it again?
(C) Do the children go with us? (D) Do you get the tickets now?

17. Bank clerk: May I help you?
Simon: Yes, where should I go to ask for a loan?
Bank clerk: ________ He's on the second floor.
Simon: Thank you.
(A) How much do you plan to ask for?
(B) What is the interest rate next year?
(C) I'm afraid that we don't offer any loans this year.
(D) The manager in the loan department can help you.

18. Wife: So, which apartment do you like?
Husband: I like the one near the post office. The best thing is it has a free parking space.
Wife: ________ I think the one near the train station is better. We can take the train to the office. And the rent is a lot cheaper!
Husband: Yeah, you're right. Let's take it.

(A) We can rest in the park. (B) But we don't have a car.
(C) It's the best choice to make. (D) But it's not cheap to park there.

19. Tim: What kind of vacation do you like the best?
Kelly: ________________ I'm dog-tired. I need a break! I just want to go to the beach, and do absolutely nothing.
Tim: Sounds good. But, I like doing things. I like to see places and go to museums.
(A) A lazy vacation, of course. (B) A shopping vacation is great.
(C) I like to go on business trips. (D) I like to work and save money.

20. Manager: Lin's steak house. How may I help you?
Mr. White: Hi, ________________
Manager: Just a minute... Yes, I have your booking here. It's 6:30 p.m.
Mr. White: That's right. Unfortunately, our trip got delayed. Is it possible that I change the reservation to Friday?
Manager: Sure. No problem.
(A) I heard that you've just updated the menu.
(B) I just want to check if you are open this Friday.
(C) I'd like to book a table for two by the window.
(D) I made a reservation under James White tonight.

Ⅲ. 綜合測驗：

以下兩篇短文，共有 10 個空格，為第 21 至 30 題，每題有四個選項，請依各篇短文文意，選出一個最適合該空格的答案。

◎下篇短文共有 5 個空格，為第 21 至 25 題，請依短文文意，選出一個最適合該空格的答案。

When should a child start to learn to use a computer? The answer depends on __21__ you ask. Some early childhood educators feel that "the earlier, the better." They believe that in modern society, computer skills are essential for every child, just like reading and counting. __22__, children should start using and playing with computers before elementary school. However, other educators believe that computers could have a negative effect __23__ the mental development of children. They say that children who play alone with a computer do not learn how to share or interact with others. Furthermore, children do not use their imagination enough __24__ the computer screen shows everything. Perhaps the best way for children to use computers __25__ to use them only for a short period of time each day. If a child uses a computer for only thirty minutes each day, she or he still has plenty of time to learn and play away from the computer.

21. (A) which (B) whom (C) whose (D) how

22. (A) Instead (B) Nonetheless (C) Otherwise (D) Therefore

23. (A) near (B) from (C) on (D) at

24. (A) because (B) or (C) so that (D) rather than

25. (A) are (B) is (C) have (D) has

◎下篇短文共有 5 個空格，為第 26 至 30 題，請依短文文意，選出一個最適合該空格的答案。

Two government projects in Taiwan provide funds for children of foreign-born parents to understand more about their parents' cultural background. The projects aim to help young people connect ___26___ their parents' home countries. These places are mostly located in Southeast Asia, where about 180,000 foreign persons ___27___ to Taiwanese citizens come from. One of the projects pays for participants to visit their immigrant parents' home countries. The purpose is to learn more about the local culture and language. ___28___ project organizes trips to Taiwanese-owned companies in Southeast Asia. Vietnam, ___29___, receives the largest Taiwanese investment. These Taiwanese-owned companies provide employment for 60,000 Taiwanese. When they hire a new employee from Taiwan, they ___30___ the person's ability to adapt to the Vietnamese culture. For many young Taiwanese with parents of Vietnamese origin, this offers an opportunity to work in their parents' home country.

26. (A) into (B) onto (C) from (D) with

27. (A) marry (B) married (C) will marry (D) are married

28. (A) Any (B) Other (C) The other (D) The only

29. (A) however (B) similarly (C) for example (D) in addition

30. (A) get off (B) get over (C) look after (D) look for

Ⅳ. 閱讀測驗：

以下有四篇短文，共有 12 個題目，為第 31 至 42 題，請於閱讀短文後，選出最適當的答案。

◎根據以下圖表，回答第 31-32 題

The Diamond Hotel is a quarantine hotel. It has seventy rooms for guests. Every room can only have one guest. This line graph shows how many of the rooms were occupied during 2020 and 2021.

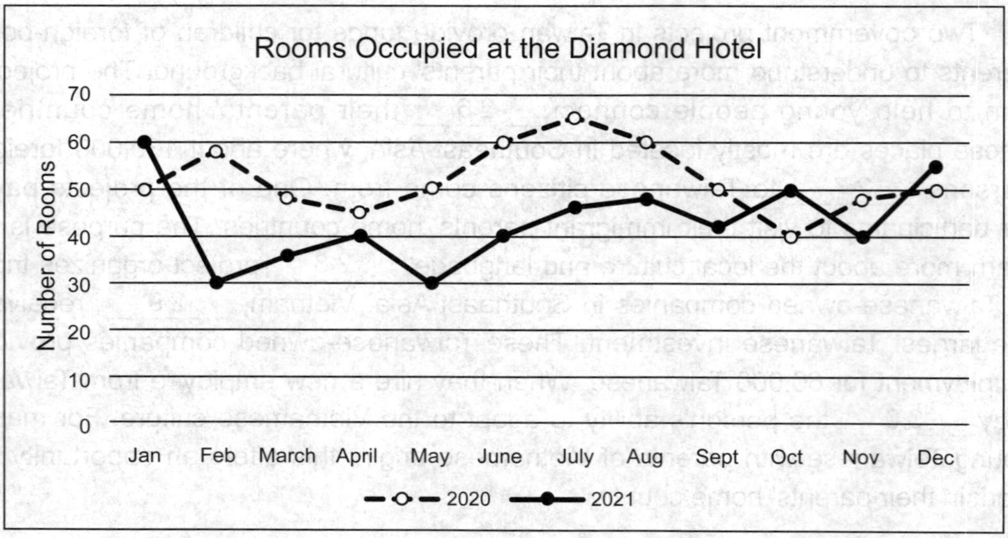

31. Since every room only had one guest, how many guests stayed at this hotel in May, 2021?
(A) 30 (B) 40 (C) 50 (D) 60

32. According to the line graph, which of the following is true?
(A) All the rooms in this hotel were occupied in July, 2021.
(B) About 40 rooms in this hotel were left vacant in June, 2021.
(C) More people were quarantined in this hotel in 2021 than 2020.
(D) More than 40 rooms in this hotel were occupied in April, 2020.

◎ 根據以下公告，回答第 33-34 題

Karano High School Video Competition

Competition Rules

ENTRY GUIDELINES

1. General
   - Participation is open only to students who are now studying in Karano High School.
   - Only one video is allowed per student / team.
   - Submit your video by September 30th, 2022.
2. Video Production
   - Videos must be one minute in length.
   - Videos must be original; use of material must be permitted by law.
3. Content
   - Must address the theme, "Karano High School – A Special Place!" describing what you love about this school and what it is like to be a student here.
   - Must be suitable for all audiences.

JUDGING CRITERIA

Judges will give points based on creativity, production quality, and how well the theme is presented.

PRIZES

Results will be announced on December 1st, 2022 during the School Anniversary Celebration, and three cash prizes totaling NT$10,000 will be awarded.

33. What is the competition about?

(A) Producing a video about student life and special education.

(B) Creating a video specially for students who love the school.

(C) Making a short video on how the school is special to oneself.

(D) Filming a one-minute video of the Anniversary Celebration day.

34. According to the competition rules, which of the following is true?

(A) Videos must be entries from former Karano students.

(B) Judges can only get points for creativity and quality.

(C) Students must hand in videos by December 1st, 2022.

(D) Participants can only use material as allowed by law.

◎閱讀下文，回答第 35-37 題

To: Molly 16th, July Sat. 12:55 P.M.
From: Jim<jim888@gmailer.com>
Subject: My volunteer trip

Hi Molly,

We arrived in Cuzco last Friday. Can you imagine? This city sits at 3,400 meters above sea level and has a population of 350,000. It's near the Andes Mountains, and about three hours by train to Machu Picchu. At the end of the four-week volunteer trip, we're going to visit Machu Picchu. I can't wait to see the mysterious Inca city!

Here, we all stay with local families. My host family is wonderful. I eat meals with them and speak Spanish with them. I also help them around the house. From Monday to Saturday, we go to a local school to work with the teachers and help them with anything they need. We teach English, and help with art, music, and sports. Also, we help repair the school, such as putting in new windows and painting the classrooms. I feel exhausted sometimes. However, when I see the children's happy faces, I know that I have made the right decision. How's your trip?

Jim

To: Jim<jim888@gmailer.com> 17th, July Sun. 10:00 A.M.
From: Molly
Subject: Re: My volunteer trip

Hi Jim,

It's good to hear that you enjoy what you are doing there. I was worried that you wouldn't get used to the weather and the hard work in Cuzco. My art trip starts from Louvre museum, Paris. We are now here to see the art display of Leonardo da Vinci, an Italian artist. His paintings are great. Tomorrow, we'll leave for the British Museum in London. Talk to you then.
BTW, don't forget to share pictures of Machu Picchu. Take care!

Molly

35. According to Jim's email, which of the following is true?
(A) There are 3,400 people living in Cuzco.
(B) Jim goes to help at school 7 days a week.
(C) Jim is staying in Cuzco for about 4 weeks.
(D) Cuzco is about 3 hours on foot to Machu Picchu.

36. Where was Molly when she wrote the email to Jim?
(A) Cuzco (B) London (C) Paris (D) Machu Picchu

37. Which of the following could be inferred from these emails?
(A) Jim can speak both Spanish and English.
(B) Jim is good at art and likes da Vinci's paintings.
(C) Molly knew that Jim would like the volunteer work.
(D) Molly likes the Louvre better than the British Museum.

◎閱讀下文，回答第 38-42 題

Carbon dioxide (CO_2) is good at holding in heat from the Sun, and even a small increase of the gas in the atmosphere can cause Earth to get even warmer. Carbon capture, usage and storage (CCUS) is about different technologies that can keep CO_2 produced by factories and power plants from causing global warming. The idea is simple, and there are only a few main steps in the process. The first step is about trapping carbon emissions from factory chimneys. For instance, a filter can be placed in the chimney, so that the carbon is trapped and it cannot go out into the atmosphere. Then, the gas is piped to places where it can be stored or used. If stored underground, it cannot contribute to the climate crisis. If used, for instance, it can help grow greenhouse plants or make soda drinks.

While CCUS projects can clearly benefit the environment, these projects are not straightforward as there are many issues to be dealt with, such as maintaining the storage site, which have slowed start-ups of CCUS projects worldwide. Thus, with only a few CCUS projects operating now, there still aren't enough to seriously help with the world's carbon emissions. Early forerunners in this technology are the US, Canada, and Norway. The good news is that CCUS has now gained **momentum** in other countries, where 30 new projects have begun in the past three years. The International Energy Agency says there must be many more to keep carbon emissions from heating the world too much.

38. What is the purpose of this article?
(A) It informs us about CCUS.
(B) It advises us against CCUS.
(C) It introduces new CCUS projects.
(D) It shows CCUS impact on technology.

39. What is the process of CCUS?
(A) To trap the CO_2, and then either keep it or use it.
(B) To use the CO_2, and then store it in greenhouse plants.
(C) To pipe the CO_2, and then trap it to cause the climate crisis.
(D) To store the CO_2 underground, and then pipe it to the chimneys.

40. Why is carbon dioxide put underground?
(A) To light up greenhouses. (B) To cool down soda drinks.
(C) To limit global warming. (D) To worsen climate change.

41. Which of the following is closest in meaning to "**momentum**" in paragraph 2?
(A) decrease (B) progress (C) wealth (D) fortune

42. What can be concluded from paragraph 2?
(A) CCUS will be stopped from now on to save money.
(B) The number of countries using CCUS may increase.
(C) CCUS benefits problems such as storage site maintenance.
(D) There are enough CCUS projects to stop heating the world.

第二部分：非選擇題（第 I 題，每格 2 分，共 4 分；第 II 到 III 題，每題 6 分，共 16 分）

I. 填充

說明：▲ 請依據中文提示，將試題內空格 ①、② 答案之完整單字（含提示之字首），分別作答於答案卷之作答欄 ①、② 之指定範圍內以完成句子。
▲ 請勿抄題，每格限填一字，超過一字者視為錯誤，不予計分。

1. 這項任務指派給對挑戰有正向態度的人。

This m___①___ is assigned to people who have a p___②___ attitude toward challenges.

① __________ ② __________

II. 句子重組

說明：▲ 請將題中 5 段提示字詞重組成一完整句子，並於句尾加上適當標點符號。
▲ 請將重組後的句子寫在「非選擇題作答區」指定範圍內，答案中不能增減字詞或修改變化字詞，請勿抄題。

2. are conducting research / fatal diseases / to stop / Many scientists / the spread of

____

____

III. 中譯英

說明：▲ 請將以下中文句子譯成正確、通順、達意的英文，並將答案寫在「非選擇題作答區」之指定範圍內，請勿抄題。

3. 健行和露營是兩項非常受歡迎的戶外活動。

____

____

110 四技二專統一入學測驗－試題

第一部分：選擇題

- I. 字彙題
- II. 對話題
- III. 綜合測驗
- IV. 閱讀測驗

第二部分：非選擇題

- I. 填充
- II. 句子重組
- III. 中譯英

第一部分：選擇題（82 分）

Ⅰ. 字彙題：

第 1 至 7 題，每題均有一空格字詞，請選擇最適合的答案，以完成該英文句子。第 8 至 11 題，每題均有一個劃底線的字詞，請在四個選項中，選擇一個與劃底線的字詞意義最接近的答案。

1. The shy little boy spoke so _______ that I had a hard time hearing what he said.
(A) bravely (B) clearly (C) openly (D) softly

2. I am terribly sorry. Please _______ my sincere apology.
(A) accept (B) ignore (C) propose (D) refuse

3. I am a _______ customer at that restaurant. I eat there at least four or five times a week.
(A) delicious (B) former (C) negative (D) regular

4. Eating too many potato chips makes you thirsty because chips _______ a large amount of salt.
(A) contain (B) control (C) contract (D) contact

5. The weather is very hot in summer, while in winter it is really _______.
(A) chilly (B) previous (C) tropical (D) visible

6. Hand washing is one of the best ways to keep healthy and stop the spread of _______ and viruses.
(A) bacteria (B) fever (C) moisture (D) sweat

7. In the admission interview, the _______ are often asked to explain why they want to enter the university.
(A) applicants (B) associates (C) receptionists (D) relatives

8. Pets, such as cats and dogs, are humans' favorite <u>companions</u>.
(A) listeners (B) directors (C) partners (D) strangers

9. The weather forecast said the temperature would <u>dip</u> from 20 degrees during the day to 12 degrees at night.
(A) dim (B) drop (C) fail (D) leak

10. Many early American Indians preferred hunting, so they lived <u>primarily</u> on buffalo meat.
(A) barely (B) frequently (C) mainly (D) scarcely

11. Marie Curie（居禮夫人）was a <u>magnificent</u> scientist who was the first woman to win the Nobel Prize.
(A) brilliant (B) believable (C) critical (D) commercial

II. 對話題：

第 12 至 21 題，請依對話內容選出一個最適合的答案，使其成為有意義的對話。

12. Anderson: Why are you studying English?
Wan-Ting: I hope to study abroad one day, so I need good English.
Anderson: Then what is the most difficult part of learning English?
Wan-Ting: ________ Native speakers talk so fast that I have problems understanding them.
(A) No problem at all. (B) Probably listening.
(C) The difficulties of living alone. (D) Speaking in my native language.

13. Waitress: Lotus Chinese Restaurant.
Customer: Hi, could I order some take-out, please?
Waitress: Sure, what do you want to order?
Customer: Sweet and sour pork, please.
Waitress: ________
Customer: Um, then I'll have the barbecued duck.
(A) Sure, here you are. (B) Sorry, we've run out of pork.
(C) Oh no, we don't have any duck. (D) OK, I'll place the order.

14. Husband: Do you like my new coat?
Wife: It looks great!
Husband: I'm glad you like it.
Wife: ________
Husband: It was on sale, 50% off.
(A) Was it a good deal? (B) Would you go with me?
(C) What was it made of ? (D) Where will you buy it?

15. Ken: Is there a drugstore nearby?
Ann: Just around the corner. Why?
Ken: ________________
Ann: Oh, no! What's wrong?
(A) I don't feel well. (B) I need a birthday cake.
(C) It's not too far, though. (D) You can pay me later.

16. Peter: I'd like to rent a car.
Clerk: Sure. What kind of car do you want?
Peter: Small, 2-door.
Clerk: Here are some 2-door small cars.
Peter: ________________
Clerk: It's NT$5,000.
(A) How is the condition? (B) What's the weekly rate?
(C) How many people does it take? (D) Are 2-door cars more powerful?

17. Ling: Do you want me to send you some pineapple cakes? They're terrific desserts.
Holly: That's great. I really like pineapple cakes.
Ling: ________________
Holly: I agree. So, why don't you send me two bags of Oolong tea as well?
(A) I prefer coffee to tea. (B) It goes very well with tea.
(C) When is pineapple season? (D) Do you need any other desserts?

18. Ms. Chen: Pam, ________________?
Pam: I work for Smart Computers. I'm a sales representative for Japan and Singapore.
Ms. Chen: Oh, international sales representative. How do you like that?
Pam: It's a great job. I like to travel, and like to work with people from other countries.
(A) are you looking for a local job (B) did you compute your travel cost
(C) would you tell us about what you do (D) can you tell me when you got the job

19. Peter: Fanny, I got it!
Fanny: What?
Peter: The jewelry job!
Fanny: Oh my God! I'm talking with a jewelry designer! Congratulations!
Peter: ________________ Pick a restaurant. It's my treat.
(A) Are you kidding? (B) It's so easy for you.
(C) Let's go celebrate. (D) How did you make it?

20. Doctor: Good morning, Mr. Lee. How are you feeling today?
Mr. Lee: Not very well. I always feel tired, but when I go to bed, I can't sleep.
Doctor: That's too bad. How long have you had this problem for?
Mr. Lee: ________ I am in advertising, and work about 80 hours a week.
Doctor: You are overworked! You need to relax.
(A) Many times. (B) Once in a while.
(C) As long as you help me. (D) Since I started my new job.

21. Teacher: Why are your class scores always so bad?
Johnny: Because... I always sleep in class, Sir.
Teacher: ________
Johnny: That's right, Sir. This is something I won't do again.
(A) Maybe you should sleep more at home.
(B) You should try and fail the next test, too.
(C) Do you stay up playing games every night?
(D) Why don't you try to study more at home?

III. 綜合測驗：

以下兩篇短文，共有 10 個空格，為第 22 至 31 題，每題有四個選項，請依各篇短文文意，選出一個最適合該空格的答案。

◎下篇短文共有 5 個空格，為第 22 至 26 題，請依短文文意，選出一個最適合該空格的答案。

When traveling abroad, it is always important to follow the local customs. Here are some tips to make sure you don't upset someone on your travels. For example, if you have dinner at a friend's house in Germany, be polite enough to eat everything, __22__ the host will think you didn't enjoy the meal. In Korea, while taking public transport, passengers should always keep quiet. Being noisy __23__ to be very rude. When visiting Saudi Arabia, be sure to eat with your right hand because most people there use their left hand for the bathroom. In Pakistan, you don't want to be __24__. This is because guests are expected to be fifteen minutes late for a meal. __25__, if you are visiting a friend's house in Denmark, don't be late. People in Denmark think it is impolite to be late. With so many different customs __26__ the world, it is impossible to know them all. If you mistakenly upset someone, make sure to say sorry.

22. (A) and (B) but (C) or (D) so

23. (A) considers (B) is considered (C) has considered (D) had been considering

24. (A) at a time (B) for all time (C) in time (D) on time

25. (A) Consequently (B) Similarly (C) By far (D) In contrast

26. (A) around (B) beyond (C) during (D) under

◎下篇短文共有 5 個空格，為第 27 至 31 題，請依短文文意，選出一個最適合該空格的答案。

The eastern part of Taiwan is a place of natural beauty. However, it is also an area __27__ earthquakes occur very often. The government has recently completed work on an undersea cable system to detect earthquakes and tsunamis. The system makes it possible for people __28__ about 10 seconds before an earthquake strikes. The purpose is to reduce __29__ and injuries. Starting in 2011, cables were put under the sea on the east coast. The location was chosen __30__ most of the earthquakes happen there. The undersea cable system stretches for 735 km, with nine points __31__ its entire length to detect the quakes. The deepest detection point lies 5,554 m under the sea.

27. (A) when (B) where (C) which (D) whose

28. (A) are warned (B) to warn (C) to be warned (D) will be warned

29. (A) dies (B) dead (C) deadly (D) deaths

30. (A) if (B) till (C) unless (D) because

31. (A) along (B) during (C) except (D) since

Ⅳ. 閱讀測驗：

以下有四篇短文，共有 10 個題目，為第 32 至 41 題，請於閱讀短文後，選出最適當的答案。

◎閱讀下文，回答第 32-33 題

The notice below is a guideline for tourists in a national park — "Leave No Trace". Read the notice and answer the following questions.

	LEAVE NO TRACE Travel Principles
	PLAN AHEAD Know the regulations of the places you're visiting
	RESPECT WILDLIFE Do not approach wildlife
	LOOK WITH YOUR EYES, NOT WITH YOUR HANDS Admire cultural / historic objects at a distance and follow paths
	WHAT YOU FIND STAYS BEHIND Shells and sand stay on the beach; fruit, wood, and seeds should be left to keep trees healthy
	WASTE & RECYCLING Learn local recycling and waste laws, ask if unsure
	BE CONSIDERATE OF OTHER VISITORS Keep noise to a minimum; allow everyone a turn to admire the sights at viewing points or platforms

32. Which of the following is <u>NOT</u> encouraged by the travel principles?
(A) Collect shells on the beach.
(B) Speak quietly to your friends.
(C) Understand the rules and regulations.
(D) Take pictures of birds from far away.

33. What do the travel principles probably want visitors to do?
(A) To study law in order to reach wildlife
(B) To allow everyone to express their views
(C) To keep nature the same as much as possible
(D) To clean their hands before touching anything

◎閱讀下文，回答第 34-35 題

Read the following job advertisements from the classified section of the website. Then answer the questions based on the given information.

(A) Auto Mechanic	(B) Hiring dependable helper
Goodcar dealership has openings for certified mechanics. Pay based on ability. Range from $160 to $200 per hour. Benefits include uniforms, health care, paid vacations. Call 06-5893642	Mature capable person to work on standard bred horse farm. General maintenance & farm work. Health care & housing provided. Call 08-7769521
(C) Want a career in real estate?	**(D) Food delivery on wheels**
No experience needed. We offer a training program for employees on how to sell land and buildings. Come in person to the main office of Royal Estate, 33 Lily Rd., Taipei. Come between 11 a.m. & 5 p.m.	No experience needed. Have motorcycle with driver license. $160/hr. Health care provided. Email: foodonwheels111@mail2.com

34. Ju-Yi is graduating from the Animal Science Department. She wants to find a job with a place to stay. Which job advertisement is she most likely to be interested in?

(A) A (B) B (C) C (D) D

35. Ming-Hua is interested in becoming a house seller. What should he do to apply for the job?

(A) Call 06-5893642.
(B) Visit Royal Estate.
(C) Email foodonwheels111@mail2.com.
(D) Mail the resume to 33 Lily Rd., Taipei.

◎閱讀下文，回答第 36-38 題

In 2020, the United Nations World Food Program (WFP) was awarded the Nobel Peace Prize for its efforts to fight hunger, to help bring about peace, and to prevent the use of hunger as a weapon of war. The WFP focuses its work on hunger and food security issues. In 1962, the organization shipped wheat, sugar and tea to Iran after an earthquake killed 12,000 people. Since then, it has been helping victims of natural disasters.

Other areas of work include the school meals program which covered about 17 million children in 2019. The WFP believes that food security and peace **go hand in hand**. The world cannot end hunger without putting an end to conflict. In 2010, the

WFP successfully resolved a conflict situation in Central Asia. Several villages on the border of two countries were quarreling over water resources. The WFP helped to rebuild water supply systems which were shared across borders and provided food for people who joined in the construction.

In 2017, millions of people in the Arab country of Yemen were close to starving in the war between rival groups. Some of these groups cut off food supplies to cause fear in the population. However, WFP workers managed to bring wheat flour to people in need, preventing the use of hunger as a weapon of war. About 100 million people received WFP food assistance in 2020. By winning the Nobel Prize, the WFP hopes that it will draw attention to the problem of hunger.

36. Why was the 2020 Nobel Peace Prize given to the WFP?
(A) For putting an end to war and natural disasters
(B) For protecting people from hunger and conflicts
(C) For preventing the use of hunger and weapons in war
(D) For persuading people to welcome food aid and conflicts

37. Which of the following is closest in meaning to "**go hand in hand**" in the second paragraph?
(A) need hard work
(B) need real action
(C) are available
(D) are connected

38. According to the passage, which statement is true?
(A) About 17 million children worked for their school meals.
(B) Groups fighting in Yemen managed to receive wheat flour.
(C) In Central Asia, the WFP ended a conflict through cooperation.
(D) The WFP donated food to 12,000 victims in the Iran earthquake.

◎閱讀下文，回答第 39-41 題

Imagine getting into your car, speaking a location into your car's computer, and then letting it drive you to your destination. The idea behind self-driving cars is fairly simple: build a car with a computer that is connected with many cameras which can track all the objects close to it, give the computer all the driving rules and routes, and then the computer should be able to drive to the destination.

There are many benefits of self-driving cars. Research shows that using self-driving cars can greatly reduce the number of cars on the street because 80% only have one person driving alone in a car. Self-driving cars can also lower the cost of transportation, which is 18% of a person's income in the U.S.A. Besides, "These cars won't get drunk, drive too fast, or take risks," said the CEO of Fastcar, John Smith.

Early estimates suggested that self-driving cars would be the standard in 2020, but instead there were only a few research vehicles on the road in 2020. As the technology is currently under research and being improved, it is likely in the near future that we will see self-driving cars move safely on public roads among traditional cars. When they arrive, their cost, safety and convenience will make them part of our daily lives. Companies that research self-driving cars which plan ahead, adjust the quickest, and imagine the most will succeed.

39. What is the main idea of this article?
(A) Setting up self-driving car companies
(B) Driving rules for self-driving cars
(C) The costing of self-driving cars
(D) The coming of self-driving cars

40. What are the key things a self-driving car needs in order to get to your destination?
(A) Objects next to the car, a camera, and a road map.
(B) Speakers, a computer, and objects next to the car.
(C) Cameras, speakers, driving rules and a road map.
(D) Cameras, a computer, driving rules, and a road map.

41. Which of the following is true about self-driving cars in 2020?
(A) Self-driving cars were everywhere.
(B) Self-driving cars were at the research stage.
(C) Self-driving cars replaced all traditional cars.
(D) Self-driving car technology was fully developed.

第二部分：非選擇題（第 I 至 III 題，每題 6 分，共 18 分）

I. 填充

說明：▲ 請依據中文提示，將試題內空格 ①、② 答案之完整單字（含提示之字首），分別作答於作答欄 ①、② 之指定範圍內以完成句子。
▲ 請勿抄題，每格限填一字，超過一字者視為錯誤，不予計分。

1. 為保持健康，均衡的飲食、充足的運動及避免過多的壓力是有必要的。

To stay healthy, it is necessary to have a balanced diet and s___①___ exercise, and to avoid too much p___②___.

① ____________ ② ____________

II. 句子重組

說明：▲ 請將題中 5 段提示字詞重組成一完整句子，並於句尾加上適當標點符號。
▲ 請將重組後的句子寫在「非選擇題作答區」指定範圍內，答案中不能增減字詞或修改變化字詞，請勿抄題。

2. in the economy / All governments / due to / predicted a decline / the COVID-19 pandemic

____

____

III. 中譯英

說明：▲ 請將以下中文句子譯成正確、通順、達意的英文，並將答案寫在「非選擇題作答區」之指定範圍內，請勿抄題。

3. 有些學校將會帶他們的學生去動物園。

____

____

109 四技二專統一入學測驗－試題

第一部分：選擇題

- I. 字彙題
- II. 對話題
- III. 綜合測驗
- IV. 閱讀測驗

第二部分：非選擇題

- I. 填充
- II. 句子重組
- III. 中譯英

第一部分：選擇題（82 分）

I. 字彙題：

第 1 至 7 題，每題均有一空格字詞，請選擇最適合的答案，以完成該英文句子。第 8 至 11 題，每題均有一個劃底線的字詞，請在四個選項中，選擇一個與劃底線的字詞意義最接近的答案。

1. You can wear sunglasses if you think the sunlight is too ______ outside.
(A) bright (B) gray (C) large (D) weak

2. Every Saturday, the library holds talks on various ______ that include friendship, career, photography and health.
(A) jobs (B) hobbies (C) products (D) topics

3. I don't feel ______ gossiping about Michael's life because it is wrong to discuss other people's private lives.
(A) annoyed (B) comfortable (C) embarrassed (D) fearful

4. Computer technology ______ people to work at home effectively without having to go to the office.
(A) attacks (B) confuses (C) enables (D) reduces

5. The shoes usually cost a lot, but now they are ______ cheap after discount.
(A) regionally (B) relatively (C) reluctantly (D) respectfully

6. Mozart（莫札特）was a great musician who started to ______ music when he was very young.
(A) compose (B) lighten (C) monitor (D) reject

7. A(n) ______ face is essential to dramatic acting because it is good at showing all kinds of emotions.
(A) expressive (B) identical (C) protective (D) reasonable

8. Henry has been very busy looking for a new job <u>lately</u>, so he hasn't contacted his family for almost two weeks.
(A) fairly (B) nearly (C) recently (D) shortly

9. Mary broke up with her boyfriend because she felt he had no regard for her feelings.
(A) concern (B) fortune (C) silence (D) temper

10. A medical report indicates that there is an association between high levels of stress and skin problems.
(A) an exchange (B) an obstacle (C) a relationship (D) a similarity

11. The government declared that the new city hall would be open to the public this summer.
(A) announced (B) discovered (C) imagined (D) predicted

II. 對話題：

第 12 至 21 題，請依對話內容選出一個最適合的答案，使其成為有意義的對話。

12. Rose: Hey, let's go to Mama's Kitchen for some food.
Jane: Sounds great. ________
Rose: No, it's next to the bank.
Jane: Oh, it's quite far from here. But never mind. Let's go!
(A) Is the food there really good? (B) Can you say it one more time?
(C) Is it across from the Internet cafe? (D) Are you sure you want to go there?

13. Alan: I've been looking for that book! Where did you get it?
Betty: ________ I just did a search on the Web and found it. It's not that difficult, you know.
Alan: Really? I must try my hand at it. Can you show me how to do it?
(A) I bought it online. (B) I paid by credit card.
(C) I left it in the drawer. (D) I finished it in one night.

14. Steve: So, have you made up your mind about a career?
Becky: Pretty much. It's going to be something with either dancing or singing. I mean it.
Steve: ________ You've always been the musical type.
(A) It makes sense to me. (B) It will never come true.
(C) I'm pretty good at music. (D) Neither of them will work.

15. Mom: I think you have too much junk in your room. Why don't you clean up right now?

Mark: Junk? There is no junk. ______________

Mom: How about these empty boxes and broken mugs?

Mark: They are for my art class.

(A) We can ask for help. (B) You can say that again.

(C) It's too late to clean up. (D) I keep things for a reason.

16. Ken: Hello. This is Ken Wang. I bought a jacket on your website a month ago. I haven't received it. Why?

Joy: Hi, Mr. Wang. Let me check. Ah! ______________ Our records show a delay in delivery.

Ken: Well, you should have called me about it.

Joy: I'm truly sorry. I'll try my best to send it out to you today.

(A) I could not find any records of your order.

(B) I phoned you last week about that order.

(C) There was no order placed for the jacket.

(D) There has been a problem with that order.

17. Jennifer: That was an interesting speech. I learned a lot!

Shu-hua: Yes, although the topic was hard to follow for a foreigner like me!

Jennifer: ______________

Shu-hua: Thank you. It's very kind of you.

(A) The speaker is from Canada.

(B) But your English is excellent.

(C) I've followed the speaker for a while.

(D) And the topic was about foreign cultures.

18. Interviewer: Have you always worked in the service line?

Tim: Yes. Ever since I graduated from college.

Interviewer: I see. ______________

Tim: Well. I think I am very hardworking but a little impatient sometimes.

(A) How do you spend your free time?

(B) What are your strong and weak points?

(C) Please tell us about your educational background.

(D) Please say something about your work experience.

19. Mike: My brother has really gone crazy. He says he wants to take up skydiving. Can you believe that?

Lily: What? ________________

Mike: I'm not. He's dead serious.

Lily: Well, you have to stop him. It's really dangerous.

(A) Am I crazy?
(B) I believe he's dangerous.
(C) You've got to be kidding.
(D) Have you talked to him seriously?

20. Bill: Nina, ________________

Nina: Not really. I'd like to check out this city. But I need to learn how to take the MRT first.

Bill: I'm going to the station. If you want, we can go together. You'll find it easy.

Nina: That would be great! Thanks.

(A) where are you from?
(B) do you have a check?
(C) how do you like this city?
(D) do you have any plans?

21. Peter: Did you hear that band Mayday（五月天）is having two shows here this summer?

Leo: Yes. And tickets are on sale this Friday. But fan club members like us can buy tickets right now. Let's see what we can get.

Peter: There are different kinds of seating in the stadium—floor, lower level, and upper level.

Leo: ________________ I want to sit near the stage.

(A) Isn't it far from the stadium?
(B) How much is the fan club fee?
(C) Why don't we go with floor seats?
(D) Can we sell tickets on the upper level?

III. 綜合測驗：

以下兩篇短文，共有 10 個空格，為第 22 至 31 題，每題有四個選項，請依各篇短文文意，選出一個最適合該空格的答案。

◎下篇短文共有 5 個空格，為第 22 至 26 題，請依短文文意，選出一個最適合該空格的答案。

Rainforests are the Earth's oldest living ecosystems. They ___22___ only a small part of the Earth's surface, about six percent, but they are very important to us. For example, they provide us with ___23___ of the Earth's oxygen and fresh water. A lot of medicines we use today to treat cancer or heart disease ___24___ from the plants that grow only in rainforests. Many items we use in our own homes come from the rainforest as well. ___25___, rainforests are disappearing at an alarmingly fast pace, largely due to human development over the past few centuries. Problems ___26___ from the decrease of rainforests include more pollutions, less oxygen, and fewer species of animals. To keep rainforests from disappearing and save the Earth for our children, we must do something immediately.

22. (A) call off (B) look into (C) make up (D) turn down

23. (A) many (B) much (C) several (D) a few

24. (A) manufacture (B) manufactured
(C) are manufacturing (D) are manufactured

25. (A) In addition (B) Luckily (C) To conclude (D) Unfortunately

26. (A) result (B) resulting (C) have resulted (D) that resulting

◎下篇短文共有 5 個空格，為第 27 至 31 題，請依短文文意，選出一個最適合該空格的答案。

In 1275, Marco Polo（馬可波羅）arrived in China. During this journey, he came close to losing his life a few times, ___27___ he kept going and finally succeeded in reaching his goal. At about the same time, Polynesians（玻里尼西亞人）were exploring the islands of the South Pacific. ___28___ the great dangers of sailing long distance in open canoes, they managed to explore and occupy all the major islands. About 200 years later, Christopher Columbus（哥倫布）left Europe to find a new way to Asia. ___29___ the earth to be flat, many people at that time were afraid that he would fall off the edge of the world. Columbus did not reach his original goal to find treasures in Asia; ___30___, he opened up a vast new world, the Americas. Every explorer needs a vision. But what ___31___ explorers to leave the security of the known world to face the dangers of the unknown? For many of them, it is simply the love of adventure.

27. (A) for (B) or (C) so (D) yet

28. (A) Compared to (B) Despite (C) Rather than (D) Unlike

29. (A) Been believed (B) Being believing (C) Believed (D) Believing

30. (A) as usual (B) for instance (C) instead (D) moreover

31. (A) drive (B) drives (C) have driven (D) is driven

Ⅳ. 閱讀測驗：

以下有三篇短文，共有 10 個題目，為第 32 至 41 題，請於閱讀短文後，選出最適當的答案。

◎閱讀下文，回答第 32-33 題

Kelly, Linda, Vivian, and Wendy are at a night market in Tainan. They are looking at the menu and talking about what they would like to eat. Everyone will order only one portion of any item she likes for herself.

Menu

Item	**Price** (for one portion)
Oyster omelet	NT$ 80
Danzai noodles	NT$ 70
Taiwanese Meatball	NT$ 50
Milkfish soup	NT$ 90
Coffin bread	NT$ 70
Bubble tea	NT$ 50

Kelly: I am hungry. I can eat a horse.

Linda: Me, too. Let's get something good to eat. I'd like to have Danzai noodles first.

Wendy: I'll get Oyster omelet. My cousin said that's a must-try. And, I also want to try Taiwanese meatball. I want to see how different it is from American meatballs.

Vivian: I'm hungry and thirsty. I'll get bubble tea and coffin bread.

Kelly: The most famous dish in Tainan is milkfish; I must try it. Besides, eating fish makes you smart!

32. What is Kelly going to order?
(A) A horse (B) Bubble tea
(C) Coffin bread (D) Milkfish soup

33. According to the menu and the conversation, who will have to pay the most if everyone orders only one portion of each item she wants to eat?
(A) Kelly (B) Linda
(C) Vivian (D) Wendy

◎閱讀下文，回答第 34-37 題

Cocoa trees were first brought to Taiwan from Indonesia by the Japanese when they ruled the island. But, the Japanese could not overcome the difficulties in growing the crop. It was not until about 20 years ago that Taiwanese farmers succeeded in growing the tropical plant.

Thanks to modern techniques, local farmers in Pingtung（屏東）are able to produce better-quality beans that can be made into fine chocolate. In order to promote chocolate industry, local chocolate makers have also created new flavors of chocolate such as tea, fruit, and pepper for the past few years. Starting in 2016, this newly emerging cocoa industry in Pingtung went on to win international fame. In years 2018 and 2019, Taiwanese chocolate makers won numerous top prizes in the International Chocolate Award (ICA)'s World Finals. The rise of Taiwan's chocolate industry and its wonderful results even gave the country the honor of hosting the ICA's Asia-Pacific competition in 2019.

Even then, the industry is facing a problem. Not many chocolate eaters in Taiwan go for local products. To meet local taste, chocolate makers have come up with a variety of fine chocolates. They hope that as more people learn to appreciate and buy fine chocolate, the domestic market will **take off**. Encouraged by their success in global competitions, the chocolate makers are also targeting at the global market. They are eager to win over chocolate lovers worldwide with the delicate flavors of Taiwanese chocolate.

34. What is the contribution of the Japanese to Taiwan's chocolate industry?
(A) They knew how to produce chocolate.
(B) They moved from Indonesia to Taiwan.
(C) They introduced cocoa trees to Taiwan.
(D) They succeeded in growing cocoa trees.

35. According to the passage, which of the following statements is true?
(A) Taiwan-made chocolate is gaining world attention.
(B) Taiwan's chocolate makers produce a single flavor.
(C) Many Taiwanese chocolate eaters like local products.
(D) Indonesia farmers planted cocoa trees in Taiwan 20 years ago.

36. What does the phrase "**take off**" in paragraph 3 mean?
(A) Remove its obstacles
(B) Become successful
(C) Appear competitive
(D) Present its challenges

37. What is the main purpose of the passage?
(A) To discuss Taiwan's problems of planting cocoa trees.
(B) To introduce different flavors of Taiwanese chocolate.
(C) To show the development in Taiwan's chocolate industry.
(D) To describe Taiwan's success in selling chocolate worldwide.

◎閱讀下文，回答第 38-41 題

Early this year, a new coronavirus（新冠狀病毒）caused the rapid spread of the Coronavirus Disease 2019 (COVID-19). Many countries began practicing "social distancing" to prevent infection spread by increasing the space between people. All over the world, social distancing brought about changes in people's ways of living, learning, and working.

Lifestyle changes due to social distancing affected almost everyone. People avoided crowded places and unnecessary traveling. In Italy, for example, church leaders spoke to followers online. Elsewhere, online shopping in Taiwan and home entertainment in China rose significantly in February.

Social distancing also had an effect on learning. In Australia, when schools were still open, teachers tried not to let students mix in common areas that included the classroom, café and library. As the crisis worsened, schools closed **one** after another. By early April, over 90% of the world's students were not attending school. In some places, such as Italy and Hong Kong, students turned to learning from home through Internet connection.

To lower the risk of infection, companies put distance between employees in the workplace and told sick employees to stay home. Offices were generally flexible in the time and place of work. Furthermore, to keep the workplace safe, the United States passed a law to provide paid sick leave for all employees. This was to make sure that workers who fell ill with the coronavirus would stay home without fear of losing their income.

In the fight against the coronavirus, people stayed apart to stay healthy. However, they all stayed connected to feel a sense of togetherness.

38. What is the best title for this passage?
(A) Less Human Contact for Good Health
(B) Better Learning with Internet Connection
(C) Flexible Time and Place for Employment
(D) Safe Homes with Popular Entertainments

39. What does the word "**one**" in paragraph 3 refer to?
(A) classroom
(B) crisis
(C) school
(D) student

40. According to the passage, which of the following statements is true?
(A) About 90% of the students stayed at home to learn to use the Internet.
(B) Social distancing measured how fast the coronavirus spreads in a country.
(C) Schools stopped students from gathering in large groups to prevent infection.
(D) A new US law stated that sick employees would be paid if they worked at the office.

41. According to the passage, which of the following is **NOT** an act of social distancing?
(A) Attending a live concert filled with people.
(B) Reducing the number of workers in the office.
(C) Holding online church meetings with followers.
(D) Watching videos at home instead of going to the movies.

第二部分：非選擇題（第 I 至 III 題，每題 6 分，共 18 分）

I. 填充

說明：▲ 請依據中文提示，將試題內空格 ①、② 答案之完整單字（含提示之字首），分別作答於作答欄 ①、② 之指定範圍內以完成句子。
▲ 請勿抄題，每格限填一字，超過一字者視為錯誤，不予計分。

1. 這炸雞很美味，但對我來說有點太鹹了！

The fried c___①___ is tasty, but a little bit too s___②___ for me.

① __________ ② __________

II. 句子重組

說明：▲ 請將題中 5 段提示字詞重組成一完整句子，並於句尾加上適當標點符號。
▲ 請將重組後的句子寫在「非選擇題作答區」指定範圍內，答案中不能增減字詞或修改變化字詞，請勿抄題。

2. stared at / who was talking loudly / the boy / on his cellphone / People on the bus

III. 中譯英

說明：▲ 請將以下中文句子譯成正確、通順、達意的英文，並將答案寫在「非選擇題作答區」之指定範圍內，請勿抄題。

3. 我表姊邀請我去參加她的婚禮。

填讀者問卷
送熊贈點

常春藤升科大四技二專系列【IA01－114】

四技二專統測歷屆英文試題完全解析－試題本（114 年版）

總 編 審　賴世雄
終　　審　梁民康
執行編輯　許嘉華
編輯小組　常春藤中外編輯群
設計組長　王玥琦
封面設計　王穎婕
排版設計　王穎婕．林桂旭
錄　　音　林政偉
播音老師　賴世雄．奚永慧
法律顧問　北辰著作權事務所蕭雄淋律師
出 版 者　常春藤數位出版股份有限公司
地　　址　臺北市忠孝西路一段 33 號 5 樓
電　　話　(02) 2331-7600
傳　　真　(02) 2381-0918
網　　址　www.ivy.com.tw
電子信箱　service@ivy.com.tw
郵政劃撥　50463568
戶　　名　常春藤數位出版股份有限公司
定　　價　320 元（2 書）
出版日期　2025 年 6 月　初版／一刷